From the ballrooms of Regency London
to the secret haunts of Washington, D.C.,
to the charming cottages of Cape Cod,
four dukes and a devil
will break all the rules.

In *New York Times* bestselling author Cathy Maxwell's **The Irish Duke**, Miss Susan Rogers had warned all London about the wickedly handsome nobleman, except the person in the most danger . . . herself.

When Gray decided to break out of her shell, she had no idea it would involve a pooch named Duke, a poltergeist, pedaling a bike through town—*stark naked*—and the perfect man, in *USA Today* bestselling author Elaine Fox's **The Duke Who Came to Dinner**.

Blake was possessed, obsessed, and dreaming of death. Only love could save him—love . . . and blood, in *New York Times* bestselling author Jeaniene Frost's **Devil to Pay**.

When the most eligible bachelor in London's marriage mart reluctantly rescues a stranded schoolmistress, the Duke of Beaufort is forced to go heart-to-heart with the spirited siren, in RITA® Award-winning author Sophia Nash's **Catch of the Century**.

India would do anything to escape a besotted admirer—even let London's most scandalous rake steal a kiss . . . and more, in *New York Times* bestselling author Tracy Anne Warren's **Charmed By Her Smile**.

By Cathy Maxwell

A SEDUCTION AT CHRISTMAS
IN THE HIGHLANDER'S BED

By Elaine Fox

BEDTIME FOR BONSAI
HELLO, DOGGY!

By Jeaniene Frost

DESTINED FOR AN EARLY GRAVE
AT GRAVE'S END

By Sophia Nash

LOVE WITH THE PERFECT SCOUNDREL
THE KISS

By Tracy Anne Warren

SEDUCED BY HIS TOUCH
TEMPTED BY HIS KISS

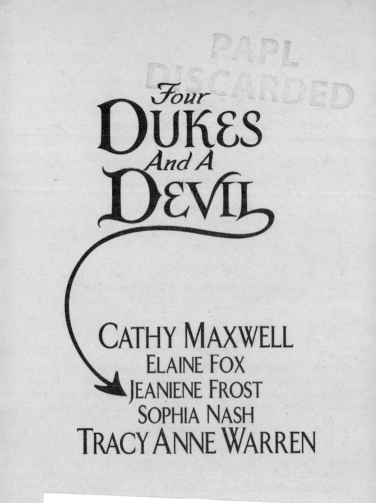

Four DUKES *And A* DEVIL

CATHY MAXWELL
ELAINE FOX
JEANIENE FROST
SOPHIA NASH
TRACY ANNE WARREN

AVON

An Imprint of HarperCollinsPublishers

AVON BOOKS
An Imprint of HarperCollins*Publishers*
10 East 53rd Street
New York, New York 10022-5299

"The Irish Duke" copyright © 2009 by Cathy Maxwell, Inc.
"The Duke Who Came to Dinner" copyright © 2009 by Elaine McShulskis
"Devil to Pay" copyright © 2009 by Jeaniene Frost
"Catch of the Century" copyright © 2009 by Sophia Nash
"Charmed By Her Smile" copyright © 2009 by Tracy Anne Warren

ISBN 978-0-06-178736-2
www.avonromance.com

First Avon Books paperback printing: July 2009

Avon Trademark Reg. U.S. Pat. Off. and in Other Countries, Marca Registrada, Hecho en U.S.A.
HarperCollins® is a registered trademark of HarperCollins Publishers.

Printed in the U.S.A.

10 9 8 7 6 5 4 3 2 1

Contents

The Irish Duke

Cathy Maxwell

Chapter One

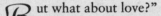

*B*ut what about love?"

Miss Susan Rogers had anticipated Lady Theresa Alberth's question. It was the mental inclination of young women nowadays. She understood because she'd also once believed love was the only true concern when it came to marriage. But now, at six-and-twenty and firmly established as a spinster, she knew differently.

Lady Theresa was Lord and Lady Alberth's only child. They sat on chairs next to their daughter and turned to Susan as if they, too, needed an answer.

Susan set her cup and saucer on the side table next to her chair. She knew her role. It was to convince Lady Theresa to obey her parents' wishes.

"Love is important," Susan agreed, very certain of herself and her message. After all, she'd given this lecture numerous times over just the last week as anxious parents with willful daughters had sought out her services. "But is it more important than compatibility? Than security? You will have children someday, Lady Theresa. What do you hope for them?"

A small frown line appeared between Lady Theresa's brows.

"I'm not going to tell you," Susan continued, "that it is as easy to love a wealthy man as it is a poor one. Or that you have obligations to your family line. I'm certain your parents have already told you all that."

Lady Theresa nodded, her expression tense. Lady Alberth had confided in Susan earlier that their daughter believed herself in love with their land steward's son, a Mr. Gerald Grover. They were hiring Susan to convince her differently. They wanted a good family for their daughter, and a title.

"What they say is true," Susan said matter-of-factly. "However, that doesn't change how one feels when one is in love."

"Yes," Lady Theresa agreed, half-sobbing the word.

Susan leaned forward, reaching for Lady Theresa's hand. The girl gave it to her. "I'm going to advise you to remember that love *must* be tested. It can be a liar, a *thief*."

Lady Theresa shook her head, but Susan pressed on. "Let me tell you my story. I was once in love. I would have willingly sacrificed everything for him. He said he loved me, too, and we were to marry. One week before the wedding, both of my parents died in a coaching accident."

"Oh, dear," Lady Alberth said. Her husband's expression had gone grim. Lady Theresa listened, that frown between her brows deepening as she placed herself in Susan's position.

"My two younger sisters and I were alone," Susan said. "The estate went to a cousin, who did not want the responsibility of us. My betrothed had told me he loved me. It was only natural I turned to him in this difficult situation. He said everything would be fine, but on the day of our wedding, he didn't appear for the ceremony."

"You were left at the altar?" Lady Alberth asked.

Susan nodded. "Publicly humiliated." The words no longer embarrassed her. She'd said them too often . . . to other girls . . . in front of other parents. "You see, my gentleman had been informed an hour before we were to be wed that my cousin refused to pay my dowry. He had other plans for the money." She gave Lady Theresa's hand a squeeze. "Don't be foolish as I was. Is it so much for your parents to ask you to participate in one Season? Is your love so fragile it would not survive a few parties, a couple of balls?"

Lady Theresa looked to her parents. "Does that mean I may marry Gerald if I go through a Season?"

"The lad is unsuitable—" her father started.

"You must follow *my* guidelines," Susan said, directing her comment to Lady Theresa but boldly cutting her father off. No good came from arguing with a young woman who thought she was in love.

To his credit, Lord Alberth shut up.

"If you believe in love, then this young man—what is his name?"

"Gerald," Lady Theresa said.

"If Gerald is the one, nothing will sway your love for him, but *you* will be certain," Susan assured her. "There is much at stake. I'm certain you wish to please your parents. And you don't want to look back in life and wish you'd had the fun and excitement of at least one Season. Just one."

Lady Theresa nodded solemnly. The frown line was still there.

Susan smiled. "So, will you join me? Just for this Season?"

Again, Lady Theresa nodded.

"You will enjoy yourself immensely," Susan promised.

"I shall endeavor to try," she said, directing her vow toward her anxious parents. "I will."

"That's all we can ask, kitten," her father said.

Lady Theresa stood. "If you will excuse me?"

Her parents nodded. Lady Theresa gave a graceful nod to Susan and left the room.

"Well done," Lord Alberth said, when his daughter was out of earshot. "We've been attempting to bring her to this conclusion for weeks."

"She is very much 'in love,'" Susan observed.

"They *all* are at this age," Lady Alberth said. "I blame myself for not having been more vigilant over her when she was around Gerald Grover."

"They played together as children," her husband said dismissively. "You couldn't have seen it coming. After all, we thought we'd raised her better than this."

"Is Mr. Grover a bad sort?" Susan asked.

"No, he isn't. But he's not *suitable*," Lord Alberth said, and that was that. He changed the subject. "You handled her very well, Miss Rogers. And you come to us highly recommended. However, I do have a concern about your fee."

"My fee is not negotiable, my lord. Over the past four years, I have seen not only to the marriages of my sisters to respected, highly placed men—" She did not need to add the word "wealthy." It was assumed. "—But also the marriages of several of your peers' daughters. Lady Theresa is not the first girl to be in love with an unsuitable man at the beginning of the Season and wed to a *suitable* man by the conclusion of it. With my guidance, of course."

"Of course," Lord Alberth said, still sounding unconvinced.

"And Miss Rogers knows a great deal, my lord," Lady Alberth chimed in, "that not even we know. Matters I wouldn't have thought of."

"Such as?" he asked.

Lady Alberth shot Susan a bright smile. "Tell him about the Irish Duke."

The "Irish Duke" was turning out to be a very fine selling point for Susan's services. It exhibited her complete knowledge of the Rules of Society. Several weeks ago she'd discovered an odd bit in the Order of Precedence, the list that determined ceremonial importance for the peers of the Realm.

She now explained to Lord Alberth. "You would be pleased if your daughter married a duke."

"Very pleased."

"But what if I told you not all dukes are the same? For example, in the Order of Precedence, the Irish Duke will always be at the end of the line."

Lord Alberth frowned. He had the same frown line between his brow as his daughter.

"For state dinners," Susan assured him, "the Irish Duke and his duchess will sit at the foot of the table if there is no one but dukes in attendance. They will be the last to enter to pay their addresses to the King and the last to be admitted to any ceremonial function. Is that what you wish for your daughter, my lord? To be last?"

"Of course not."

"I thought not," Susan agreed. "And that is where my services are most appreciated. I will steer your daughter away from the Irish Duke. I will keep her safe from his attentions." She didn't add that there were only two Irish dukes in the world and both safely tucked away in Ireland. Besides, one's title had been attainted for plotting rebellion and the other was so old, a wife would have been useless to him.

"Let us also remember how good Miss Rogers was in handling Theresa," Lady Alberth reminded him.

Susan could see his reluctance and held her breath. The very well respected Lord Alberth was not a man who liked to spend money. But with a commission from him, there was no telling what wealthy doors might open to her. She might finally be able to afford a small house on Beech Street and a few other creature comforts—

"Yes, very well," his lordship said. "Didn't know about the Irish Duke. I don't want my daughter last at anything. Besides, I've never been fond of the Irish. Keep the fellow and that dratted lad Grover away from my daughter," he ordered, rising.

"I will, my lord," Susan said, also coming up to stand. Keeping unwelcome suitors away from precious daughters was all part of her services. "Thank you for your trust in me."

Lord Alberth grunted a response and left the room. It was left to Lady Alberth to clap her hands, and say happily, "I can't wait to tell Claire Bollinger that we, too, have hired you. She thought she was so special, but now, we'll see which daughter marries first."

She and Susan finished the arrangements. Her fee would be paid at the end of the Season, with a bonus if Lady Theresa married a "suitable" gentleman.

Susan was quite pleased with herself when the butler escorted her to the door, and she went out into the damp February afternoon—until she saw the coach and footman waiting for her.

For a second, Susan was tempted to go the other way, but knew it would be useless. The coat of arms on the door told her it was her sister Ellen this time.

Susan went down the steps and walked to the coach door a footman held open for her. She climbed in, not surprised when her sister launched into her without preamble.

"What were you doing at Lord Alberth's? Susan, don't tell me you were peddling yourself to the Earl of Alberth?"

"Fine, I won't." Susan reached for the door handle.

Ellen grabbed her arm. They were three years apart, Susan being the oldest. They were both honey blondes who looked enough alike with their gold-brown eyes for people to think them twins, except that the cut of Ellen's clothes was far more expensive than Susan's.

"I didn't mean it that way," Ellen snapped.

Susan shrugged.

Her brows coming together in consternation, Ellen said, "You must stop this. You mustn't keep going around amongst people of Dodgin's set and offering yourself for hire." Dodgin was her husband, Lord Dodgin. He was some twenty years older than Ellen and a rather strict man. Susan hadn't realized how strict when she'd arranged Ellen's marriage to him. She'd feared Ellen would be miserable. Instead, Ellen had turned out to be just like him.

"I have no choice, Ellen. I must support myself."

"We've offered you room."

"In the country," Susan objected. "And with the role of playing companion to Dodgin's eldest sister. No, thank you."

"I can't believe you are so ungrateful—"

"I can't believe you've forgotten everything I've done for you. I sold everything we had to bring you and Jane to London. I took care of you. Without me, the three of us would still be penniless in Little Hereford."

"And we do appreciate you," Ellen assured her. "If

I could return the favor, I would. However, Dodgin doesn't want my spinster sister idling around. You know how he is."

"I've learned. And I've learned how Jane and Sir Alec are, too. I refuse to be a charity case in my own family. I value my independence, Ellen, and you'd best warn Dodgin to become accustomed to hearing my name in his circles. This Season will make me a success, especially after I find a husband for Lord Alberth's daughter, and you'd all best come to peace with it."

"We'll do everything we can to stop you," Ellen answered.

"You may try your best," Susan responded, and opened the door. She climbed out of the coach, refusing the footman's hand, and marched down the street, head held high for the first time in years.

Chapter Two

Two weeks later . . .

"It's the Irish Duke."

"What's *he* doing here?"

"I don't know. I was certain Bollinger told me he was *not* invited."

"Ummm, the Irish Duke."

Susan heard the rush of excited whispers around the ballroom floor. They were saying something about an Irish duke, but she wasn't certain she was hearing correctly because she was far too preoccupied searching for Lady Theresa.

The girl was a trial. Her beloved Gerald had followed her to London, and he was most adept at sneaking his way into every social occasion. The only time Susan hadn't caught sight of him was when Lady Theresa and several of her other charges were presented at Court—

and that was probably only because Susan wasn't there herself.

He wasn't completely unrespectable. In fact, he was rather handsome and had a charm about him. It was also obvious he was madly and completely in love with Lady Theresa.

Gerald had shown up at the ball this evening. Last night at the Barrington ball, the young couple had wanted to dance, and it had taken all of Susan's persuasive powers to convince them a public spectacle would only make Lady Theresa's father angrier. Reluctantly, they had agreed she was right, but Gerald wouldn't leave until he knew he could spend a few minutes with Lady Theresa sometime over the next few days. Before Susan knew what she was doing, she found herself agreeing to chaperone Lady Theresa for a rendezvous.

It was a devil of a promise and one Susan knew she'd have to renege on. She'd feel bad for doing so. She liked Lady Theresa, and Gerald seemed the sort of man who would make a good husband. If only he had money or prestige—

A tingling at the nape of her neck brought her thoughts to a halt. Some inner sense warned her that something was amiss. She didn't experience it often, but when she did, she paid attention. She prayed it wasn't a disaster with Lady Theresa or one of her other eight charges.

Susan turned, looking around the crowded room for the reason her every sense had gone alert—and then she saw *him*.

For a second she could barely think, let alone move.

A tall, dark-haired man with a square, masculine jaw, broad, *broad* shoulders was staring at her with such intensity it was as if his gaze reached across the distance between them and touched her. He was the most handsome man she'd ever laid eyes on.

She knew she should look away, but she couldn't.

Feelings she'd long thought dead to her forever, feelings of desire and lust and yearning, reared their ugly heads and reminded her she was still young, still alive.

And it wasn't just his looks that attracted her. There was a presence about him that seemed to make all other men fade in comparison, a presence that made her feel vulnerable, something she'd vowed she'd never let happen again—

"Miss Rogers, please don't be upset with me, but it was my brother who brought the Irish Duke to the ball. Miss Rogers? Miss Rogers, are you all right?"

Susan had to give herself a little shake to make Miss Arabella Riggins's nasal voice make sense. The young woman, a slender, fluffy blonde who often acted completely helpless, stood before her, hands clasped in worry.

"I'm fine," Susan said, knowing she sounded a bit dazed. "I just had something else on my mind. What were you saying? Something about someone's coming to the ball?" She glanced over her shoulder and was disappointed to see that the dark-haired gentleman no longer stood where she'd last seen him, and there was no time to search for him because Miss Arabella was prattling on again.

"The *Irish Duke*, Miss Rogers. I didn't know Archibald was going to bring him, or I would have warned you."

The Irish Duke? Susan shook her head. "Miss Arabella, please don't worry. There is no Irish duke here tonight." *Because there is no Irish duke in England.*

"Oh, but there is," Miss Arabella assured her. "I know because he is a friend of my brother."

Susan thought Miss Arabella a bit of a silly goose, but making up an Irish duke was behaving beyond goosey.

And then their hostess, the silver-haired Lady Bollinger, skillfully slid up to Susan to say, with a smile on her face but desperation in her eyes, "I had to admit *him*. *He* and my husband are friends. I pray you to forgive me. I didn't send *him* an invitation, but *he* is here all the same."

"Who's he?" Susan asked, confused.

"The *Irish* Duke," Lady Bollinger said, the purple plumes in her hair shaking with her agitation.

"You mean, there *is* an Irish duke?" Susan said.

"Of course there is," Lady Bollinger answered. "You knew that. You told us about him. The Duke of Killeigh. You've warned all of us against him."

"We've attempted to do everything we could to avoid him," Miss Arabella said. "But he is on a hunt for a wife. Lady Elizabeth had to run from the room last night at Lord and Lady Barrington's ball or else she would have been forced to take the floor with him."

"Run from the room? Away from a duke?" Susan was stunned. That was shocking behavior. Her charges should not behave that way, but then where had she been last night when all this was going on—?

She'd been having a very sincere and frank talk with Lady Theresa and her Gerald.

Lady Bollinger flipped open her fan. "You needn't worry. The girls managed to skirt any of His Grace's advances quite successfully." She made a rather nasty laugh. "My husband will be furious the duke is here tonight. He has reconsidered their acquaintance after you explained the Order of Precedence and no longer wishes to speak to him."

Susan groped for words, horrified at the rudeness. "But he's a duke."

"And he is also, as you very rightly pointed out, *Irish*. An Irish duke. Lord Bollinger opined to me yesterday evening that considering the Irish dukes have fomented rebellion since time began, the Crown would be better off without them. I answered that was a very astute opinion and urged him to see what he could do in Parliament."

"He would talk to Parliament?" Susan raised a hand to her forehead, trying to make sense of all this. "We must remember," she said, forcing herself to smile, an expression that actually hurt at this moment, "that Killeigh is still a duke. Irish dukes are important."

Lady Bollinger dismissed her words with a wave of her hand. "But not important enough for *my* daughter. She will not be last for anything."

"I don't want to be last either," Miss Arabella injected.

Susan could have buried her face in her hands in frustration. Who would have thought that her clever little speech to convince parents that they needed her services and to pay her handsomely for them would be taken so literally?

Who would have thought there was an Irish duke in London?

"Of course, there is nothing we can do about his presence now," Lady Bollinger opined. "However, I wanted to warn you, Miss Rogers, to be on the alert. The Duke of Killeigh is a handsome man—"

"*Very* handsome," Miss Arabella echoed.

"You need to keep our precious little pigeons away from him," Lady Bollinger finished, giving Miss Arabella a motherly tap on the arm with her fan. "We can't have his handsome countenance luring them away."

"I shall do my best, my lady," Susan replied, more than overwhelmed at the moment.

What a devil of a mess.

She needed to go somewhere to think. She needed to concoct a new story, one that didn't brand the Irish Duke an Undesirable.

Lady Bollinger had spied someone she knew who was more important than Susan and gone floating off, fan and purple plumes waving in the air. Miss Arabella was claimed by her next dance partner, a pockmarked baronet's son who would never be as good a catch as a duke, Irish or not.

Seeing that all her charges, including Lady Theresa, were on the dance floor with proper partners, Susan moved toward a corridor. She needed a moment of solitude to consider this new twist with the Irish Duke.

However, she'd not taken more than a few steps when a strong hand clamped down on her arm. She turned with a start to realize that the dark-haired stranger had come up silently behind her.

"Don't speak, don't even think until we are outside alone," he said. The lightest trace of Ireland accented his words. He opened the glass door leading out into the garden.

Susan attempted to dig in her heels. She feared what that accent could mean. "I do not know you, sir. I shall not go off alone with you."

"You don't know me?" the gentleman repeated. "And yet everyone is quoting what you've said about me. Let me introduce myself, I'm the Duke of Killeigh."

With those words, he whisked her outside to the seclusion of the winter night.

Chapter Three

Miss Susan Rogers was not like any spinster of Roan's acquaintance, especially those with the charge of other people's children.

He'd pictured either a robust dumpling of a woman or a thin, spare one, both with gray hair and frown lines.

Instead, he found himself commandeering a woman with golden blond hair, full curves in all the right places, and brown eyes alive with intelligence. He'd noticed her immediately when he'd entered Bollingers' ballroom. She'd stood out like a beacon from all other women there—and it made him unreasonably angry.

He didn't want to be attracted to her. Not after what she'd done to him.

Roan Gillray, the fourth Duke of Killeigh, had come looking for a wife. Other men who frequented the round of balls and parties comprising the Season laughed about the Marriage Mart, and many vowed to steer clear of matchmaking mamas—but Roan wanted to be ensnared. He was ready to marry.

Perhaps it was because he'd been to war. He knew how short and precious life was. There had been times on the battlefield when he'd doubted he would make it out alive . . . and many lonely nights when he'd longed for the grace of female companionship. He wasn't thinking about sex. He'd never lacked for bed partners. What he wanted, what he needed was something *more* . . .

And then he'd been blessed to inherit the dukedom from his cousin, an ill-humored, bitter man who had shut out all in the family. No one had been more surprised than Roan when he learned he was his cousin's heir, and not just to the title but also the old miser's carefully hoarded fortune.

Well, Roan had plans for that fortune. He was anxious to throw off the mantle of soldier and take up the hoe as farmer. He wanted peace and a place on this earth that was all his. He liked the idea of knowing where his bed would be at night and having a woman who understood his ways and cared for him sleeping beside him in the middle of it. She didn't need to love him—Roan had seen too much of the cruelty in men to believe there was such a thing as love—but he wanted a woman who *liked* him. Now there was a good word. He wanted someone in his life to like him.

Except now, everyone acted as if he was a pariah, and it was all because of this woman, who had the longest lashes he'd ever seen—

Miss Rogers jerked her arm away from his hold, and he let her go, half-expecting her to march inside and denounce him. It was anger that had driven him forward, but the cold air had slapped some sense into him.

However, instead of storming inside, she stood her ground. "You are angry," she said, "and you have every right to be." She straightened her back. "I have unintentionally maligned you. Please accept my apology, Your Grace."

"Unintentionally, Miss Rogers?" He gave a bitter laugh, his anger welling inside him all over again. "You singled me out, and you don't know me."

"I didn't single *you* out. I was talking about Irish dukes in general."

"There aren't that many of us."

"Yes, and frankly, I didn't expect that there would be one in London."

"So it would be acceptable to malign my title if I wasn't in London?" he asked, a bit confused by her reasoning. "Or were we just never supposed to leave the island?"

Miss Rogers sighed and moved away from the door as if she didn't want to be overheard. "I only told everyone the truth about the Order of Precedence. The Irish dukes do follow the English and Scottish dukes."

"Yes, but we are ahead of all the marquises and viscounts and everyone else of any country."

"I know," Miss Rogers agreed. "But I've discovered no parents want their daughter to be last in anything. It really is quite extraordinary, but it has worked to my advantage. You know what I do for my living, do you not, Your Grace?"

"You see that young women introduced to society are successful in their hunt for husbands."

"I would frame it a bit more gently, but yes, that is what I do. And I am very good at it. But this year, because of my pointing out the Order of Precedence, I have had more parents than usual seek out my services. I didn't mean to blacken your name although it has been an excellent selling scheme."

Her honesty was refreshing. It had seemed to Roan

that every woman he'd met in London spoke in riddles and hidden meaning. Miss Rogers didn't flinch at plain speaking.

So he felt completely within his rights to say, "I'm certain it has been a wonderful scheme, but now you must tell your employers the truth."

"But I *have* told the truth," she informed him.

"Yes, but they don't understand that an Irish duke is as good if not better than most the other peers of lower rank," he answered.

"Isn't that matter open to debate?" she suggested.

"It is *not* open to debate," he replied.

"We are debating it right now."

Roan frowned, mentally taking back everything he'd thought about plain speaking.

"Miss Rogers, you say you mean no disrespect, but you refuse to clear up the misunderstanding you created."

She crossed her arms, looking out into the night before countering, "I am sorry for the misunderstanding, Your Grace. You seem to be every inch the gentleman. However, I have not misled anyone about the Order of Precedence. If they chose to take it to the extreme—well, what can I do?"

"You can tell them they are wrong," Roan answered, his temper returning.

"But they are not."

"They *are*."

"No, I've studied my *The New Peerage*. I am correct, although I regret no mention was made of your holding the title. My copy is several years old."

"Or is it that you do not wish to look the fool, Miss Rogers? You would rather I play that part."

Even in the moonlight, he could see her blush. She crossed her arms as if cold. "It is my livelihood after all," she murmured.

Roan could give her that. Having been one of the genteel poor, he understood her position, and he came to a decision. "I understand. However, I find it insulting to have young women run from me when I ask them to dance."

"It was extremely rude of Lady Elizabeth, and I shall take her to task. If you wish, she will be happy to dance with you this evening."

"I'm not interested in taking her to task," Roan said, an idea coming to him. "However, *you* could dance with me. I believe that would settle the matter."

"*Me?* Dance with *you?*"

Roan nodded.

"Oh, no, Your Grace, I couldn't."

"Why not?"

"Because if I did that . . ." She let her voice trail off.

"Then it would be the same as admitting you were wrong about the Irish Duke," he finished for her.

She took a worried step away from him. "I am to be here for my charges, not for my personal entertainment."

"Oh, this wouldn't be personal, Miss Rogers, and you know it. It would be a matter of settling business between us."

"But then everyone would question what I'd said about the Irish duke."

"Exactly," he agreed.

"And I can't let that happen. I don't receive payment for my services until the Season is over."

"That's ridiculous," he said.

"It is a risk," she admitted, "but I'm paid more money that way."

"And making me the outcast of society is about money."

"*No.*" Miss Rogers made an impatient sound. "I had an idea and . . . it didn't work for you. But I will rectify the situation if you will give me a bit of time."

"I don't want to give you time," Roan said, enjoying the game. "I want a dance."

"I can't give you a dance. It would ruin me."

He moved in closer. "Or it would make us *both* the talk of London—"

The door opened, and a young couple all but tumbled out the door they were so anxious to throw themselves into each other's arms. Unfortunately for them, Miss Rogers was there.

"*Miss Rogers?*" the young girl said in surprise.

"Lady Theresa," Miss Rogers said in tones of disapproval. "Good evening, Mr. Grover. The two of you come with me."

And before Roan registered what was happening, Miss Rogers marched the hapless lovers back inside the door . . . and escaped him.

Susan was relieved to be free of the Duke of Killeigh's overwhelming presence. The man was a menace to her.

He was also devilishly attractive.

But she couldn't dance with him. Not until this Season was over. Her creditability and livelihood depended upon it.

So, she laid into Mr. Gerald Grover with great enthusiasm. Anything to put distance between herself and the Duke of Killeigh's disturbing challenge.

A dance? How ridiculous. How *dangerous*.

The hapless Gerald was happy to slink off when she was done. Of course, Lady Theresa was in tears, so it took a good part of an hour to placate her and extract further promises to behave. She really was a good girl but infatuated with her Gerald. Fortunately, Lady Theresa had been so shocked to see Susan, she hadn't noticed the duke.

After the reprimand, Susan had to hurry back out to the ballroom to check on her other charges.

All in all, it was a very hectic hour . . . but she did notice that the Duke of Killeigh was gone. He'd left. Apparently he hadn't wanted that dance after all.

Susan stood alone by a potted palm, away from those enjoying the ball, and was surprised by how disappointed she felt. She knew she shouldn't. Hadn't John taught her how men made promises they had no intention of keeping?

Except, for some irrational reason, she hadn't expected that from the Duke of Killeigh.

With a shake of her head, she told herself she was being silly. She couldn't dance with the duke. It was better he'd given up on her—

A footman carrying a silver salver approached, interrupting her thoughts. "Miss Rogers?" he asked.

"Yes."

"This is for you." The servant bowed and offered the salver. On it was the Duke of Killeigh's card.

Susan picked up the card and caught sight of the bold, slanted handwriting on the back of it. She waited until the footman had withdrawn to read what had been written.

I _will_ have my dance. Killeigh

She folded the card and slipped it into her glove. Life had suddenly become very complicated.

And more than a bit exciting.

Chapter Four

*I*f he was to claim his dance with Miss Rogers, Roan needed to be at the balls she attended with her high-born charges. There was the problem.

Her nonsense about the Irish Duke and the Order of Precedence had effectively cut him off from society, or at least that corner of it.

He stewed on this matter for a good three days. When not stewing, he made it a point to learn everything he could about Miss Susan Rogers, and what he learned, he liked.

She was actually from a good family. Her sisters were married to Lord Dodgin and Sir Alec Lawson or *Loud-son*, as Roan liked to think of him. Sir Alec was one of the most annoying people of his acquaintance, and rumor had it that Dodgin wasn't much better.

Perhaps that was why Miss Rogers lived in a modest

set of rooms off Olivia Street. She might have decided poverty was better than living under either of their roofs. Certainly they would have extracted their pound of flesh for supporting her.

At last, his stewing hatched a plan so devilishly delightful, he knew every door in London would open to him, especially the ones hosting Miss Rogers.

The next day, he enlisted the aid of his friend, the Honorable Mr. Reen Trenholm, and they went to White's. Roan chose a time when he knew the club would be the most crowded.

"I need Raggett," Roan informed a staff member. Raggett was White's proprietor, "And the Betting Book."

At the words "Betting Book," heads turned. The book was the most famous in London. There wasn't a man in the room who didn't enjoy a good wager, and Roan planned to make a brilliant one. It helped that Lord Alberth and Lord Bollinger sat not too far away at a table with a group of their cronies who were probably clients of Miss Rogers, too.

Roan could not have asked for a better opportunity.

Raggett wasted no time answering Roan's summons, the Betting Book under his arm. "Your Grace, it is a pleasure to see you today," he said with a bow.

"We wish to enter a wager," Roan told him. He and Trenholm stood in the middle of the room, and he knew many were listening.

"Very well," Raggett said, crossing to a secretary, where there was pen and ink. He dipped the nib of the pen, and said, "Your wager, Your Grace?"

"One hundred pounds," Roan said, then stopped for dramatic effect, wanting every ear in the room on him. The talking had died down. "No," he said, "make that one *thousand* pounds—" Now he had their interest.

Of course, the color had drained from Trenholm's face. "—That I will dance with Miss Susan Rogers before a fortnight has passed."

Even Raggett blinked in speculative surprise at him. The stalwart proprietor had certainly heard of Roan's dilemma. There wasn't much that was discussed under White's roof that escaped him. He lowered his head and recorded the bet.

Trenholm did his best to look brave. He didn't succeed until Roan leaned close, and, in a side voice, assured him, "Don't worry, I'll cover both bets."

His friend broke into a smile and immediately nudged Raggett. "And I'll wager *two* thousand pounds that the lady will not dance. What do you say, Your Grace?"

What Roan had to say, he'd save for later, when he and Trenholm were alone. As it was, he had no choice but to match the bet.

Of course, there was no one within earshot who was not listening now.

All Roan had to do was say nonchalantly, "Is there anyone else for this wager?" to find out exactly who was listening. A host of men jumped at the opportunity and placed their wagers on both sides of the bet. Alberth and Bollinger were not among their number, but that was fine with Roan. He thanked Raggett for his attention to the matter and, with a nudge to Trenholm to follow, left the club.

Outside, he wasted no time in saying, "*Two* thousand?"

Trenholm grinned. "I thought since you were being expansive . . ."

Roan grumbled under his breath, but he wasn't angry. The size of the wager alone was enough to make it the talk of London.

"Do you believe this will work?" Trenholm asked, suddenly sober.

"It will," Roan said confidently. "Few can resist a wager or the opportunity to make a little mischief. I will have an invitation to a ball Miss Rogers will be attending by nightfall."

And he was right. Where once no messengers had come to Roan's door, the invitations now came pouring in. He had only to pick and choose. Some of the hostesses had written personal notes, assuring him that Miss Rogers would be in attendance.

His plan had worked better than he could have imagined . . . because as much as the *ton* adored putting on airs, they loved a good wager more.

Susan couldn't put her finger on it but there was something in the air. She looked around yet another ballroom, keeping a watchful eye on her charges but also aware that everyone else seemed to be keeping their eyes on her.

It was very disconcerting—especially since after that night at the Bollinger affair, she'd half expected to see the Duke of Killeigh again, and hadn't.

She'd told herself she was being silly. No duke, not even an Irish one, would worry himself over a nobody like herself. Besides, the Duke of Killeigh had been spitting angry with her when last they parted. Still, that hadn't stopped her from looking at his card every night before she went out—

Miss Arabella came running up to her, interrupting her thoughts. "Have you heard the news, Miss Rogers?"

"What news?" Susan asked. The girl was so flushed with excitement, Susan wouldn't have been surprised to hear that Napoleon had been defeated.

"About the wager the Irish Duke has made that he will claim a dance from you."

"He made a wager?" For a second Susan felt faint. No wonder everyone was staring at her.

"In the Betting Book at White's," Miss Arabella said, and was quickly seconded by the other girls who had joined them. They all started speaking at once about what they'd overheard and from whom.

Susan was horrified. Such notoriety could ruin her business.

"Miss Rogers?" Lady Alberth's voice intruded on her disturbing thoughts. "May we have a moment?" She was flanked by Lady Bollinger and Lady Riggins, Arabella's mother.

Susan raised a hand to her forehead. This was not going to be good. "Of course."

They left their daughters behind and found a private spot in their hosts' library.

"You've heard about the wager?" Lady Alberth said.

"I have," Susan admitted. "Just this moment."

"I am not pleased. I discussed this with the other mothers, and they are as unhappy as I. A genteel woman should not have her name listed in the Betting Book at White's."

"My lady, I did not seek this out—" Susan started.

"That may be true," her ladyship said, "but we've been talking amongst ourselves and we believe this sort of nonsense deflects attention away from where it should be—on our daughters."

"You are very right, my lady," Susan hurried to agree. She could not afford to have everyone walk off. Her dreams of her little house on Beech Street were fading quickly.

"Furthermore," Lady Bollinger chimed in, "you convinced us and our daughters that the Duke of Killeigh was unacceptable. Now he has singled you out, has announced to everyone he wishes to dance with *you*. I wonder if you had an ulterior motive all along. Perhaps you wanted him for yourself?"

"We did not believe we were hiring a fortune huntress when we engaged your services," Lady Riggins jumped in.

"You did not," Susan assured her. *This is madness. Why is the duke doing this?*

"Then you shall see this matter is set right?" Lady Alberth said.

"I shall attempt to do so," Susan promised.

"'Attempt' is unacceptable," her ladyship countered. "You *will* set it to rights or not see a shilling from my husband."

"And whatever you do, *don't* dance with the Duke of Killeigh," Lady Bollinger said, pointing her fan at Susan for emphasis.

"Or else you will set the wrong example for our daughters," Lady Riggins agreed. "*You* can't marry a duke. Why, you are of the working class now. I've had enough trouble explaining to Theresa why she must not be so moony-eyed for her Gerald without having to explain your infatuation with a duke."

"My infatuation? Lady Alberth, I have not encouraged the duke or gone in search of his attention—"

"It doesn't matter," Lady Alberth said. "You have it, and you will end it."

"And we want proper husbands for our daughters. We are paying for it, and we expect it," Lady Bollinger added.

Susan could have pointed out that they weren't paying for it yet, but they weren't in a listening mood.

The peeresses left the room. However, the moment the door closed, it opened again to let in her sisters, Jane and Ellen.

"I warned you," Ellen said.

"Were you listening at the keyhole?" Susan accused.

Jane dismissed the charge with a wave of her hand.

"One did not need to eavesdrop to know what was being said in this room. Alec warned you that you would embarrass us, and so you have."

"I have done nothing of the sort," Susan said.

"Your name is in the Betting Book at White's," Ellen replied with a self-righteous lift of her chin.

"Many women have their names in that book. The club members wager on everything from who will marry whom to who will drop her baby first to who has the bluest eyes." A headache was starting to form behind her eyes. "This is ridiculous. One should expect at least a measure of support from one's family."

"You were offered the opportunity to live with Dodgin's aunt," Jane pointed out.

"I don't call that support," Susan muttered mutinously, and started for the door.

"Wait," Ellen said. "We are not finished talking to you."

"But *I* am finished talking to you," Susan answered, her hand on the door handle.

"But we didn't come about the scene in the library," Ellen said. "One of your charges, Lady Theresa, I believe, was crying her eyes out in the Ladies' Retiring Room. We thought you would want to know."

"See? We do offer you our support," Jane said, cattily.

Susan didn't make a response but opened the door and left the room.

In the corridor, she tried her best to think clearly. It was hard when she was so hurt and angry by her sisters' response to this crisis, and it was a devil of a fix. The best solution was to avoid the duke completely, which shouldn't be hard. After all, because of her, he wasn't being invited to anything.

The realization was a calming balm for her frantic thoughts. For the first time since she'd heard news of the wager, Susan drew a full breath and released it. All would be well. She needed to focus her attention on her charges. The Duke of Killeigh could take care of himself.

She hurried to the set of rooms set aside for the convenience of the ladies. Lady Theresa was not there, although the attending maid had seen her earlier, "Sobbing her eyes out." Susan left to search for her in the ballroom.

However, just as she entered the ballroom, the butler announced, in grand, round tones, a new arrival to the ball. "His Grace, the Duke of Killeigh."

Susan froze. She dared not take another step into the room. Was it her imagination that everyone turned almost as one and looked right at her?

Almost as one the crowd stepped back, creating a direct line between her and the duke standing proudly in the doorway. He looked magnificently handsome in his tailored black evening attire. That irrational, confusing pull between them was even stronger than it had been when first they'd met.

This wasn't just any man; this was one she had been fated to meet.

And then she thought of the wager . . .

Chapter Five

$\mathcal{R}$oan savored the moment. All eyes in the room, including those of the musicians, who rumor said had put down a quid or two of their own on the wager, were on him and the lovely Miss Rogers.

He had to admit, she had been amazingly easy to conquer. He'd barely even had to lay siege. One wager to catch the imagination of the *ton*, and she hadn't stood a chance.

He walked forward.

Miss Rogers stood completely composed, but there was a gleam of anger in her golden brown eyes. She didn't like losing any more than he did.

However, she'd been neatly outflanked.

As for himself, he'd never felt more alive in his life. He could literally feel the rush of his own blood through his veins, the pounding of his heart.

He didn't bow. He was a duke, after all. But he inclined his head and offered one gloved hand. "Miss Rogers, would you do me the honor of a dance?"

The room had gone so silent, his words seemed to echo off the wall—or was that because in one split second, he'd found himself anxious as to her response, and not because his pride was on the line.

No, he wanted to know how she'd feel in his arms. He had a sudden need to know the scent of her skin and feel her move close to him in harmony.

Her long lashes swept down toward her cheeks.

The room seemed to hold a collective breath, one Roan discovered he held himself.

Her gloved hand came up to rest in his as she dipped into a small curtsy. "I would be honored, Your Grace."

Triumph shot through him—and not because of the wager.

It was as if something he'd long sought was now in his sights. This woman was unlike any other. He knew it with a conviction that went all the way to his bones.

The room had come alive with her response. He could hear murmurs around him and knew those who had wagered against him must be spitting with frustration at how easily she had yielded to his request.

Roan turned to lead her to the dance floor. Their audience stepped back to allow them passage. They'd not taken more than two steps when Miss Rogers made a sharp gasp of a pain and started to fall forward. She caught herself before he could and straightened, placing all her weight on one foot.

Those demure long lashes at last raised for her eyes to meet his. "I'm so sorry, Your Grace. I seem to have twisted my ankle. I won't be able to dance." She let go of his hand and limped back a step, practically hopping on one foot to demonstrate. "I beg you, please find another partner."

She didn't wait for his response but hobbled awkwardly away from him.

Now, he'd been outflanked.

Worse, the majority of people in the room knew, too. Many outwardly grinned.

In two steps he came up beside her. Hooking her arm in his, he said, "Please, let me help you, Miss Rogers. I feel completely responsible for your accident."

She tried to disentangle herself. "It is not your fault, Your Grace. I pray you, please choose another partner."

He tightened his hold. "I would be less than gallant to desert you after causing such an injury."

"Your Grace—" she started to protest, but he cut her off by swinging her up in his arms.

"Let me carry you to a chair," he said, moving toward a set of chairs in a corner of the rooms.

Laughter started all around them. Bright spots of color appeared on Miss Rogers's cheeks. There would be hell to pay once she could set her tongue loose on him, but Roan now had the answer to some of his questions: She felt good in his arms, and there was no perfume that smelled better than the scent of her.

Realizing their audience, he enjoyed making a great show of making her comfortable in a chair. He had a servant fetch a footstool, but instead of setting her foot upon it, he sat himself, reached for her ankle, and rested it on his thigh.

"Your Grace," she protested, trying to pull her foot away from him. He held fast, even going so far as to slide her kid slipper off her foot. "This is unseemly," she whispered furiously at him.

"We must be careful," he said with a straight face. "A twisted ankle is quick to swell. I think it must be wrapped. Fetch bandages," he ordered the footman.

She leaned forward, speaking for his ears alone, "I don't need it wrapped. Please, Your Grace. It will be fine."

"You don't want me or the rest of this fine company to believe you have twisted your ankle accidentally on purpose, do you?"

She studied him a moment, then looked around, realizing that even though the music and conversations had started up again, they were being closely watched. She settled back in her chair, turning her head away from him. "This is ridiculous."

"Yes, isn't it?" Roan agreed with mild amusement although he didn't mind having Miss Rogers's foot in his lap. She had a nice foot, as attractive and well formed as the rest of her. He couldn't resist covertly running his thumb along the inside of her arch.

Her toes curled, but she pressed her lips together, stoically—and he had a flash of insight.

"It isn't just me, is it? Or this Irish duke nonsense. You want to keep all men at bay."

She turned to him, her eyes widening. For a second, she was speechless, and he knew he was right even before the denial reached her lips. "I wish I hadn't started this nonsense," she murmured.

"Yes, it's bringing me too close."

Her brows came together in a frown. "Would you stop that? We are in a roomful of people with prying ears."

"No, I don't believe I will," he said. "I'm ready to be done with games or guessing." He leaned forward. "And I don't care that we are surrounded by people. In fact, I welcome it because what I'm feeling right now is real. Surprisingly real."

She pulled back, resting her hands on the armrests. "Please, don't speak to me that way, Your Grace."

"Why not?" he asked evenly, watching her every move, every breath.

"Because . . ." She looked away.

He waited.

Her gaze swung back to meet his, her vulnerability clear in the depths of her somber eyes. "I don't trust what I feel when you are near," she whispered.

Her candor went straight to his heart, momentarily stunning him by the intensity of his own reaction.

When he didn't speak immediately, she rushed on, "There can never be anything between us—"

Roan found his voice. "Why not?"

"Because," she said as if it were an explanation.

"Because I'm Irish?" he demanded.

"*No,*" she hurried to say. "Because you are a duke. Because you could do so much better than I. Because I've made choices in my life that have been unconventional—" She paused, and a shudder went through her before she finished, "Because I'm old."

Roan had been listening to her litany of objections, but that she thought herself old startled him enough to laugh. He regretted his response the moment the lines of her face tightened.

Not wanting her to form the wrong impression, he reached for her hand. "Anyone believing Miss Susan Rogers is so ancient as to be on the shelf is a daft fool," he said. "As to the others, let me be the judge of the sort of wife I want. I don't live my life for others, and advise you to follow my lead. Most people don't know what they want, so they settle for rules and the opinions of others. Be brave, Miss Rogers. Be bold."

"If only it were that easy, Your Grace," she said sadly.

"*It is.*"

Abruptly, her whole manner changed. She pulled her hand from his. "Lord and Lady Alberth."

Roan could have cursed the interruption. He had been so intent on Miss Rogers, he'd forgotten they were in a crowded ballroom. He rose, placing Miss Rogers stockinged foot on the stool. "Alberth," he said greeting.

His lordship did not acknowledge him. Instead, he snapped to Miss Rogers, "Have you seen our daughter?"

Miss Rogers pushed herself out of the chair. "I was looking for her, my lord," she said. "When I was—" She broke off as if words failed her. "Distracted," she finished weakly, awkwardly slipping on her shoe.

Roan offered a hand to help her, but she ignored him.

"I want my daughter," Alberth said, his voice tight with rage. "I want her now."

"My lord," his worried wife said. "We don't know that she could have run off with Gerald Grover—"

"She shouldn't have been given the opportunity," Alberth said. "*She*"—he nodded to Miss Rogers—"was supposed to keep her eyes on her."

"Let us adjourn this discussion to a more private place," Roan said, moving to stand between the very angry Alberth and Miss Rogers. Too many people were taking an avid interest in the conversation.

"The only thing I'm going to do is find my daughter, Your Grace. This woman was supposed to watch her."

"Alberth, you are working yourself up over nothing—"

"*Nothing?* She's my only child, Your Grace. I must protect her. And while I worry, this woman"—he nodded toward Miss Rogers—"is-is *diddling* away with—with—" His voice broke off as if he realized he'd best think better of what he was saying.

"With *me?*" Roan asked pointedly, daring Alberth to go further.

"Please, Your Grace," Miss Rogers said, taking a step forward.

Roan held up a protective arm, wanting to shield her

from Alberth's ridiculous accusations. However, before any of them could go further, a group of young women pushed their way through the growing audience around them.

"Miss Rogers," one of the girls said. "Here is Lady Theresa."

A very attractive dark-haired girl came forward. "Father, I'm right here," she said in a low, embarrassed voice. "I've never left. And Gerald wasn't here either."

"Where have you been?" a worried Lady Alberth demanded. "I've been looking everywhere."

Lady Theresa glanced around at the number of people surrounding them, then whispered in her mother's ear. Lady Alberth's eyes opened in surprised delight. She whispered to Alberth, whose anger evaporated.

"Haven's son?" he repeated. The Earl of Haven's son was said to be the catch of the Season.

"She was in the supper room with Haven's son," Alberth told the room at large.

There were appropriate murmurs of appreciation at the coup, and Lady Theresa blushed appropriately. "After Miss Rogers talked to me the other evening, I started to think that perhaps she was right. Perhaps I should be open to the addresses of other gentlemen." Her gaze softened when she looked at a young blond-haired fellow, Haven's son, who had joined the crowd around them.

"Well," Roan said, "it appears someone is owed an apology."

"Your Grace," Miss Rogers protested.

Roan shook his head. "No, the man made accusations that were unjustified, and he should apologize." He turned to Alberth. "Won't you, my lord?" He edged his words with a hint of steel.

"She should have known where my daughter was," Alberth answered.

"*You* didn't even know where your daughter was," Roan countered, and received several nods of agreement from their audience.

Alberth was not one to enjoy apologizing. He hedged and shifted his weight, then said, "Very well. I regret the misunderstanding."

It was not a graceful apology, but Miss Rogers bobbed a curtsy, and replied, "Please, I beg you not to think of this again."

His lordship shrugged, then walked over to meet Haven's son. Lady Alberth followed him, and the crowd focused their attentions upon other matters.

Roan was pleased. In fact, he felt a bit heroic for standing up for Miss Rogers. He turned to her, expecting gratitude and, instead, he found her surrounded by Lady Bollinger and others.

Miss Rogers did not appear pleased, and he was puzzled.

The women walked off.

He approached. "Weren't they happy Lady Theresa was found?" It seemed a safe question.

It wasn't.

Miss Rogers turned to him with angry tears in her eyes. "No, they weren't happy. In fact, I've been given the sack by all of them. I'm ruined. Everything I worked for is gone."

"Miss Rogers, I don't know what to say—"

"Don't say *anything*. Not one word. You've said enough. You've done enough." She turned and started walking away.

Roan went after her. Out in the foyer, he demanded, "What have I done wrong?"

She paused long enough to explain, "Have you ever seen one of those tightrope walkers? That's what I do, Your Grace. I walk a tightrope between respectable society and not-so-respectable society. A gentlewoman at this level of society doesn't work. My sisters warned me. I knew the risks I ran. I thought I could keep my balance, but this evening . . ." She shook her head. "You shouldn't have paid attention to me. I'm not worth it. Losing my livelihood isn't worth it."

"Susan," he said, using her Christian name because it was more direct, more intimate, "I wasn't trying to harm you—"

"But that is what happened," she replied, cutting him off. "Excuse me. I've been ordered to leave."

She all but ran out the door, not waiting for her cloak. Roan stood for a second in confusion. He didn't understand how everything had just gone wrong. He charged after her, but was waylaid by a footman who wanted to give him, "My lady's cape."

By the time Roan made it out the door, Miss Rogers had disappeared.

He needed to find her, but first he wanted a conversation with Bollinger and his wife.

Susan was furious with herself. What a *fool* she'd been. Her mistake had been in forgetting her place. She'd allowed her infatuation with the Duke of Killeigh to be too obvious. Too public.

Lady Bollinger and the others had not minced words. She had been deemed "unsuitable," and they were right. Ellen and Jane had warned her.

Of course, it didn't help when she returned to her lonely rooms and realized that the sharp words had not been what had hurt this evening.

No, what had pierced her like a lance was her own

realization at how foolish she had been. Sitting with the duke, having him pay court to her, had actually led her to believe that there might be more to his intentions than some wager, or even pure lust.

She'd wanted to believe he cared for her. Wanted him to *love* her.

Susan shook her head, crossing her arms and pacing the parameters of the room. There was no such thing as love. It was a phantom, a myth, *nonsense*.

But wouldn't it be a blessing to have a man like the duke in love with her? To have him *care* for *her*?

She raised a hand to her forehead, remembering the way he'd defended her to Lord Alberth. Not even her sisters would dare to speak out for her.

Of course, she could blame the duke for causing the incident . . . except that she truly, deeply valued those moments they'd spent together.

The man was dangerous. She lost all common sense around him. He'd destroyed her commissions. She was impoverished. Alone.

And yet, she was also in love.

The word snuck up on her. Startled her. Made her think she was going mad, and yet she knew it to be true.

She'd fallen in love with the Duke of Killeigh.

Susan sank into a chair, startled by the depths of her feelings. She barely knew him . . . and yet, this evening, they spoke as if they'd known each other forever.

Of course, no duke could ever be in love with her—

A knock sounded on the door.

Susan frowned. She rarely had visitors. It was probably one of her sisters, with an ultimatum for disgracing the family. They'd probably been stewing over it for hours.

She went over to the door and hesitated. She should

not answer it. Ellen and Jane would only make her feel worse. They would accuse her of disgracing them, and they would be right.

Her unknown visitor knocked again. "Miss Rogers, *Susan,* please, open the door."

The voice belonged to the Duke of Killeigh.

Chapter Six

Roan knew she was on the other side of the door. He could literally feel her presence through the wood. The pull between them was that strong.

He did not know what he'd do if she denied it.

Nor did he know what he would say if she did open the door. He had her cloak. He'd grabbed it from the footman at the ball, thinking to use the return of it as an excuse.

It was a pitiful substitute for the true reason he'd come for her. Silly even.

Roan had faced French fire. He'd been surrounded by screaming heathens wielding knives and scimitars ready to skin him alive. But he'd never been more afraid than in that moment when, slowly, the door handle turned—and he found himself face-to-face with Susan.

Susan. Even her name felt good to him.

She was still dressed in her evening clothes although

she'd taken the pins out of her prim, tightly arranged curls so that her hair tumbled down around her shoulders. She appeared young, defenseless . . . and frightened. She'd been crying.

It broke his heart.

For a long moment, they stood, and it was in that moment, Roan knew what he felt was true and right.

He loved Susan Rogers.

But did she love him?

He tossed the cloak to the floor and held out his hand. "Will you dance with me?"

"You don't need to do this," she said. "It's over. You won."

"No," he answered. "It's just beginning."

She didn't mistake his meaning. Her eyes, still shiny with tears, softened. "We mustn't. You could do so much better than I, Your Grace."

"Roan," he corrected. She didn't understand so he explained. "I will not have the woman I want for my wife to call me 'Your Grace.' That is reserved for inferior beings. My wife will be my other half. My conscience, my delight, my soul."

The tears now poured freely from her eyes.

Roan didn't know what to make of it. Was she telling him no? He'd never felt so vulnerable. So lost.

He sank down to his knees. "Susan, marry me."

"But you barely know me." She was smiling now . . . through the tears.

"Aye, and the poets say that sometimes we must risk all for love. Susan, I want to spend my life knowing you."

She came down to the floor in front of him. Her arms came around his neck and she kissed him full and hard on the mouth.

Roan wasted no time kissing her back. He kissed her in a way he'd never kissed a woman. He wanted her to know this wasn't just about passion. What was between them was something sacred.

And then she placed his hand on her breast, and he knew she still didn't understand.

It took all his will to pull his hand away. He cupped Susan's face in his hands. Her eyes were wide with confusion. "I want you for my wife. Do you want me for a husband?"

"I believe I started falling in love with you from the moment I laid eyes on you. But, Your Grace—"

"Roan," he insisted.

"Roan," she repeated. "Roan, Roan, *Roan*." She placed her hands on his shoulders. "I can't let you do this—"

"Do you not love me?"

"I said I love you, with an intensity that is almost frightening—"

Roan cut her off with a kiss. He loved the taste of her, the feel of her, the scent of her—

She broke off the kiss. Her breathing matched his own fevered pace. "I'm not worthy of you. There, I've said it. Please, Roan, this cannot happen."

It felt as if she were cutting out her heart to turn him away. What Susan had felt for her long-ago suitor paled in comparison to her feelings for the duke.

For the first time in her life, someone had come after her. Someone had cared what she was feeling, worried about her, wanted to be there for her.

It was a powerful gift.

"For too long, Roan, I've felt as if I've had the weight of the world on my shoulders—first with my parents' deaths, then protecting my sisters. And then, seeing to my own welfare. I am humbled and deeply thankful for your offer. Indeed, just for your presence."

He watched her intently as she spoke. He was so handsome, so noble. So wonderful. However, now a frown had formed on his brow. He leaned back. "Do you love me, Susan?"

She started to hedge, knowing that if she truly cared for him, the best thing she could do would be to stop him from this foolishness.

But as she started to open her mouth to explain, he demanded, "I don't want common sense. Or what you believe you should do. I want to know, lass, do you love *me*? Not the duke, but the man."

"I love the man," she said, unable to hold back her feelings any longer.

"Good. Then I've made up my mind." He rose to his feet, taking her hand and bringing her up with him.

"Your mind about what?" she asked as he picked her cloak up off the floor.

"About us," he said, placing her cape around her shoulders. Without warning, he swung her up in his arms. "We are going to elope."

She opened her mouth to protest—

"No, Susan, for once think of yourself. Make me a happy man and come with me to Scotland. To Gretna Green, where we can be married in a trice, and no one can say us nay. We'll be there before dark tomorrow."

He was completely serious.

And for once, she thought of herself. "Yes. Yes, I will be your wife. Yes, I will go to Scotland. Oh, Roan, and, yes, I love you so much it hurts."

He sealed her promise with a kiss, and before she realized it, they were out the door and on their way. He hired a coach with fast horses at the nearest coaching inn, and as the sun came up on the morning, they were a quarter of their way to Scotland.

If she'd had any doubts about him or a marriage

to him, they were dispelled on the ride. Roan opened himself completely to her, and she returned the favor, sharing with all that was inside her, all she'd feared telling another. They held each other, content with the promise that within hours they would belong to one another.

The drive was uneventful. Their marriage took place at eight the following evening in a low-ceilinged taproom with candlelight all around them. Roan paid each of the witnesses a hundred guineas before taking Susan's hand and leading her up the back stairs to the room waiting for them.

Susan knew she should pretend shyness. She was a virgin after all. But her love for her husband made her eager.

The moment the door closed behind them, she kissed him with abandon.

"I shall never tire of kissing you," Roan promised when they came up for air.

"But there is something more, isn't there?" She noticed how he'd restrained himself on the coach ride. She'd known, because she'd had to struggle to keep her own desire for him in check.

Well, no longer.

"I don't want to hurt you, Susan," he began. "They say this can be painful for a woman—"

She shut him up with a kiss.

After that, there was no restraining either one of them. Laces were fumbled with and finally undone. Buttons freed. Clothes dropped to the floor. The clean sheets felt good against the heat of her body. But nothing could compare with the feeling of her husband lying naked beside her.

Their kisses grew more heated. He was strong in ways she'd not imagined. He held off his own pleasure to please her—and that's when the last traces of doubt left her. This man was a gift from God.

Susan wasn't completely certain what to expect. She had a general idea, but ideas were not the same as experience. What she discovered was that the act of coupling was far more fun than she could have imagined.

Roan tickled her with his tongue, caressed and soothed her with his fingers, and kissed every place that was kissable.

And then, the games between them were over. Her husband's weight rested on top of her. The length of him pressed intimately against her.

He brushed back tangled strands of hair from her face, his expression serious. "I love you, Susan," he said, then kissed her, fully, deeply before entering her in one smooth, strong thrust.

The sensation of him caught her off guard. She gave a small gasp of surprise. Immediately, he was repentant.

"I'm sorry. Here, let me leave you alone—"

Susan stopped him from pulling away by placing her hand on one firm buttock. "You'll go nowhere, husband," she said, "until you've finished what you've started." Her body had adjusted to him. In fact, he felt quite nice . . . but she knew there had to be more.

The worry left his expression. "I think only of your pleasure," he whispered.

"Then begin pleasuring," she answered, the words turning into a soft purr as he did exactly that.

Susan knew she would never forget the joy of this first coupling. Roan was everything she wanted in a lover. He knew what she needed before she was even aware herself.

She clung to him, trusting him. He did not fail her. He took her to places she'd never imagined. Their bodies moved as one until that bright, shining moment when she gave all.

Her whole being vibrated with her love for him. Tears came to her eyes from sheer joy.

And then she felt him join her. He thrust deep and hard as if reaching to her very center before finding his own blessed release.

For a long time, neither moved. They held each other tight.

Susan found her voice first. "May we do this again?"

Her question startled a laugh out of him. He rolled off her, bringing her up so she rested on his chest, her legs intertwined with his. Flipping the bedcovers over them, he nuzzled her nose, and promised, "Morning, noon, and night."

And so they did.

Three days later, they finally left their marriage bed— but Susan was no longer the same woman she had been that first night.

Then, she'd been shy and uncertain of Roan's love.

Now, she emerged a woman deeply loved and confident that, at last, she'd found her place in this world . . . by his side.

Epilogue

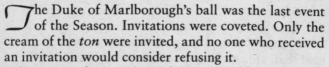

The Duke of Marlborough's ball was the last event of the Season. Invitations were coveted. Only the cream of the *ton* were invited, and no one who received an invitation would consider refusing it.

Consequently, it was a night to see and be seen.

However, when the butler announced the arrival of the Duke and Duchess of Killeigh, conversation stopped. After all, Killeigh had been a bit infamous at the beginning of the Season, with all that talk of his being an Irish Duke and the Order of Precedence. There were few who didn't know the story.

But no one had heard he had married.

Whispers started from people wondering who the lucky woman was. Word had gone around that Killeigh had purchased one of those new homes in Mayfair and was in the process of buying the best of furnishings.

The debutantes were the most curious. Their Season had not gone well. Many missed the wise counsel of Miss Rogers. She'd known exactly what to do and what to say in every circumstance. The most unhappy was Lady Theresa. She missed Gerald Grover and wished she'd not tossed him aside for Lord Haven's vain and stupid son.

She wondered if she had the courage to defy her parents.

Two people who were not curious were Ellen and Jane. They had been relieved not to have to worry about their sister. She had apparently taken off. Run away. They agreed it was rude of her, but at least they wouldn't have to worry about her.

They turned to see who would appear at Killeigh's side as his new bride just as a matter of idle curiosity—and then Ellen dropped her punch cup in surprise. It landed on Jane's new satin slippers, forever staining the fabric, but Jane didn't care. She was just as shocked as Ellen.

Their sister stood on the step beside the Duke of Killeigh.

Susan looked magnificent. Diamonds at her throat, her ears, and nestled in her blond curls sparkled in the candlelight. Her gown could only have come from Madame Lucia's, the premier dressmaker in London. It was a white muslin trimmed in blue lace. On her feet, she wore sandals made of silver cords.

Jane leaned close to Ellen's ears. "Everyone will be wearing those sandals by tomorrow."

Ellen nodded. "She looks positively stunning. Who knew Killeigh had so much money?" She frowned. "Of course, can you believe she just took off without telling us?" she muttered.

"I can believe we'd best do what we must to beg her forgiveness," Jane answered, and Ellen knew she was right.

The person most relived to see them was the Honorable Rees Trenholm. He was the first to approach Roan. "Congratulations, Your Grace, on your marriage." He bowed to Susan. "Killeigh could not have chosen a more beautiful woman for his bride."

Susan blushed but she was actually very nervous. "I pray you, Mr. Trenholm, how does the wind blow? Will there be much gossip?"

Rees laughed. "Of course there will be, but what do you care? The two of you look absolutely happy with each other."

And they were.

"As for myself," Rees said, "I am happy to see you show your face at last, Your Grace. There is a matter of a little wager on the Betting Book at White's." He raised his voice so all could hear. "The matter of a dance has not yet been resolved. And there have been several who have come to me for their money," he added under his breath.

Roan laughed. "Then let me solve the matter now. Your Grace?" he said, offering his hand to his wife.

She placed a gloved hand in his, and he led her to the dance floor. The crowd moved back, and the other dancers stepped back, leaving the floor for them.

"That must have been quite a wager," Susan murmured.

Her husband smiled. "My lips are sealed."

The music started, and, for a second, Susan was lost in the perfect wonder of the evening. They moved as one, and she was so caught up in the music and being in the arms of the man she loved, she forgot about their audience. She forgot her past. She forgot about everything but her present and her future.

Too soon, the music came to an end.

Both Roan and Susan were startled, and very flattered, when the crowd clapped for their performance. Susan knew she had been accepted.

Her husband leaned close. "Don't be too ahead of yourself," he warned. "After all, we have to sit *down* the table from Marlborough and the others."

Susan rewarded his impudence with a kiss that delighted the crowd, who swooped in on them with their well-wishes. Ellen and Jane found themselves standing on the fringes of the crowd.

Rees couldn't help but smile. He was relieved he wasn't going to have to make good on all those bets.

Lady Theresa stood by the doors leading out to the garden watching all this. Miss Rogers looked so happy, so loved.

And she felt so alone.

Tears threatened. She slipped outside, wanting a private moment alone. If her father saw her crying, he'd be very annoyed.

She swiped her cheeks with the back of her hand. She'd been such a fool. Gerald had loved her, and she'd treated him badly. What she wouldn't give to have his love back—

"*Theresa.*"

It was her beloved Gerald's voice. At first, she thought she was imagining things, but then she saw him. He stood in the night shadows by the garden gate.

Without hesitation, she lifted her skirt hem and ran to him. His arms around her were strong and secure. They kissed, and she wept, overwhelmed with her love for this man. Her parents would never approve of him . . . but she could love no one else.

"I was so wrong," she declared, but he shushed her with a kiss.

When they could speak again, her beloved asked, "Will you go to Scotland with me, Theresa?"

She turned, looked back at the glittering company in the ballroom that could be seen through the glass doors. Her heart twisted at the thought of her parents—and yet, this was her life.

She chose Love.

"Now," she answered Gerald. "This very minute."

And so it was that on that March night, a new set of lovers eloped.

Because in the end, the measure of a well-lived life is not titles or riches. It's not even measured by the people we please, especially at the cost of our own souls.

No, the true measure of a well-lived life is how well we love . . . and how well we are loved in return.

CATHY MAXWELL spends hours in front of her computer pondering the question, "Why do people fall in love?" It remains for her the great mystery of life and the secret to happiness. She lives in beautiful Virginia with her children, horses, dogs, and cats. Fans can contact Cathy at *www.cathymaxwell.com*.

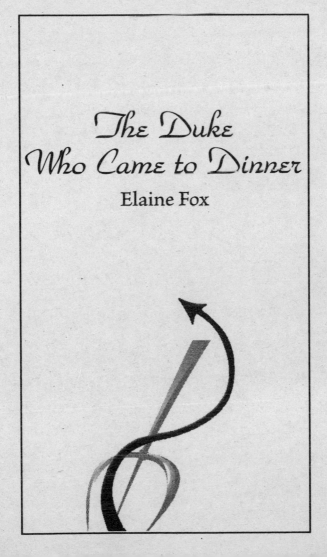

The Duke
Who Came to Dinner
Elaine Fox

Chapter One

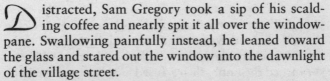

Distracted, Sam Gregory took a sip of his scalding coffee and nearly spit it all over the windowpane. Swallowing painfully instead, he leaned toward the glass and stared out the window into the dawnlight of the village street.

Pedaling a bicycle with all the determination of Dorothy's Wicked Witch of the West was a slender, fairhaired, stark-naked woman.

Stark, he marveled, forgetting his coffee.

Naked.

He moved right, nearly overturning a table lamp, to look out the next window as she sped past.

Her hair streamed out behind her in long, damp curls, some clinging to her naked back, some bouncing past her shoulders. A few strands adhered to her face. Her trim legs pumped hard, and he realized she wore the barest of panties in the palest of pinks—an odd conces-

sion to the perception that nudity might not be appropriate for a bike ride.

Sam craned his neck and let his temple touch the windowpane as he watched her cycle past the house.

Other than the panties, she was quite obviously naked.
Firm, perky breasts pointed forward as she pedaled, her
eyes looking neither left nor right but trained on the
street in front of her as if willing herself invisible.

That she was beautiful was abundantly clear. As was
the fact that she was nuts.

It only occurred to him after she'd rolled out of sight
that she might have needed assistance. Like a robe, he
thought, looking down at his tattered flannel. Or a car,
he thought, glancing at the faded Nissan pickup in the
drive.

It was too late, however. She was gone. Like a bizarre
dream. The ghost of Lady Godiva, he thought with a
smile. On a Schwinn.

Gray Gilliam nearly flung the bicycle into the shrubs at
the end of the driveway and sprinted to the back door.
She'd left it unlocked, but it balked as she pushed before
she turned the knob, then refused as she turned the knob
and pulled, then opened with a bang against the inside
wall as she turned, pushed and stumbled into the mudroom.

She panted, a stitch in her side so sharp she pressed it
with one hand and bent forward.

She had never been so humiliated in her life. Though
she'd kept her eyes forward as she'd ridden home, she
was sure somebody somewhere along the way had wit-
nessed her disgrace. Now she'd have to wonder every
time she got a strange look from someone if they'd seen
her naked.

Breath finally slowing close to normal, she flip-flopped

out of the mudroom, across the kitchen, and headed for the stairs. Despite the fact that she was inside, goose bumps rose on her naked skin. She decided it was because of the chill inside the house and not because she felt as if she were being watched. The house was always cold, she reasoned.

And she always felt like she was being watched, another voice in her head volunteered.

While it was true, it was silly, she told herself. It made no sense to feel watched in this house. For one thing, the place sat on close to ten acres of private beachfront land, so no one was looking in the windows. And if there'd been someone inside the house, the creaking floorboards and unoiled door hinges would have alerted her to their presence immediately.

She shivered. Her thin Virginia blood was simply unused to June in Massachusetts.

She had just donned her fat white terry-cloth robe when the phone rang. She sprinted to the kitchen where the lone receiver was.

"Do you love it?" her friend Rachel asked.

Rachel almost always started a phone conversation in the middle, something Gray both enjoyed and wondered if she should disapprove of. She'd been taught to ask politely if someone was otherwise engaged before assuming a conversation was mutually agreeable.

"The house," Rachel elaborated. "Isn't it perfect for a summer away?"

"Of course it is! But oh, Rachel, you won't believe what just happened to me!" She hunkered down into the plush leather armchair in the music room. It was her favorite chair, even though it put her in mind of how it must feel to sit in a giant leather baseball glove. "This morning was so beautiful I decided to go for a bike ride. And I was standing on the shore, over by the bay outside of town, and it was gorgeous and the water felt so warm, and I was thinking I really needed to be more like you—"

"Gray, I hate it when you say things like that." Rachel's voice showed her displeasure.

"I know you do, but it's true. I'm way too self-conscious, for one thing, so I decided what you would do would be to—"

"Wait! Let me guess. You stripped naked, went swimming, and got bitten by a shark."

Gray laughed, almost wishing that had been the outcome. "All but the last bit."

Rachel gasped. "No way. You? You got naked. In public."

"It wasn't exactly public. There was no one around. But yes, I went swimming. Skinny-dipping."

There was a pause. Then, "All right, who are you really and what have you done with Gray?"

Gray laughed again. Leave it to Rachel to cheer her up even on the heels of her biggest mortification. "Very funny."

"So, how was it, acting like me? Rewarding? Or did something bad happen?" Rachel's voice was wry.

"It was *very* rewarding," Gray said, realizing she'd gone about this story the wrong way. "At first it was positively divine, and I could see why you follow your impulses, why physical freedom is so exhilarating. But then . . ." She felt breathless anew at the embarrassing memory, flushing hot again. "Oh Rachel, you won't believe this, but a dog stole my clothes!"

"A—what?"

"As I was swimming, I saw this beautiful white dog running up the beach. I'd seen the dog before, actually. In fact, I saw it just yesterday on the beach, with a guy in a long, heavy coat. I remember because I thought it was strange that the guy was wearing a winter coat in June. Anyway, before I could do anything, this dog picked up my sundress and ran off. Just . . . *ran off*. I couldn't believe it. I started whistling for it. Calling it. But it disappeared up the beach without a backward look."

"Oh my God." Rachel paused, and was obviously having a hard time restraining laughter. "What about the guy in the coat? Was he around?"

"I didn't see him, but I did wait for him for quite a while. 'Til my fingers got pruney, and I thought I'd freeze to death. Then I ran out of the water, grabbed my underpants—thank goodness he didn't take those too—and pedaled home as fast as I could."

Rachel was openly laughing now. "Did anyone see you?"

"No! At least I don't think so. I didn't see a soul, thank God. Not that I was looking."

Rachel hooted. "And you had to go through town, didn't you? What other way is there?"

"I don't know! I went through town. It was *mortifying*. Imagine it."

"Oh I am," Rachel said through guffaws, adding, after Gray moaned, "Come on. It's *funny*. And nothing bad happened, did it? I mean besides being embarrassed."

"No, I just kept my eyes on the road and my feet on the pedals." Gray hesitated, struck by the idea that being embarrassed didn't really qualify as something "bad" happening. "I guess I was only embarrassed."

"And seen by no one, as far as you know."

"As far as I know," she repeated ominously.

"Gray, I promise you, if anyone saw you, they were struck dumb by your beauty. It's not like you know anyone anyway." She chuckled again. "Besides, you were probably pedaling so fast you were invisible."

Despite herself, Gray laughed. "It *was* the fastest I've ever ridden."

"The fact is, I should try to be more like you," Rachel said. "This is exactly the kind of thing that would happen to me, except the town would have been throwing a parade, and everyone would have seen me."

Gray scoffed. "You don't want to be like me. I'm sick to death of who I am. Uptight and cautious and—well, my students call me the Gray Ghost. That should tell you something."

"It tells me they remember the time you caught them drinking beer in the woods."

"No, it means I'm practically invisible. I've spent a lifetime actually striving to be invisible. God forbid I ever *made a show of myself*, as my mother used to say. And now look at me. I'm scared of my own shadow."

"You are not."

"Trust me, I am. Coming up here was the gutsiest thing I've done in years, and right off the bat I do something stupid."

"What you did, Gray, was—was *make a show of yourself!* And wasn't it kind of fun? You're already getting out of your shell, not even a week into your summer."

"Maybe," she conceded thoughtfully. Out of her clothes, out of her shell . . . same thing. "But mark my words. I'm going to change myself this summer. I'm determined. I'm going to loosen up. Follow my impulses. Be brave."

"Gutsy Gray! And you're off to a great start!"

Gray laughed. "I don't know about great. But getting naked in public *was* a start."

Rachel cracked up again, before getting down to the reason for her call. "Listen, I'm wondering if you've seen any sign of the so-called ghost yet."

"Not unless the ghost is an obnoxious sundress-stealing dog." Gray crossed her legs and picked at a terry-cloth pill on her robe. She wished Rachel hadn't brought up that damn ghost. She had just been starting to feel comfortable. If it weren't for all the talk about this place being haunted, she was sure she wouldn't be imagining herself watched at every turn.

"Nope, the ghost is the Duke of Dunkirk. At least according to legend. Supposedly, he's buried right where our house was built."

One of the reasons Gray was house-sitting this summer was because Rachel and her husband, Robert Kinnistan, were trying to sell their house in the Cape Cod town of Wellfleet, Massachusetts. The trouble, according to their Realtor, was that the place was old and rumored to be haunted. Rachel thought that if someone were living in it, that might prove to the squeamish it was both comfortable and ghost-free.

Before Gray arrived, she hadn't believed any of those reasons were why the house wasn't selling, most particularly the ghost. She'd thought their Realtor was lazy. Or maybe the squeamish one herself. But the opportunity to get out of DC and reinvent herself was more than she could pass up. Though she hadn't told her friends, she was thinking of moving there if she could find a job.

It wasn't until she'd gotten to the house that she'd been consumed by creepy feelings. Talk about the power of suggestion. She didn't even *believe* in ghosts, so it was ridiculous to feel spooked.

"Why would a ghost haunt the place it was buried?" Gray asked, exasperated. "I mean, really, you'd think they'd haunt the place they died. Or the people who were responsible. These things never make sense."

"I know, ghost legends are all the same. Although I think some people say he didn't actually die until he reached the shore. And where he reached the shore is supposedly right where our house is. Others say he died in a house that stood where ours is. I just don't know."

"So have you ever noticed anything odd when you've been here?"

"Well..." Rachel's tone was reluctant. "I haven't, but Robert says he has. I can't remember what, exactly."

Gray swallowed. "Ask him if he's ever noticed this: every now and then I smell something burning. Not like the house is on fire but like a pipe or a cigarette. But when I look around, I can't find anything. It's weird."

The line went silent. Gray wondered if they'd been cut off. A chill swept through her again.

"Hello? Rachel?"

"I'm here," she said. "I'm thinking. You know, Robert might have mentioned something about a pipe smell..."

Despite herself, Gray shivered. This was stupid. She wasn't the superstitious sort. She was more interested in figuring out *why* the house was considered haunted than whether or not it really was. Because she knew the answer to that. There were no such things as ghosts.

"Then it must be something explainable. Like a light socket overheating or something caught in a radiator," she reasoned. "So who was the Duke of Dunkirk, and what was he doing here?"

Rachel sighed. "I don't know. Robert could tell you. All I know is, the duke is supposedly our ghost, and that bar in town, Dunkirk's Den, is named for him. Personally, I think it's Covington Burgess."

"You think someone named Covington Burgess is haunting your house?" Visions of an old sea captain or a long-dead fisherman pacing the crow's nest filled her head.

Rachel laughed. "No, he's all too alive, in my opinion. I think he's the one who took the legend of this duke and attached it to our house, saying it was haunted. He's also the rat who bought the Neely home for a song after claiming it was sinking into the marsh, and he's been after Robert's house for years. I guess we should feel lucky he hasn't sicced his engineering firm on us yet. No doubt he'd get them to claim four hundred feet of cliff face is getting ready to give way and send the place into the ocean. Though that would be easier to refute than the ghost thing."

"Covington Burgess," Gray repeated. "I'll remember that name."

"Do. And if you hear anything about him wanting to buy, let me know. Oh darn. Gray, the baby just woke up. I've got to go. I thought we'd have more time to chat."

"Don't worry." Gray felt a pang. She missed her friend. "I've got to shower anyway. We'll talk soon. And I'll let you know what I find out about this supposed ghost."

"Good," Rachel said, then finished, laughing, "And remember: go with guts."

Chapter Two

The swelling strings of a Puccini aria were spilling out of his stereo speakers when Sam heard the scratching at his back door. No doubt the dog had finally realized he'd taken off this morning without getting his breakfast first.

Sam finished wiping the windowsill where he'd spilled his coffee and glanced outside once more as if the woman might still be there.

Strange things happened all the time once the summer people came to the cape, but he had to say he'd never seen a woman riding naked through town on a bicycle before. In his opinion, it was an improvement over the typical tourist problems of drunkenness, litter, noise, illegal parking, and a formidable line outside The Lighthouse for breakfast.

Wadding up the paper towel in his hand, he headed for the back of the house and pushed open the screen door. The large white dog trotted in manfully, for all the world as if a fanfare of trumpets heralded his arrival.

"Good morning, Duke. Up to no good?" Sam asked conversationally.

One of Duke's ears flicked in Sam's direction, the only sign that he'd heard.

Sam had found the dog a year ago on the beach up near Truro. He'd been wearing no collar and sported neither a tattoo nor, as the shelter discovered, a microchip. Sam posted signs all over the cape and checked in with animal shelters from Hyannis to Provincetown, but nobody ever claimed him, so Sam decided to keep him. Or the dog had decided to keep Sam. One way or the other, they'd stayed together.

The name Duke had come easily. For some reason it was the first one that sprang to Sam's mind, and the dog responded to it immediately. Ever since then, however, Duke had acted as if Sam were born to serve him. With his thick white coat, pricked ears, and high, curling tail, the dog had an attitude of authority that one found oneself obeying before giving it any thought.

Duke, indeed, Sam had thought on many occasions. Still, he was a gentle animal, who rarely caused trouble. He just went where he wanted, when he wanted, and nobody could stop him.

Sam studied the dog's coat for evidence he'd been rolling in dead things, but aside from a shower of sand from his feet and a few bits of seaweed clinging to his fur, he appeared as white as when he'd left.

Grabbing the broom, which was always at the ready, Sam swept the offending grit out the door. Then he stepped onto the porch to sweep the sand into the grass behind the house. The yard was small, only about fifteen feet deep, but it was enough to buffer the house from the marsh beyond. He stood for a moment, looking at the morning sun on the water, the fresh smell of salt water mixing with the warmth of the soil making him take a deep, lung-expanding breath.

Between the view and the Puccini, he felt like the day promised something special. Something the bizarre spectacle of the morning had only portended. He smiled, surveying the yard. He was proud of the new bronze sculpture he'd bought that spring, an abstract that stood near the edge of the marsh, echoing the feel of the cattails and grasses. He planned to add more art pieces when he had the funds, maybe some iron and stonework, too.

As he turned to go inside, something on the grass near the short gravel drive caught his eye. For a moment Sam thought the white heap was a plastic shopping bag, but it looked too big for that. He stepped off the porch and strode toward it, thinking, *Sure enough, litter hits the town the same time as the tourists*. It was like clockwork.

But when he reached the mass he saw that it wasn't white, but pale yellow. And it wasn't a plastic bag but an article of clothing. He plucked it from the ground with two fingers and held it aloft. Covered with sand and sporting bits of kelp, he saw that it was a dress. A woman's sundress, to be precise.

He looked from the dress in his hand toward the back door of his house, putting two and two and two together. And getting a mess.

Low laughter started in the back of his throat. A runaway dog, a naked bicyclist, and the sudden appearance of a dress all pointed to one thing: somehow Duke had stolen that poor woman's clothes. No wonder she'd been pedaling so fast. She wasn't an exhibitionist; she'd been robbed.

He took the thing up in both hands and shook it. Much of the seaweed and a lot of sand showered onto the ground at his feet. It was a flimsy little affair, made of some knit material with spaghetti straps and a three-button vee at the front. Pale yellow. Like the woman's hair.

He folded it over an arm and headed back to the house. The chances of his figuring out where she was staying were slim. For one thing, he didn't have a lot of time this week to be searching out the rental houses along the oceanside. He had three articles to write for various publications on the latest classical music releases.

For another thing, something he'd noted in the woman's posture told him she'd probably rather be without the dress than know that someone had seen her riding naked through the streets at the crack of dawn.

What the hell, he thought. He'd wash it anyway. She'd probably be gone at the end of the week, and he'd never see her, but just in case he ran into her, he'd have it ready. Why should she care if some stranger had seen her panicked flight this morning? It wasn't as if she'd ever see him again.

Gray stood looking at the sign for Dunkirk's Den, the bar where all the locals reputedly hung out. Had she been interested in being herself, she would have gone to Aesop's Tables in the middle of town. With a lovely front lawn filled with tables, and the cozy lounge upstairs, it was just the type of place Cynthia Gray Gilliam of McLean, Virginia, would have patronized.

But tonight she was just Gray, of Gull Cottage Lane, Wellfleet, and despite her friend's protests, she was still convinced that trying to be more like Rachel was a good idea.

Look at this morning, she told herself. So what if

she'd had to ride home naked on a bicycle? She'd had twenty minutes of exhilaration first.

She briefly put a hand to her forehead to forestall the automatic blush the memory incited. It was only embarrassment, she reminded herself. And embarrassment did not count as something bad happening.

She'd had an incredible, early-morning swim, learned what it felt like to be naked out-of-doors— something she was sure she hadn't done since she was a toddler, if then—*and* she had a hilarious story to tell her friends. No harm, no foul, as her ex-boyfriend Lawrence would say.

She shook her head to rid it of Lawrence. It had been over a year since their breakup, and in that time he'd gotten married. It was past time to get him out of her mind.

Still, her stomach somersaulted at the idea of going into the basement bar. It looked dark and seedy. She bet it sold only Budweiser. The bathrooms were probably disgusting. But music blared happily from within, and if she wanted to be different than herself, well, this seemed to be the place. Not to mention that somebody here might be able to tell her the story of the Duke of Dunkirk.

Go with guts, she thought, straightening her shoulders.

She doubted if even Rachel or Robert had ever come here.

In deference to the venue she'd chosen, Gray had dressed down. She wore jeans with her Etienne Aignier flats and carried a small, Coach clutch purse. Her hair was pulled back in a ponytail, and she wore only the barest of makeup with her white Ralph Lauren sweatshirt. Simple diamond studs adorned her ears, her only jewelry other than a Cartier watch.

It was as casual as Cynthia Gray Gilliam got. And while she knew it was not what some would consider Dunkirk's Den material, she had to content herself with the fact that her mother would have tackled her at the front door if she'd been around to know her daughter was actually going out in these clothes and not painting the house.

Not that her mother was here, of course. No, she was home in Virginia, disapproving of Gray telepathically, as usual.

Inhaling deeply—*go with guts, go with guts*—Gray headed for the door just as a large man in a small tank top pushed out of the bar and belched into the balmy evening air.

"Oh, excuse me," Gray said automatically, as if she'd interrupted a private moment.

The man grunted as she took the weight of the door from him. He gave her a look as if he meant to turn around and follow her back in, but she scooted past him into the bar.

"No problem," he slurred belatedly, as the door shut in his face.

The place was dark and undistinguished. Chrome stools with black vinyl seats surrounded a horseshoe bar, around which tables lined the dark-paneled walls. On the far side was a tiny dance floor with, incongruously, a dartboard on one side. Gray had a moment of imagining the mishaps that could occur if the two activities went on simultaneously, then reminded herself that she was not the Safety Inspector or anyone else who needed to care about such things.

She made her way to the bar and sat gingerly on one of the stools, half-hoping the enormous sumo wrestler behind the bar wouldn't notice her.

He did.

He sauntered over, pushed a cocktail napkin in front of her, and asked, "What can I get for yah?"

She licked her lips. "Um. Could I, uh, get a glass of wine?" Her voice rose at the end as if expecting the man to scoff at anything other than an order of beer, or maybe a pirate-sized shot of rum.

"Sure. What kind?" He looked at her passively.

She smiled in return. Of course they had wine. She was being ridiculous. Every place had wine. "Oh, let's see. Maybe a chardonnay—or wait, a Pinot Grigio, I think." She smiled again. "If you've got it?"

He chewed for a second on what she hoped was a piece of gum, studied her, then said, "What kind, white or red?"

Gray flushed from head to foot, wished she could flee, then said in a small voice, "White, please."

He leaned toward her, music bouncing all around them. "Did you say 'white'?"

She nodded and glanced around so self-consciously she didn't actually see anyone as much as hope to make them look away from her.

The man took a glass down from a rack overhead and filled it from a tap with a white handle. Next to it was a tap with a red handle. And below the taps Gray was sure were two large boxes of something labeled WINE.

He deposited the full glass in front of her, and asked, "Want to start a tab?"

Still frozen with embarrassment, Gray could not imagine fishing into her purse for money at that moment. "Uh, sure."

He nodded and moved to the register.

Gray exhaled a long, slow breath.

* * *

Across the bar, Sam Gregory eyed the young woman with great curiosity. She was, without a doubt, the most beautiful woman he'd ever seen in this bar. Which was saying nothing. But she might also be the most beautiful woman he'd ever seen in Wellfleet. Or in Massachusetts. Hell, maybe anywhere.

In the light from the neon Budweiser sign over the bar, her skin glowed like a white sand beach in moonlight. Her wide eyes shone like sea glass under elegantly lean brows. Add to that her thick wavy hair and ballerina bearing, and he was turning into a poet trying to justify why he couldn't take his eyes off her.

Then there was that demure little smile with the upraised lashes she'd given Roy. Roy, who'd thought she'd ordered "some Grecian formula" when she'd said "Pinot Grigio."

He chuckled to himself. She was a fish out of water, all right. Though not as out of water as she had been that morning.

For unless he missed his bet, he was certain this was his Schwinn-riding Lady Godiva. And he'd be a fool not to come to her aid now that he'd been given a second chance.

The question was, how did you go about mentioning to a woman you'd never met that you had her clothes?

Gray sipped her wine fast, eyes darting around the bar, trying to pick out who wouldn't scare her to death if they came over to talk. Or who, if it came to it, she might consider going to talk to herself. She hadn't really considered what to do once she'd braved the door, and was wondering if perhaps throwing out one's entire personality was really the route to take to become someone new.

But really, didn't she owe it to her commitment to change to give it everything she had? Surely riding naked through town on a bicycle had been the start of something momentous.

Then again, it might have been enough for one day.

A stringy-haired woman in the corner nursed a brown drink in a short glass, but she looked glassy-eyed and despondent, and seemed already to be talking to someone despite the fact that no one was near. It seemed naïve to think she might be wearing a Bluetooth when her shoes didn't match.

There were two men drinking and watching ESPN on the TV, but neither of them looked particularly friendly. In fact they both looked a little tough, with their thin hard faces and sinewy tattooed arms.

There was a guy playing a pinball game, and another playing video poker, and then there was the sumo-wrestler bartender, who had not indicated any sort of interest in a conversation with her beyond "red or white."

Finally, there was a tall thin guy in worn khaki shorts and a faded red tee shirt coming around the bar with a beer in his hand. A Budweiser, of course.

Where had he been? she wondered. She hadn't noticed him before, but then half the bar was so badly lit it was hard to see beyond the glare of the oversized TV hanging in the corner of the well where the liquor bottles were.

He was normal-looking, she thought, eyeing him covertly. Which was a good thing because it looked as if he were coming toward her.

Sure enough he sat down next to her, straddle-legged on the stool, facing her.

"What's a nice girl like you doing in a dump like this?" he asked pleasantly. His voice was low and had a husky quality to it that made the cheesy come-on seem more intimate than it would have otherwise.

Make up that line yourself? she wanted to ask, but that would have been rude. And despite the fact that Rachel would have said it, Gray smiled, and said, "Do you think this is a dump?"

His eyes, light-colored and sharp in a face that was otherwise friendly, made a slow loop around their surroundings and lit back on her. "I think it defines 'dump.' Don't you?"

People were awfully blunt here. Must be a northern thing, she guessed, and chalked it up as something else she needed to try. Bluntness.

"I suppose I do," she said, her tone emerging primly.

She picked up her wineglass. The beverage was more like grape brine than wine, but for Gray it beat cheap beer.

"But it's fun. You know, kind of." She looked uncertainly around again. "Is it always so empty? I thought there'd be more people here."

"It's early." He placed his beer on the bar next to him. "This place doesn't really get going until after ten or so."

He didn't have the same hard edges as the rest of the patrons, and from what she could tell from their brief exchange, he seemed educated. She wondered if he was a tourist or a resident.

"So what are you doing here, if you think it's a dump?"

He grinned, and Gray was struck by the thought that he was nice-looking. Strange thing not to notice right off. The smile did it, though. Deep dimples and appealing crow's-feet made him distinctly handsome.

"I like dumps." He tilted his head. "But I don't think that's true of you. Which leaves only one conclusion."

She eyed him while sipping her wine again. "Which is?"

"You're slumming."

"Slumming?" Gray tried unsuccessfully to look surprised. It was exactly how she felt. Still, she didn't need to admit it to this guy. Something told her he'd hold it against her. Heck, everybody in the room would hold it against her, but she got the feeling this guy was testing her. And she'd never failed a test in her life.

He cocked a grin at her. "Aren't you?"

"Are you judging me, Mr. . . . .?" She knew calling him "Mister" anything was ridiculous, but it was the closest she could come to his cheeky banter.

He laughed, and she thought again that he was nice-looking. In a Jekyll-Hyde kind of way. "Sam. My name is Sam. And I am being something of a jackass. I apologize. It's just that I've never seen a woman who looked like you in this place."

She looked at her drink, unwilling to be flattered, if that was indeed what he meant. It was hard to tell. "So you were judging me."

"Aren't you judging me? Aren't we all judging each other?" He flagged the bartender.

"Sounds like barroom philosophizing to me." She took another sip of her wine, which she was pleased to note had become almost palatable. It meant she could finish it and leave. She'd gotten out of her comfort zone, been gutsy for one full drink; maybe she could give herself a break and have a nice dinner at Aesop's Tables.

"Sometimes that's the only kind of philosophizing that makes sense," Sam said.

She picked up her purse to retrieve her wallet when the bartender placed another drink in front of her and one in front of Sam.

"Oh, I didn't order that," she protested.

"I know." The sumo wrestler pointed to Sam. "He did."

Sam picked up his beer and saluted her. "Cheers," he said. "Ms. . . .?"

She gave him a brief, undecided look, then picked up the glass. What the heck, she thought. It beat going back to her haunted home. Besides, if she couldn't be gutsy with this brazen fellow, who could she be gusty with?

"My name is Gray," she said with a smile.

"*Gray?*" He started to chuckle.

She shot him a warning look that had no effect on him whatsoever. Oddly, this made her feel better about his teasing.

"I'd've pegged you for more of a Saffron. Maybe even a Magenta. But Gray?" He shook his head, smiling. "No way."

"It's a family name."

"The Crayola family?"

"My first name is Cynthia," she explained, trying to clarify—what? That she was not in fact a crayon? He was *joking,* for pity's sake, and she was acting like the schoolmarm she was.

"Ah." He nodded, picked up his beer, and took a long pull from it.

She was boring him. She was a humorless snob. He was thinking her name suited her perfectly.

"So what's a nice guy like you doing in a dump like this?" She straightened her shoulders and tried to look confident.

He smiled slyly, looking at her from the corners of his eyes. "Slumming. What else?"

She laughed—*see? I get jokes*—and her glance grazed him from tee shirt to sneakers. "You don't look like you are."

He burst out laughing, and she blushed. She hadn't meant to insult him, but of course she had. Lord, she couldn't play this game. She had no idea how to flirt. When she'd met Lawrence, she'd been set up by friends. At a wine tasting. At the National Gallery. All she'd had to do was talk coherently about the Impressionists, and that was easy.

"Touché, Gray. You're tougher than you look. So, are you here on vacation?"

"I'm summering here." She twisted her glass in the condensation on the bar. The bartender had forgone the formality of a cocktail napkin with drink number two. "What about you?"

His smile curled ironically.

She shook her head, sighing. "What did I say this time?"

"What do you mean?"

"I mean you're looking rather . . . condescending again."

One long-fingered hand touched his own chest. "Me? Condescending? I promise you, Gray, I didn't mean to . . ." His words petered out, and he laughed at her skeptical look. "Oh okay. It was 'summering.' That word. Nobody but debutantes and doctors' wives use seasons as verbs."

"And nobody but reverse snobs throw 'debutante' around as an insult." She socked away another gulp of wine and felt proud of herself. It was an awkward parry, but still. She wasn't taking any of this guy's guff. "Not to mention that you were wrong. I was neither a debutante nor am I a doctor's wife."

The look he gave her kicked up a surprising team of butterflies in her stomach. Appreciation and amusement. It made her feel that not only was he looking at her, but he was really *seeing* her.

"I'm very glad to hear that."

The words made her feel hot. She took a calming

breath. "Okay, so, what does one typically do in a place like this?"

Sam gave her a conspiratorial smile. "I'll tell you what 'one' does," he said, "in a place like this."

She looked up quickly to find him laughing at her again, but this time it was overt, not smug. She chuckled.

"One does clams." He motioned for the bartender again.

"Clams? What do you mean?"

"I mean fried clams. The Den may not do much right in the way of food, but they have some of the best fried clams on the Cape. And the onion rings are first-rate." He put one foot up on the lower rail of her stool. "Besides, it is what one does here. Can I order you some?" She hesitated, and he took the opportunity to flag the bartender. "Two clam plates with onion rings. And put it on my tab."

Gray smiled. It was chivalrous, in a way. And because she didn't want to drink two glasses of wine on an empty stomach, she was grateful. "Thank you."

"You're welcome. Don't want you leaving the Cape without trying all the delicacies."

"You're actually a nice guy, aren't you?" She looked at him quizzically.

He laughed. "Was there ever any doubt?"

Chapter Three

Sam looked at that perfect porcelain-doll face, smiling up at him with lips that cried out to be kissed and eyes that challenged, despite something naked in their depths, and felt a tightening in the pit of his stomach. This girl was uncomfortably beautiful. And she was a helluva lot sharper than he'd given her credit for, even if he was still certain she was former debutante material.

But hey, she wanted slumming, he could give her slumming. And maybe be entertained in return. After all, any woman who would be in a position to have her dress stolen by a dog had to have some wildness in her.

The clams arrived, and they feasted, then had another round of drinks. She was looking just the slightest bit tipsy when she held up a hand, and said, "Enough. I can't consume another bite or take another sip of anything. Except maybe some water."

Sam ordered a couple of waters.

"So what do you do up here?" Gray asked him, her eyes glowing in the dim bar light. "If you're not just 'summering.'"

She gave him a saucy look, and he marveled at the flawlessness of her features. Strands of hair had come loose from her ponytail and trailed next to her face, framing it as if planned for a photo shoot. One of the longer tendrils caressed the slender column of her neck, and he reached a finger up to touch it, felt the softness of her skin. A corresponding heat filled his core.

"I'll tell you what I'd like to do," he said. "I'd like to take your picture. Right here, right now, just the way you are."

Unplanned perfection, that was what she radiated.

He was unprepared for her burst of laughter. "Oh my, that's almost as good a line as your first one!"

He took back his hand and put it in his pocket. "My first—?"

"'What's a nice girl like you . . . ?'" She dissolved into laughter.

He couldn't help smiling with her. She was tipsy, no doubt about it. "Now who's judging whom?"

She reached a hand up to touch his cheek and sobered, looking deeply into his eyes. Sam swallowed as the blood stalled in his veins.

In a low, fake accent, she asked, "Would you care to look at my etchings?" She fell into laughter again.

This time he couldn't stop himself. He took her hand from his face, held it tightly in his, and leaned toward her, his lips capturing hers.

In the time they had eaten, the bar had filled with people, and the music had grown correspondingly louder as the night had worn on. But Sam hadn't noticed. And now, as Gray's lips opened under his, the whole place could have blown away around them, and he wouldn't have known the difference.

She leaned toward him, which surprised him, and one hand grasped the front of his tee shirt. He stepped into her, the barstool hitting him in the thighs, and ran a hand around her back. His fingers felt the trim curve of her waist and tightened around it.

After a second he pulled back and looked into her pale blue eyes, pupils huge in the dim bar. "Want to get out of here?"

For a moment she appeared suspended in time. Her lips glistened from his kiss, and she gazed up at him as if momentarily stunned. Then the corners of her mouth curved, and she dropped her head. A second later she put a hand to her mouth, and he realized she was laughing.

"Sorry! Sorry!" She looked up through her lashes at him, eyes alive with mirth.

"Let me guess. Another cliché you've heard a thousand times." He tilted his head and looked at her, at once amused and mildly embarrassed.

" 'Want to get out of here?' " she repeated. " 'What do you say we get some air?' 'How about we go someplace more comfortable?' 'Did I tell you I have all of Sinatra's albums on vinyl?' " She giggled again.

"Okay. How about, Let's blow this pop stand. Whaddya say, Gidge?"

"Much better!" She beamed and stood up, her body lengthening along his in the crowded space. Her barstool tipped over behind her but was righted by someone who immediately occupied it. She fumbled on the bar for her little purse and grabbed his arm hard enough to make him totter. "Okay, Moondoggie, let's go."

They went up the stairs and out into the star-flung night. It was so much darker there than at home, Gray noticed, and the air smelled heavily of sea salt, tinged faintly with decaying fish. She breathed deeply as the breeze lifted the hair from her neck.

She felt good, she realized. More relaxed than she'd been in years. Of course, she'd had a little more to drink than she'd intended, but so what. She was of age.

"'*I'm just mad about Saffron,*'" Sam sang under his breath, "'*Saffron's mad about me . . .*'"

Gray laughed and looked up at her companion as they headed toward the harbor. Sam's long-legged steps were easy beside hers, and she envied the way he seemed so at home in his own skin. Casual, yet in control at the same time.

Interesting, she thought. And interesting that she was there beside him. She, Gray Gilliam, who never went out on a date without first getting a résumé and references on whoever the lucky man happened to be, was walking beside some guy named Sam she had met in a bar.

On the heels of that thought she realized that she had done it. She had done the gutsy thing. She had come to a place that was outside her comfort zone, met a guy who was totally not her type, and had managed to come out of it feeling more like herself than ever before.

She tucked her purse under her arm and pushed her hands into her pockets, glancing at Sam again from the corner of her eyes. He was definitely not the type of guy she would fall for. He was challenging and lively and a little bit unkempt. She'd had to be tough and on her toes as never before just to talk to him. But she'd done it! She'd verbally sparred with him, and she had not come out feeling like a ninny. Instead, she felt triumphant. *Gutsy!*

She inhaled deeply again and turned slowly around in a circle as she walked, looking up at the stars. From the harbor came the clink of riggings against masts and the soft splash of water on rocking hulls.

"Oh I could just drink this air in forever. Isn't it wonderful?" She beamed up at him.

He looked down at her, his eyes crinkling with his smile, and she thought what a pity it was he wasn't her type.

"It's damn near perfect," he agreed, but his grin was ironic.

She shook her head. "Too bad you don't really appreciate it."

"What do you mean? I'm the one who may actually end up drinking this air forever." He half faced her as they walked. "You're only drinking it for the summer, remember?"

She liked the way he did that, the way his shoulders angled toward her as he talked. He really did have an innate kind of polish, perhaps even some chivalry. He had, after all, bought her dinner and ordered water after they'd had those drinks. She caught herself staring at him a moment too long and looked down the street.

"That's true," she said, opting not to tell him of her tentative plans to stay. "So maybe you just take it for granted." She shrugged, fearing she was losing the energy to keep up with his banter. She was, after all, a beginner.

A corner of his mouth lifted. "That's a little presumptuous, don't you think?"

"According to you, that's what we do, isn't it? Judge each other all the time?" She lifted a brow in his direction and was gratified to hear him laugh.

He had a terrific laugh.

She could notice things like that, she reasoned, despite the fact that she would never fall for him. She could appreciate his appeal. His gait, for instance. It was agile and aloof, like a Thoroughbred that could take off at any moment with great speed, even though at the moment he was simply walking along beside her. She wouldn't want to be the one with her hands constantly on the reins, however. She had the feeling she'd end up with leather burn.

"It must be wonderful living here all the time." She sighed, impulsively linking her arm through his. "It's so . . . free."

She heard him chuckle and turned to look up at him.

"That might be the person, more than the place." Sam squeezed her arm gently with his own. "You seem to be getting into the swing of your summer vacation pretty well."

Gray shook her head. "No, it's the place. I've taken vacations at other places and never felt like this. Like I've shed something heavy I've been carrying for a long time."

A broken heart, for example, she thought. She could just imagine what Lawrence would say about her walking along so chummily with a guy she'd just met. A guy wearing unpressed khaki shorts and running shoes that had obviously seen many miles.

Though it was more than that. It was something heavy within *her* that she'd lost. Inhibition, maybe. A claustrophobic sense of self.

"So what *do* you do? For a living, I mean," she asked, kicking a rock ahead of them and watching it bounce into the scrub grass by the side of the road.

He paused and looked down. Gray stopped walking before her arm slipped out of his.

"I have the feeling what you would consider a living and what I would are considerably different." He reached out a hand to her other arm and drew her toward him.

"I don't know about that." Gray let him link his hands behind the small of her back. "If you're eating and have a roof over your head, I'd consider that a living. And we know you're drinking."

He laughed.

She placed a hand on his tee-shirted chest and was surprised by the solid feel of the muscle beneath. She was also surprised at how comfortable she felt in his arms, despite knowing that he wasn't her type, that this wasn't a romantic evening, that he surely didn't think she was the right woman for him either.

"I—" he began.

"That you, Sam?" The gruff voice came out of the darkness and startled them both.

Sam exhaled slowly a moment, then said, "Yeah. Covington?"

Gray's head whipped around in the darkness at the name. *Covington Burgess.* Hadn't Rachel said that was someone to look out for?

A small man, with wild white hair and glasses on a cord around his neck, stepped from the shadows. He wore baggy dungarees and rubber boots, with a thick, nubby sweater.

"What ah you doin' out heah?" The old man's voice, in addition to being laced with a strong New England accent, was distinctly annoyed.

"I could ask you the same thing." Sam stepped back, ending the embrace but sliding one hand down Gray's arm to catch her hand in his.

"Me! I live here, dammit, that's my house right there as you well know."

Sam chuckled. "Yes I do. I'm wondering what you're doing out here in the middle of the night."

"Seeing what all the ruckus is about, obviously." One gnarled hand clutched the glasses at his chest and put them to his face. "Who's that with you? I don't know this person. Who ah you, young lady?"

Sam looked down at Gray, and she could see the light of amusement glittering in his eyes. "This is Gray . . . uh . . ."

Embarrassment flooded her. She'd been caught canoodling with a guy who didn't even know her last name, and it couldn't be more obvious to the little man standing in front of them. She dropped Sam's hand and stepped toward Covington Burgess, extending her right hand to shake.

"Gray Gilliam, Mr. Burgess," she said, perhaps a bit too forcefully. She'd been in too many moods this night. "I'm house-sitting for Robert and Rachel Kinnestan. At Gull Cottage—"

"I know the house," he grumbled, looking suspiciously at her hand. Or at least it seemed suspicious to Gray, the way shadows fell over his grizzled eyebrows to mask his eyes. He took her hand and shook it once in a warm grip. "Place is a terror, you ask me. They oughta do somethin'. Thought they had it up for sale."

She straightened. "They do. And I don't know what you mean, the house is perfectly lovely."

"Hmph. You ain't heard it yet, I gather." Covington turned to Sam. "You two should go home. It's the middle of the night. Guess I'll have to drive you, young lady, seein's how you both been drinking."

"What? No, I have my car." Gray shook her head. "I can give Sam a ride."

"Uh, Gray," Sam said, "I live right there." With a motion of his head he indicated the building behind them, directly across the street from Covington Burgess's.

Gray looked at the frame clapboard house with the little front porch. Behind it lay the water, calm and gleaming in the moonlight like a spirit.

"You live there?" She turned fully to take the place in.

"I drink it in day and night." His voice was tinged with humor.

For some reason, seeing his house made him seem more like a real person and less like someone useful on her road to personal change.

"It's lovely," she said wonderingly, gazing at the wrap-around porch. Beyond it, marsh grass dark as pen-and-ink slashes stood against the canvas of water. A silent black pier stretched out from the shore.

As she stared, a white dog appeared from behind Sam's house and trotted up the street, away from them.

"Hey!" she said, recognizing the plumed tail from the morning's clothes-robber. She started to point, then thought better of it.

"What?" Sam turned just as the dog disappeared around the bend.

She shook her head. "Uh, nothing. I just thought I saw something. Never mind."

The last thing she wanted to do was explain to these two what had happened that morning. With a start, she realized she had ridden past this very spot, past both Sam's and Covington Burgess's houses, stark naked.

Glad of the darkness, she pressed a hand to one scalding cheek.

"Gray, I think you should take Covington up on the ride. We have had kind of a lot to drink."

She turned to him, panicked at having to ride with the strange little man. "I know but . . . *Sam*," she finished, her voice urgent.

How could she say she didn't want to get into a car with the man when he was standing right there?

Sam gave her a reassuring look. "I'll come with you. Just to be sure you get home all right."

"Oh yes," she breathed. "That would be nice."

"I'm gettin' the keys." Covington turned and shuffled off toward his darkened house, looking for all the world like a Hobbit heading back to his Hobbit-hole.

They stood, awkwardly silent, next to each other in the dark. She wondered where the dog had gone. If she came back the next day and found it, would she also find her dress?

Distantly, she heard water lapping at the shore across the street. Did Sam hear that in his bedroom when he went to sleep at night?

"How well do you know Covington Burgess?" she asked, crossing her arms over her chest. The evening's chill had penetrated her sweatshirt.

Sam shrugged, pushing his hands into his pockets. "Well, I live right across the street from him, but I wouldn't say I know him well. He's got pretty much a hand in everything around town, too, from the school board to the town council, so it's hard not to have some dealings with him if you live here. How do *you* know him?"

"I only know of him. Rachel said something about him being . . ." She hesitated, realizing Sam might consider him a friend. "She, uh, she just said he might be . . ." Her wine-addled brain couldn't come up with an alternative to the truth.

Sam laughed, and angled toward her, adding in a low voice, "A pain in the ass?"

She smiled, relieved. "Something like that."

The rumble of an engine came from behind Covington's house, and headlights illuminated the driveway. Two widely spaced headlights, Gray noted, before an enormous, seventies-era Oldsmobile crept into the light from the streetlamp.

"Oh my God." Unconsciously, Gray stepped closer to Sam. "Is he okay to drive that thing? How does he see over the wheel?"

She could feel Sam's warmth as he took her hand again. "Telephone book," he whispered.

The three of them sat on the long bench seat in the front, Gray in the middle, leaning heavily into Sam, her hands clutching his forearm as they bounced over the gravel-and-sand road that led to Gray's house by the sea. When it came into view, the place loomed in the inky night, a hulking, sprawling shape against the shore. Gray blinked, a sinking feeling in her gut. The place couldn't have looked more ominous. Surely it was the power of suggestion. Though Covington Burgess hadn't said much, his *You ain't heard it yet, I gather* was enough to confirm that if he hadn't started the rumors about the house being haunted, he at least had heard them.

Why hadn't she left any lights on? she wondered, feeling trepidation to her core. Then, *hadn't* she left lights on? She could swear she remembered turning on the outside floods before she left, knowing she'd be driving home in the dark. Had something happened? She glanced uneasily from window to window as if she might catch a glimpse of Mrs. Danvers from *Rebecca* in one of the windows, about to set fire to the place.

"Here you go, missy," Covington said. "Don't know how you stay here, myself. Place has always given me the creeps. Might want to leave some lights on next time you go out."

"Th-thank you." Gray slid across the seat as Sam opened the door and got out, gently pulling his arm out from under her clawlike grip. She glanced at the elfin man beside her. His face, lit only by the dashboard light, looked vaguely malevolent, like the face of the house. "For the ride. It was nice meeting you," she added, taking Sam's hand to rise from the car.

"You be careful, now." Though the words were kind, he said them as if irritated at having to remind her. Covington dipped his head to look out the passenger door. "Sam, you ready?"

The car drifted forward with a groan of ancient brakes, and he threw it in PARK. The machine lurched against the transmission.

She stumbled into Sam as the car moved. "You gonna be all right?" Sam asked, steadying her.

"Would you mind coming in with me?" she asked, voice low, eyeing the darkened house anxiously. "Just for a minute. To make sure everything's . . . okay?"

"Sure." He smiled softly. "Hey, are you all right? You're shaking."

She forced a little laugh. "I'm just cold. And it's so dark."

He nodded, looked at her an extended moment, then leaned down to look in the open car door at Covington. "Hey, Cov, why don't you go on back? I'm going in with Gray just to check the place out."

"I can wait," the man snarled. "Long's you ain't plannin' on painting the livin' room or nothin' while you're in there."

"No, no. I don't want you to wait. I can ride her bike home. It's not that far. You go on back to bed. I'm sorry we woke you."

"You didn't wake me. I was awake anyway. Just 'cause you wah makin' more noise than a flock a geese don't mean I wasn't awake already. Damn arrogant," he finished, muttering the final words.

"Uh, okay, good. Glad we didn't wake you. I'll be fine here, really. You go on."

Covington's fuzzy head began to shake, and a sound like wheezing emerged from his throat. A laugh, Gray realized after a moment of alarm.

"I see what yah up to. Young men nevah change," he crowed. "All right, then. I'll go on."

He shifted the car into reverse and nearly took Sam's head off as the car lumbered backward. He slammed on the brake.

Sam took hold of the door, said, "Thanks for the ride!" and closed it.

Covington pulled backward out of the drive. They were alone, in a pitch-black night, with the sea roaring softly in the background and a possibly haunted house standing sentry in the foreground.

"How do you know that I have a bike?" Gray asked suspiciously.

Was it her imagination, or did he look abashed?

"Everybody's got a bike around here. Lots of times they come with the rental house." He took her arm. "Come on. Let's check this place out."

They walked down the drive, sand crunching softly beneath their feet and the ocean growing louder as they approached the house. The place was perched high on a cliff, but tucked behind a dune covered in sea grass, making the beach from ground level just the ghost of an idea beneath the sliver of moon.

"I love this old place," Sam said, as they pushed up the dune on the ocean side of the house by mutual yet unspoken assent.

"You know it?" she asked, as the sea came into view, whitecaps folding in on themselves against the shore below.

"I've known it since I was a kid. My family used to come here on vacation—I grew up outside of Boston— and we always made up stories about this old place, not that it doesn't have enough stories all on its own. The fact that it's situated all by itself on such a big plot of land made it look especially old. Like even time had given it a wide berth."

"Do you know about the ghost, then?"

He turned, and she caught the flash of his smile in the moonlight. "The Duke of Dunkirk?"

"Yes, exactly! So you know the tale? Rachel thought Covington Burgess had made it all up, to keep them from getting a good price on the house."

"Cov?" He shook his head. "Nah. That legend's been around for decades. Not that it isn't exactly the kind of thing he'd do. But I remember reading about the duke in an old book when I was a kid."

"But the supposed fact that he was buried here, under this house, that's just crazy. Why would a duke be buried here?"

"Well, he wasn't a duke when he got here. Or rather, he didn't know he was a duke."

"What do you mean?" She shivered in the cold.

"Do you want to go inside?" He reached an arm out for her, and she tucked herself into his shoulder, smiling.

"No. I want to hear the story."

They gazed out over the ocean.

"All right, then. The duke was apparently born a younger son. Not, in other words, destined to inherit the title. So, being an adventurous young man, he decided to come to the New World and try his hand at whaling. While he was gone, though, both his father and his older brother died, making him the duke. The sad thing is, he never knew it. He died on a whaling expedition, and his buddies brought him back here to bury him. Legend has it he walks the earth as the ghostly Duke of Dunkirk because he never got the chance to be duke while he was alive."

"But surely once he died, the title fell to someone else. Making the whole 'walking the earth as the duke' thing kind of pointless."

"That's just it. When he died, the title died with him. He was the last of the line. So I guess his mission is to keep the Duke of Dunkirk as alive as he's able to be."

Gray snuggled into Sam's side. It was amazing how comfortable she felt with him. His arm around her shoulders felt just right, and their bodies fit together in a lovely, cozy way. She had the brief thought they might fit in other ways, too. She shivered, but not with cold.

"Come on," Sam said. "Let's get you inside. You're freezing. I'll just check the place out and go."

As they started to turn toward the house something caught Gray's eye, and she froze, staring down at the beach.

"What?" he asked.

She peered into the darkness, unsure if she was losing her mind or not, but the beach was now empty. A second ago she could have sworn she'd seen the white dog loping along the sand.

"Nothing," she said, scanning the beach for the man in the long coat. But whatever she'd seen was gone. Or had never been there. She laughed, looking up at Sam. "I think all this talk of ghosts has gone to my head!"

Chapter Four

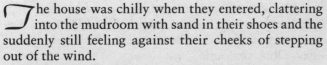

The house was chilly when they entered, clattering into the mudroom with sand in their shoes and the suddenly still feeling against their cheeks of stepping out of the wind.

"I thought I left the heat on," Gray said. "And some lights. That's so odd."

"Maybe it's a fuse." Sam waited a beat while they moved into the kitchen from the side door. "Or the ghost."

She laughed nervously. "You don't really believe all that stuff, do you? About the dead duke and all?"

He looked around the kitchen as they stepped from the mudroom. It looked just the way he'd always pictured it. Painted cabinets, high ceiling, old but solid-looking appliances, hardy wood counters. "Hey, anything's possible."

She flipped a switch, and the kitchen lights came on.

He raised his brows. "That rules out the fuse."

She sent him an eye roll. "Reality rules out the ghost. I'm just going to check the thermostat."

She headed for the dining room, and Sam followed, nearly plowing into her when she stopped suddenly, sniffing the air. "Do you smell that?" She turned slowly in a circle, nose in the air.

"What is it, Lassie?"

She shot him a half-amused glance. "It's the weirdest thing. Every now and again I could swear I smell smoke. Not like the house is on fire, but cigarette or pipe smoke. It's happening again now. Don't you smell that?"

He sniffed.

"See what I mean?" She watched him intently.

"Yeah." He walked the perimeter of the room. "Actually, yeah. It's faint but . . ."

"Do you think something's burning?"

He shook his head. "Doesn't smell like wood burning. It's like you said, more like a pipe or something. You know . . ." he added, "the Duke of Dunkirk was rumored to be an avid pipe smoker . . ." He gave her an intense look of doom.

She went motionless, eyes wide. "Really?" Her voice was close to a whisper.

God, I am an ass. He smiled and shook his head. "I have no idea. I was just messing with you."

She let out a breath, her shoulders sagging, but he could see amusement in her eyes.

"Thanks a lot. I wasn't even thinking it was the ghost." She moved to the thermostat. "Here's the problem. It's pushed down below fifty. No wonder it's not on."

She moved the plastic lever to the right, the furnace kicked on with a thump and a groan.

"Do you mind if I look around a little?" he asked.

"I've been curious about this place my whole life, always wondered what it looked like inside."

"Sure, go ahead." She watched him walk from the room and admired his physique. She was glad he wasn't in a hurry to go home. Even better, while he was looking around, she'd have the chance to clean herself up a little. She had the feeling her hair was wild, and her makeup definitely needed touching up.

Ten minutes later she found him in the music room. At least, she called it the music room. It was where the ancient stereo and crateful of record albums were. She'd found some old Duke Ellington and Ella Fitzgerald, one with Louis Armstrong, and had been playing them since she got here.

He knelt before the crate, flipping through the albums. When he heard her enter, he turned his head and grinned at her. "Hey, you *do* have all of Sinatra's albums on vinyl. There's some really good stuff in here."

She knelt beside him. "I know. The old jazz is my favorite."

"Oh, man, this is *great*." He pulled an album from the back and flipped it over, reading.

"What?" She leaned close, brushing his shoulder with hers.

"Rubenstein, playing the Emperor Concerto." He glanced at her. "Beethoven. Does this thing work?" He lifted the plastic cover over the turntable.

"Yes. I've been playing it every day since I got here. I was amazed the needle was still good. The thing looked like it hadn't been touched in a decade."

"Okay, go stand over there. Midway between the speakers. This is going to blow you away."

She looked at him curiously, and he gave a sheepish smile. "Sorry. Don't mean to order you around, but trust me, you'll love this."

"I didn't feel ordered around." She stood and moved to the center of the room. "I just didn't realize you were a classical music buff."

"All my life." He handled the album gingerly, careful not to touch the surface. "My parents told me I was born humming Bach. Now, close your eyes."

She smiled. "Okay."

Moments later she heard the low *thump* of the needle making contact with the record and the *pop* and *hiss* of vinyl. The opening orchestral chord made her jump, then the hands of a master descended on the piano keyboard. From the opening arpeggio, she was enraptured. Sam had turned the music up so loud that the notes seemed to travel both up her spine and the keyboard in unison, swelling around her, buoying her upon a wave of sound.

It was marvelous. As the music built to crescendo after crescendo, piano and orchestra merging and dancing against one another, she felt a form of delirium take her. She'd never experienced music like this before, thunderous enough to drown out all her thoughts, yet so beautiful it filled her with joy. As if the strings had been plucked within her, vibrating her emotions.

Behind her, she felt Sam move close, the nearness of his body creating ripples of sensation within her even though he didn't touch her.

She turned her body to face him and found him looking down at her, eyes gentle in warm light. She was overcome with the desire to touch him, to feel him touch her, to make a connection with this man who really had very little to do with who she was or what she wanted. Yet he felt so familiar, as if she'd known him for years.

Whatever part of herself she had shed earlier in the evening was the part that had determined this man was not her type, and all that was left was the impassioned woman here before him. A woman enraptured by the music, and the night, and his presence, and the very air around them that still trembled with the last notes of Beethoven.

In the silence, her fingers rose to his chest and traced the outline of his breast pocket. "Thank you for that. It was . . . incredible. I've never heard anything like it."

"I'm glad you enjoyed it." He said it quietly, as if he meant it, *really* meant it. As if for him it wasn't just something to say.

"Thank you, too, for coming in with me tonight," she said, adding, chagrined, "I was nervous."

Slowly, he reached out, and his hands came to rest on her hips. "Are you nervous now?"

The low tone of his voice set her nerves atremble.

She looked up into his face, complex, changeable, expressive. She felt like she could look at that face forever and never be bored.

With a tightening of his fingers, he pulled her close, his body against hers, and bent his head down to catch her lips.

The fire was immediate and furious. The fire between them, that was. If she'd thought she'd smelled smoke before, this was an all-out conflagration.

His hands moved up to cup her face, his mouth probing, his hips pressing hers. Against his hard body, hers went soft, melting into him, going hot and liquid to her core.

Could she possibly be this reckless? What on earth could stop her? She had never in her life slept with someone on a first date—and this hadn't even been a date. But she was consumed by a desire so fierce she didn't recognize herself. Her hands roved up his back, then down to his hips, clutching the taut muscles of his buttocks and pulling his hardness against her.

His hands dropped to her breasts, pushed up under her sweatshirt, then under her shirt. She felt his hot palms on her flesh and moaned with relief. She had to have him, she could not—*would not*—stop herself.

At first she thought he had moaned in return, and registered it as vaguely odd that she'd seemed to feel it in the floor. But when an inhuman wail vibrated up the walls, she froze.

Sam did, too.

They both looked over at the turntable. It had turned itself off.

"What the hell was that?" Sam's voice was almost as low a rumble as the furnace.

"I . . . I have no idea."

You ain't heard it yet, I gather.

Fainter now, but still audible was a weary *woo-ooo-ooo,* a sound for all the world like something a cartoon ghost would make at a Halloween party.

"Do you think this is this what Covington Burgess was talking about?" She gripped his arms with rigid hands.

Sam pulled back and raised one brow. "Let's not go invoking ghosts just yet. Seems to me it has to be the heating system. Have you used the furnace before?"

"Yes, I've had it on most nights since I got here. So, five nights, not including tonight."

He looked at her in bemusement. "Gray, it's June."

"Sam, it's cold. Don't forget, I come from Virginia. Where summer means *warm* weather. Besides, I've never heard anything like *that* before."

The sound had stopped, but inside Gray's head it echoed like a threat.

Sam's eyes scanned the room. "I'll go check it out. Is there a basement? And a flashlight?"

"Yes to the basement. I'll look for a flashlight."

She rummaged through some drawers in the kitchen

until she came up with an old but solid Maglite. She watched him make his way down the wooden steps to the basement. It was really more of a cellar, with a packed-dirt floor and rough stone walls that looked as if the long-ago builders had chipped the foundation out of the earth with miners' picks.

"I'll wait here," she said, as Sam opened the door to the basement.

He glanced back at her, amused. "Good idea."

As Sam disappeared into the dim light of the single-bulbed cellar, Gray sat on the top step. The sound had stopped, but the chill in the house remained. Didn't they say you felt a chill when a ghost was around?

She laughed at herself. She didn't believe in ghosts. Besides, it seemed pretty obvious this was a furnace problem. But what about the smoke smell, she wondered, then shook her head against the thought. This was what came of getting way overheated only to be left to cool off on her own.

Which brought her to the bigger issue of Sam. Ten minutes ago she'd been ready to jump into bed with him. Had he felt the same? Certainly he had seemed to.

A puff of air brushed by her cheek, and she smelled smoke again. She sat up straight, put a palm to her face, and sniffed the air, her heart racing. A second later the hairs on the back of her neck rose, as if someone stood just behind her. She twisted, pushing her back against the doorjamb.

The kitchen behind her was empty. Silent.

In fact, the basement was silent, too.

"Hey, how's it going down there?" she called, peering down the stairs. She was starting to creep herself out. "Sam?"

The ensuing silence sent her pulse racing. She stood, one hand gripping the handrail, and stared at the six square feet of basement visible from the top of the stairs as if she could conjure him.

She heard a rustling, briefly imagined Sam wrestling with an ethereal nobleman, and took one step down the staircase.

"Sam?" Her voice was reedy. She cleared her throat. "Sam!"

A moment later he appeared at the bottom of the steps. His hair was tousled, his shirt collar askew, and what looked like a large spiderweb clung to one sleeve.

"It's definitely your furnace." He wiped at the web with one hand, making a face as it clung to his fingers. "The filter looks like it's been there since the turn of the century, but there's a valve on it I've seen go bad before. That's what made the woo-woo whistling sound. I can come back tomorrow with my tools and fix it up."

"Oh good." She took a deep, relieved breath. Just seeing him put her at ease. She looked at his hands, imagined them taking their time . . . exploring . . . She shook herself, dragged her eyes to his face. "It's strange that it was so *loud,* though. Do you think that's why people have said this place is haunted?"

"Maybe. The noise travels up through the ducts, so that probably amplifies it, makes it echo. And then there's your smoke problem."

She noticed he held something. "What's that?"

He grinned and lifted the narrow box in one hand. "The ghostly pipe. An old carton of cigarettes hidden behind the furnace. Somebody here must have been a closet smoker."

Gray tilted her head. "I don't think Robert smokes, Rachel would hate that."

He shook his head. "These are old. The box and a couple of the packs inside are a little singed from the heat, but you can still see that this is not modern packaging. Take a look. They're probably ten years old."

"Is the furnace that old?"

He made a sound between a scoff and a laugh. "That furnace is ancient. I'm surprised they haven't had to replace it. I can patch it up, but it's a miracle it's still working."

He started up the stairs, holding out a deep purple box with the words *Pall Mall* on it, along with some sort of crest.

"Ooh." She took the box in both hands. "My grandfather used to smoke these. I was devastated when he died."

"Lung cancer?"

She gave a dire laugh. "Yeah. Go figure."

"I guess we've solved the mystery, then. Laid the ghost to rest, as they say. You going to be around tomorrow?"

She startled. "Uh. Around? Sure. Maybe not awake, considering it's going on 2:00 A.M. now." She laughed, dragging her mind back to the problem at hand. Her brow furrowed. "You know how to do that? Fix furnaces and stuff?"

"Sure, I do it all the time."

Ah, she thought. *He must be some kind of plumber.* "Well, great."

She stepped back from the doorway as he reentered the kitchen, unsure what to do. Gray placed the cigarettes on the counter, and the flashlight, then they stood there for an awkward moment.

Gray thought he might move in to kiss her again—pick up where they left off when the "ghost" moaned—but instead he pushed his hands into his pockets and looked toward the door.

"Well, I guess it's getting late. I should let you get to sleep."

"Oh." She didn't mean to sound surprised, so she covered it quickly. "Yes, definitely. I'm exhausted. It . . . was nice to meet you."

She cringed inwardly. If that wasn't the most clumsy thing she could have said, she didn't know what was.

He looked at her, brows raised. "Yeah. You, too. Bike's in the garage?"

She crossed her arms over her chest. "Yes. Are you sure you'll be all right riding back? It's so late. . ."

"Oh sure. You should turn that furnace off for the night, probably, just to keep it quiet. Wouldn't want you getting spooked in the middle of the night." A grin shot across his face.

She laughed. "Too late. It *is* the middle of the night."

"True." For a second he looked as if he might kiss her again, but he just took a deep breath, and said, "All right, then—"

Steeling herself, she blurted, "You could stay, you know. On the couch I mean. Because it's so late. If you wanted."

He pressed his lips together and dropped his gaze. "I appreciate it, but I should probably just take the bike."

Disappointment sank in her gut as she followed him. "Okay."

"Hey, what's your phone number?" he asked. "I'll call you tomorrow about fixing that thing."

She nearly stumbled over her feet to write down her number, wondering if she should offer to pay him. She'd cross that bridge tomorrow, she thought, glad that she would see him again despite this awkward ending to the evening.

Once at the back door, he turned and gave her a crooked smile. "It really was nice to meet you, Gray."

"Yes, it was. Nice to meet you, ah, too. As I said." She grimaced when he turned to open the door.

What an idiot. How could she be so shy with him now when not half an hour ago she had her hands on his ass while his were under her shirt?

He had just walked down the steps and taken the bicycle from where it leaned against the wall when she felt the prickle of someone watching her again. She glanced behind her into the kitchen, but of course it was empty.

"Hey, Sam?" she called, just before he got on the bike.

"Yeah?" He paused, looking at her with brows raised expectantly.

"What year was it that the duke supposedly died here?"

He furrowed his brow and thought a minute. "Around 1813, I think. Why?"

She swallowed hard. "And when was that Beethoven piece written? The one you played tonight?"

A slow smile started across his face. "Written around 1810, but I don't think it was performed until close to 1812."

She nodded, stomach quaking with nerves.

"You're not thinking we woke the ghost with his favorite piece, are you?" Sam asked with a grin.

She forced a smile in return. "No, no. I was just . . . curious. Good night, Sam."

He waved a hand and, with one foot on a pedal, swung his other leg over the seat and took off into the moonlight.

Little had she known this morning when she was cycling madly home naked that the very same bike would be carrying a handsome stranger back to town early the next day.

Once he was out of sight, she moved back into the

music room and plopped into the leather chair, frowning. She was tempted to play the Beethoven again because she wanted to remember the feel of Sam's hands and mouth and body on hers. Had he changed his mind? She'd opened the door to his staying, offering him the couch, which everyone knew could mean anything. But instead he'd chosen to leave.

He'd chosen a cold bike ride at two in the morning rather than staying in her house. With her. Alone.

She sighed. He might have gotten rid of her ghost but that didn't mean she wouldn't be haunted tonight.

Chapter Five

The following day was stunning. Warm and sunny, with a cooling breeze flowing through Sam's open windows. Summer was finally here.

Duke heard him stir and sat up straight next to Sam's bed, panting in his face. With his brown gaze trained on Sam, Duke conveyed to him that someone's needs were not being met, and if Sam were smart, he would attend to them fast. Specifically, Duke wanted outside.

"I know, buddy," Sam said, stretching. The last thing he wanted to do was get out of bed. Instead, he lay listening to Duke's breathing and remembering the feel of Gray Gilliam's body against his.

Had he been foolish or fortunate? It was hard to say.

He glanced at the clock, nearly nine o'clock. He'd better get a move on. Recalling Duke's early escape yesterday reminded him that he'd left the dress—*Gray's* dress—in the washer overnight. He pushed out of bed and padded down the stairs in bare feet. Retrieving it from the washer, he shook it out, then took it out back to hang it on the clothesline. If there was one thing he'd learned from the last woman he'd dated, it was that girl clothes often did not take kindly to the dryer. In addition to having his dog steal Gray's dress, he was not willing to compound the problem by ruining it.

Not that it would matter if he never got up the nerve to give it back to her. He'd had plenty of opportunities last night to mention that he had it, but it never seemed like the right time to embarrass them both.

Duke trotted around the small yard, content this morning to do his business locally. Sam scrounged up a couple of clothespins and hung the yellow sundress on the line, where it waved like a conquering flag in the freshening breeze. It had been a long time since he'd had a woman's dress in his house, and he couldn't help thinking how nice it would be to have the woman who owned this one there, too.

Then again, she could turn out to be a nut. Last night had been a lot of fun, but it was only one evening. He'd misjudged people with more time than that to observe them. Carolyn, to name one. The woman who'd taught him, by throwing an antique vase at him, that women's clothing should not go in the dryer.

That was one thing that had occurred to him last night as he'd been looking at Gray's furnace. She was beautiful, and intelligent, and certainly seemed nice, but he didn't know her at all. If they had slept together, and she'd turned out to be different than she seemed, it would have made for a very long summer.

If he was honest, though, the real reason he had decided not to spend the night was that he was afraid she *was* everything she seemed to be. That was, the kind of girl he could really fall for, and the last thing he needed was to fall for someone who was leaving in a month or two.

That said, it had been hard to leave her. With her wide blue eyes and kitten-soft hair, not to mention her killer body, he'd damn near had to tear himself away.

From inside the house, Duke barked, and Sam jogged up the back steps to find the dog at the front window, tail sailing back and forth like the white flag of surrender. Inexplicably, his nerves jumped, as if he knew Gray was at the door. He felt the conflict of wanting desperately to see her and yet not wanting to ruin the memory of the night before by seeing her again. What if she wasn't what she'd seemed?

He was being stupid, he thought, and opened the door. But the porch was empty. He took one step out and saw someone move around the corner of the house, clearly heading toward the back. He caught a fleeting glimpse of blond hair, and excitement rippled through his chest.

It *was* Gray. Had she gotten a ride in somehow? Was she looking for her bicycle? Or him?

On the heels of that thought, he realized that she was heading for his backyard. The very place her dress hung drying in the summer air.

Laying his head back, he closed his eyes and cursed.

Duke barked and ran for the back door. Sam followed, squinting his eyes as if that might change the view. Out the window he saw Gray, in a short white tee shirt and clamdiggers, standing by the clothesline fingering her dress.

With a deep, bracing breath, he opened the back door. Duke bounded out, tail high and wagging wildly.

Gray turned toward him, and on her face he read shock, then surprise as she spun toward the approaching dog.

"He's friendly," Sam called, sensing doom. This was the part where she suspected him of doing something awful. Where he had to explain the unexplainable—really, the dress just showed up on my lawn—with an excuse as flimsy as "the dog ate my homework."

Duke bounded toward her, but rather than looking afraid, Gray knelt and extended her hand, palm up, for Duke to inspect.

"Is this where you live, you naughty thing?" she said, laughing. She turned a bemused expression on Sam. "This is *your* dog?"

He shrugged ruefully. "If I say yes, are you going to be mad at me?"

"That depends," she said, rising. Duke sat on her feet and leaned up against her thigh, snowy head bent back to look up at her adoringly.

Traitor, Sam thought. He should be over there ripping the dress off the line, to show her how he'd done it.

"Why do you think I'd be mad?" She eyed him suspiciously.

Too late, he realized that by admitting he knew this was her dress, he was divulging that a) he'd seen her naked on the bicycle and b) he hadn't told her. His mind worked furiously, as his face warmed with shame, but all he could come up with was the fact that he was pretty much screwed any way this played out, so it was probably best to stick to the truth.

"Are you blushing?" she asked, eyes wide. Then she closed them, putting one hand to her brow. "Oh my God. You saw me, didn't you? You saw me riding home yesterday morning. Is that why you came and talked to me at the bar last night?"

"I—well—it's—the thing is . . ." There was no way out of this. Yes, he'd seen her, but that wasn't his fault, was it? And yes, it was why he'd talked to her at the bar, but he'd have talked to her anyway. She was gorgeous. And yes, his dog was the reason she'd had to ride home naked to begin with, but it wasn't as if he'd trained Duke to do that kind of thing. He'd been as shocked as anyone when he found the thing in his yard.

With both hands, she covered her face and bent over at the waist. For a horrified second he stood frozen, watching her shoulders shake.

Good God, he thought, *she's crying. She's going into hysterics.*

Beside her, Duke stood up, still wagging his tail and hopping lightly off his front two feet to lick her arm.

"Gray, I'm sorry." He strode toward her, hands outstretched. "I don't know how it happened. Heck, I can't even imagine how he got the thing off you to begin with. But I swear, I had nothing to do with it. I—"

She straightened and he saw that her face was wet with tears. But instead of the desperate look of unhappiness he'd anticipated, he saw that she was *laughing.* She'd been bent over at the waist, convulsed with laughter.

His heart lightened immediately. "What?"

"I can't believe it." She giggled through a hand now at her mouth. "Of all the people . . ." She laughed again, then tried to sober, wiping her eyes and stifling her mirth. "That *is* why you talked to me last night, isn't it?"

"Gray, I would have talked to you anyway. My God, you stood out at that bar like an angel in a tar pit. But believe me—"

"Did you even think about telling me you had my dress?"

"Of course!" He threw out his arms. "But tell me, how do you do that? How do you say to someone you just met that, by the way, you have her clothes at your house."

She arched a brow. "It beats having her *find* her clothes at your house."

He inclined his head. "I'll give you that. I'm sure it looks . . . odd."

"I'll say. Just tell me this. Were you down there? On the beach? Did you watch me . . . ?"

"What? Oh, no. God, no. Believe me, if I'd seen Duke take your clothes, I'd have gotten them back to you right away. I found the dress right over there"—he gestured toward the spot—"late yesterday morning, after he got back to the house covered with sand. But . . . how did he even get the dress? What were you doing without your clothes?"

It was her turn to blush. "Acting totally out of character. For which I was punished severely." At his confused look, she added, "I was skinny-dipping."

The visual this statement brought with it made his lips curl into a smile. "Okay, now I have to confess that had I seen that, I would definitely have returned the dress. But I can't say how quickly."

Incredibly, she laughed. Then, with one hand scratching Duke's ear, she reached out and touched her dress again. "Did you actually wash it?"

"Yeah, it, uh, looked a little the worse for wear when Duke brought it home."

"You named your dog Duke? What is it with this town and the Duke of Dunkirk?"

"I didn't name him after that duke. I didn't name him after *any* duke. It just, well, I don't know. Maybe I did. Come to think of it, the name just came to me, and it seemed to fit."

"It does fit." She leaned down and looked Duke in the eye as she buried her hands in his fur. "So you're the guy in the long coat I've seen walking with him on the beach."

Sam frowned. "Uh, no. Probably not. I don't own a long coat, for one thing. And lately I've been too swamped with work to walk him much."

"Does he go with you to your jobs?"

"My, uh, jobs?" He frowned, shook his head. "No, I work at home."

She cocked her head. "I thought you were a plumber. Because you were going to come fix my furnace. You have—tools. You know what to do with pipes and stuff."

He chuckled. "No, sorry. I'm nothing so useful. I'm a music reviewer. Classical, for magazines, mostly. CDs, concerts, DVD performances."

Her expression cleared. "That's how you knew that Beethoven piece."

"Everybody knows that Beethoven piece." When she flushed, he added, "Everybody who's into classical music, that is. Hey, listen, I was going to call you. How 'bout I come work on that furnace this afternoon, if that's all right with you."

She beamed. "That'd be great!"

"I can bring your bike, too, when I come. I'll just throw it in the back of the truck." He indicated the pickup next to the garage. "How did you get here this morning?"

"I walked."

His brows rose. "That's quite a hike."

"Oh, I love to walk. And it's a gorgeous day."

He gazed at her, knowing that a besotted look had settled onto his features. "Gorgeous," he agreed.

She smiled. "I was thinking, when you're done with the furnace, I could treat you to dinner. As a thank-you. I'm a pretty good cook."

A gratified warmth spread throughout him. It was easy to say he didn't want to get involved with someone who was leaving, but when faced with this amazing girl, it was getting too hard to say no.

"That sounds perfect."

She nodded once, smiling, and turned to go. A second later she turned back. "Oh, and Sam? Could you also bring my dress when you come?"

He laughed. "No problem. I'll send Duke over with it the minute it's dry."

Several hours later, Sam emerged from Gray's basement, a bag in his hand and the heater humming, if not quietly at least effectively, behind him.

Gray turned from the stove where she was sautéing onions and couldn't help grinning at the handsome, disheveled man before her.

"Have you exorcised my ghost?" she asked.

"That should be the last you hear of him." He held aloft a bag full of clanking parts. "No more ghostly wailing. No more cigarette smoke. Do you think you'll be lonely?"

"Hardly. Relieved is more like it. So how do you know how to do all that stuff?" She wiped her hands on the towel over her shoulder.

"Hey, you live in old houses long enough, you learn how old stuff works." He leaned a hip against the counter. "That smells great. What is it?"

"We're having shrimp scampi. I hope you like garlic."

He grinned. "Only if you're eating it, too."

Gray blushed with pleasure. "It's only fair."

They stood there a moment, both wearing dopey smiles and goggling at each other, before Sam said, "So, you mind if I take a shower?"

"Oh no, not at all. The bathroom's at the top of the stairs."

"Great." He dropped the bag on the counter and

headed for the stairs, leaving Gray to cook and think about the naked man being caressed by warm soapy water not fifteen feet above her.

It was only about ten minutes later when Sam called down to her.

She moved to the bottom of the steps and saw his wet head poking out of the steamy bathroom. "Need someone to wash your back?" she teased.

That fabulous smile overtook his face again. "Actually, I was looking for a towel, but if you're offering . . . ?"

She started up the stairs. Ah, the temptation. The linen closet was right next to the bathroom, and he watched as she retrieved a clean towel and handed it to him.

He took it with one hand, his fingers covering hers on the terry cloth, and pulled her closer, the door shielding all but his head and one shoulder. He kissed her, damply but chastely, and smiled. "Thank you."

Her gaze caught and held his. "You're welcome."

They stared at each other a long moment, then both leaned simultaneously in for another kiss.

Feeling gutsy, as was so easy with this guy, Gray pushed the door wider with one hand and stepped into his embrace. Sam deepened the kiss, pulling her close to his wet body, the length of it hard against Gray's. She felt his arousal stiffen against her and pushed her hips into his. Her hands held his head, fingers woven through the wet tendrils of his hair.

Heat fired between them, and it wasn't just because of the hot shower. Sam's hands rode down her back, then around her waist and beneath her shirt.

Gray let her fingers run down his ribs and around his hips to the hard evidence of his desire. "Let's go into the bedroom."

Sam pulled back. Gray had just enough time to worry

that he might refuse, when he smiled, and said, "Lead the way."

They fell onto the bed in a flurry of passion. He pushed at her shirt until she sat up and pulled it swiftly over her head. Sam went for the button on her pants, and a second later she was naked.

"Incredible," he exhaled.

Gray thought the same thing as she pushed him back onto the bed and lay her body over his, flesh against flesh, the delicious sensation of one body meeting another for the first time. He had the physique of an athlete. Her hands covered his pectorals while his reached up and touched her hair where it cascaded toward her breasts.

"You are. . ." he breathed, but he didn't complete the sentence as Gray cupped his hardness and stroked.

He inhaled sharply. "My God."

She smiled, and his hands moved over her breasts, across her ribs and stomach. One hand tucked itself between her and where she rested atop his hips, his finger immediately finding her center.

She bit her bottom lip. Oh, she needed him. *Now.* She felt none of her usual inhibition, required none of the usual coaxing to bring the act to fruition. All she felt was hot, naked hunger.

She propped herself up on her knees and his fingers dove inside. She gasped, then sighed, her hands caressing the evidence of his desire.

"I . . . let's . . ." She couldn't form the words, but her hand directed him toward her heat.

"Jeez," he exhaled. Then added, "Have you got . . . ?"

She reached over toward the bedside table and opened the drawer. She had just put the condoms in that morning, hoping for this occasion but doubting it would actually happen.

He rolled slightly and took the tiny envelope from her.

As he moved, she had the opportunity to note just how well muscled he was, despite being lean. He fumbled with the wrapper, then tore it open with his teeth.

Gray laughed, and a second later his hand was back on her and her head began to spin.

He donned the condom in one swift move, then pulled her decisively over him. She wavered just a second. But when she saw him tilt his head at her hesitation, felt him stroke her thigh like a filly that needed calming, she gave a small smile and rose up to cover him.

She came down slowly, causing them both to moan with pleasure. But before she could turn up the pace, he'd caught her around the waist and flipped them so that she was on the bottom.

"I want to look at you." His eyes were intense upon her face. "You're the most beautiful thing I've ever seen."

With that he took her, long and hard, answering her need with his own, her impassioned cries, her clutching hands and gripping legs, with his hunger and need and power. Just as Gray was arching into him, splitting into a thousand spectacular pieces of satisfied desire, he thrust one final time, his arms trembling where they held him above her, and made a sound of release.

Then he lay alongside her, his body warm and enveloping, holding her close.

They'd been silent a while when Gray asked, in a small voice, "Why didn't you stay last night?"

She felt the breath leave his chest in a sigh. "I thought . . . I was worried . . . the truth is, Gray, I was afraid you were just the type of girl I could fall for. And you're only here for the summer. I wasn't sure about getting involved."

She propped herself up on one elbow and looked down at him quizzically. "And now, what? You've decided I'm not the kind of girl you could fall for?"

He laughed, and his gaze skittered away. "No." He exhaled again and met her eyes. "Now I realize that I've already fallen. And there's nothing I can do about it."

She laid her head on his shoulder. "You don't have to sound so dire about it."

He laughed, and she could hear it in his chest.

"To tell you the truth," she said hesitantly, "I'm not altogether sure what my plans for the future are. When I left home, I thought if things worked out here, I'd stay. I have the summer off to decide, but . . ." She shrugged. "If a teaching opportunity came along, I'd be interested."

Sam raised his head and looked down at her. "Really?"

She raised her eyes. "Yeah."

He grinned. "If that's the case, you should talk to Covington."

"Covington! What on earth for?" She propped herself up on one elbow again.

"He's head of the school board. He'll know about jobs, and he might even recommend you. He was nicer to you the other night than I've ever seen him."

"*That* was nice?" She frowned. "He's a strange little man."

Sam laughed. "You don't know the half of it."

They got out of bed and headed back toward the kitchen, Gray feeling lighter and more confident about the future than she'd felt in a long, long time. "I hope you're hungry," she said.

Sam grabbed her around the waist as she turned the heat back on under the pan on the stove. "Always."

She laughed and turned to kiss him.

"Gray Gilliam, I am very happy to have found you."

"And I you," she agreed. "Not just because you fixed my furnace and rid my house of a ghost, either."

They smiled at each other and kissed once more before a scratching at the back door made them both jump.

"Who could that be?" Gray wondered.

Sam moved to the mudroom and opened the back door. In trotted Duke, tail aloft and a wide grin on his canine face.

"The Duke who came to dinner!" Gray laughed.

Sam reached down to pet the dog, then straightened, expression suddenly alert. His eyes scanned the walls and the ceiling.

"What is it?" she asked. Then, with a sniff, she froze.

Sam turned in a circle, nose in the air, and faced her.

At the same time, with identical incredulous smiles, they said, "Do you smell pipe smoke?"

ELAINE FOX grew up in Maryland in a family of avid readers and talented writers. After receiving her B.A. in English, she spent several years working in academic and corporate environments before deciding to pursue her dream of writing a book. Fox is now the *USA Today* bestselling author of fifteen contemporary and historical romances and four anthologies. She lives in Virginia, where she is currently at work on her next book.

Devil to Pay
Jeaniene Frost

Chapter One

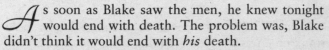

As soon as Blake saw the men, he knew tonight would end with death. The problem was, Blake didn't think it would end with *his* death.

"I don't want any trouble," he said, realizing the stupidity of those words. It was after midnight, he was in a derelict alley with three thousand dollars' worth of crack cocaine on him—and that was the good news.

"You lost?" one of the men asked, coming closer.

The other three from the opposite end of the alley drew closer, too. There was no way out. Blake could feel *him* rouse, sensing the danger. He didn't have much time.

"You need to leave," Blake said, fear setting in as he felt that familiar buzzing start in his head.

Another of them laughed. "Give us those bags you just bought, bitch, and we'll leave."

For a split second, Blake hesitated. He'd bought the

crack with the last of his money, and he needed it. Not because he was an addict; Blake had never touched drugs in his life. No, he'd intended his first use to be the last thing he ever did.

But that buzzing in his head was getting louder. *No. Not yet. Not until I can get away from these people . . .*

"Take it and leave me alone," Blake ground out, yanking the bags from his coat.

One of them took the bags, then shoved Blake. He staggered and fell, tasting blood as his mouth banged against a fire escape.

That rustling in his head got louder. It was too late.

"Kill me," Blake gasped.

Confusion was stamped on the faces peering at him. "He crazy," someone muttered.

Blake glanced around. No one had a gun or knife drawn. This was a dark, gang-infested alley in Columbia Heights, DC. Couldn't one of them stab him or shoot him?

Blake began to yell the most incendiary thing he could think of. "What're you standing there looking at? You recognize me from last night, when I was fucking your mother?"

"Oh, *hell* no," one of them said.

They surrounded Blake, kicking him. Blake twisted, making no move to defend himself. Instead, he arched toward the blows. Fear rose, but not of dying.

Break my neck, Blake thought savagely. *Or take a pipe and smash my head open!*

They didn't, though one of them did smash his foot into Blake's face, breaking his nose. Blake coughed up blood even as his whole body clenched. *He* was almost here. Blake tried to force him back, but *he* was too strong.

"What's the matter with you?" Blake roared with his last ounce of strength. "*Kill* me!"

A hard kick snapped Blake's head back before his world went white. For a brief, blissful moment, Blake thought he'd finally gotten to die, and he felt overwhelming relief.

But when Blake came back to reality, there was blood everywhere. A few people were gathered at the end of the alley. Blake didn't know how long they'd been standing there, but their eyes were wild, faces chalky with shock. They'd probably never seen anything like this, even there, in one of the worst parts of the District.

Blake let out a howl of despair as he stared at the thick red blood coating his hands and the bodies around him. *Damn you,* he silently screamed at the monster inside him. *Damn you to hell!*

But that was the problem. Hell was where the devil inside Blake came from.

Elise's living room began to shake, but she barely noticed it. She was so used to the vibrations every time a train zoomed by that it was more attention-grabbing when there were extended periods of calm.

The fifties song "Jump, Jive and Wail" played on her iPod, a recent gift from her sire, Mencheres. Elise would have continued to listen to music on her records, no matter how many times the trains made the needle jump and scratch them, but one of Mencheres's most common lectures was to embrace the changing world. Some vampires, as they got older, withdrew from society and became hermitlike, clinging to the things from their original time period. Eventually those vampires could become so disconnected that hatred for the ever-advancing world was a side effect.

Elise was already a loner. She lived under a metro tunnel, didn't socialize much with other vampires *or* humans, and far preferred big-band music to the noise on the radio these days. All things considered, Mencheres had reason to be concerned about her sliding down that hermit road, but she didn't hate the modern world or its changes. She was just happier by herself.

More shaking of the walls announced the arrival of the six-fifteen train. Elise put her book down with a sigh. Time to shower and eat, activities that required her to leave her comfortable home.

She put on a tank top and pants, adding a jacket over that in spite of the warm temperature outside. Fewer clothes meant more attention, and Elise wanted to talk to as few people as possible. She pulled her hair into a ponytail, put on a baseball cap, and opened the creaking metal door.

A blast of smells hit her as she went into the tunnels that connected the defunct section where she lived to the operating metro tunnels above. At least she didn't need to breathe; the residual odors from the indigent who used these places as a temporary residence and bathroom, combined with the stench of rotted food, dead rats, or other animals—were bad enough.

The few homeless people who were in the tunnels at that hour didn't look at Elise as she walked by. Every so often, a newcomer would approach her. One who hadn't been warned about her by the others, or who hadn't listened. Elise didn't feed from any curious newcomers—smelling them was bad enough—she just slammed them with the power in her gaze and compelled them to leave her alone. If one was stupid enough to attack her, well . . . that person didn't live long enough to regret it.

Tonight it was only the regulars, so Elise passed by without incident. She walked out of the tunnel and through the station platform, keeping her head down, not needing to look to know the way. It was so familiar to her, she could have made the trip in her sleep.

Once free of the closeted atmosphere, Elise's steps became longer and more relaxed. She even hummed as she made her way down Connecticut Avenue to the fitness club. The girl behind the counter barely glanced at Elise when she came inside, but a nod indicated that Elise didn't need to show her membership card. She was such a regular sight there, few employees asked to see it anymore.

Elise went upstairs to the multitude of exercise machines. Her size would never be any different than it was now, but the club employees asked too many questions if she didn't at least pretend to exercise. After twenty minutes on the treadmill, Elise went to the locker room. She stripped and showered, then brushed her teeth with the toothbrush she kept with a few other items in a locker. After a quick blow-dry of her hair, she was ready to move on to the next item in her routine.

Some nights, when Elise was lucky, she fed from whoever was alone in the locker room. It only took a flash of her gaze for the woman to forget Elise had just cornered her and drunk her blood. But most evenings were busy at the gym. It was easier for Elise to walk the city, and find someone alone—or accompanied by fewer witnesses to brainwash.

Tonight, Elise found her meal along 7th Street, a young man who wandered away from his friends in the Sculpture Garden. She drank from him, closed the holes with a drop of her own blood, and sent him back to his companions inside of two minutes. He'd be sleepier from the pint she drained from him but otherwise unharmed. It was only in the movies that vampires needed to kill to feed, along with other falsehoods like wooden stakes and sunlight being harmful to them.

As a nod to her sire's admonishments to get out more, Elise then sat and read at a local coffee shop instead of just buying more books and going straight home. She even exchanged a comment about the weather with someone who sat across from her. There. No one could say she wasn't interacting with humans except to bite them.

When the coffee shop closed, however, Elise gratefully headed home. She walked through the Capital Lawn, taking comfort in the familiarity of the gleaming white buildings and older structures. Then she followed the line of the tracks through the city until she reached the station where the tunnels connected.

She'd made it past the few remaining travelers and into the inoperative tunnels when she smelled something unmistakable. Blood, seasoned with the distinctive tang of death. Elise quickened her pace, her sneakers making hardly any sound at all. There were very few homeless left in the tunnels at this hour, though their wariness was unfounded since Elise never killed one who hadn't attacked her first. Still, those who guessed what she was didn't linger long after dark. *Silly humans*. Just because she preferred to go out at night didn't mean she was trapped inside during the day.

The smell became stronger the deeper Elise ventured inside the tunnel. Even over the sound of an approaching train, Elise could hear a heartbeat just ahead. Whoever it was had slunk back into one of the old maintenance alcoves but would soon find out that a sneak attack was a bad idea.

When the man stepped out onto the track with his back to her, she paused in surprise. Whoever this was didn't seem even to know she was there, let alone be lying in wait. That stench of blood and death came off the stranger, but even stronger was despair. He balanced on the edge of the track as if in indecision. The train would be here any second. The fool wouldn't try to cross the tracks now, would he?

The man clutched his head, muttering, "No, not yet!" several times. The tunnel vibrated as the train approached. With growing awareness, Elise saw that the man was going to jump right in front of it.

Even as she charged forward to snatch him back, something happened. The despairing scent pouring off him changed to the choking stench of sulfur. His mouth opened in an impossibly wide snarl as he whirled, gripping Elise with more strength than any human should have. Pinpoints of red shone in his eyes, like sparks before a fire, and before her gaze, his skin seemed to turn to a waxy ashen shade.

"*Vampire*," he hissed, reaching for her throat.

Elise didn't pause to wonder what was going on. She punched him in the head, watching in relief as he collapsed to the tunnel floor.

Chapter Two

Blake's first thought on waking up and seeing duct tape around his hands instead of fresh blood was, *Thank God*. A year ago, the same sight would have shocked and terrified him. Now it was a better start than most days.

Then it occurred to him to wonder where he was. Or who the blond woman watching him with an unreadable expression was.

Blake glanced around, noting with relief that the room was empty of blood or bodies. It was also empty of windows, and it was shaking with a powerful vibration.

Was he still in the District? How long had the most recent episode lasted?

"You need to get away from me," were Blake's first words. He eyed his bound hands and feet. *He* would feel threatened as soon as this registered. Blake tensed, expecting that buzzing in his head to start up, but so far, there was silence. *Still time for the woman to get away.*

"Why did you try to jump in front of the train?" she asked.

Blake closed his eyes. That's right, the last thing he remembered was the train.

"Did you stop me?" he asked incredulously. "Damn it, *why?*"

She raised a brow. "You could say thank you."

Blake wanted to slap her. So close to being free, and she ruined it. "You don't know what you've done, but you'll be making a bigger mistake if you don't leave right now."

She gave a pointed look at his wrists and ankles. "You think you can hurt me?"

The memory of being shoved in a police car, hand-cuffed, flashed through Blake's mind. He'd been fighting the encroaching noise in his head and hoping desperately that the cuffs and the reinforced backseat would hold.

The next memory followed without pity. The crashed police car, kicked-in barrier between the front and back-seats, and the mangled remains of the two officers.

"I'll kill you." Blake's voice was hoarse with self-loathing. "Leave now, before it's too late!"

"You can't kill me," she said, a sort of detached amusement in her tone. "I'm already dead."

As Blake watched, her eyes changed. They became impossibly green and began to glow, bright as traffic lights. Her smile widened to show more of her teeth, where her front two incisors extended down to form sharp, pointed tips.

Blake found himself smiling. A vampire had kidnapped him. *Today might be a good day after all.*

* * *

Elise watched the man's reaction with interest as she revealed her inhuman nature. Surprisingly, he didn't look afraid. In fact, the strangest expression of relief crossed his face.

He tilted his head back. "All right, then. Kill me."

She wrinkled her nose. "You think I'm going to bite you? Not with how you smell."

He made an impatient noise. "So plug your nose while you drink my blood. But hurry. I don't know how long it'll be before *he* takes me."

Elise considered him. She'd met suicidal people before but none who gave off the kind of vibes this man did. Considering what she'd seen after she grabbed him back from the oncoming train, Elise had a good idea about what was driving him to kill himself. She'd never personally come across someone in his condition before, but in her long life, she knew people who had.

"You're possessed, aren't you?"

Elise asked it matter-of-factly. His eyes widened as if he'd been struck.

"Yes," he whispered. A spasm crossed his face, too raw to be labeled pain. "For about six months now."

He didn't look to be the type to play with a Ouija board. Maybe he was one of those foolish humans who trifled with spirits, seeking to tap into the dark power of the other side. "How did it happen?"

"A car accident." Her brows went up, but he just sighed. "I was driving home from work when this woman jumped in front of my car. I called 911, tried to help her, but she died in my arms. Witnesses cleared me of being at fault, and I thought it was just a terrible accident. About three weeks later, the blackouts started. I'd hear this buzzing in my head, then wake up in places I didn't remember going to, with no idea what I'd done. I thought I was crazy. Then—"

He stopped and swallowed hard, looking like he was about to throw up.

"The demon started taunting me. Leaving notes in handwriting I didn't recognize, making videos of me doing things I couldn't even imagine, let alone remember . . . I can't live like this," he summarized, voice hardening. "That demon's made me a murderer, a fucking monster! I tried seeing a priest, getting an exorcism—nothing's worked. It won't even let me kill myself. If you understand what's wrong with me, kill me now. You'll save lives if you do, believe me."

Blue eyes stared intently at Elise from under black, scraggly hair. It was hard to tell what he really looked like under the dirt and grime that said he'd been living on the streets for a while. He looked to be in his midthirties, but what might have been an athletic, attractive physique was now hunched with guilt, fear, and despair.

Killing him would be an act of mercy, Elise reflected. *It wouldn't be hard to do.* Humans were so fragile; one flick of her wrist would snap his neck before he'd even realized she moved. After all, she'd killed before, and for less noble reasons than this.

She'd almost decided to do it when Mencheres's face flashed in her mind. Was she becoming one of those vampires who forgot what it was like to be human? How precious those years were *because* they were so short?

"What's your name?" she asked, rising.

The hope on his face as she approached was heart-wrenching. "Blake Turner. Will you . . . will you leave my body where it can be found? I still have family who might want to know what happened to me. . ."

"Blake Turner," Elise said slowly. "I'm not going to kill you. I'm going to help you."

Chapter Three

B lake looked around the tunnel. "I'm not sure about this."

"I need help to figure out whether you're salvageable or not," was Elise's curt response, as they continued down the passageway. "Keeping you cooped up in my house isn't a workable solution."

"Can't you just call someone?" Blake asked, thinking *house* was a generous word to describe the place where she lived. *Oversized coffin* would be more appropriate, since it was tiny, underground, pitch-black aside from some sparse lighting, and lacked any kitchen, toilet, shower, or other amenities.

Still, it was a perfect place to keep Blake locked up and away from people, which was why leaving it didn't appeal to him. Who knew he'd be unable to convince a *vampire* to kill him? So much for the bloodthirstiness of their legend. Blake also couldn't understand why the demon hadn't taken over yet. Every other time Blake attempted to kill himself, the demon showed up and stopped him. Could it sense that the vampire wouldn't kill him? Was that why the demon was biding its time?

Or was it waiting for a better opportunity to appear? Like now, as they were heading toward the metro station and all the innocent people inside.

"This isn't safe," Blake repeated for the dozenth time.

She kept walking, her grip on his hand like a cool vise. "My sire will know what to do. I'll use the pay phone at the station to call him. It's safer if you come with me than to hope you'll still be at my house when I get back."

"He's strong when he takes over," Blake said, almost spitting the words out. He hated what he'd been turned into—a host for the worst kind of evil. If death was the only way to stop the demon, Blake would gladly die. His life had been ruined beyond repair anyway.

Just seven months ago, he'd been a successful stockbroker. He'd had a beautiful house, great friends, and was even on good terms with his ex-wife. Now he'd lost everything, was wanted for multiple murders, and the only way for him to stop the demon was to kill himself. It was a far, far cry from the days where his biggest concern had been the fluctuating market on Wall Street.

"I'm stronger," Elise said.

Blake looked her over with doubt. Elise was about five-four, and if she topped a hundred pounds, it wasn't by much. Furthermore, she had an ethereal quality to her small-boned frame that hinted at fragility. Combined with her beautiful, pale face, Elise reminded Blake of one of those antique dolls his ex-wife used to collect. Elise was the type of woman men tripped over themselves to protect, not the type who could outwrestle a demon. Fangs could only reach so far, after all.

"You said you've never encountered a demon before. How do you know you're stronger?"

Elise shot him a sideways glance. "You talk so much," she muttered. "It's tiring. Can you stop for a while?"

Blake bit back an amazed snort. *This* was the woman who was supposed to stop the demon when it showed up? Someone who couldn't even carry on a brief conversation without getting tired?

"I think we should go back," Blake said, as they rounded a corner and the metro station came into view. "This isn't—"

A roar of buzzing filled his mind all at once. Blake had only a second to clutch his head at the pain when his vision went white. He didn't even get a chance to warn Elise before the demon took him.

Elise was startled when Blake grabbed his head as if his brains had just exploded. His one hand was still in her grip; but just as she smelled the sulfur, he yanked it away. And then ran like a proverbial bat out of hell.

She cursed herself as she chased him. With the demon controlling him, Blake was *quick,* streaking up the tunnel and into the station in barely the amount of time it took to blink.

But Elise had superhuman abilities as well, so she stayed close behind him. The demon burst through the station, knocking over anyone in its way. At 5:00 A.M., there weren't many commuters, but enough to make exposing her real nature a risk. Elise kept her eyes and fangs under control, knowing her speed was bad enough, but at least that wouldn't announce "vampire!" to the general public. She plowed through the people just as roughly as the demon had, not letting it gain any ground. *Keep running,* she thought coolly. *Once we're free of all these humans, I can quit playing nice.*

The demon broke out of the metro station and darted onto the sidewalk, pumping Blake's legs like pistons. Elise kept it just ahead of her, letting it think she wasn't fast enough to overtake it, until they reached a less-monitored part of the neighborhood. Then she sprang forward with all of her undead speed, tackling the demon from behind and bashing its head into the street.

Blake's body went limp, the sweet smell of fresh blood replacing the previous stench of sulfur. Elise flipped Blake around, giving his injury a quick evaluation. *No skull fracture. The surface wound on his forehead can be healed—and his nose was broken before, anyway.*

She opened one of Blake's eyes. No more swirling red. His skin lost that waxy-ashen look as well, and he didn't smell like anything except blood and unwashed human. The demon was gone. For the moment.

Elise let her fangs out just enough to drag her thumb across one, welling up blood. Then Elise smeared her blood over the three-inch split in Blake's skin, watching with satisfaction as the wound slowly closed like a magic zipper had formed in his flesh.

It wouldn't do to feed Blake any of her blood. That would heal him more thoroughly, like getting rid of the concussion he no doubt had, but it would also make him stronger. The demon inside Blake was already pushing his body to limits no human should be able to sustain. Elise wasn't about to add to that.

But now, what to do with Blake? She couldn't just sling him over her shoulder and walk to the nearest pay phone; that would attract too much attention. Nor was she about to leave him there and risk the demon's coming back while she was gone. If only it was a little later in the morning, then she could grab the first person walking by with a cell phone and hypnotize them into compliance while she called Mencheres.

Creaking drew Elise's attention to the end of the street. A homeless woman slowly pushed a shopping cart overflowing with various items along the sidewalk. Elise smiled, then picked Blake up and tucked him under her arm like a football.

"Good morning," she called out. "How much do you want for that shopping cart?"

Chapter Four

*B*lake awoke to a horrible smell. With that stink and everything being dark, for a moment, he thought he was in a garbage dump.

Then he heard her voice. "Quit squirming, people will notice."

It took a second for him to recognize who spoke. It was the vampire, Elise. Blake blinked, his vision clearing enough to realize it was dark because something was over his face. Something that reeked of body odor and things he didn't even want to name. Add that to a headache worse than he'd ever experienced, and Blake thought he might throw up.

But he was still with Elise, even after the demon had taken control of him.

"Did anyone get killed? Hurt?" Blake asked, dread spreading through him.

"No. Now quit talking."

At those words, Blake didn't care about her brusqueness, his cramped position with his knees mashed to his chest, the stink, or the throbbing in his head. The demon had taken control of him—but the vampire had kept it from harming anyone. For the first time in months, Blake felt a stirring of hope.

Whatever he was stuffed into vibrated. From the feel of it, Elise was pushing him along an uneven surface. It was hot, too, and with the reeking dark material covering him, hard to breathe.

Blake pulled the rancid material off him and looked around. They were in a cemetery, of all things, and from the looks of it, Elise had stuffed him into a shopping cart.

"A shopping cart?" Blake said. "Whose stuff is piled on top of me?"

"It belonged to a homeless woman, but don't worry, I paid for everything," Elise said, shrugging. "It was a good way to transport you without drawing notice."

"Why didn't you just . . . commandeer a car or something?" Blake asked, getting out of the cart. His bones creaked once he was freed from that cramped position.

Another shrug. "I don't know how to drive."

Blake looked at her with more shock than he'd shown when he found out she was a vampire. "You don't know how to drive?" he repeated.

Elise seemed amused at his disbelief. "I never got around to learning."

Waking up in a homeless person's shopping cart was still better than waking up to the sight of dead bodies. No matter his current circumstances, Blake was grateful for that. He still didn't know how Elise thought she could help him, but she could apparently keep him from killing when the demon possessed him. And since she was taking Blake to meet her sire, maybe *that* vampire would put him out of his misery even if Elise refused to. It was something to hope for.

It was ironic, Blake reflected. Before becoming possessed, he'd never thought much about death beyond having a life insurance policy and exercising to stay healthy. Now, Blake lusted after death as though it were a beautiful woman. Death meant he'd never hurt anyone again. Death meant his family would be safe. Death meant his remaining friends never had to open their doors and see a demon standing on the other side of it, concealed in Blake's skin. Death was Blake's only way of beating the thing inside him, and Blake wanted to beat it more than he wanted anything else.

Elise's whistling shook Blake from his dark ponderings. She was whistling "Beautiful Dreamer" in a soft, melancholy way, the notes as perfect as if they were coming from a flute. Blake wondered how a vampire, who supposedly didn't breathe, could whistle. He wondered how Elise was out in the daylight without spontaneously combusting, or how it was that vampires even existed at all. So many things he hadn't thought were possible turned out to be true. Vampires? They existed. Demons? Real, too. If aliens landed at the Capitol tomorrow, he'd only be mildly intrigued.

"If sunlight doesn't hurt you, why do you live underground in a tunnel?"

Elise kept whistling. Blake thought she'd decided to ignore him, but when the last strains of the song ended, she replied.

"I don't do so well around people."

Her voice was soft, too. Filled with a sort of disconnected regret, as though her lack of social skills made her sorry, but she didn't understand why. She started to whistle that same song again. Blake sat down, leaning back against a tree, and closed his eyes. He could almost imagine he was somewhere else, listening to the sweet and haunting tune.

"You won't let me hurt anyone, will you?"

Elise paused. "No." She continued whistling, the sound and her answer lulling him, making him feel almost . . . safe.

Blake did something he hadn't done willingly for weeks. He let himself fall asleep.

Elise listened as Blake's heartbeat and breathing became more relaxed with slumber. She kept whistling, even though she wasn't used to breathing this much. Still, the song seemed to soothe him, though why that mattered to her was a mystery. *His being quiet will draw less attention,* she told herself, knowing that was a lie. They were in Arlington National Cemetery. There weren't many people around to notice if Blake caused a stir, except perhaps the ghosts.

It was so odd, this protective feeling. Once she'd made up her mind to help Blake, her long-dormant emotions awoke. Elise couldn't help but admire Blake's concern for other people, even over his own life. *You won't let me hurt anyone, will you?* It had been a long time since Elise had cared that much about other people, especially strangers.

When DC's homeless or criminal element attacked her—which happened every few months—she killed them. It didn't occur to her *not* to since she reasoned that by doing so, she was saving someone else from that person's future attack. Blake wasn't responsible for what the demon inside him did, but he was willing to die in order to prevent other people from getting harmed. His strength of character under these extreme circumstances held up a mirror to hers, and Elise didn't like what she saw reflected there. *Mencheres is right,* she realized. *I've let myself slip away. How much of the person I was is still left? Can I salvage the remains before apathy eats away at the rest of me?*

She'd start with Blake. Maybe by helping to save his soul, she'd earn a reprieve for her own.

Chapter Five

A black Volvo approached, driving along an area where vehicles usually weren't allowed. Elise felt the encroaching power from inside the SUV.

"Here they are," she told Blake, waking him.

The SUV stopped next to them, interrupting whatever Blake had been about to say. Two people got out, the man radiating a crackling power that announced him as a Master vampire, and a redheaded woman who seemed human.

"Bones," Elise said, bowing her head in the deference he deserved as co-sire of Mencheres's line. Elise might have been out of touch with vampire society, but every undead person knew about Mencheres's merging lines with Bones several months ago.

"Elise," Bones replied, with a nod. "This is my wife, Cat."

Cat smiled and stuck out her hand. Elise shook it,

thinking the famous half-breed didn't appear as she'd pictured her. With Cat's reputation and nickname of the Red Reaper, Elise had expected a more imposing presence, but Cat looked no more threatening than a Hollywood actress.

Blake looked at the two newcomers warily. "Are they both vampires?" he asked Elise.

"He is," Elise replied, glancing at the redheaded half vampire again. "She's more . . . complicated."

Cat laughed. "That's one way to put it." She extended her hand to Blake, but before he could even twitch, Bones batted it away.

"Don't touch him, Kitten."

The cold menace in Bones's voice had Cat blinking in surprise even as Elise felt her anger flare.

"The demon doesn't have him now," Elise said. "There's no need to act as if he's foul."

"It's all right," Blake said, looking down at himself with sadness and disgust. "I *am* foul. If I were he, I wouldn't want my wife touching me, either."

"It's not your filthiness that concerns me, but she's half-human," Bones said, his hand still on Cat's arm. "Demons can't possess vampires, but so little is known about half-breeds that I'm not risking the possibility."

"Aren't you being a *tad* paranoid, Bones?" Cat asked. "You told me on the way over that the host had to die before a demon could jump. Well, he looks alive to me."

"Heart attack, aneurism, blood clot, stroke." Bones ticked the items off his fingers. "He's human, so he could drop dead in seconds just while he's standing there. This is why I didn't want you coming with me, Kitten."

Cat rolled her eyes, giving Elise a look that clearly conveyed her exasperation. "Paranoid," she repeated. Then she turned her attention to Blake. "Sorry to meet under these circumstances, but we're going to take you to Mencheres and hopefully he–"

"No!" Blake screamed, his hands flying to his head.

Elise knew what that meant by now. She flung herself onto Blake even as a blast of sulfur filled the air.

Bones also launched forward, wrapping one arm around Blake's throat and the other across the heaving man's chest. The fiery red lights were in Blake's gaze again, his skin turning sallower with each instant.

"*Let me go,*" the demon hissed in a voice that sounded nothing like Blake's. It was hoarse and sharp, like glass being ground together.

"Kitten, start the car," Bones directed, not taking his attention off the demon.

Cat turned and walked to the car. The demon's eyes followed her, then it let out a laugh.

"*Catherine.*"

The redhead froze at the suddenly older, feminine voice coming from Blake's mouth. She turned around, eyes wide.

"Catherineeeeeee. . ." the demon drew out in that same voice, but now with a pleading undertone. "Please don't leave. Help us. There were creatures at the door asking about you, Catherine. They're hurting us. Make them stop. No, don't, let my husband go! No, don't touch him, don't . . . NO! Joe, oh God, JOE!"

"Grandma," Cat whispered, tears in her eyes.

"Bloody sod," Bones snarled, clapping his hand across the demon's—Blake's mouth. "Don't listen to it, Kitten."

She still seemed shell-shocked. "That was my grandmother's voice, Bones!"

"It's a trick," he said firmly. "That's why the best thing to do is take this poor bastard out to the salt flats and kill him."

"No one's killing him," Elise said at once.

Bones leveled her with a glare sizzling with green. His power expanded until it felt like it was burning her.

"Don't be a fool." Each word was scalding. "The only reason I'm not snapping this bloke's neck now is because there are too many living creatures around the demon could jump to. But his life will end on the salt flats. The only way to get rid of a demon is to kill the host."

Elise was frail compared to the power emanating off Bones, and as her sire Mencheres's coruler, Bones was also in a position of authority over her. But that didn't mean she was giving up on Blake.

"Mencheres told me I could bring Blake to him," she replied, her voice hard. "So that's where we're going, not to any salt flats."

Bones's mouth curled. "You were always stubborn."

Elise just stared at him. *You don't know me,* she thought. *And you might technically be my Master now, but you're not going to win this one.*

"Shouldn't we be going?" Elise asked.

The demon's eyes locked onto hers. Evil. Knowing. Anticipating.

You're not going to win, either, Elise silently vowed. Determination welled up in her, stronger than any emotion she'd felt in decades. *I won't let you.*

Chapter Six

Elise hadn't seen her sire in months. That wasn't unusual, except in this case, Mencheres had been the one to keep himself secluded away. One glance showed that the toll from the recent war that resulted in Mencheres's long-estranged wife being killed still hung over him. Physically, Mencheres looked the same. His waist-length black hair was just as lustrous, his creamy skin still held the amber tint of his Egyptian heritage, and his features were as handsome and regal as ever. But sadness clung to him in a tangible way, making the familiar lines around his mouth seem more likely to form a frown than a smile.

She hugged him, feeling none of her normal aversion to close contact. At the feel of his arms around her, the same peace washed over her that Mencheres always inspired. *Father, I've missed you.*

When he let her go, Elise touched his face. "You look terrible."

Mencheres gave her a strained smile. "True, but I will be better in time."

All things heal with time, he'd told her shortly after turning her into a vampire. Elise still wasn't sure she believed that, but things did *numb* with time, at least.

"Tell me about the man," Mencheres said.

Blake wasn't there; Bones had taken him directly to the basement, where the vampire cell was located. Every permanent vampire residence had a reinforced room for confining new vampires while they fought to control the initial blood craze. If a new vampire couldn't break out of it, Bones had reasoned, neither could a demon.

"He's back to himself now," Elise replied, shuddering at the memory of their hours-long car ride. The demon had continued to torment Cat by mimicking her grandparents' voices on what had—apparently—been the scene of their murder by vampires. Bones couldn't keep his hand over the demon's mouth the entire time, either. Not with the demon biting Bones and trying to drink vampire blood off the wounds. Or choking when Bones gagged him. Several times, Elise had worried that Bones's temper would snap, and he'd kill Blake, but they'd all made it in one piece, though Cat was still outside composing herself.

Mencheres studied Elise. She looked away from his probing gaze. Finally, a heavy sigh came from him.

"You've come to care for the human."

It wasn't Mencheres's mind-reading skills that betrayed her. Those only worked on humans, not other vampires. Mencheres just knew her too well.

"It makes no sense," Elise admitted. "He has no value in this world, no reason to go on. Plus, he *wants* to die.

But I was like that, too, once. Maybe more than once."

The silence stretched between them, filling with the unspoken memory of their history. Mencheres didn't need to be reminded that Elise had also been desperate to die when she was human. After all, it was how they'd met.

"I will try," Mencheres said at last. "But there may be nothing that can be done."

Elise laid her hand on her his arm. "Sire . . . *father* . . . thank you."

Mencheres's dark gaze was bleak. "You may not thank me when this is over."

The metal clamps bit into Blake's wrists, ankles, and waist. Bones had shackled him to the wall in a way that let Blake know the vampire wasn't concerned whether he was bruised in the process. Add the green glinting in Bones's eyes and the fangs curving where normal teeth had been, and Blake knew he was staring death in the face.

"No one's here," Blake said quietly. "You could say it was an accident, that I tried to get away."

Bones shot him a single glare. "Mate, if killing you were an option, you'd have met your maker hours ago. But I'm not giving that foul beast inside you the satisfaction of freeing it. Not until there's nowhere for it to run."

Elise's entering the room with a tall, foreign-looking man stopped Blake's reply. She had her hand in the stranger's, and Blake wondered if this was her husband or boyfriend. Oddly, he didn't like either thought.

"You tried to control his mind?" the stranger asked Bones, traces of an unfamiliar accent in his voice.

Bones grunted. "Too right. Filthy get wouldn't shut

up in the car, and for some reason, he kept after my wife the whole bloody trip."

The stranger looked thoughtful at this information. Blake winced.

"I'm sorry."

The stranger moved to the side, and Blake saw he had a dog behind him, of all things. Elise shut the door. It was just the four of them and a mastiff in the room. *What now?* Blake wondered.

The stranger's eyes narrowed on Blake, then went green. So bright, like looking into the sun, but a different color. Staring into his eyes, Blake felt as if he were spinning, but that was impossible, since he was manacled to a wall. His heart began to pound, and a weird feeling of panic rose.

Elise moved to stand close to him, not touching, but her presence was soothing anyway.

"This is my sire, Mencheres," she said softly. "He's going to help you."

No one can help me, Blake thought, then almost recoiled at the blast of invisible bands that gripped him. What the hell?

"Something's . . . squeezing me," he gasped out.

Mencheres kept staring at him with those hypnotic eyes. "I am."

The pressure increased until lights danced in his vision, and he could barely breathe. *This is it,* Blake realized. *I'm dying.*

"Sire," he heard Elise say, sounding agitated.

Don't worry, Blake wanted to tell her, but didn't have enough air for the words. *I'm not afraid. Thank you for everything you've done. It's not a bad way to go, actually, looking at your beautiful face . . .*

"What is your name?" Mencheres asked. His voice

sounded far off and echoing. Amidst the encroaching darkness, unable to breathe, Blake wondered how the guy expected him to answer.

"What is your name?" the question was repeated, with more emphasis. Mencheres's face filled Blake's vision, those ghastly glowing eyes boring into his. *Get away,* Blake thought. *Let me see Elise again. She's the only one in this room who gives a shit about me.*

"*What is your name?*" With a harder squeeze. Everyone but Mencheres faded out of Blake's sight. Blake's lungs were burning, his chest jerking in a vain attempt to coax air into it.

"Xaphan," someone hissed. Surprisingly, the voice was clear to Blake. Should he be able to hear things while he was dying?

"Xaphan," Mencheres repeated. More power slammed into Blake, until there was nothing in his vision but black, and he couldn't feel the pain in his lungs anymore. "Leave him."

An ugly laugh echoed across Blake's mind. "No, little Menkaure. And you're not strong enough to force me."

Another squeeze. It seemed like so long since he'd breathed, Blake didn't know how he was still even alive to register the viselike grip.

"Leave him."

That awful buzzing filled his head, indicating the demon was about to take over. Blake wanted to scream, but he couldn't move, couldn't see, couldn't talk. What if this was hell? Was he already dead and paying for all the things he'd done?

A string of words in a language Blake had never heard somehow penetrated his consciousness. The weirdest thing was, it was in a feminine voice, and it wasn't Elise.

Mencheres growled. That's how it sounded, anyway,

and something so heavy and hard pressed against Blake that he prayed for mercy. *Please, no. Too much. Stop. Stop!*

"Come out of him!" It was a roar that Blake felt in his bones. Then he was falling, blinding lights streaking by. For a few incredible seconds, Blake felt free of everything. Even sound faded into silence, leaving blissful, peaceful, welcoming silence. *At last . . .*

Then feeling came back in a rush of pain as something pressed on his chest, and his lungs felt like he'd inhaled fire. This time, when he opened his eyes, he saw Elise's face over his. Her mouth came down, not in a kiss, but to blow air into him.

Blake coughed, tilting his head because all of a sudden, he needed to gulp in breaths. Her hands—pale, cool, soft—touched his forehead.

"Are you all right?"

Blake couldn't reply, too occupied with gulping oxygen to try to form words. A dark head leaned over him, black hair falling around his shoulders.

"I can't save him," Mencheres stated flatly. "The demon inside him is too strong."

Chapter Seven

The sun had set an hour ago. Elise was tired, lack of sleep from this morning starting to catch up with her. Still, she didn't take Mencheres up on his offer to have someone else guard Blake while she rested. It seemed too cruel to pass Blake off to a stranger just so she could sleep, especially since people were acting like Blake was already dead.

She took Blake to the kitchen, knowing there would be plenty for him to eat. The humans who lived with Mencheres as willing blood donors for him and his entourage meant that the kitchen was stocked. Blake was ravenous, wolfing down three plates of food before looking embarrassed at his excess. Elise's stomach growled as well, but not for what Blake was eating. She pushed down her hunger with the same ruthlessness she'd used to forgo sleep. Blake didn't have long to live. The least Elise could do was to make these last days as comfortable as possible.

With that in mind, she'd refused to pack Blake up and start the journey to the salt flats tonight. There'd be time enough after Blake was fed and rested, she'd insisted to Mencheres, and he didn't argue. Bones was less agreeable, muttering that every minute they hesitated, the demon had a chance to possess someone else, continuing its carnage through a new person.

Elise could see Bones's logic. Even a couple days ago, she'd have agreed with it, but a lot had changed in the last twenty-four hours. Blake's first thought ever since she'd met him had been about what was best for other people. Well, Elise would be the one to think about what was best for *him,* and tonight, that wasn't loading him up in a car to drive to his death. Death would come soon enough for Blake, and that knowledge gnawed at Elise worse than her hunger or lack of sleep. It wasn't right. Long ago, Elise had been given a second chance. Why couldn't one be found for Blake?

Mencheres walked into the kitchen, silent as a shadow. Elise was sitting next to Blake on a barstool by the countertop, close enough that she could feel *and* see Blake tense when he noticed the other vampire.

"What did you do to me before, in the other room?" Blake asked Mencheres, his voice almost casual.

"I suffocated you until you were between life and death. It was my hope that I could use your weakened condition to force the demon out and send it into the dog," was Mencheres's equally calm reply. "It didn't work. I'm sorry"

"And you did all that without even touching me." Blake sounded bemused. "You must be one powerful vampire."

For a second, Mencheres looked weary. "Not powerful enough. The demon in you is ancient and strong. It will grow stronger with each person it destroys, so I can't let it go free."

"No, you can't," Blake agreed, his jaw tightening. "I know better than anyone about the horrible things it will do. This needs to end."

Mencheres stared at Blake. "You're a very brave young man. I do regret what must be done."

Elise glanced away. She felt a stinging in her eyes, even if it had been longer than she could remember since the last time that happened.

"Mencheres, I need a razor," Elise said abruptly. "After Blake showers, he can shave."

Blake gave her a surprised look, but Mencheres's expression was grim.

"You can't leave him alone with the razor," Mencheres said. "The demon will know what we've planned. Xaphan will try very hard to kill Blake, so he can escape into an unknown host before Blake reaches the salt flats."

Blake snorted. "Before, the demon wouldn't let me kill myself. Now he wants to do the honors? And what are these salt flats I keep hearing about?"

Mencheres opened his mouth, but Elise answered, unable to keep the huskiness from her voice.

"Demons can jump into any living thing once their host dies, even an animal that's several miles away. So when we . . . when you die, there can't be anything alive nearby for miles."

"Wouldn't it be okay if the demon were to possess an animal?" Blake asked. "I mean, a possessed armadillo couldn't do much damage."

"Animal possession is very temporary," Mencheres replied. "The demon's goal is to get back into a person.

It's easy to compel an animal to kill itself once people are around. Haven't you ever noticed that some animals seem to throw themselves into traffic? The driver of the first car to strike a possessed animal would, by virtue of closest contact, then become the next person the demon possessed."

Blake sighed. "It just keeps getting more twisted, doesn't it?"

"There's only one type of place where it's safe to force out a demon," Mencheres went on, filling the loaded silence. "The salt flats. Salt is a natural element for containing a demon. Once the host dies, the salt limits a demon's range to only a mile in every direction, and there are no humans or wildlife living on the salt flats."

Elise wished she knew what Blake was thinking so she could . . . what? Tell him things would work out? They wouldn't. There were so few things she could do to help him, and that knowledge made her feel worse than useless. Not only had she failed to save him, she'd be one of his executioners.

"Okay." Blake nodded briskly. "That makes sense. I'm glad you guys know how to stop it. I wish I had found you sooner."

"It seems like fate that you found us at all," Mencheres said, staring at Elise. "Demons feed on rage, hatred, jealously—all our lesser emotions. Once they've consumed everything they can out of a person, they move on. Elise tells me you were possessed when a woman ran in front of your car several months ago. You understand now what happened. The demon used her up, then it let her kill herself to find a new body. It would have eventually done the same to you."

Mencheres paused, his gaze flicking back to Blake. "You must be very strong. As a rule, humans don't last long before the demon controls them completely. For you to still have periods of control against a demon of Xaphan's caliber—remarkable."

Blake shoved his plate away and held out his hands. "Do you see the blood still staining these?" he asked, intensity pouring off each syllable. "There is *nothing* remarkable about being a murderer, and that's what this thing has made me."

Elise wanted to tell Blake that no, he wasn't the killer. He was the weapon, and weapons didn't have a choice. But even though she believed that, the words eluded her.

She stood. She might not be able to say anything to ease Blake's guilt, but she could still do something.

"Let's clean the blood off you, for a start."

Chapter Eight

*B*lake stood under the hot spray of the shower and closed his eyes. This felt good. Normal. It used to be his routine every morning and night. Now he couldn't remember the last time he'd had a hot shower. The stall was big, too. One of those upscale versions where there were multiple heads and two entrances to it. These vampires sure lived in style.

He was lathering his hair for a second time when Elise stepped into the shower. Blake froze so completely that he didn't even wipe his eyes when the suds trickled down to them.

She was naked, her body slender and sleek and so unbelievably beautiful that Blake wondered for a moment if he were hallucinating. Elise took the shampoo off the alcove in a nonchalant fashion, pausing to let her gaze sweep over him.

"Without all that dirt, you're younger than I thought

you were," she said, sounding faintly surprised. Her hand swiped his face, brushing the soap from his eyes and flicking his sudsy hair back. "You look completely different."

I could say the same thing about you, Blake thought, unable to tear his eyes away from her pale skin, long legs, petite round breasts, and tight cluster of hair between her thighs. His cock noticed, too, waking up and stretching as if to get a better look.

Blake spun around. Despite everything he'd been through, it looked like embarrassment wasn't beyond him after all.

"Uh, Elise, I don't think you should be showering with me," Blake managed.

He heard the water hit her as she moved closer. God, the thought of how Elise would look with rivers of water streaking down her skin made him harder. All at once, the shower stall felt far too small.

"Why not? I have to keep watch over you, and I needed to shower. I left you alone to relieve your bodily functions, but it's more efficient for us to shower together."

She sounded utterly clinical, as if discussing carpooling versus taking a bus. Obviously, being naked in the shower with him meant nothing to Elise. Was it the demon in him that made her consider him as less than a man? Or was it the fact that he was human, and she was a vampire?

Either way, Elise's complete dismissal made anger flare in Blake. He turned around, his erection jutting out and almost hitting her in the stomach.

"As you can see," Blake began, "there's a problem with your *efficiency* strategy."

Startled, her gaze traveled over Blake in an entirely different manner than it had before, pausing at his chest and stomach before moving lower. With her mouth half-open and the water clinging to her just as sensuously as Blake had imagined, his cock jumped, like it was begging for her touch.

She turned and walked out of the shower without another word. Blake closed his eyes and let out a slow sigh. Then he began to attack his hair with the shampoo again.

Elise was shaken by her reaction to Blake in the shower. Seeing a naked man *shouldn't* have had any effect on her. Becoming a vampire tended to kill modesty along with a heartbeat, so the sight of bare flesh didn't hold the same provocative taboo that it did for humans. Plus, she was used to showering in front of strangers, considering she took the majority of her showers at the fitness club.

So the wave of need that hit Elise when she saw Blake naked was a complete surprise. Blake was long-limbed and muscular, his thinness making his body look chiseled instead of gaunt. The dark, crisp hair that covered Blake's chest narrowed when it reached his stomach, then led in a trail to his groin before lightly dusting his thighs. Looking at Blake, Elise had been overwhelmed by an urge to touch him. She'd stroked his face and flicked her fingers through his hair before she could even stop herself.

It never occurred to Elise that Blake would want her. She was a vampire, he was human. Plus, she was participating in his death, a fact Blake was well aware of. For all his agreement over why he had to die, still, Elise's position as one of his executioners would hardly warrant affectionate feelings.

Of course, maybe that desire was Blake's natural reaction to a naked woman—any woman, even her, cold lifeless thing that she was. The thought relieved and saddened Elise. *Just stop,* she told herself. *It was one thing when you were forcing yourself to care about Blake to keep from killing him. Now you're caring too much. Why can't you feel things like a normal person, instead of it constantly being all or nothing?*

Blake's coming out of the bathroom interrupted her mental chastisement. He had a towel around his hips, his black hair touching his shoulders and curling from moisture.

"Sorry," he said, blue eyes steady. "Maybe group showers are just what vampires do, but they're more than I can handle."

Elise had to look away. Blake's earnestness made her heart give an odd lurch, like something was yanking at it.

"I'm the one who's sorry," she replied, fighting to keep her voice cool. "It won't happen again."

Blake cleared his throat like he was about to say something, then stopped. Elise glanced up, waiting, but his mouth was set in a tight line. Whatever it was he'd been about to say, he'd decided against it.

"Here." Elise indicated the chair across from her. "Sit. I'll shave you."

Mencheres had dropped off those essentials along with some clothes for Blake, since they were close to the same size. Blake didn't argue about shaving himself. He just sat in the chair and tilted his head back.

Elise approached, her gaze fastened on the long line of Blake's throat where his pulse throbbed so temptingly. She licked her lips. What would it be like to taste him?

Stop it, she rebuked herself at once. *He needs your help, not your selfishness.*

She lathered Blake's neck, working quickly with the razor so she didn't have to be so near to him. Blake's scent was a mixture of nervousness, weariness, and something else. Something spicy Elise couldn't name since she hadn't been able to determine Blake's natural scent underneath the camouflaging odors of blood and death before. His pulse increased every time she made a stroke with the razor. Was he worried about a vampire holding a sharp object to his throat? Wondering whether she'd be overcome with bloodlust if she accidentally nicked his skin?

"You're in no danger of my feeding from you," Elise told him after he twitched when she leaned in close to shave under his jaw. Even with the dabs of shaving cream clinging to his face, without his former shaggy beard, he was more handsome than Elise first realized.

"Do I still smell too bad?" he teased.

No. You smell wonderful, and I'd like to bury my fangs in your throat and hear you moan while I suck your blood.

"I'm not, ah, hungry," Elise stuttered. Where had her icy aloofness gone? Why was he affecting her so much?

She finished with a last upward stroke of the razor, jumping back to gesture to the clothes on the bed.

"These are for you. I'll leave while you change."

Elise almost ran from the room, slamming the door and leaning against it while clutching the razor in her hand.

Chapter Nine

The largest salt flats in the United States were in Utah. Flying would have been the quickest way to get there, but even though Mencheres had a private plane, he didn't choose that option. Maybe he was trying to give Blake a couple days to prepare for his death.

Driving was another possibility, but that came with its own set of difficulties, the least of which was comfort. Stuffing Blake into a backseat for over two days while driving him to his execution was cruel. Also, the demon had a greater chance of causing an accident and killing Blake—with plenty of people around to jump into—if they were all crammed into a car.

Therefore, Elise was relieved when Mencheres said they'd take a train. It would just be the three of them. Bones had muttered something about it being too soon since the last train he'd taken, whatever that meant, and since he still held a grudge against the demon for its hours of tormenting Cat, Elise was glad Bones and Cat weren't going.

Mencheres booked two bedroom cabins for the journey. It would take them almost three days to get to the Bonneville Salt Flats in Utah. Once they boarded at Union Station, Mencheres closed himself in the cabin with Blake and ordered Elise to sleep in the other one. She'd stayed awake during the night and through the morning to watch over Blake. The demon hadn't taken him again, however, and Blake had slept like he'd been drugged. It seemed with his fate sealed, he felt relieved, while Elise was the one struggling with anger and doubt.

Once alone in the cabin, Elise didn't think she'd be able to sleep, but her body had different ideas. The rocking of the train felt comfortingly familiar, lulling her to sleep even though her mind kept whirling. When she woke up, the sky was turning dark shades of orange and blue. *Almost dusk.* She'd slept the rest of the day away.

Elise bolted out of the narrow pull-down bed, guilt filling her. There went six of the fifty-five hours remaining of Blake's life, and she'd spent it slumbering while Blake had been shut in a cabin with a vampire he barely knew. True, he barely knew her, either, but compared to the time Blake had spent with Mencheres, Elise was an old friend.

She was on her feet and whipping the door open to the neighboring cabin in the next second. Blake looked up in surprise to see her in the doorframe, but Mencheres just raised a brow.

"With your haste, one might think you were afraid I'd lost him."

Blake was staring rather fixedly at her midsection.

Elise glanced down and felt a spurt of embarrassment, of all things. Not at the fact that she was shy over only wearing her shirt and underwear, but at how that revealed her anxiousness to see him as soon as she'd woken.

"I . . . thought I heard something," Elise lied.

Her sire gave her a look that said he knew better, but Blake seemed to buy it. He dragged his gaze away from her and coughed.

"I was about to go to the dining cab and get dinner. Did you want to come with me?"

"Yes," Elise said at once.

A smile spread across Blake's mouth. It transformed his face into something dazzling, but it also looked so unfamiliar on him, Elise realized this might be the first time she'd seen him smile.

"You might want to put something else on."

"Oh." There went that flash of embarrassment again, as if the clock had magically rewound, and she was a girl with her first beau. "Of course. I'll be back soon."

Elise returned to her cabin, shaking her head at the strange way she was acting—and feeling.

Blake leaned back in the chair across from Mencheres. There was a pull-down table between them that doubled as a chessboard. They'd played seven games, and the vampire had beaten him every time.

"She likes you," Mencheres said quietly once Elise left the cabin.

A snort escaped Blake. *I wish.* "She can hardly tolerate speaking to me for longer than five minutes, so you'll excuse me if I disagree."

"Youth," Mencheres muttered. "So blind. Speaking of that, checkmate."

Blake looked at the board. *How the hell?* "You tricky bastard," he said, seeing the trap he'd fallen into.

Mencheres gave Blake a tolerant look. "I was alive before chess was even invented. If you could beat me, then I wouldn't have learned much in my years, would I?"

And Blake knew Mencheres had been around for a *lot* of years. Over four thousand, the vampire had stated casually, as if that wasn't a staggering number. He'd also told Blake about the history of vampires. How Cain had been the first after God cursed him with forever drinking blood as a reminder that he'd spilled his brother Abel's. That they lived in structured societies ruled by a head Master, and—contrary to Hollywood's frequent assertion—wood through the heart was ineffective in killing them. Blake didn't ask why Mencheres was so free in divulging this information. Who was Blake going to tell? He'd be dead soon.

Elise came back. Her hair was wet, making it appear a darker blond. Her cabin must have had a shower in it like this one did. She wore drawstring cotton pants, which seemed to be her norm, but instead of a zip-up hoodie over her tank top, her arms and shoulders were bare. Blake's gaze lingered over her pale, radiant skin, remembering what it looked like without clothes covering it.

Figures he'd meet a woman like Elise now, when he was at the lowest point of his soon-to-be-ended life. Blake wished he could have met her before the demon, when he'd be able to take Elise to a real dinner, not just a quick bite on the train's dining car. Or to a Broadway play, or hell, to a swanky blood bank, if that's what she liked. Elise had shown him more compassion than most of the humans he'd come across in the past several months. He only wished there was something he could do to thank her.

There wasn't, of course. All he could do to show his appreciation was to make the last chapter of his life as easy on her as possible. So few things were still within his control, but he could meet his end like a man. No whining or any of that bullshit. Plenty of people died before their time. Because of the demon in him, Blake had been responsible for some of those untimely deaths, in fact. Fair didn't count for a damn thing when it came to life—why should he cry about not getting fairness in death?

"I'm ready," Elise said, holding open the sliding door.

Blake stood. "So am I." *And I'll prove that, Elise, when the time comes.*

Chapter Ten

*E*lise picked at her plate, eating a few bites just to look normal to the other humans in the dining car. Blake had been intrigued that she could eat at all.

She was silent throughout most of dinner, struggling to think up something to say and failing. Blake didn't seem to expect her to chat, either. Elise felt frustrated. Couldn't she even make small talk to ease his evening? Was she so out of practice with how to act in a social setting that she'd been stricken mute? She was a vampire; she could lift the train car and carry it if she had a mind to! Yet she couldn't come up with a way to start a single, pleasant conversation. *How humbling.*

"Things have been quiet for almost twenty-four hours," Blake said.

Shame stung her, forcing out a blur of words. "I'm sorry. It's just that I'm not very good at conversations. For years, I hardly talked to anyone aside from

Mencheres, and he knows me so well, few words are needed. I would like to speak with you, Blake, but I find it extremely difficult coming up with the proper words to say."

He stared at her, his mouth quirking. "I meant the *demon* had been quiet for almost twenty-four hours, but . . . you want to talk to me?"

If Elise had still had blood pressure, she'd have blushed. *Of course* Blake had been referring to the demon. She was the only one focused on herself, narcissistic fool that she was.

"Never mind," she murmured.

Blake's hand slid across the table, touching her arm. "I'd like to talk to you, too," he said. That little quirk to his mouth faded, making his face very serious. "If that's all right."

His fingers were warm. Blake wore a white button-down shirt, the neck open, showing off his beautifully sculpted throat and collarbones. Black pants fit him well, emphasizing not only his leanness but also the strength in his legs.

Elise downed her water in a gulp. This was bad. She hadn't felt this way about a man since—well. And that had ended horribly, too.

"Elise?" Blake was still staring at her. "Is that all right?"

No. Because if I don't pull back now, if I don't distance myself from you this moment, I'm going to hurt like I haven't hurt in decades. My coldness and apathy are all that can save me.

But just as Blake was helpless over the fate that brought him ever closer to the salt flats and the end of his life, neither could Elise bring herself to turn her back on him. Some things had to be done, no matter their cost.

"I'd love to talk to you," she said. "Let's go back to the cabin."

Mencheres wasn't in the cabin when Blake entered it. Elise didn't seem concerned about his absence, however, so Blake didn't question it. Maybe the vampire was getting some overdue sleep. Or finding his own dinner.

"Here." Blake gestured to the bench across from him. "It's comfortable, if you have a good imagination."

She smiled, showing pretty white teeth without that curve of fang he knew lurked in her mouth. Even though her hair was still damp, and she didn't wear a speck of makeup, Elise's beauty was obvious. She seemed unmindful of the looks she garnered, though. Hell, Blake had thought the train porter was about to ask her out when he dropped off the check.

Was it real? he wondered. The movies hadn't been right about much concerning vampires thus far, but what if Elise's looks were some sort of illusion? A predator's mirage in order to lure her prey closer?

"Is that your real face? Or do you look . . ." Blake paused, trying to choose an inoffensive word, "different?"

She frowned. "I look different when I shed my human disguise, if that's what you mean."

"Yes, that." So he'd been right about the glamour. What was under it? "Can I see you? The *real* you?"

Elise's blue eyes began to swirl with green, growing brighter, until they were pure emerald and cast a glow in the small cabin. She opened her mouth enough so that Blake could see the tip of her tongue touch two white fangs that hadn't been there a moment ago.

"This is me," she said, voice soft and almost hesitant.

Blake waited for more. When nothing happened, he

was confused. "I've already seen you like this, right after we first met, remember?"

"I remember." For a moment, she looked as confused as he'd felt. "I thought you must have forgotten, since you asked to see the real me . . ."

Blake couldn't help himself. He laughed, which made her eyes glow an even more vibrant shade of green.

"What's funny?" She sounded pissed.

Blake waved a hand, controlling himself. "I thought maybe you were using some sort of spell to look so god-damn beautiful, but it's just you. No wonder Mencheres changed you into a vampire. Who wouldn't want to keep you around forever if they could?"

Her mouth was still open, but now, it looked more like in disbelief. "You think I'm beautiful like this? But you're human!"

She said it as if that was a logical reason he shouldn't. Blake sighed. "Doesn't mean I'm blind."

She seemed to shrink a little in her chair, and she looked away. "I'm a vampire. I drink blood, I don't breathe, and my heart doesn't beat. Don't I scare you?"

Blake thought of all the things he'd seen—and done, though thankfully he didn't remember those parts—the past several months. Elise, scary? She couldn't be less frightening to him.

"You don't scare me." His voice was rough. "In fact, I think you're the closest to an angel that I'll ever get."

Something glittered in her eyes, making them brighter. It wasn't until a pink tear slid down her face that he realized what it was.

"Oh, God, Elise, don't cry," Blake said. He moved the short distance across the cabin to take her in his arms, half-worried she'd shove him away.

She didn't. Her arms wrapped around him, amazingly silky skin pressed against his cheek. Elise felt cooler than he did, but not in an icy, lifeless way. No, the supple, soft touch of her flesh felt as alive as his. If he hadn't known what she was, Blake might have thought the air-conditioning was just set a little low.

"I'm sorry," she whispered. "It's so wrong of me to burden you with my tears. Please, let me go."

Blake didn't want to. Holding Elise felt more right than anything he'd done in . . . well, he couldn't remember how long.

"I need this, too," Blake said.

Once, he'd have been too guarded to admit to such vulnerability to a woman he didn't know very well, but now those games seemed like a waste of time. Time he didn't have.

She moved so he could sit on the narrow bench with her instead of balancing over her. Blake pulled Elise onto his lap, resting her head under his chin, and closed his eyes. In the quiet, pressed close to each other in their mutual need for solace, there was more honesty than Blake had experienced in all his other relationships. *She's what I've been missing all my life,* Blake realized, but not in remorse. It was in deep appreciation that he'd been allowed to meet her before it was too late.

"I was engaged in the fifties." Elise's voice was barely audible over the rumblings of the train. "Edmond didn't know what I was. I'd told him I couldn't have children, but he said that didn't matter. I thought he'd accept the rest of me, too, if I could show him I truly loved him. Mencheres urged me to tell Edmond what I was, not to start our marriage with such a great deception between us. So, the night before our wedding, I showed Edmond my true nature."

She was trembling. Blake smoothed his hands down her back.

"He was so horrified." It was a pain-filled whisper. "He called me defiled, unclean, a hell-spawn. He wouldn't listen, no matter what I said. He ran off, but I thought with a little time, his fear would ease, and he would come back. He did come back, the very next morning. I woke up and Edmond was in the room with people I'd never seen before. They all had wooden stakes, one as long as a pole, and . . ."

Elise's voice broke. Blake's arms tightened around her.

"Edmond had them hold me down. I didn't struggle, because I thought if Edmond saw I wasn't fighting them, he'd realize there was nothing to fear from me. I kept pleading with Edmond to stop, but . . ." Elise's voice changed. Became flat and emotionless. "Edmond shoved a stake through my heart. I stared into his eyes the whole time. He was furious when I didn't die—he kept stabbing more wood into my chest. I couldn't think through the pain, and at last I fought back. Edmond's neck snapped when he hit the wall. The others were injured, but they lived. They ran away, and I left my house to live below the train station in the tunnels. I've mostly avoided people ever since, because if I didn't care about anyone, then no one could hurt me."

Chapter Eleven

*E*lise waited for Blake's reaction. Only Mencheres knew this part of her life, but as a vampire and her sire, he was obviously biased when it came to his opinion of what she'd done. What would Blake think, knowing she'd killed her human fiancé on their wedding day?

"I can't believe he'd do that to you," Blake said. His hands never paused in their soothing path along her back. "I understand why Edmond ran. Being afraid of what you don't know—yeah, I get that. But I will never understand why he tried to kill you when he came back. How could Edmond do that to you, no matter how shocked he was?"

Something inside Elise burst. It must have been her last line of emotional defense, because the feelings running through her left her dizzy with their intensity. Who would have thought this virtual stranger's acceptance would be the grail of forgiveness she'd sought all these long, lonely decades? And why was it that she'd only found him now, just to have to lose him so cruelly in the next two days?

"I lost someone I loved, too," Blake said. "I married Gail right out of the army. We were both young, didn't have a clue how to make a marriage work. I got a job in commodities and worked my way up to being a pretty successful broker on Wall Street. Gail finished college and began teaching. She wanted to start a family; I wanted to wait so I could keep advancing in my career. I was so busy climbing the corporate ladder, I ignored what mattered to Gail. I don't blame her for divorcing me. Sometimes you have to lose everything to know what you had."

Elise was familiar with that. She'd lost everything when she was human during the Great Depression, then again with Edmond, and now she had the feeling that when Blake died, she'd lose everything once more. *Why couldn't there be another way to defeat the demon inside him, aside from killing him?*

"Elise." Blake drew away enough for her to look at him. "Will you drink from me?"

"What?" She couldn't have been more startled if the demon had suddenly appeared.

He sighed. "I don't have much time, and that's all right. But I'd like to think something of me will last. If my blood is inside you, then it'll live on for as long as you do . . ."

Fresh tears came to her eyes. How could she feel so much pain when just a few days ago, she'd been empty inside?

". . . but only if you want to," Blake continued. "I don't know if the demon in me makes it too disgusting to–"

Elise sealed her mouth over his throat, the suddenness of her movement cutting his sentence off. Blake's heart began to beat with an excited, increased pace that heightened her hunger. She let her tongue probe his neck, tasting his skin. Caressing his pulse. Deciding just where she'd penetrate with her fangs.

Blake's breathing accelerated, his chest rubbing hers with its rapid movement. His hands clenched on her back in the same rhythm that she flicked his neck with her tongue.

"Is this, ahh, going to hurt?" he asked, his voice catching when she pressed her fangs against his throat.

Elise smiled. "You'll see."

She let her fangs pierce him slowly, savoring the exquisite splitting of his skin and the hot, luscious blood that followed. Blake shuddered, a groan escaping him that she heard and felt against her mouth. She waited, letting the euphoric venom from her fangs spread farther into his bloodstream, before drawing in a long, deep suction.

Blake's back arched and he gasped. Elise moaned at the slide of his blood down her throat, warming her. Igniting every preternatural sense in her. She took in another swallow, getting as much pleasure from the way Blake's hands gripped her as she did by the sweet taste of his blood. His breath came in gasps, the thundering of his pulse against her mouth mirrored by his heartbeat next to her breasts. The rich, spicy scent of him increased, wrapping around her. Intoxicating her. Urging her to take more.

"God, yes," Blake moaned, his voice rising. Elise grabbed his head, arching his neck farther back, and bit into him again.

A hoarse cry came from him, like a lover might make. Even as Elise gave a last, longing swallow, savoring his blood, she drew her thumb across a fang and held the cut to the holes she'd made. They closed before the final sounds faded from Blake.

She leaned back to see his face. His eyes were closed, dark strands of hair tumbling over his forehead, and he had a sensual, lethargic—and surprised expression on his face.

His eyes opened in the next moment, coriander blue and beautiful. "That didn't hurt at all," he said, a grin tugging at his mouth.

Elise laughed, bright and filled with the unexpected happiness inside her.

The smell of sulfur woke her. Blake had fallen asleep in her arms, both of them reclining on the narrow pullout that masqueraded as a bed. Elise wasn't drowsy. She didn't want to miss a second of her remaining time with Blake.

When that awful, burning stench enveloped Blake, her arms hardened and rage filled her. She was prepared to keep the demon from harming Blake—or escaping—so she was taken aback when all the demon did was open his eyes.

"You and I need to talk," Xaphan said in a low, gravelly voice.

Elise watched with loathing as Blake's skin turned that waxy, sallow color, and red replaced the lovely blue in his eyes.

"I don't think so," Elise growled.

His lips curled back in a condescending sneer. "Stupid little vampire, don't you see? I'm your only hope of saving this mortal."

Even though she knew better, hope sparked in her. "How? You'll willingly leave him?" That would mean the demon would get away, but then Blake would be free. God forgive her, she would be okay with that.

"If I could do that, do you think I'd still be here, kept by two bloodsucking vermin? I'm too deeply buried inside this body to leave while he still has life, vampire. But I'll make a bargain with you."

Don't listen. You can't bargain with evil. It will always win if you do.

"What's your offer?" Elise asked softly.

Those malevolent eyes glared into hers. "I'll give you the rest of this mortal's natural life span if you get us away from the other vampire. When the mortal eventually dies, then I'll be free to find a better home."

"Liar," Elise bit off. "You'd try to kill Blake as soon as we got off this train."

Xaphan sighed. The sulfur smell from his breath would have gagged Elise if she'd still been human.

"The years this mortal has left are no more than a tick of the clock to me, but they mean something to you, don't they? This is a fair offer. If you refuse, try to force me onto the salt flats, all of you will die. You can't hope to beat me; I am one of the first Fallen. I was around before Cain was even turned into a vampire."

Icy fear slid up Elise's spine as she stared into the demon's eyes. There was nothing left of Blake in them. They were ageless, evil, and swirling with red embers. It was as if she'd been afforded a glimpse into hell. How could she and Mencheres think to kill something as old, as powerful, as Xaphan? What if all of them *did* die on the salt flats, their bodies left to rot under the harsh sun, because she didn't take the only chance they had at surviving? Could she truly kill Blake anyway, after what he'd come to mean to her?

Elise thought of having Blake with her for forty, fifty, maybe even sixty years. That would be more happiness than she'd ever allowed herself to believe she'd find in all her undead lifetime. Xaphan might win anyway, if she persisted in taking Blake to the salt flats. Maybe if she took his deal now, in the future, they'd find another way to vanquish Xaphan without killing Blake *or* letting the demon possess someone else.

Really, wasn't this the only possible solution, even if it meant bargaining with a devil?

"If you care at all for his life—or yours—you'll see this is the only choice . . ." Xaphan drew out.

Blake's face flashed in her mind, looking completely different than it did now with the demon piloting him. *I can't live like this,* he'd said when they first met. Blake had proved countless times that he'd rather die than let the demon get away. In the end, this wasn't her decision. It was Blake's—and he'd already made it.

"No deal," Elise said, hardening her resolve. "If we all die sending you back to hell, then so be it."

The demon howled, becoming a mass of livid movement and flinging both of them up to the ceiling of the cabin in a blur. Elise didn't let go, wrapping herself around him and letting their hate-filled gazes meet.

"I'll kill you," Xaphan hissed.

Elise didn't blink. "You will try."

All at once, the demon froze. Elise relaxed even though the new flood of oppressive power squeezed her. Mencheres came into the cabin.

"You did the right thing, my child," he said to Elise.

She wasn't surprised that her sire had overheard the entire exchange. "I had no choice."

Mencheres came closer, forcing the demon back into the corner of the small room. "Yes, you did. And you made the right one."

Elise wondered if she'd still think that later.

Chapter Twelve

$\mathcal{B}$ lake looked at the clock. Eight-thirty in the evening. He had less than twenty-four hours left to live.

Elise sat across from him, her tenseness palpable. Mencheres had forced her to leave this morning to get some sleep, but Elise had come back looking like she had spent the three hours in the other cabin wide-awake. Blake wanted to assure her once more that she'd done everything she could, but maybe talking about it would only make things worse.

Her blond hair was loose, falling just past her shoulders, and she wore another tank top with yoga-style pants. Blake had been studying her while she looked out the window, trying to memorize her features. Small, straight nose. The mouth that looked more sensual than pouty. Those high cheekbones and smooth forehead. Her beautiful, mesmerizing, blue-green eyes.

Yes, if there was an afterlife, Blake wanted to bring the memory of Elise with him.

"Chess?" he asked, gesturing to the board.

She glanced away from the window. "I don't know how to play."

"Hmm. You don't know how to drive or to play chess. What have you been doing with all your time?"

His tone was teasing, but her face clouded. "I listen to music," she said slowly. "Read a lot of books. When I get restless, I walk through the city. It's been sufficient."

It didn't sound sufficient. It sounded lonely. Elise had said she'd been living like that since the fifties, but what had she been like before then? Blake knew she was much older than he, even though she looked to be in her early twenties. *How much older?* he wondered.

"How old are you?"

She appeared to think about it for a second. "Altogether, including the years before I became a vampire?"

Blake nodded.

"Ninety-nine in September," Elise said.

That number was so at odds with her lovely, youthful appearance, Blake had to smile. "You don't look a day over ninety-two," he said with wry humor.

Elise shrugged. "Some days, I feel even older."

Today was one of those days, if the stress on her face was any indicator. Blake sought to lighten her mood. There was no need for either of them to bemoan what was coming.

"How about I teach you to play chess? It's not hard. By the time the train arrives in Salt Lake tomorrow morning, you'll be a pro."

"I don't want to learn to play chess," Elise snapped, then she grabbed the edge of the built-in metal board and ripped it out of the cabin wall.

Blake stared at her. "Don't do this."

Suddenly she was in front of him, kneeling in the empty space where the pull-down table had been.

"You don't have to die." Her voice was ragged. "I can take you with me and keep you safe. Keep the demon from hurting anyone else . . ."

Blake took her beautiful face in his hands. "You can't watch over me every second of every day, and I won't let that thing get away to ruin more people's lives. Aside from you, the only thing that's made me happy these past few days is knowing that I've finally scared it for a change. That demon is going to regret what it did to me, because I'm the man who's going to bring it down. Don't try to take that away from me, Elise."

Her eyes were bright, pink tingeing the corners. Blake couldn't stop himself from what he did next. He kissed her, needing her taste like he was the vampire, and she was fresh blood. To his relief, her mouth opened at once, her tongue raking his while fangs sprang out of her upper teeth.

Blake didn't care about her fangs, even when those sharp tips scored his tongue. Elise sucked at the blood while kissing him, her raw need matching his and driving his passion to a fiery level. He pulled her up on his lap, groaning when she wrapped her legs around his waist.

His hands went under her tank top, tugging it up in impatience. Then he blinked when it was wadded on the floor with her bra in the next moment. Blake didn't bother to contemplate how fast Elise had taken it off, however. He cupped her breasts, tearing his mouth from hers to kiss them. Her flesh was soft and sleek, her nipples so hard by comparison. When he sucked and bit them gently, Elise moaned, ripping at his pants.

They split open, torn to the knee. Blake pulled them off, kicking the remains free. Her pants were gone in another blur, as was his shirt, until there was nothing separating her skin from his.

He grabbed her hips and arched forward, his mind exploding at the squeeze of her flesh as he thrust into her. Oh God, oh yes! He kissed her again, bracing his legs against the chair across from him, moving deep and fast within her. Elise rocked with him, gripping him so tightly it almost hurt—but he never wanted to end.

He held her, moving faster, knowing this would be the closest he ever came to heaven.

The whistle at the station sounded like a death knell to Elise. She gripped Blake's hand. If it were possible for vampires to throw up, she would have gotten sick as the train ground to a halt.

"Salt Lake City," the attendant cheerfully called out.

Blake squeezed her hand. "It's okay," he said, and squared his shoulders.

I won't cry, Elise promised herself. *If he can be this brave, so can I.*

She didn't feel brave, though. She felt like silver was spearing her through the heart. How she'd ever get through the day, she had no idea.

Last night, she'd cast about for any other option than Blake's death. Turning Blake into a vampire wouldn't work, Mencheres reminded her when she brought that up. Changing Blake into a vampire required that he be drained of blood until he was *almost* dead. Then, still clinging to life, Blake would drink Elise's blood, which would trigger his undeath. Since natural death didn't happen, becoming a vampire wouldn't force the demon out. No, it would mean Xaphan would have a back door into possessing a vampire instead. With Blake as a possessed vampire, who knew what new horrors Xaphan could wreak? They'd be handing the demon more power than he'd ever dreamed.

I won't let the demon free, he'd stated flatly. Mencheres had agreed that only human death, without any vampire blood in Blake, could force Xaphan out into the merciless trap of the salt flats.

But without any vampire blood in Blake, his death was irreversible.

They exited the train. Elise kept hold of Blake's hand because she couldn't stand not to touch him, but Mencheres's hand on Blake's shoulder was for a different reason—to restrain him in case the demon tried to make a run for it again. Xaphan had taken over Blake last night, going ballistic and trashing the interior of the cabin before Mencheres stilled him. Elise had to green-eye the train workers so they didn't call the police at the disturbance. *You'll all die tomorrow,* Xaphan had spat before crawling back into whatever hole he'd burrowed inside Blake. No, they hadn't heard the last from Xaphan.

Elise didn't know what the demon had in store for them, but she knew he wouldn't go gently into that good night. Still, Xaphan wasn't scaring her with his threats. He was just solidifying her resolve to do anything to make sure Blake had his victory over the demon. If Blake was willing to die for that, so was she.

Mencheres had two vehicles waiting for them in the parking garage. One was a regular four-door sedan, but the other was a large van. Elise's heart clenched at the thought of loading Blake's body into the van afterward. At least he wouldn't be stuffed into a trunk. That indignity she couldn't stand.

"Wait a few days until you mail my letters," Blake said to her quietly. He'd written to his family, apologiz-

ing for what they thought he'd done and telling them he
loved them.

"All right."

She didn't tell Blake that she had no intention of mail-
ing those letters. She'd deliver them in person and make
sure, with all her inhuman power, that they didn't think
less of the amazing man walking next to her.

Mencheres stopped by the van. "I'll drive this one,"
he stated. "You and Blake follow me in the car."

Elise didn't move. *No, no,* was running through her
mind in a roar. Blake leaned down and, very gently,
kissed her cheek.

"Don't come apart on me now," he breathed.

She nodded and forced her legs to move, one step after
the other. Somehow, she made it into the car, Blake in
the driver's seat next to her. Mencheres started up the
van, and Blake followed him out of the parking lot into
the bright morning sunshine.

Chapter Thirteen

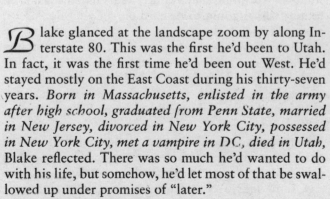

B lake glanced at the landscape zoom by along Interstate 80. This was the first he'd been to Utah. In fact, it was the first time he'd been out West. He'd stayed mostly on the East Coast during his thirty-seven years. *Born in Massachusetts, enlisted in the army after high school, graduated from Penn State, married in New Jersey, divorced in New York City, possessed in New York City, met a vampire in DC, died in Utah,* Blake reflected. There was so much he'd wanted to do with his life, but somehow, he'd let most of that be swallowed up under promises of "later."

Now that there was no more "later," Blake couldn't help the sadness washing over him. He wished he'd spent more time with his family. Gotten to know his friends better. Let go of jealousies and resentments a lot quicker. *All that time, so much of it wasted,* Blake thought. *What I wouldn't give to live it all over again, especially with Elise by me.*

Even as the regret filled him, Blake pushed it back. He'd chosen his life, such as it was, and he'd been allowed to meet the most amazing person before the end of it. Plus, what he was doing now was the equivalent of jumping on a grenade to save dozens of people, if not more. Blake harnessed the same mentality that had seen him through a two-year stint in Iraq during the First Gulf War. *Complete your mission. Don't fail your unit.* Right now, Elise was his unit. He'd make her proud of him.

"I don't want you going back to your home in the tunnels," Blake said.

She looked at him, her eyes wide. "What?"

"I don't want you going back to your home in the tunnels," he repeated, emphasizing each word. "I don't want you spending the next fifty years like the last fifty. I know this is going to be hard on you, but don't let it push you back to how you were, avoiding everyone so you don't have to care for anyone. I can stand dying, Elise, but I can't stand the thought of that."

Her jaw flexed, and she blinked a few times, but she didn't reply.

"Promise me," Blake said, hardening his voice.

"I promise."

Her words were choked. Blake looked back at the road, something tight inside him easing. Elise would go on. She'd live long enough for both of them, and one day, some lucky bastard would come along and make her happy.

And whoever he was, Blake hated him. Guess he wasn't finished being jealous after all.

Blake started to whistle to distract himself from that line of thought. Oddly enough, he found himself whistling that same tune Elise had earlier in the week,

"Beautiful Dreamer." After a few minutes, some of the stiffness left her frame.

"I love that song," she murmured. "It was my favorite as a child."

"It's been around that long?" Blake asked, teasing.

She gave him a melancholy look. "Longer. My mother used to sing it to me before I'd fall asleep. Funny, I can't remember her face, but I remember her voice."

Blake swallowed hard. In time, she'd forget his face, too.

"How did you become a vampire?"

Elise fixed her gaze on Mencheres's van in front of them. "I was twenty-one when the Great Depression began. My husband, Richard, lost his job that first year, along with so many other people. After several months, we lost our house, too. My parents were dead, but his mother was alive, so we stayed with her for a while. I gave birth to my daughter, Evangeline, during that time. Two months after she was born, Richard's mother died. She'd been behind on her house payments, so the bank took it, and there was no life insurance, so we were turned out into the street. Some friends of Richard's lived in Hoovervilles in Central Park, so that's where we went."

"What's a Hooverville?" Blake asked.

"It's what everyone called the tent villages, after that bastard, President Hoover. Richard scraped together enough cardboard, wood, and trash-can scraps to make a shelter. Every day, he looked for work, but there wasn't any. Winter came, and my baby got sick. I took her to the hospital, but they sent us home. She died three days later. Two weeks after that, Richard jumped off the Brooklyn Bridge."

"Oh, God, I'm sorry," Blake said, imagining Elise as the young, grief-stricken woman she must have been.

She swiped at her eyes. "I try never to think about that time." Her voice was amazingly steady. "It hurts too much. It hurt too much then as well, which was why shortly after Richard's death, I jumped off the Brooklyn Bridge, too."

Blake gasped. "What?"

Elise nodded, a faraway look on her face. "I don't remember hitting the water. I just remember the cold. There had been chunks of ice in the East River that day. I should have died; most people who jump off that bridge do, but Mencheres found me floating in the water and saved me . . ."

Her voice trailed off—and then she screamed, "Stop!"

Blake slammed on the brakes so hard, his head almost hit the steering wheel. He looked around, but there was nothing in the road or any other reason he could see for her reaction.

"Jesus," he exclaimed. "Don't do that again. If I hadn't been wearing a seat belt, I'd have gone straight through the windshield and made Xaphan's day!"

Elise swung to look at him, her eyes blazing green and an expression he couldn't name on her face.

"The river," she muttered. "The ice. Of *course*."

Blake felt like she was speaking an unfamiliar language. "What are you talking about, Elise?"

In reply she kissed him. Then she shot out of the car, turning the ignition off and taking the keys with her.

Elise stood next to Mencheres. The two of them were outside by the car, close enough that they could quickly reach Blake if Xaphan took him over but far enough away that Blake couldn't hear what she was saying.

"You told me when you first found me in the river, I didn't have a heartbeat," Elise said in a rush. "For all intents and purposes, I was dead, but the river was so cold that day, it gave me hypothermia. My body slowed down to clinical death, but when you pulled me out of the river, you warmed me, gave me your blood, and *brought me back*. If we induce severe hypothermia with Blake, his heart will stop, as will his breathing. He'll be dead enough to force Xaphan out onto the salt flats. Then, once the demon is gone, we'll bring Blake back. It's a long shot, but it could work."

Elise desperately wanted Mencheres to agree. But he'd had so much more experience with demons than she did; maybe there was something she was overlooking. What if it took too long from when Xaphan was expelled from Blake's body until his essence was destroyed? How many minutes *could* Blake be dead before there was no pulling him back from it?

"Come with me," Mencheres said.

He led her around to the side of the van. Elise's heart sank. Was Mencheres taking her out of Blake's eyesight to tell her that this couldn't be done? Did he want to give her privacy while she broke into tears when he delivered that hammer of a verdict?

Mencheres opened the back of the van. Inside it was an oblong container several feet long, with various medical devices she didn't recognize stacked around it. But the generators and portable defibrillator she knew at a glance, and there was only one reason they'd be there.

"You knew," she whispered. "You knew all long that there was a chance Blake could be saved this way. Why didn't you tell me?"

"Because you had to believe you would lose him in order to realize what he meant to you," Mencheres replied. "It's been so long since you cared for anyone. I wanted that for you again."

Elise looked once more at the items in the van. There were no guarantees that this would work, and she had a lot to learn in a short amount of time, but there was hope. At last, there was hope.

"All right," Elise said. "Let's get started."

Chapter Fourteen

The Bonneville Salt Flats looked like a white, desolate ocean. They stretched for miles in a peninsula that was bordered on the west by the mountains and on the south by the interstate. Mencheres drove by the sign at the end of the access road that told visitors to park and venture on foot into the tourist section. Blake knew why they weren't stopping at the tourist section; they were heading for the middle of the flats, where two and a half miles was the closest distance between him and the end of the salt barrier.

It was blazing hot outside, but in this case, that was a bonus. In the spring, Mencheres said, the salt would be turned to mush in places, making driving on it impossible—and they needed the van with its cache of equipment. But in the middle of the summer, the salt was hard, like crystallized gravel, allowing the van to ride easily over its flat, sparkling surface.

Blake sat between them in the front. There were too many instruments in the back that could be used to kill him, if and when Xaphan appeared. Blake had no doubt the demon would come forth at any second. In fact, he wondered what Xaphan was waiting for.

At last, Mencheres stopped. Blake glanced around. There was nothing to see except miles of white and the mountains to their left. Steeling himself, Blake took in a deep breath.

"Okay. I'm ready."

Despite Elise's optimism about being able to bring him back, Blake didn't think it would work. Chances were, when he died, he'd stay dead. Successful resuscitation happened in less than half the cases, he knew that from his army days when they taught him field triage. Still, he didn't share his doubts with Elise. Let her think he died believing he'd be saved. Why make this harder on her?

Blake went into the back of the van. There wasn't much room with all the equipment around. Mencheres opened the doors and set up the generators outside. No need to ruin even his slim chance with carbon-monoxide poisoning.

Elise gestured to the large rectangular piece in the van, which looked to Blake like an elaborate, water-filled coffin.

"It'll be easier if you take your clothes off . . . most of them, at least."

She looked almost shy saying that, as if he'd take her suggestion as perverted voyeurism. Blake's heart squeezed. *I'll miss you forever,* he thought, staring into Elise's beautiful blue-green eyes.

He stripped to his boxers, then took her in his arms. She hugged him back tightly, her whole body shuddering like something inside her was trying to break out.

"I know this makes no sense, since we've only known each other less than a week, but Blake . . . if I could spend the rest of my life with just one person, it would be you," she whispered.

Blake pulled away. Looked at her face and saw the naked vulnerability, emotion, and need there. He smiled, brushing back a strand of her blond hair.

"No, Elise. We've known each other forever, because that's how long I'll love you."

Then he kissed her, trying to imprint the feel of her on his mouth, hands, and body before death came to take him away.

Elise knelt next to the hydro chamber. Blake had been immersed in the glacial water for over fifty minutes. His initial, massive shivering had slowed, as had his pulse and breathing. Confusion was starting to set in even as his eyes kept fluttering closed.

"Where am I?" he mumbled to Elise. "Too warm. Need to get out."

"He's entering the last stages of hypothermia," Mencheres said in a low voice. "His body is past feeling cold and is suffused with a false sense of heat instead. It won't be long now."

Elise touched his forehead, but Blake didn't seem to feel it. His face and neck were open to the air, but the rest of him was submerged in the freezing water. All the better to bring about hypothermic cardiac arrest.

If she could have traded places with Blake, she'd have done it a million times over. The past forty minutes had been hell, watching him suffer in the container. Her only comfort was knowing that Xaphan would suffer, too. He'd taken Blake over as soon as Blake lay down in the chamber. Xaphan had thrashed around, trying to break everything he could touch. Mencheres restrained him with his power, holding Blake's body immobile even though the demon writhed and fought inside him. Xaphan had been gone for the past thirty minutes. Elise figured the demon was resting up for one last stand.

Blake's heart skipped several beats. Elise tensed, meeting Mencheres's eyes. *Soon. Very soon.*

Panic made Elise want to snatch Blake out of the water and start to warm him up now. What if this didn't work? What if this was the last time she'd ever see Blake? Dear God, how could she stand her heart being demolished yet again?

Blake said something she couldn't understand. Elise bent closer until his mouth was almost next to her ear.

"What is it, darling?"

"Elise." Her name was garbled and breathy, like Blake had barely the strength to form it. "Sing me to sleep."

Blake's eyes were closed, so Elise didn't have to worry about him seeing her tears. She started to sing, dipping her hand into the freezing water so she could hold his.

Blake's breathing became shallower, the intervals between his breaths extending longer and longer. His pulse was erratic, too, at times speeding up in bursts, then growing more and more sluggish. By the time Elise reached the last line of the song, Blake's heart had stopped completely.

She stared at him, feeling more frozen inside than the icy water that brought about his death. Blake's eyes were dilated, no spark of life in them. Just glassy, like a doll's eyes.

Elise thought she'd been prepared to see him this way. That she was strong enough to handle it, but something inside her shattered. She ripped off the cover of the chamber and grabbed Blake up in the next instant.

Mencheres's hands shot out, stopping her. Keeping

her from lifting Blake all the way out of that awful, killing water.

"Wait," he said.

"No," Elise snarled. "I have to bring him back!"

Mencheres didn't loosen his grip, and she felt his hold on more than just her arms.

"Not. Yet."

Elise would have fought him, her own sire, whom she trusted more than anyone in the world. But a blast of power in the air around them stopped her. Sulfur fumes seemed to crawl up her nose, and a howl of rage filled the van until it shook.

"You fool," Xaphan hissed.

The words didn't come from Blake's mouth. They came from behind her.

Chapter Fifteen

Elise didn't have time to turn around before the doors blew off the van, and Mencheres was sucked out into the sunshine. She dropped Blake, careful to make sure his head was hanging outside the chamber, and ran out of the van.

"Mencheres!" she screamed.

Nothing was around but miles of empty, ominous white salt. Where was Mencheres? Her sire was the most powerful vampire she'd ever met, how could he simply *disappear*?

Something slammed into her from behind. Elise fell, getting a face full of salt. Then she was propelled up and flung into the side of the van, hard enough to make it tilt on its tires.

"Bring him back," Xaphan growled near her ear.

Elise whirled, but there was no one there. Another

blow knocked her into the van again. Then another and another, all made by someone she couldn't even see.

Elise tasted blood where her lip had split. The bright afternoon sunlight, naked of any cloud cover, felt like needles on her skin. Something seized Elise's hair, grinding her face into a ragged piece of metal from the dent her body had made.

"Bring him *back*," Xaphan said again, and she was shoved into the van.

Blake was still slumped over the chamber, motionless. Elise pulled him all the way out of the water, laying him on the van's floor. He was as white as the salt outside, all the color gone from his skin, and his skin was cool enough to feel like he'd been carved out of ice.

The van gave a violent rock that had equipment sliding into the corner.

"Stop it!" Elise snapped. "If you break everything in here, I can't save him."

"Do it now," that horrible, disembodied voice ordered.

Her hands trembled as she set the breather over Blake's mouth, turning on the machine that would pump warmed, humid air into Blake's lungs. *We must reheat his core slowly,* Mencheres had said. *Too much artificial warmth to his extremities will make lethal gases fill Blake's bloodstream.*

Therefore, Elise didn't use the hot packs with Blake yet. She covered him with blankets and set up the IV to fill an artery with heated blood. Another IV was inserted for a warmed saline solution. Then Elise began CPR, forcing Blake's stationary heart to pump.

An invisible hand slapped her across the mouth. "Faster," Xaphan said.

The demon's voice seemed to rise and fade at the same time. Elise took out a syringe with an elongated needle, punching that needle through Blake's breast-bone to inject epinephrine directly into his heart. Then she began compressions to his chest again.

"Bring him back *now*," Xaphan roared. The van lifted off the ground a foot and smashed back down, shattering the windows.

Elise paused to take a long, poignant look at Blake's face. *That demon is going to regret what it did to me,* he'd told her. *Don't try to take that away from me, Elise.*

That was what she was doing right now, taking away his choice because it hurt her too much to honor it. Searing pain tore through Elise's heart. *I can't do it. I love you too much to betray you like that.*

She kissed Blake's cold lips, then sat back. "It's over," she told the demon.

A viselike grip settled around her throat, lifting her until her head banged on the ceiling.

"You will obey me," Xaphan said. Waves of sulfur curled around her, the odor so thick, it felt like it was slithering inside her.

Elise could barely talk with the pressure on her throat, but she managed to force out her reply.

"Go . . . to . . . hell."

The van shook, metal curling back from the frame, before it was lifted and slammed repeatedly to the ground. Elise used all of her strength to tear away from the force that held her. She crawled toward Blake, covering him with her body when she reached him. Shielding him from metal shards that sliced through the air, ripping into her flesh and gouging the equipment around them. For a few nightmarish minutes, it felt like the entire world was being shaken and ripped apart.

A piercing shriek scalded her ears, causing Elise to lift her head and look in its direction. In the open doorway of the ruined van, a cloud of black flame appeared. It stretched into the form of a man with long, smoke-tipped wings coming from his back.

"Die," the demon hissed. That cloud of burning sulfur shot straight toward Elise and Blake.

Elise braced herself but didn't try to escape. She wouldn't leave Blake, even if it meant her death.

Mencheres suddenly appeared in front of her, his power crackling the air around him. The flames reached him—and stopped, dissolving into smoke mere inches from his body.

"You're not strong enough anymore, Xaphan," Mencheres stated. "Your time is up."

Xaphan screamed, but even as that awful noise reverberated, the smoke from the tips of his wings spread. It engulfed his legs, dissolving them out from under him. Then his arms, his torso, and finally, his sneering face, until there was nothing left of Xaphan but the faint scent of sulfur in the wind.

Elise closed her eyes for a second. The demon was gone. He couldn't hurt Blake—or another innocent person—anymore.

Then her eyes snapped open. "Help me," she said to Mencheres, scrambling to get the equipment set up again.

Mencheres moved quickly, gathering up the pieces of equipment that had been scattered around the van, but the outcome was soon obvious. Everything had been damaged. The generators weren't working, which meant no heated oxygen, blood, or saline, and most of the IV lines had been shredded. Elise looked at the wreckage of their medical supplies with numbing panic. They'd never get Blake to a hospital in time, even if Mencheres flew him there, and they needed these things to bring him back to life.

Elise made her decision in the next moment, a steely determination filling her. *I won't let you die. I won't.*

She grabbed the nearest unbroken syringe she could find and rammed it into her throat, drawing out her blood. Then she plunged that same needle into Blake, injecting her blood into his artery.

"Begin compressions," she directed Mencheres, blowing into Blake's mouth.

Mencheres gave her a look she couldn't read, but she didn't care, whatever it meant. She kept blowing air into Blake's lungs, pausing only to draw more blood from her to inject it into Blake. After five minutes, she had Mencheres stop, but Blake's heart was still silent.

"Let's warm him up more," she said, and gathered everything that still held heat and piled it around Blake. All remaining warmed blood and saline bags were pressed to his armpits and groin, plus more blankets were piled on top of him. Elise even hauled the broken generators over to place Blake's body on top of them, since they were still warmed from their recent activity.

"Again, more compressions," she said, and injected another syringe of her blood into Blake.

Mencheres complied, manipulating Blake's heart while she continued to blow air into his mouth. After another several minutes, Blake felt warmer. Elise's hopes leapt when his heart made a few faint, erratic beats, but then it fell silent again.

"Come on," Elise shouted in fear and frustration. "You're not ready to die yet!"

"Elise . . ." Mencheres said.

"No," she cut him off. "I'm not giving up on him."

She looked at Blake—silent, pale, beautiful—and did the only thing she could think of. She bit into his neck, right at the jugular.

"Begin compressions," she said to Mencheres. Her tone dared him to argue.

Mencheres pressed on Blake's chest in those measured, controlled pumps. Elise sucked, drawing Blake's blood into her with the help of Mencheres's actions. She drank deeply, chilled by the temperature of Blake's blood but not stopping until what she'd taken from him would have been lethal if he wasn't clinically dead.

"Now," Elise said. "We're going to transfuse my blood to Blake. All of it."

Mencheres found a catheter that wasn't broken and set up the line in Elise's throat, positioning the other end of the IV in Blake's jugular. Once it was set, Elise closed her eyes, willing her blood out of her body and into that narrow plastic tube.

It took ten minutes for Elise to drain herself into Blake. When she was done, she felt light-headed, as if she hadn't fed in weeks. She found the portable defibrillator under the remains of the car seat and charged the electrodes, pausing only to send up a silent plea. *Please. Don't take him from me.*

Then she sent the volts into Blake's chest. His heart fluttered again for an extra few beats after the shock, but then stilled once more. Elise charged the defibrillator and hit him with another set of volts. Blake's heart responded, beating on its own for a full minute, then it quieted again.

Mencheres touched her arm very lightly. "You've done all you can. Even if this worked, Blake's heart won't restart enough for him to live as a human again. He will either rise as a vampire, or he will stay dead."

Elise put her arms around Blake. "So now we wait?"

Her sire nodded. "Yes. We wait."

Epilogue

*E*lise looked around at her home under the defunct train station in the District. In a lot of ways, she would miss this place. But a promise was a promise.

She hefted her books into a double-plied leaf and lawn bag, thinking she'd leave the bed and chair for another lost soul to make use of. Maybe her former home would provide the same kind of refuge to someone else that she'd needed these last few decades. The thought pleased her.

An arm slid around her waist, the muscled flesh the same temperature as her own. "Ready to go?"

Elise smiled and turned into Blake's embrace. He was faintly flushed from a recent breakfast of plasma, but the new silky luminescence to his skin looked very different than when he'd been human.

"I'm ready now."

Elise was ready for a lot of things, the first of which was living with the man she loved. And maybe next was learning how to drive. Or how to play chess.

Now that she had Blake, the possibilities were suddenly endless—and wonderful.

New York Times bestseller **JEANIENE FROST** lives with her husband and their very spoiled dog in Florida. Although not a vampire herself, she confesses to having pale skin, wearing a lot of black, and sleeping in late whenever possible. And, while she can't see ghosts, she loves to walk through old cemeteries. Jeaniene also loves poetry and animals, but fears children and hates to cook. She is currently at work on her next bestselling Night Huntress novel.

Catch of the Century
Sophia Nash

To Philip Vanderbogart Nash,
a handsome devil and a most beloved uncle . . .

Chapter One

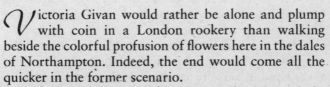

Victoria Givan would rather be alone and plump with coin in a London rookery than walking beside the colorful profusion of flowers here in the dales of Northampton. Indeed, the end would come all the quicker in the former scenario.

Lord, how she loathed the countryside. A casual observer would never guess that the turmoil of worries tumbling through her mind this fine spring day rivaled the stories to be found in the sole possession Victoria carried—a book of *Canterbury Tales*.

This was her last thought before the shrill blast of a carriage horn interrupted all. "Take heed. Make way!" A driver's voice rang out from one of the three regal coaches barreling down the turnpike.

For the fifth time that hour, Victoria hurried her three young charges to the edge of the road to avoid being trampled. Spirited horses shook their heads, and polished brass and metal traces jangled in the air as the lead team jigged closer at a spanking pace. At the last moment, the first carriage swerved toward them, and Victoria spied the silhouette of a masculine profile beyond the gilt-edged window. The rear wheel passed perilously close to her boots, and a flag of wind whipped over her as she stumbled back.

The trio of adolescent boys reached to steady her and murmured words of concern. She coughed and sputtered amid the clouds of dust kicked up by the departing entourage. What sort of uncaring person had the audacity to nearly run them down without even a—

There was a shout, and the impressive set of equipages came to a dead halt a hundred yards away, before she could catch her breath and quell her frustration.

A stylishly liveried driver from the lead carriage jumped down and opened the highly lacquered door.

"Wait here," she admonished the boys. She strode forward a few paces, then stopped—her legs shaky, her composure even more so.

A tall, daunting gentleman unfolded his frame from the polished carriage, his gloves and hat fisted in one large hand. It was obvious even at this distance that he was as dashing in his elegant clothes as she was uncommonly shabby in her faded gray gown. His long, loose strides ate up the distance between them, and suddenly, he was right in front of her, his gold quizzing glass gleaming as it lay amid the starched shirt linen between the lapels of an austere dark blue superfine coat.

He ran his fingers through his dark hair and replaced his lustrous brushed-beaver hat before he finally glanced down at her. His brows drew together.

Victoria's breath caught in her throat. *Good Lord.* His eyes were the most arresting shade of pure blue— deep and devastating. They spoke of seduction even in this overly sunny florist's fantasy of countryside buzzing with all manner of perverse insects.

Not that she knew the smallest particle about seduction. The closest thing to temptation unleashed had been her introduction to chocolate several months ago courtesy of her benefactor, the Countess of Sheffield.

He perused her form in a slow, unsettling fashion, appraising her from the top of her sensible and very old chipped straw hat down to the toes of her very new and very fashionable calfskin half boots, courtesy of another good friend.

"Well?" she asked, collecting her wits in the face of such magnificent masculinity. From the expression decorating his extraordinary face, it occurred to her that most likely he had rarely been brought to heel for anything in his life.

"I should like to apologize for the ill example of driving my heretofore excellent coachman just exhibited, madam."

"I've seen drunken sailors after a decade out to sea show more care behind a team."

He pursed his lips for the barest moment, and Victoria was uncertain if it was in annoyance or in humor. "You've the right of it, madam. Shall I have Mr. Crandall keelhauled at the next port, or shall I have him tied to the nearest tree so you can lash him yourself, straightaway?"

She snorted.

"My thoughts exactly."

He undoubtedly agreed with her only to deflate her. But she refused to retire her displeasure. The day had been far too awful, and this was the proverbial last straw. "It's easy to accept guilt when it falls on another's shoulders and not your own."

"Quite right. That's just what I told Crandall when

he tried to blame the poor pheasant running across the road just past your party. Shall I dismiss him without reference?"

"Of course not!" She nearly shouted in frustration.

"Or perhaps you'd prefer me to go after the bird?"

She ground her teeth together.

"Well, then, since you clearly possess the heart of a saint"—she would swear the corner of his lips twitched just the barest bit—"the matter is settled. I'm so glad you escaped injury, madam. Good day to you. I do apologize again for any inconvenience." He bowed and began to turn away.

It was her muttering that probably stopped him in his tracks. "Did you have something further to say?"

That habit had always got her into trouble in her youth. There was no excuse for it really. "Nothing, nothing whatsoever."

"Are you in need of aid? Perhaps a bit of compensation is in order for all the trouble?" She could sense rather than see the wariness in his eyes as he fished in his darkly patterned waistcoat and produced a gold guinea.

She gripped her beloved book to stop herself from taking the much-needed coin. "Absolutely not." Her voice sounded tense and high-pitched to her own ears. "I don't need money, and I certainly would never accept it from you if I did."

"Are you sure? You would be doing me a favor, really—easing my conscience." His blue eyes appeared even more vivid as he finally displayed a dazzling smile, which only served to irritate her further since it caused the most annoying fluttering in her stomach. It must be hunger.

She tried to shrug off the importance of his offer—and wavered. Pride lanced need. "No, thank you."

He raised the handsome quizzing glass to his eye and stared at her.

She felt rather like a moth under a magnifying glass. A dusty one. She had never been good at hiding her emotions. And today was obviously no different.

"Here, take it," he said quietly as he advanced the coin and lowered his eyepiece.

The man hadn't even condescended to ask her name. Only her tacit forgiveness had been required, and a guinea offered to enable him to forget her all the faster. But then, on the playing fields of the rich and titled, mere mortals of the working class did not require names. She should know that much by now. She turned on her heel to see to the boys. "Good day to you, sir," she tossed over her shoulder.

Christ, the dark auburn-haired siren had robbed him of his ironlike grip on his wits. Who would have guessed snapping, green-eyed beauties could be found scampering about the back of beyond in intriguing, fashionable little boots and a hideous gown barely fit for the ragman? This species of female did not exist in town. It bore further inspection.

He easily caught up to her as she reached the trio of boys, who silently gazed at her with complete adoration in their eyes. Apparently, her charms worked equally well on the younger members of his sex.

She turned around again, her vivacious eyes spearing him. They were the color of spring. Of life. They were the eyes of some mysterious stubborn female tribe—one he'd heard tell of but never encountered. All the ladies he met were well-mannered, exceedingly accommodating, and possessed of a certain fondness for riches. *His riches.* But facing him now was an outspoken hellcat, bent on countering his every word despite her station. She was also the worst liar he had ever seen. She was altogether quite refreshing in an exceptionally impolite fashion.

"Madam, my manners have gone completely begging. Would you be so kind as to favor me with your name?"

"*Another* favor? I rather think you've used up your allotment today, sir. Everyone knows too many favors breeds complacency, which only leads to dissolute behavior. I won't have the ruination of your character on my conscience."

John Varick, the newly minted ninth Duke of Beaufort, nearly shouted with laughter. He couldn't stop himself from going after her again when she herded the boys past him. They followed her despite their evident desire to gawk further at his carriages. The smallest boy was lagging and looking parched.

He said to her back, "I beg your pardon, ma'am. Look, I know we got off on the wrong foot, but it's apparent one of your party is ailing. May I offer all of you some refreshment? Water at the very least? You know, it wouldn't be any trouble a'tall to escort you to your home."

She stopped in her tracks, and her shoulders slumped forward for the briefest instant before she arched her back again. Only the crickets could be heard, and a horse pawing the ground. Without turning to face him, she said softly, "All right."

He took a deep breath and came 'round the little group. He bowed properly. "John Varick—your servant. May I ask who I will have the pleasure of escorting?"

She lifted her chin. "May I present Gabriel, Matthew, and Peter? Masters Towland, Smithson, and Linley." Each boy ducked his head at the mention of his name. The last and littlest looked at him reverently.

"And the name of the," he paused, "*lady* escorting this troop of apostles?"

"Victoria Givan." Her voice was lyrical and soft when she allowed her ire to cool.

He waved to the driver near the horses. "Crandall, please arrange space for Masters Towland and Smithson in the other carriages. I shall take up Master Linley and Mrs. Givan."

"*Miss* Givan," she corrected.

John Varick knew well how to hide from the world the humor he felt tickling his mind. He stole another glimpse of her pretty boots.

Soon enough the boys were settled, and he offered his arm to hand Miss Givan into the carriage. "And where shall I direct Crandall? To the Pickworth estate down the road, or perhaps somewhere else in the neighborhood?" Surely she was a governess out taking the air with her charges, although that did not explain the impractical elegant footwear.

She settled on the bench beside the young boy he had carefully chosen as their chaperon and rested the large book on her knees. As he ducked inside to join them, she lowered her mossy eyes. "It's a bit farther down the road, Mr. Varick. We're on our way to Derbyshire actually. Wallace Abbey to be precise."

He nearly missed the last step. The forward motion propelled him into the seat across from her and the boy. "*Wallace Abbey*? Why, that's *sixty* miles from here." He should have known better than to have been lured by an unusual face.

His amused driver of the last decade and a half cracked a rare smile upon hearing her direction and shut the carriage door, leaving no escape. There had been quite a dry spell since Crandall had last won a round in their association.

"Really? Sixty miles?" she said, lifting her small pointed chin, "I hadn't known it was quite so far."

"Miss Givan, were you planning on walking the entire way?"

"Of course not." Her mien, voice, and eyes violated all ten rules of honesty.

The carriage moved forward, picking up the pace a few moments later. A long silence ensued, during which John poured a glass of water for the boy, who downed it eagerly. Her hand wavered a bit as she accepted another glass from him. "Miss Givan, dare I mention that Wallace Abbey burnt to the ground over two decades ago? You weren't planning on spending the night there on your, ahem, *pilgrimage*?"

"I'm well aware of that. I'm escorting the boys to Derbyshire to take up their new positions there as apprentices to the architect Mr. John Nash. Perhaps you know of him? He's quite famous."

"Certainly."

"Wallace Abbey is to be rebuilt and will serve as an extension of the foundling home where I'm employed in town. I've promised to settle the boys in a refurbished cottage near the abbey and to hire several servants for Mr. Nash's colleagues, who will oversee the boys and the rebuilding."

"I see." He removed his hat, turned it upside down, and slipped it between the parallel leather straps running the length of the carriage's high ceiling. He debated how far he would be willing to accompany the pretty woman and her charges. It would be simpler, nay, more prudent, to arrange passage for them on the next mail coach. "Are you ever going to tell me how you came to be walking on this road—so far from London?"

Victoria Givan, orphan, teacher, and all-'round manager of dozens of little-men-in-training, concentrated on steadying her breathing. All it had taken was a glance at the golden *B* above the famous royal crest on the carriage's outside door to confirm her suspicions. How on earth was she to think properly with the freshly anointed Duke of Beaufort sitting across from her?

Good God.

Every morning and afternoon his sobriquet blazed from all of the newspapers—*The Catch of the Century*. Sometimes every letter was capitalized if the columnist was especially overawed. His story was oft repeated; as a young man he had taken his modest maternal inheritance and formed a seemingly never-ending string of brilliant foreign schemes and investments leading to a fortune that rivaled the royal families of Europe. And all this before it became apparent that he would, indeed, succeed to the illustrious title since the former duke, his uncle, had never sired a son.

And he was ridiculously handsome—a man in his prime. His mesmerizing blue eyes were said to have caused a multitude of ladies to swoon dead away in his presence. Silly schoolgirls composed poems about his awe-inspiring smile and his even more dazzling riches. Victoria sighed.

His ability to withstand the onslaught of ambitious ladies flung at him by their determined relations over the last decade or more was one of the most popular topics under the swagged edges of the *Fashionable World* columns. Why, his every movement and his every word were recorded in biblical proportions. And the gossip had reached its zenith this past month, when the former Duke of Beaufort had died unexpectedly, investing the man before her with the title he wore with such ease.

He began to tap the side of his well-muscled thigh in exasperation while waiting for her answer. What had he asked her? More importantly, how was she to cajole this gentleman into taking them all the way to Derbyshire? There was nothing except common decency to prevent him from leaving them at the next signpost. His

Grace did not look the sort who suffered fools lightly. And Victoria felt little more than a fool after today's events.

She stopped biting her bottom lip when he raised his quizzing glass to his eye again, evidently to intimidate her into an answer.

"Do you need spectacles, Mr. Varick? Peter would be happy to lend you his, won't you dearest?" The boy nodded and produced his small pair straightaway.

He lowered his quizzing glass. "I do *not* require spectacles."

"It's entirely understandable, you know. Failing sight is a common ailment among many gentlemen of your advanced years, and—"

"Advanced years?" he said, one corner of his mouth curling the merest bit.

"Why, yes. Ah, please forgive me, I should never have suggested you are . . ."

"What, Miss Givan?"

"Well, I do have the greatest respect for the wisdom one acquires with gray hair and all."

"Gray hair? I do not"—he sat up straighter and blinked—"Miss Givan, I'm not in the habit of enduring people who evade questions. Now, will you favor me with your certain-to-be-woeful tale instead of these tedious observations of yours, or not?"

Young Peter Linley's head had been swiveling back and forth in an effort to keep up with the conversation. "I'll tell you, sir."

The duke fastened his penetrating gaze on the boy. "I knew I could count on you, Peter. Men must stick together. Spill it."

"Well, it was like this. Me and Gabe and Matthew—"

"Gabriel, Matthew, and I," Victoria instinctively corrected. "Really, this is the most tiresome story."

He ignored her. "Go on, Peter."

"Right," the boy said. "We were at the last inn. The one in Quesbury. Do you know it, sir?"

"Yes."

"You see, Miss Givan was haggling with the innkeeper because he was askin' too much for the bread and cheese, then the mail coachman's horn sounded and, well . . ."

"Yes?"

"That's when it got really interesting."

"Peter . . ." she tried her best 'I shall make you rue the day' voice. Lord, make this day end, please.

"Go on."

"Well, another gentleman, actually he didn't quite look like a gentleman—more like a laborer really since he had lots of dirt on his clothes—anyway, he took up for Miss Givan when the innkeeper winked at her and said she could pay off the debt in another fashion since he fancied red hair. He even pinched her"—Peter darted a glance at her and hurried on—"and the laborer darkened the daylights out of the innkeeper. For some reason that made the rest of the men there join the brawl. We had to crawl out on our hands and knees and had a jolly time of it . . . until we saw that the mail coach was gone without us and we had to walk."

"And all your belongings?"

"Oh, all of Miss Givan's coins were lost in the brawl, and our belongings are still on the coach, sir. But that's for the best, Miss Givan said. Easier to walk without havin' to carry much." The boy grinned, and the duke ruffled his hair.

Victoria tried to laugh. Tried to appear good-humored. In fact, she was an ugly combination of mortified and anxious. She knew she had only one way to get all the boys to Derbyshire safely, and that would involve engaging the bemused interest of the richest man in England for the next sixty miles or so. It was all that separated the boys and her from spending a hungry night or three under the stars, blanketed by a hedgerow, and all manner of insects and wild animals prowling this *jungle*.

For the first time in her life, she felt very much beyond her depth. If she could just make his blue eyes a plain shade of brown, and eliminate, oh, say a few hundred thousand pounds from his staggering wealth, then she would feel much more capable of making this paragon of bachelorhood come around to her way of thinking.

She also wished for one day and one night of quiet reflection so she could make a bargain with her maker: to get her out of this detestable countryside in exchange for an end to her ridiculously romantic dreams. It was too bad the angel charged with guarding over her took such delight in sabotaging her wishes at every opportunity.

Chapter Two

*J*ohn glanced up from the large stack of documents he had been perusing for the last fifteen miles only to find the boy fast asleep in Miss Givan's luscious little lap. Each time he had allowed his concentration to waver, he had studied her lovely, even profile while she gazed out the carriage window at the day's gloaming. Worry emanated from every stiff inch of her. And he inwardly cursed.

Didn't he dole out enough tithes and coin each year to an endless string of venerable institutions to discharge his conscience? He didn't want to have to take a personal interest in any one person in need. There were too many people who suffered, and he could not be responsible for all. He tightened his jaw. It was much more productive to remain apart from others and concern himself with his endless correspondence, investments and speculations that could ultimately benefit many.

Despite the fact that she was a fascinating creature,

he didn't have time for this. He had but a week or so to sort out an impossible dilemma in his newest venture if he was going to be ready to take on autumn's cornucopia at the proposed mill. He couldn't spare a moment on an unusual-looking, sharp-tongued teacher wearing mysteriously fashionable half boots. Who on earth had given them to her? A cast-off lover, perhaps? He glanced up from her footwear to find her exotic green eyes flashing at him.

He suddenly realized his carriage had lurched to a stop more than a minute ago. *Christ.* What was taking Crandall so long? "Wait here, Miss Givan." John wrenched the door open and jumped from his carriage without waiting for the steps to be moved into place.

One of his outriders, who was waiting in the Gray Fox Inn's yard, leapt to attention. "The owner said the roof gave way after the rain two nights ago, Your Grace. The next inn is twenty-five miles from here."

"And?"

"And the innkeeper said he and his wife would be willing to give you the only habitable room—their own— for a pretty penny. Mr. Crandall is having a look."

"Of course there is no second room." There was not a hint of a question in his voice, only barely restrained annoyance.

"Correct, Your Grace. Although there is plenty of room in the excellent stables."

"Have Crandall pay the man for the room if it is suitable and get everyone settled."

The man cleared his throat. "Shall I have Your Grace's affairs brought to the innkeeper's room—or is the *lady* to occupy—"

"Bring my portmanteau inside. And order whatever dinner can be served for everyone as soon as humanly possible."

His outrider darted a glance beyond him and dipped his head.

John turned to find Miss Givan standing there, silent.

"I thought you were to remain in the carriage, madam. Do you ever do what you are told?"

"Rarely. I'm more used to doing the managing. Of the children, of course." She looked pensive and slightly unnerved. "Look, I want to thank you for taking us this far. The boys and I will continue on our way from here. I'm certain it's not that much farther."

"Miss Givan, if you think I will allow you to go trotting off down this obscure country lane, into the darkness, you can discard that idea straightaway." He brushed an invisible piece of lint from his sleeve. "You have never ever been out of London, have you? Do you not know how many bears, mad dogs, boars, and wicked men are lurking about at night?" He hoped she was as ignorant as he thought she might be of the benign nature of the countryside. Why, there hadn't been a wild bear lumbering in England's woods the last century or more.

There was a symphony of skittish doubt in her expression. "We shall sleep in the stable, then."

"Glad to hear it. Can't abide straw ticking myself," he drawled. "Come along now, Peter. Madam, I shall leave it to you to gather the rest of your charges. Dinner awaits." He captured Peter's smaller hand in his own and took a chance by walking away from her.

An hour later, John stared in wonder at the adolescent boys seated around the hastily arranged table in the only chamber untouched by the calamity aside from the kitchen. "Impressive. Who knew dwarfs were capable of consuming an entire side of beef at one sitting?"

"They're of a *growing age* and not used to such abundance," Miss Givan said defensively, as the boys giggled.

It had not escaped his notice that she'd eaten very little. "Come now, Miss Givan," he said, nodding almost imperceptibly to the manservant. "You can do better than that crust of bread. We must keep up your strength if you're to have a prayer of keeping this next generation in line." The servant transferred a juicy slice of meat to her plate at the same moment Crandall entered. His loyal driver produced a bottle of the finest brandy one could buy from seasoned French smugglers. John never went any great distance in his carriage without a case of it well-cushioned in fine English wool. A crystal glass appeared.

Silence reigned as Crandall carefully poured the nectar of the gods. It was the only thing John had looked forward to this entire problematic day. If he couldn't have a taste of the auburn-haired siren, and his conscience and good sense suggested he couldn't, then he would at least let the amber waves of balm claim a portion of his monumental concerns.

He suddenly realized everyone's eyes were upon him for some odd reason.

"Boys, Mr. Crandall, would you please give me a moment with Mr. Varick?" Miss Givan rose and urged the boys from their chairs.

"Varick?" his driver said, righteously. "Why, he's the—"

"That will be all, Crandall," John cut him off curtly. As the servants and boys exited the room, John lifted the ambrosia to his lips and savored the intoxicating scent.

"Sir," the spitfire said with hauteur, "I would ask you to refrain from consuming spirits in front of the boys. They're of an *awkward age*, and easily impressed by gentlemen they might admire."

"So they're of a growing age *and* an awkward age?" he asked dryly. "How inconvenient."

"It would not do to give them the idea that they should spend any monies they might one day find in their pockets—on . . . on gin or any form of the devil's brew."

"Gin? Why, this is the farthest thing from that vile poison."

She stared at him silently, mutinously.

"Miss Givan, are you truly asking the gentleman who has taken you up in his carriage to forgo the one and only bit of heaven to be found in this godforsaken excuse of an inn?"

"Well, I'd thought—"

"And here I was considering taking you and the boys miles out of my way tomorrow to deliver you safely to Wallace Abbey." He lowered his voice. "And I was also considering how best to share the one and only room available here." He said the last to provoke her. Her eyes were flashing again. It was definitely how he liked them best.

"Why, I wouldn't share this room if it were the only one in all of England. And furthermore, *Mr. Varick,* I want you to understand that I intend to repay every last farthing for this meal, the carriage ride, and for all the trouble you have so *generously* taken on today."

"Really?" He enjoyed the animated play of her delicate brows and relaxed in his chair to savor another long taste of his excellent brandy. He wondered if she had truly deduced who he was. "And how do you plan to accomplish that, Miss Givan?"

"I shall write to my benefactor, who will forward any and all monies due you straightaway." She pushed back her shoulders. "With or without your further aid."

"You have a benefactor, do you?" He glanced at her elegantly tooled footwear.

"Of course," she said, the tiniest blush finally cresting

her cheeks. "And you shall be happy to learn that I have already asked the innkeeper, who I have found to be considerably more civilized than *most* men I've encountered since leaving town, to provide a pallet for me in the kitchen, which he has graciously consented to do. I would never dream of asking for the use of this room. I shall be perfectly comfortable with the innkeeper's wife in the kitchen."

"And the boys?"

"Will be in the stable."

He looked at her shrewdly for a long moment.

"It's very rude to stare," she muttered.

"I'm debating the wisdom of informing you that there will be ten times as much drinking going on in that stable than in this room—what with the number of ostlers, drivers, and servants occupying the outer building."

She strode over to the table and retrieved the brandy bottle by pinching the neck with two fingers as if it were three parts distilled poison to one part pure evil. "Well, Mr. Varick, I must thank you for setting a better example."

"Miss Givan, has anyone ever told you '*no*'?"

She hid the bottle of brandy he had spent a small fortune on, along with the nearly empty glass, in a rude armoire in the corner. "I've never put myself in a position to have to hear it."

"Who gave you those boots you're wearing?"

Miss Givan whipped around. The smallest crease of a wrinkle appeared between her brows. "A good friend."

A *very* good friend, indeed, John thought as he ground his molars together.

John stared down at the sleeping form of Miss Victoria Givan on a pallet far from the innkeeper's wife in the kitchen. She had obviously been placed in his path to bewitch him.

The frayed hem of her simple shift had risen above her knees; the thin blanket discarded completely in the balmy night air. He could not drag his gaze from the moonlit sight of her slender thighs and calves, and her pretty, feminine feet. No wonder her lover had given her those damned boots. The better to ogle her elegant ankles.

Christ, he had always prided himself on his ability to keep his baser instincts in check. He obviously needed to engage a mistress, just as Crandall was hinting. Of course, his driver probably suggested it to keep him in a better frame of mind. John had taken for granted the convenient arrangement he had had for so many years with Colleen, the beautiful Duchess of Trenton, possessor of three yapping dogs, two indolent children, and one husband old enough to be her grandfather. But she had become melodramatic of late, insisting they should marry when poor Trenton cocked his toes. He had had to end it.

Miss Victoria Givan rolled onto her back in sleep, and his mouth became dry as chaff. The scrap of her shift eased off her shoulder, exposing one creamy breast to taunt him.

He groaned and squeezed his eyes shut. Surely he deserved a place beside the saints for not acting on the impulse. Heaven wasn't worth it, the devil on his shoulder shouted.

Damn it all to hell. He leaned down and gathered the woman in his arms to carry her to the room. If he couldn't sleep, he might as well give her the bed. Without the brandy to fortify him, his manners had become far too accommodating, and he had invited the three boys to sleep in makeshift beds the innkeeper had placed in the tiny sitting room beyond. Unfortunately, he hadn't known boys made such a ruckus in slumber.

She was so soft in his arms. So different from the harsh angles she seemed to possess when she was wide-awake. She slept like a bear in hibernation. Must be a result of sleeping near a gaggle of snoring infants for decades in the foundling home.

His own life had been spent in the reverse manner. All alone for the most part. No brothers or sisters, no mother. Merely a father, who, while very kind, had not been much in evidence in their country home due to the demands on his time in London. But John had learned to enjoy the peace of solitude.

She muttered something when he placed her in the middle of the innkeeper's soft bed. He leaned close as he tucked the bed linens around her form, only to hear two blasted words. Well, only one was a true word . . . a name.

"Oh, *John* . . ." she whispered on a sigh as she settled.

He straightened awkwardly, resolutely. No. He would not be gulled like some rich, wet-behind-the-ears buck first come to town. He knew better than to put himself in such a situation with an unmarried miss in an almost public place. He'd had enough brushes with the altar of late.

Why, in the last three months alone, an impoverished marquis had tried to sneak his daughter into John's sleeping quarters, and he had been forced to ferret out the truth behind a very determined widowed countess, who had deliberately planted scandalous rumors linking herself to him. She had made the mistake of thinking he would leg shackle himself to a pretty lady he had never even met—all in the name of honor. The last event had caused a new fever pitch in the gossip columns.

John studied the luscious morsel bathed in moonlight before him. She was all soft curves, rosy flesh, and tangled locks of shadowy plum hair. He couldn't resist touching those dark loose curls of a shade he'd never seen. Surely they would be silken. His palm stroked the glossy locks, bringing him closer to those irresistible lips of hers.

He closed his eyes against the sight, but his mind refused to be denied the remembrance of that full bottom lip below the lovely bow of her lush upper lip. And suddenly he noticed her scent of warm crushed roses. He couldn't have stopped himself from dipping lower to follow the trail of sweetness if his life had depended on it.

And then, he didn't want to be blind from the potency of the moment. He opened his eyes, only to encounter her sleepy, half-closed expression. She said not a word to stop him, and he inched forward at her silent encouragement. It would really be just a promise . . . of a hint . . . of a taste . . . of a kiss. Very innocent, of course. There were boys snoring in the closet-sized room beyond after all. And the innkeeper's wife in the kitchen.

He swept his lips across hers, side to side, feather soft. And then he molded his upper lip in the crevice where her lips met and teased the softness he found there. A soft moan came from her, and it was all he could do not to gather her again into his arms. Every part of him— well, the key parts of him—of any man, really—came awake at the sensuous sound.

And then she whispered it again . . . "Oh, *John*—"

"Darling," he returned quietly as he trailed kisses to the sensitive spot near her temple.

And then without another sound and with the swiftness of a pickpocket in London, she grabbed his ear and sent him to his knees. "*What are you doing?*" she hissed.

"Let . . . go . . . of . . . my—" he rasped out.

"I should have known better than to trust you," she interrupted in a harsh whisper. "All men are perfect scoundrels. My good friend always warned me, and I should have listened."

He wrenched away from her and stood stiffly, his body trying and failing to take in the reversal of intentions. "And all women are incomprehensible."

"Well, that's not very nice of you to say given that I just woke up to find myself in *your* bed. You were trying to press your attentions on me."

"No. I was offering what you seemed to request," he gritted out. "When ladies whisper my name in the middle of the night, certain assumptions are made."

"I did not do any such thing. I was sound asleep."

He looked at her shrewdly. "I suppose you are now going to suggest I do the honorable thing?"

"Why, yes I am." She shook that magnificent mane of hair back. "Get out of here. Or perhaps it would serve better for you to wait here while I cut a switch and tan your—shush . . . are you laughing?"

"So you're not going to ring a peal and demand a proposal of marriage before the innkeeper and his wife?"

"Why on earth would I want to marry *you*, Mr. Varick?" she hissed. "And I would ask you to lower your voice if you don't care to awaken anyone."

"So, you're not attracted to me?"

"Absolutely not."

"Really? And what sort do you favor? Poor sods who grovel at your pretty feet?"

"No. Agreeable sods with better manners."

He rubbed his sore ear. "I beg your pardon. I've been told I'm actually something of a catch, so to speak."

"Is that what silly females say to get the coins in your pockets?"

"No," he said with a low wolfish growl. "That's what they say to get beyond my pockets."

She did not miss a beat. "Vanity is not an attractive trait in a man."

He choked on his pent-up laughter. She was impossible. *Impossibly alluring*—in an outrageous, spirited manner. No woman had ever dared to speak to him in such a fashion. He'd always managed to endear himself to the females of his childhood—the housekeeper, the cooks, the housemaids; and he'd been equally up to the task of erecting a polite distance—the size of the Roman Empire—toward the marriage-minded females of his adulthood.

In all his five-and-thirty years, he'd never found a woman who refused to be charmed if he chose it, or at the very least behaved with extraordinary politesse and god-awful fawning. Of course, he was fated to meet the first truly intriguing woman of his life only to find she would have none of him.

That hair of hers was a dark halo in the moonlight, framing her pale, beautiful shoulders. And he knew precisely what lay beyond that ridiculously flimsy shift.

Perfection.

"Madam," he said quietly, "pardon me. I think I'll retire for the evening. I find that considerable rest is required in one's dotage." He turned on his heel and strode to the door.

As he rounded the corner, he could have sworn he heard her utter something about the benefits of warm milk and honey . . . *for gout.* This was followed by the barest ripple of low, throaty laughter.

He decamped as fast as possible. To sleep in the stable. In the damned straw.

* * *

John Varick, the ninth Duke of Beaufort and well-doc-umented Catch of the Century, withdrew a square of linen and sneezed. Across from him within the confines of his luxurious ducal carriage, Victoria noted it was about the twentieth time he had done so that day.

And she was perversely glad. Humor was the only thing that kept her from succumbing to an advanced state of anxiety as young Peter Linley, seated beside her, turned another page in her beloved book of *Canterbury Tales*.

Not as lost in thought as Victoria had surmised, the duke glanced up at her from the intimidating pile of documents and letters on his lap. His impossibly blue eyes met hers, and for a moment, she felt in danger of drowning in their depths. He was so very handsome. He studied her until she felt heat crest her cheeks. Before he returned his attention to his papers, he formed just the smallest hint of a knowing smile. She nearly burst with frustration.

He had kissed her.

It had been her first kiss, and she was fairly certain she had missed at least half of it. Of course, it would happen that way. She had decided recently that she would end up kissing the cheeks of St. Peter at the Pearly Gates before she would ever kiss a living, breathing man. Her station in life forbade it. And she had never really believed the romantic courtly rags-to-riches sto-ries between the covers of the book Peter was reading. And so for many years she had had to be satisfied with her imagination.

His lips had been gentle, so very unlike what she had imagined. Warm and knowing . . . and *lazy* almost. She swallowed.

In the blink of an eye, she had woken from dreams of

him and immediately deduced what he was about. In the haze of that poignant lime and bay scent of his, she had dragged herself away from the tide of his overwhelming magnetism.

Those same lips, which appeared to have been formed to drive all females to distraction, now tempted her less than three feet away. And with each uneven passage in the road, his long, muscled legs molded in biscuit-colored pantaloons, brushed against hers. She determinedly turned her attention out the window, where rain tapped a steady tattoo.

He had been reading the entire day. Not one word had left his lips, even when they had stopped for a midday meal. She had worried he would leave them behind when he strode into the private dining quarters. She had surely infuriated him to the extreme boundaries last evening. But no. Mr. Crandall had reemerged from His Grace's private room and said dinner had been arranged for her and the boys in another chamber.

And after, the duke had reappeared and Mr. Crandall had bustled her and the boys back into the carriages.

And then it had started to rain.

For the last three hours she had been calculating to the minute how many more miles to Derbyshire as the drizzle turned into sheets of rain. If she could just get within a few miles of Wallace Abbey, she would relax. She and the boys could walk the rest of the way if need be. It had taken all of her patience to curb Peter's curiosity and enthusiasm for the new sites beyond the carriage window, and to encourage him to read in complete silence.

Finally, she spied it, the distinctive weathervane of the Cock & Crown Inn at Middleton, which was supposedly very close to Wallace Abbey. It had been described in detail to her by her benefactor, the Countess

of Sheffield and by the lady's fiancé—a man for whom
Victoria had carried an unrequited longing in secret for
a good portion of her life. She shifted in her seat, determined to put such impossible thoughts from her mind.
She had tried to squash those dreams the day she had
befriended the lovely countess. And she had irrevocably
buried those same dreams in a grave six feet closer to
China the day the countess and Michael Ranier de Pey-
ster had formally announced their engagement. There
was not a person alive who could not love the extraor-
dinarily compassionate Countess of Sheffield. They had
never discussed Victoria's sensibilities toward Michael,
but somehow she was certain the countess knew. And
yet, that had not stopped the beautiful lady from assist-
ing the foundling home.

Victoria felt the duke's gaze upon her once more, and
she could not resist the challenge he unconsciously presented. She turned her face away from the sodden scen-
ery. Even rain appeared more dreary in the country as
opposed to the liveliness of town.

"And precisely where is this cottage?" he asked quietly.

"I believe it's less than a mile from here, according to
the directions given to me." It was time to end this cat-
versus-dog game. She had amused him to some degree
for dozens of miles yesterday, and for her part, she had
had the pleasure of experiencing about five seconds of
pure, unadulterated lust last eve.

At least she had managed to retain her innocence—
little good it would ever do her—even if she had lost
a portion of her sanity. Truth be told, she would have
enjoyed just a few more seconds . . . or perhaps a full
minute or three of his kisses. "As I told Mr. Crandall
during the last change of horses, it's the small dower
house a mile or less from the abbey's ruins, *Your
Grace.*"

His expression was impenetrable. "Your attention to protocol certainly makes a late appearance."

"I beg your pardon if I've offended in any way. We are, all of us, most grateful to you for taking us up."

"And?"

"And, what?"

He withdrew his handkerchief and sneezed.

She continued, forced gratitude edging her words. "Thank you, too, for arranging our meals, and . . . and for our *lodging*."

"And?"

She snapped with the tension and ill ease. She had not slept above one half hour after their interlude. "I will not thank you for the use of the bed last night. I was not given the choice of refusing it! And I said I would repay you for all the trouble we've caused you."

Peter's eyes were round in his face.

"Now you've done it," the duke said, then looked at the boy. "Let this be a lesson to you, Peter. As some of the *Canterbury Tales* suggest, no good deed goes unpunished."

The carriage rumbled to a stop, followed by the other two ducal conveyances.

"I'm sorry, Your Grace," she said with a stab at sincere contriteness. "I truly am very grateful. I—I don't know what I would have done without your coming to our aid."

His eyes narrowed, and she had the oddest sensation that he didn't take any pleasure from her show of solicitous gratitude.

He made a movement to remove the edges of his hat from the straps above them, and she stayed his arm with her hand. "No. It's dreadful outside, and I'd rather not be the cause of any further inconveniences." In truth, she wanted to remember him like he was now, ensconced in ducal plushness—or like last night in the moonlight.

He looked at her for a long moment, ignored her request by tugging his hat onto his head, and opened the door to jump out. Apparently chivalry could not be repressed in a duke.

It was pouring like the afternoon deluges of foreign jungles she had read about. Peter and she watched as he grasped the umbrella Mr. Crandall offered, then dodged mud puddles to reach the cottage door. The umbrella offered little protection from the storm.

A man who appeared to be marked with a great many stains on his clothing stood waiting in the already open doorway. Much gesturing and talk emanated from the man. None emanated from the duke.

It seemed an age before the man in the doorway bowed deeply, and the duke returned to Mr. Crandall. The noise of the rain drowned out their conversation, but Victoria used the moments to collect the book from Peter, button his plain coat, and straighten her gown in preparation for their descent.

And then, with a rush, the duke was back inside the carriage, water running in rivulets down every part of him. He was as wet as a school of fish in the River Thames. And he did not appear happy about it.

"Well, madam. It appears you are to move about all of England with an epic portion of ill luck." He used one of the carriage blankets to ineffectively swipe at his large wet form, which seemed to take up more than half the carriage.

"Whatever do you mean?"

He glanced between Peter and her before picking up a walking stick to rap three times on the carriage roof. Before she could utter another word, the carriage jerked forward, and they reentered the roadway.

"Wait! Please stop the carriage. I assure you we don't mind getting a little wet. The boys and I—"

"Miss Givan?" he interrupted, his face set.

"Yes?" she replied.

"Do you know the location of the closest structure with four empty beds?"

"Yes. It's behind us."

"No. That insult for a cottage features crumbling walls within and certainly not a single bed, cot, or pallet. There's been a delay. Some sort of illness has forced most of the men from their labors. And those selfsame men lie abed in every last corner of every last inn in the neighborhood."

She was speechless for the first time in her life.

"The nearest place with four empty beds is Beaulieu Park—*my* home, Miss Givan, which is miles from here."

"I see," she said, her voice low. "Well, we shall just have to make do." She grabbed the walking stick from the corner where he had placed it and struck the carriage ceiling again three times. She fell forward onto his lap when the carriage came to an abrupt halt. "Please arrange for Mr. Crandall to turn around. We'll sleep on the ground in the cottage. It's really not such a hardship. We are not used to *feather beds*, I assure you." She did not know why she had such an ungodly urge to provoke this man, who had shown so much kindness to them.

His face now as dark as the storm clouds in the sky, he grabbed the stick from her stiff fingers and rapped the ceiling yet again in rapid succession. The carriage jerked forward, and the duke's head bumped into hers, causing her to see stars. She bit her lip to keep the tears from her eyes.

When she finally allowed their eyes to meet, she saw

for the first time a flash of displeasure there—just the barest flicker before it disappeared. She had to give him credit. He had more command of every inch of himself than Wellington before the French army.

"The cottage has a quarter foot of water lining its floors due to the storm. And the second and third levels require better supports. It seems there are no doors or windows yet in the rear. And it stinks of the gutter inside. Now, Miss Givan, I have just one request."

"Yes, Your Grace?" she whispered.

For a long moment he was silent. Peter's fingers crept into hers. "You will not refer to me as 'Your Grace' when we are in private. For some insane reason it has the hollow ring of an insult coming from your lips."

"I assure you it's unintentional," she said quietly.

"Now, it's all arranged. The four of you are to stay at Beaulieu Park for the next fortnight until the cottage is aired and habitable." He paused and brushed off the inconvenience. "It's not an imposition of any sort. The number of apartments in Beaulieu rivals the royal pavilion in Brighton. I shall assign two dozen maids to see to you and the boys to maintain a level of *un-questionable* propriety, since any breaches in decorum could result in actions already deemed unpalatable . . . to *all* of us."

She burst out in a little breath. "Of course."

"At any rate, I shall be in residence a mere week or so. I've only come to resolve a long-standing dispute between the former Duke of Beaufort and our neighbor. Then I must return to London. You shall then have Beaulieu to yourselves." His eyes had become lazy and half-closed, his amusement returned. "I trust you not to cause too much damage in my absence, ma'am."

She hated having so little chance to exercise the smallest measure of pride. Poverty did that to a person. "Of course, Your Grace."

His eyes darkened with displeasure.

"I mean, yes and thank you, *Mr. Varick*." When his gaze did not waver from hers, she snapped. "What?"

"I find even 'Mr. Varick' sounds like an affront, coming from you."

"Well, then what on earth am I to use when addressing you?"

"*John*." His gaze never wavered, his voice decisive yet cool. "When we are in private, of course."

"I beg your pardon? I—"

"Think of it this way, your demands will take on an entirely new level of importance with such equality of station."

"I rather doubt I shall ever rival your rank."

"Well, you can't say you weren't given a rare opportunity last night."

She looked away, only to encounter Peter's confused expression—another reason to change the subject. She cleared her throat. "What sort of dispute do you have with your neighbor? Perhaps I could at the very least offer an impartial opinion—if only to erase the smallest dab of our debt to you."

He studied her for a few moments before he retrieved the thick sheaf of papers, which he had placed in a cubby on the side of the carriage. "My neighbor, the Earl of Wymith, refuses to allow a road to be built at the northernmost minuscule corner of fields he has left fallow."

"And?"

He rubbed a hand over his face. "And for decades my family and all the tenants of Beaulieu, as well as the nearby village, have had to travel nearly twenty miles to circumvent Wymith's property to arrive at Cromford Canal, where barges stop to transport goods to market. And I had hoped . . ."

"Had hoped what precisely?"

"Well, the last time I visited my uncle here—just before he died—I saw that the area has become more and more depressed. Many families have lost their men to the war—and those husbands and sons who have returned have lost their tenancies to others."

"Well, what are you going to do about it?" She was instantly contrite about the note of insistence in her voice. Really, she had no sense of reticence when it came to injustice.

He sighed with a great show of tolerance. "I was about to tell you. I had planned to construct a large mill on the edge of Beaulieu. It would be an ambitious project, designed to bring employment and wealth to the people of Derbyshire. But we will need the easement to encourage others to mill their grains here. If we could create the road, the distance to the canal would be negligible."

She felt a sudden rush of affection for this man before her. He was not like most aristocrats she had known, always after amusements and loath to promote commerce. Victoria had never understood why great men and ladies viewed honest work and industry with such contempt. "Why does your neighbor hate the Beaufort family so much?"

"According to the Earl of Wymith, my uncle almost killed his father two decades ago when the former earl was trying to retrieve wounded game—a duck—he had shot from a blind on his property. According to my uncle, who never failed to repeat this story ad nauseum at every opportunity, the earl was trespassing in search of Beaulieu-raised pheasants, and he had every right to shoot at him. My uncle was, ahem, fanatical about hunting and very particular about poachers. Thank God he was also a very poor shot."

"So, your uncle wounded the earl?"

"Mostly his pride. According to the apothecary who tended him, the earl sustained a small flesh wound on his arm that did not require stitching." The duke shook his head. "I recently sent an apology to the new earl, but he would not accept it. And when I tendered an offer to buy the tiny yet critical eighth of an acre to build the road, Wymith said he would sooner give land to a Frenchman than sell it to a Beaufort. I've pressed members in the House of Lords to use their influence, but the man won't see reason."

"So this entire dispute is over a nicked arm and a lost duck?"

"Or a pheasant." He shook his head. "Can you imagine what I've offered through an army of solicitors to soothe the Wymith feathers?"

"I'm not sure I want to hear this."

"Fifteen thousand pounds."

Something caught at the back of her throat, and she could not stop a fit of coughing that overcame her. Peter came to her aid, pounding her back. She could not manage to stop. She wasn't sure if she was more embarrassed by her coughing or shocked by the outrageous amount he had named. Why, fifteen thousand pounds was nearly thirty *years'* worth of food for the foundlings at the home in London.

Through her tears, Victoria saw Peter eyeing the duke. "Do you think you could spare a bit of the, uh, *water* in that silver flask you keep trying to hide, Your Grace? I think Miss Givan might need it."

Chapter Three

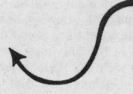

For nearly five days, John Varick avoided Victoria Givan and her merry band of boys. It was the sanest course of action. For some absurd reason, he just didn't have the heart to find out the truth behind this irritatingly tempting female. She was either a spirited but virtuous young woman with a tenuous hold on a position in a foundling home, or she had a mysterious *benefactor* who supplied her with fine footwear and a position in the foundling home, no doubt to provide an outlet for her boundless reserves of energy. In the first case, he refused to lead an innocent down the path toward ruin, and in the second case, just the idea of her in the bed of another man made him want to unleash every last one of his bloodthirsty Beaufort character traits and hunt down the bastard.

And so, he had shunned temptation for both their sakes.

It had been easy to do given the acres of paneled, gilded, and richly furnished rooms between them and the mounds of documents in his study. Oh, he had played the perfect host—in absentia. His housekeeper had reported that she had, indeed, given Miss Givan and the boys a daylong tour of Beaulieu. Apparently, her young charges had taken particular delight in the hundreds of fallow deer racks, and the battlefield paintings by masters and demimasters attesting to the family's vicious feudal beginnings. Only the stuffed, mounted, and framed remnants of the past remained. In overwhelming quantities.

Surprisingly, the bewitching young woman had not made a single effort to engage his notice. Quite the contrary. Safely ensconced in the easternmost wing of Beaulieu, she had taken her meals with the boys and occupied them inside and outside of these walls, keeping out of sight. He should be grateful. But for some perverse reason it only served to irk him. For it proved he had not had the same effect on her as she had had on him—which was a deviaton from the swarms of females in his past. And if there was one thing John Varick detested, it was aberrations of any sort.

Well, she would be gone soon enough, and the memory of the entire episode with the exquisite green-eyed beauty and the less than exquisite words flowing from those lush lips would fade. He had done his duty by retrieving her party's battered possessions from the inn where the north road mail coach driver had at last seen fit to deliver their bags. And at the appropriate time he would arrange for one of his carriages to transport them to the refurbished cottage at Wallace Abbey.

Closeted in the vast study that was now his alone to prowl, John tried for the third time this morning to bury himself in the mountains of problems he had always relished untangling. If he hadn't been allowed the honor of serving his country in the war against the French with his body—and his powerful uncle had forbidden it given John's future station—then he had long ago decided to serve his countrymen with his mind.

A sound drifted from the open window, and he stood abruptly and strode to look outside. She was there . . . walking from the direction of the stables, her cheeks glowing with exertion, and her well-worn straw hat hanging from its black ribbons down her back. She was even lovelier than he remembered.

Oddly, she was alone, a look of consternation worrying her brow. Shading her face, she stopped and gazed past the rise of the formal gardens.

He hated seeing her ill ease. Despite the clamor in his mind—much like a midnight church bell, warning of disaster, he closed the distance to the ornate door and all the barriers between them to join her outside.

"Miss Givan?"

She whirled around to face him. How could he have forgotten how vibrant and beautiful she was? The force of it nearly knocked the wind from him.

"Oh, Your Grace . . . I mean, oh, please excuse me. So good to see you." She tugged her hat back onto her pretty head, her deep plum-colored locks flooding her shoulders and back like a schoolgirl. At a guess, all her pins were lost hodgepodge about the countryside.

"May I be of service? I spied you from my study and you appeared overanxious."

"Well, you see . . . well, the thing of it is—I can't seem to find the boys and—and"—she bit her lip— "Oh, John—I fear they're lost. They're quite taken with this first taste of the country. And, I'll admit I'm not very good at negotiating the hills and vales, and I don't doubt the boys are very ill at it as well." She appeared embarrassed. "All the dales look the same—very green, very beautiful, but *endless* and quite, quite barren of the wonderful signposts in town. Oh, botheration— *where* could they be?"

"Slow down. Try to catch your breath, Vic."

"What did you just call me?" She appeared stricken. "Please don't call me that. You may use Victoria if you like, but not the other."

What in hell? "Come, I shall help you find them. Do you know where they set out to go?"

"I was trying to find the lake." The smallest crease of a wrinkle appeared between her brows. "The stable master said he spied them walking there."

"Come." He politely offered his arm.

She stared at it. "Really, there's no need. I'm perfectly capable of walking unaided. I just need your direction."

"Well, that's a first. I never thought I'd ever hear you ask for my direction." His lips curled into a smile as they set off. He dared to glance at her profile discreetly from the corner of his eyes as they walked, a hand's width of air between, and an acre of tension.

She worried her lower lip and refused to be provoked into conversation with him.

He found he could not stop himself from goading her again. He began to lengthen his loose strides, covering more ground than she. She had to add a kick to her step to stay abreast. Halfway up the second long hill, he noticed she had fallen behind, and he slowed, appalled at his puerile maneuverings to force her to speak. Perhaps she was well and truly terrified for the boys.

And then suddenly, she was running past him—No, *racing* him up the huge hill.

And he began to laugh—to laugh harder than he had in two decades. But it did not stop him from accepting her silent challenge—and passing her shortly thereafter.

A dozen steps from the top, he slowed to an exaggerated snail's pace to allow her to win. It was the gentlemanly thing to do.

Without warning, two hands shoved his back hard from behind. He lost his footing and landed face-first on his hands and knees before he rolled onto his seat.

"I'm so sorry, *Your Grace*. Did you trip? Do you need my help? My goodness, perhaps you would do better to carry your walking stick. Balance suffers and bones become brittle late in life, you know."

He looked up to see her at the top, her hands on the lovely curve of her slim hips, and her lively green eyes brimming with laughter. "You're perfectly right. I should take better care." God, he had missed the sight of her these last five days.

She came toward him, full of life, and he lifted his arm to catch the hand she offered. "Up we go, now."

She made the mistake of ignoring his superior angle, and he jerked her down into his lap. And found himself face-to-face with the most tempting female in all of Christendom. His body was thirteen steps ahead of his mind, registering the small round bottom pressing against him. And suddenly there was no more laughter between them.

The air seemed to thin, and they stared at each other, time suspended. Her hat lost somewhere down her back, her lovely dark auburn locks framed her heart-shaped face, bringing perfection within far too easy a distance.

He forced himself to break the tension eddying through and all around them, its current pulling at them. "Well, perhaps we should—"

His words were cut off when she swooped in and stole a quick kiss—just the smallest brush of her divine lush lips against his own before she pulled back. She apparently had not only lost her humor, but now also her nerve. She pushed against his chest to rise.

When he tightened his grip on her arms and wouldn't release her, her eyes widened.

"I've never known you to do anything so halfheartedly, Victoria." He stroked the side of her cheek, and whispered, "For God's sake, don't start now."

And then he took control.

He meant to leave her without a shred of doubt about who was in charge of matters concerning efficient ways to implode every last one of her scruples and his. All the good reasons he had lined up quite orderly to keep her at a distance were effectively forgotten as he held this magnificent, vivacious woman in his arms.

The bow shape of her upper lip had distracted him hour upon hour in his carriage and he lost no time familiarizing himself with the delicacy, as well as its plush mate below. God, she was so sweet—all pliant femininity. Without knowing what he did, his hand found its way behind her head to hold her steady while he teased the seam between those delectable lips of hers. He felt her harsh exhalation of surprise on the hollow of his taut cheek as he delved beyond. And in that moment he learned the truth about Victoria Givan. She was untutored in the art of a kiss; she was without doubt an exuberant, unforgettable, yet very *innocent* siren. No one else had ever kissed her this intimately, and the male in him growled at the thought of anyone else ever considering it.

With no surprise, Victoria Givan learned the sinful intricacies of a kiss far more quickly than was proper for a lady. Suddenly, it was *her* hands that were gripping his back, urging him closer. And it was *her* delicate tongue torturing him . . . tempting him to madness. John deepened the kiss, for once in his life allowing himself to get lost in the woman he held in his arms. Without thought, he caressed her curves and the pebbled crests of her breasts through the thin, high-necked gray dress she wore. He was losing every inch of his famous control, losing every battle in his—

With the suddenness of a spring shower, and just as drenching, he was left grasping at air.

"Yes, well . . . It appears"—she straightened her gown—"the *resuscitation* has worked. *Marvelously.*"

"The *what?*" He imagined the feel of her luscious neck squeezed between his hands.

"The re-sus-ci-ta-tion," she repeated. "You don't need a hearing horn, do you?"

He would bury her right here. Alive.

"You fell, don't you remember? Perhaps your memory is failing, too."

"Victoria," he growled, "so help me . . ." Better yet, he would make love to her so long, and so well that she'd be unable to form another ridiculous observation . . . for at least a full week. Good God. What was he thinking? He shook his head, disgusted. He had to regain rational thought.

"Oh, *there* it is," she said, out of breath and on her tiptoes, pointing at the lake on the other side of the hill. At least, her high-pitched voice proved she was not as immune as she wished.

"Yes, I know," he said, dripping with irritation as he stood up awkwardly. Inwardly, he cursed his breeches, which were not cut to accommodate what they were being forced to accommodate.

She closed the very short distance to the immense body of water. He edged behind her and was at least grateful she didn't turn around. He wasn't sure if he still wanted to wrap his hands about her throat to choke her or seduce her within an inch of her bloody virtue. Lord, what had he become?

Just like a female, she pretended not to notice his annoyance, while she searched the distant opposite end of the lake.

"Perhaps they're in that little hut over there," she said as cool as you please, indicating a nearby rude structure. "The stable master said that the gamekeeper had offered to show them how to shoot yesterday. That's his lodging, isn't it?" Her eyes wouldn't meet his.

"Yes," he gritted out, loins still aching.

"I'll be right back."

Now was the time for all good men to regain their sanity and strength of will. He casually bent to retrieve a few flat stones. He sent them skimming over the glass-like surface of the lake and cursed again. He'd cursed more in the last week than he had in his entire life.

Victoria had not spent many years among boys without knowing precisely what John Varick was about. And she'd been warned, and echoed the warning to dozens, nay, hundreds of girls. She should know better than this. She sighed.

Lord, it had been exciting—far more exciting than anything she could have ever possibly dreamed. Oh, he had brought to life in her the very thing that was supposed to have remained dormant for a person of her class. He had stirred passion into being deep within her.

Well, this was what happened to females who dallied with desire. She had wanted to experience a man's kiss, and for once, her wishes had been granted.

She picked up her pace toward the half-hidden structure and prayed for regulation of her thoughts before temptation got the better of her. But really, why was she trying so hard? Her virtue was about as important as the spots on a laying hen. She began to stomp harder as she continued forward. Not one single person would even care what a spinster teacher in a foundling home did with her life. It was all so pointless, really. Except to her. She would know.

But she had always despaired at the idea of going to her grave a virgin spinster. She could bear the truth that she would remain a spinster her entire life. But did she have to add insult to injury by remaining a virgin, too? Was she never to know intimately what it was like to be a woman?

She had dutifully said her prayers every morning, every evening, and over every dreary meal she had ever endured. And ever since she had turned thirty years old last year, she had prayed for one opportunity—just one—to understand what it would be like to be held, to be cherished—well, to do a bit of holding and cherishing in return to a man who entranced her.

The very thing she had wished for was before her, and she was struggling mightily to resist it. And for what reason? He, the Catch of the Century, would be the last person to reveal her wicked weakness of character. Oh, what was wrong with her?

The tiniest sting stabbed at the tender skin above her ankle as she strode along. She reached down to jerk her gown away from the bramble she was sure she would find. "Oh!" As she jumped back, the end of a large snake slithered under the woods' decaying leaves of winter. Edging many feet away from the ghastly creature, she investigated her flesh. Her thin stocking was down about her half boot—the binding thigh ribbon had apparently lost the fight against gravity during the race with him or more likely when she had lost the fight to keep herself away from him.

Two punctures marred the skin just above the half boot and wayward stocking. That vile reptile had bitten her. Of course.

"Hey . . . Are you all right?"

She looked up to find him there. Immediately lowering her shift and gown, she had the oddest dizzy sensation as she stood up.

"Is it a thorn? Here now, let me have a look." He sat on his heels and reached for her boot.

She was so stunned, she let him. "I . . . I think it was a snake. Actually, I *know* it was a snake."

In the blink of an eye he was carrying her into the gamekeeper's hut, and she felt like some sort of foolish, improbable damsel in distress straight from the pages of her book of *Canterbury Tales*. It didn't feel nearly as exciting as she had always dreamed, especially when he abruptly dropped her onto a rustic bed and yanked aside her skirting to examine her calf.

He bit out, "Stay still," very unlike any of those heroes she sighed over. "What did it look like?"

The room spun, her vision blurring before the reality of the blood on her leg. "I didn't see it very clearly." Botheration, her flesh blazed with pain. Now there was no question about it. She truly, positively, absolutely *detested* everything about nature. "It was sort of tawny. Very, very long . . . And there was a darker pattern on it."

His face became ashen. "A pattern? What sort?"

Her stomach roiled, and the most awful queasy sensation gripped her. "I think it was speckled . . . Or perhaps there were little dark diamond shapes? I don't know, really. It disappeared quickly." She shivered, involuntarily.

He was staring at her, his expression stark, his eyes hard. She had never seen him so serious. Only now, he was fishing about in his pockets.

"I've only heard of one instance of a harmless snake biting anyone," he muttered. "They would have to be truly provoked."

"I think I stepped on it. Is that enough provocation?" She was doing a wretched job of camouflaging the ball of fear growing in the pit of her stomach. "What are you doing?"

He extracted a small pocketknife and unfolded the tiny lethal-looking blade.

She backed away on her bottom to the end of the cot.

"I told you to stay still. Victoria, do as I say. Look, I promise I'll never force you to do another blasted thing in your life ever again," he said quietly, in complete opposition to the ironlike authority she saw in his face. Whatever he had in mind, it was going to happen with or without her permission. She thought the former might hurt less, and so she lowered her leg for his inspection.

When she saw the glint of the knife, she squeezed her eyes shut.

Two slashes of raw pain sliced through her, and she yelped a vile oath but remained very still.

"Good girl," he bit out.

A warm pressure replaced the vicious blade, and she reopened her eyes to see his dark head covering her leg. Lord, he was kissing her leg. *My God . . .* she thought she might faint.

And then she felt him sucking the raw wound with a vengeance. "Oh please, stop . . ." she moaned, her leg throbbing.

He turned his head away and she heard him spit upon the earthen floor. "Hush," he said breathlessly, before he reapplied himself to the task.

It wasn't so awful after all, she thought, her head spinning on some unseen axis. Once the throbbing stopped, and the numbness settled on her flesh like a warm blanket, her mind rationalized the horridness of the situation. He efficiently drew the venom from her until she became worried he would be ill from it.

Finally, he lifted his mouth from her, but shaded the area from her view. Withdrawing a handkerchief, he wrapped it about her ankle and tucked the ends in place. "There now."

He stared at her, his expression blank, his eyes glassy. "Here." He reached into his coat and withdrew his ornate flask with a royal crest etched into its silver side.

And then she saw it. His hand shook, just the slightest bit as he extended it to her.

God. *She was going to die, and he knew it*. She was going to die from tromping about the so-called benign countryside. After all those years walking near the so-called lethal dangers outside of Mayfair in town.

She'd never drunk so much as a single drop of spirits in all her life. She grabbed the flask he offered and, without a pang of remorse, drank long and deep—which wasn't nearly as long or as deep as she would have liked. A clog of fire engulfed her throat, and she coughed through the fires of hell. And drank a lot more.

"Victoria," he whispered, despair lacing his words. "That's enough."

"Then *you* drink," she said, summoning up false bravado.

"*Now* you want me to drink?"

"This is a wake, correct? It's why you offered me your brandy, isn't it?"

He didn't laugh, which only served to make her even more scared. He put the flask on a table just out of her reach and surreptitiously glanced at her bound leg. Her ankle and calf throbbed with the sensation of hundreds of pins and needles poking at her.

"There, now. You're just overcome. And no, I've given

up spirits. Did you not say it's bad for my gout?" With this forced amusement from his lips, which contrasted with the grave concern in his expression, she knew then, without a single doubt, that she was through with life.

"Oh . . . John," she whispered again, her mind softening from the brandy. And then she couldn't stop the words guaranteed to make her a fool. "I wasn't supposed to die yet."

"Victoria—"

"This is not the way it was to happen. I was supposed to live a long, dreary life, and become a gray old maid after raising hundreds of foundlings. And they would have put a plaque in the chapel in my honor." She felt very light-headed as she rushed on. "Oh, I regret so many things. Worst of all, I'll never experience . . ." She stopped abruptly, her mortification complete.

"Never experience what?"

"*Nothing.* Nothing at all." If she could blush any deeper, fire would erupt from her veins.

"Tell me."

"I'll die a—a . . . Well, *you know* . . ."

He blinked.

"Darling," he said, "don't be ridiculous . . ."

"Ridiculous? I think I have the right to say or act any way I like when I'm dying. Was that or was that not a poisonous serpent that just bit me?"

"There are no serpents in England—only snakes— mostly grass snakes."

"Don't you dare change the subject, John. Was I or was I not just bitten by a deadly poisonous snake?"

"Perhaps." It was better she didn't know the conclusions he'd drawn. If the snake was a mature viper, which it most likely was, he would never reveal how painful and how very fatal it could be.

"Did you or did you not just extract venom?"

"Possibly," he said reluctantly.

"Which snakes in England have venom?"

"The one that prefers shaded woody areas—the *V. berus.*"

She appeared near shock, her face and hands white and clammy. "Just because I spent my life within a foundling home doesn't mean I can't decipher Latin. Oh God, it's *V.* as in *vipera,*" she moaned.

"Now, don't leap to conclusions. The grass snake is speckled."

"And, let me guess," she said, her pupils dilated unnaturally. "The viper has dark diamond shapes."

"Look, there's a possibility you could become ill for a while, but there's every reason to believe you will recover. You are young, and very strong and—" His words were bringing naught but more worry to her expression, and so he gathered her in his arms, and she finally gave in to the tears that had been slowly gathering in her glassy eyes. He prayed the last words he had spoken were well and true. And he also hoped his throat ached from tension and not venom.

He leaned over her and kissed her temple, then her wet cheeks, then her . . . God, he wanted to chase away those tears with every fiber of his being. He would do anything to wipe away the horror of the moment. He wanted to comfort her, assure her that she was cherished for once in her life.

"Oh, please, John . . ." she whispered, trembling. "*Lie beside me.* Kiss me. Hold me."

He knew exactly what she asked and exactly what he could not do. He might want to offer her raw physical comfort more than he'd wished for anything in his entire structured, ordered, carefully constructed existence meant to distance himself from every last bloody conniving, marriageable female in England, but she knew naught of what she asked.

God. She might very well be dying. Or not. Either way, this tiny hut in the middle of the wood was the last place he would deflower the woman he wanted as the future Duchess of Beaufort—if she lived through the next day and night.

He shook his head to clear it. What had he just thought? Christ, who was he trying to fool? Right here, right now, whether she was dying or not, he was going to stop avoiding one primary fact.

He adored her. Could not stay away from her no matter how hard he tried. She might just be the most impertinent female in all of creation, but hell, there was a certain charm to that, for there wasn't a man or woman alive who had even dared to *think* he or she could manage him.

Still kneeling beside her, he rested his forehead against hers. Sometime within the next two hours to two weeks he was either going to bury her or marry her. Either option seemed better than keeping himself from this ball of fiery woman and even her battalion of boys who had entered his refined domain.

John repressed a groan. God, he was going to give her everything she had never asked for . . . and more. So much more. He would give her his name, something he'd thought he would never do before years of careful reflection, and even more painstaking negotiation with a score of solicitors.

But what he dared not give her was what she asked for now. However, he could give her a taste of what was to come if she lived through this wretched afternoon. The idea held five parts despair to one part passion. He prayed his body would obey his mind.

He cradled her head with one hand and dipped down

to drag a trail of kisses on her feverish cheeks. Victoria's ragged breath caught in her throat as he valiantly tried to chase away her fears with a kiss designed to enchant. A slow kiss, and a slow stroke along the inside of her arm, down the side of her rounded, perfectly shaped breast.

She was so damned responsive. After long minutes, her obvious panic receded slightly, and he wrestled with the first spark of desire igniting between them. She was gripping his arms, urging him closer. "Oh, John, do hurry. I feel faint—so hot, so cold. Shivery . . ."

She must be near delirium. "It's best not to rush on so," he murmured.

"But if we don't rush," she said breathlessly, "I might never experience it."

He didn't know whether to laugh or cry. Instead, he tucked kisses under her high collar as he worked the buttons free down the bodice. He would shower her with just the smallest bit more pleasure, before a long retreat. Settling his mouth over the coral-fleshed peak that had plagued his thoughts day and night, she immediately moaned. Her excitement drove him to the brink of madness, and he unconsciously bunched the skirting of her gown high above her slender thighs.

Surely she was dying. Victoria's head was spinning, and dimly she thought it was from the venom or from the brandy she had consumed—probably both. And all she could think with dark humor was that this was a perfectly lovely way to die even if it wasn't honorable. It was probably going to weigh heavily against a lifetime of pious living.

But it was worth it.

She could barely breathe when she looked past half-closed eyes to find his lips encircling the sensitive tip of her breast. His mouth tugged at her, and her body arched toward him. A well of longing . . . and something else spiraled within her as she stroked the dark locks on his head. She would have liked to have had a child with those long, black lashes, and that raven hair of his. And those eyes that were so deeply blue they reminded her of the candied violets in the forbidden bakeries of her childhood.

And suddenly, he was moving his lips back to her neck, his deft fingers covering her bared breast with the edge of her gown. He whispered all manner of lovely words meant to soothe her. Lord, he was retreating.

"John, I swear that if you stop now, I shall never, ever forgive you," she whispered.

"Victoria," he groaned, grasping her face. "You don't understand." He stilled her lips with his fingers as she tried to argue. "I don't want to hurt you further. And certain things must be said. I would insist we—"

"Don't you dare say another word." She pulled on his neckcloth until he was forced to lie atop her on the small bed. The feel of his overly starched shirt and coat against her breast was unbearably erotic. And then she suddenly noticed that, just as she asked, he had stopped speaking. His expression had grown primal, and stark—all raw man. A man whose last ounce of control staggered on a stone precipice that broke away as he leaned down to possess her lips once again with his own.

The haze of passion ebbed but a moment, when she realized he had risen slightly, and the rustling was the sound of him unfastening his breeches. All thoughts of flowers, and lashes, and the children she would never see flew from her. He moved above her, and she instinctively opened her legs to accommodate his body. Oh, this should be beyond embarrassing, if it were not so shockingly elemental, and right . . . as nature intended. It was as if fate had ordained that she would bind her body and soul to his on this very day.

Her body ached for him to press closer to her. But just as she thought she might die from craving his touch, from wanting the mystery of him, he stopped. Again.

She opened her eyes to find a guilt-stricken look in those now dark eyes of his. She spoke before she could even think. "Would it help if I told you I forgive you in advance? Or perhaps a touch of anger would spur you. Just think of the headlines . . . Catch of the Century— CAUGHT!"

"Victoria . . ." he rasped. "You are the most confounding . . . plaguing . . . irresistible woman."

"Such flattery. The words a lady longs to hear—"

He interrupted by lowering his mouth to hers. And then his kiss became so all-consuming, her thoughts tangled, and she lost her grip on the moment.

It all came crashing down, as he nudged more snugly into the cradle of her legs, the fabric of his breeches slightly abrading the tender skin of the inside of her thighs.

And then, he flexed his hips slowly. It was the oddest, most intimate sensation—as if his entire body was kissing hers, molding to hers—filling her in a place he alone was meant to forge.

And before she could take in the magnitude of what was happening, he was rocking gently, and she was turning to molten liquid. "Hold on to me, darling," he whispered into her ear. "Tighter." And for once, she obeyed him, followed his wishes to the letter.

Pain suddenly lanced her and left her flesh throbbing.

He went stock-still. "Give it a moment," he groaned. He was deep inside of her, that part of him thrumming to the beat of her heart.

She registered his hand stroking her head, and slowly a nearly primal desire to move even closer to him—to advance, and retreat—enveloped her. Her fingers tightened again on the bunched muscles of his broad back.

At her signal, he proceeded, in gentle, then increasingly powerful, thrusts to fulfill all her dark-as-the-night flights of fancy. And then all thought was lost as she splintered into a thousand stars like those of a spring night. He plunged deeper than she thought possible, then gasped and became still, his heart racing inches above her own.

The heat of the afternoon, the brandy, and the poison wound 'round her senses. The inevitable guilt from what she had just forced upon him soon followed, and she surrendered to the magnitude of it all.

As he carefully rolled to her side and gathered her in his arms, John desperately hoped he had given her a measure of pleasure and chased away her darkest fears for at least a few moments. God, he had sworn he would not do this. So much for his famous discipline. His last vestige of self-control had vanished in the face of her sweetly ardent desire. She had, with her poignant show of puffed-up bravery and innocence, uncovered a desperate need he hadn't known he'd possessed. She was as vital as the air he breathed to sustain him.

He looked down to find her unconscious now, her face pale and still. Her breath caught ominously, and an ache of the acutest kind dragged over the part of him he hadn't ever known could register pain—his heart. Ah . . . it was surely being torn asunder.

She exhaled roughly and worked to drag another lungful inside of her. She was clinging to life as courageously as she had lived her life.

God . . . He felt as wretched and ancient as she had repeatedly jested.

The smallest sigh drifted from her. And then another that seemed to gurgle and shudder endlessly. *A death rattle* . . .

A loud snore rended the air.

He bit his lip and looked up at the roughened timber crisscrossing the ceiling. For Christsakes. When had he turned into such a melodramatic idiot? Oh, he knew the answer . . . It was the precise minute he had met the impossible yet perfect creature before him now snoring as deeply as a two-ton longshoreman after an encounter with a barrel or two of poorly distilled whiskey.

Chapter Four

Victoria had never, ever, *ever* been so mortified. Why, she had for all practical purposes *begged* the Duke of Beaufort to make love to her. And so she did what any rational woman would have done. She refused to see him for three days.

At first he had come to her bedchamber door at Beaulieu in person—every three hours, like clockwork. One solid knock followed by ten seconds of silence. Then his voice would call out, at first filled with anxiety, then with frustration, and still later with cool resignation.

The kindly maid had explained it all to her. The boys and the duke had *escorted* her from the lake after they had found her there. Did she not remember tripping over the fallen tree limb? Hitting her head and falling unconscious? Her dreadful headache?

Oh, she remembered the last part, all right. Actually, she remembered every single last embarrassing detail of their encounter until she had slipped into the comforting arms of drunken oblivion.

So that was how he had hidden the truth. He had obviously concocted the main story, then found the boys to provide a side helping of decorum while he carried her back.

At this point, her dignity was so far removed from her that she rather doubted it could ever be recovered, in even the smallest quantity. That stung almost as much as her loss of virtue to the man from whom she most longed to hide the tangle of tender feelings curling around her heart.

It would take a century before she could face him. She, who had recently prided herself on her ability to play the nonchalant heroine.

And so it went for three days. She'd secretly hoped he would break down the door in the middle of the night despite the fact that two footmen and one maid were stationed outside her door per her request.

After the first day, *notes,* versus his person, arrived with each meal tray. She returned them unopened.

She spent her time brooding, and sometimes lurking behind the silk drapery framing the tall windows in her chambers. Often, she saw him playing games with the boys outside. First he taught them nine pins, perfecting their aim and showing them how to address the pins with the heavy ball. Then it was on to rounders. He was very adept at swinging the odd-shaped, heavy wooden bat. Of course, he did it within sight of her window. He would turn his head toward her apartments every so often, and she would scurry back like the pathetic mouse she had become.

Yet all along, she had known it would not last. During the gloomy afternoon, when she tried for the fifth time to bury her nose in the *Canterbury Tales,* the one book that had never failed to enthrall her until now, she heard the sound of several pairs of footsteps scurrying away and the click of the lock echoing from the door. She held her breath.

He strode forward several feet, and all the air immediately seemed to desert the chamber. He seemed to have forgotten that for once, it was up to him to close the door since he had obviously dismissed the army of servants. He returned to shut the door, then closed the distance between them. Three feet from her bedside, he came to a halt and stared down at her. "How are you?" The faintest grooves appeared on his forehead.

"Much improved," she murmured, then glanced at her hands, which she forced still.

"Victoria—" he began.

"No," she said, "Don't say it."

"What do you suppose I was going to say?"

"What you hinted at while we were in that vile little hut, and I was pretending to die. You remember, the same place I became foxed to the gills and forced you to . . . to have your way with me." The vision of her tightly entwined fingers became blurry.

"Actually, I think it was *you* who was having your way with *me*, Vic," he said, dry humor itching his words.

"I told you not to call me that."

"Very well, *Victoria*. The physician privately reported to me that you are fully recovered in body if not in spirits." He was standing very stiffly. "I'm sorry, more sorry than I can say, that you suffered through that scare with the snake, which, in hindsight was quite obviously a grass snake and—"

"And what?"

"And I'm sorry I hurt you." He seemed hardly able to get out the last words. "I'm sorry that I offered you the brandy. Sorry I—"

"What? Followed my directions?"

"No. You have absolutely no share of the blame for what happened. But now we must be sensible. I don't want to argue with you. You see . . . we must marry. I *want* to marry you straightaway. I've already arranged a carriage to leave today to take us back to town—with the maid you've come to like—Mrs. Conlan."

Oh, this was worse than she had envisioned. He was dissembling. He was also rambling, quite obviously stricken with the knowledge of what his honor, as a gentleman, demanded.

"You know," she interrupted, "I should let you do it, if only to teach you a lesson."

He stood stock-still. "What on earth are you implying?"

"I mean, really, why ruin one life when two can be ruined so easily?"

Anger flooded his normally impassive expression. "Is this your response?"

She continued as if she hadn't heard him. "But I find I can't do it. Yes, I find I'd rather spend the rest of my life teaching orphans than tending to your failing health."

"*Victoria* . . ." His tone was menacing, low. "So help me God—"

"He won't help you, I assure you. I find He deserts me at every critical hour. I suppose it's my complete and utter lack of principles in the face of temptation—oh, what is the use? Look, I'm sorry I seduced you against your will."

He quickened his speech. "Tell me now, straightaway. Are you uttering all these ridiculous things to warn me off? Victoria . . . does your heart belong to another?"

She answered without pause. "Yes." She could not stop her eyes darting away from his.

"Have I ever told you that you are the absolute worst

liar plaguing Christendom? Now who in bloody hell gave you those ridiculous boots? Is he the one who calls you 'Vic'?"

"Oh, for pity's sake, *Your Grace*. I'm a commoner. I could be the product of a Covent Garden light-skirt and a pandering drunk for all you know."

"Actually, I'm guessing your father was an army captain, and your mother a prim but luscious school-teacher, what with those charmingly dictatorial ways of yours."

She started. Why, she knew precisely who her parents were and he was halfway closer to the truth than he would ever know. When she'd become a teacher and gotten access to the foundling home's private records, the first thing she had done was search for clues.

Her father had, apparently, been one of a vast wave of men in the Royal Navy—a Captain Givan. In her dreams, she envisioned him as a formidable officer spitting at his archrival's feet as he died an honorable death.

She'd forced the details about her mother from the older matron at the foundling home. Mrs. Kane had still remembered the day a scared young maid had tried to deposit Victoria in the front hall with an almost il-legible petition signed by a Mrs. Givan. The matron had explained to the maid that infants could not just be left without a formal review and acceptance by the governors. The girl had silently left, but within minutes, the matron had found nine-month-old Victoria propped against the gates of the home along with the petition. No trace of the young maid or Mrs. Givan had ever been found, and so Victoria had been absorbed into the sprawling foundling home's system.

The petition, written on nearly translucent paper, suggested Mrs. Givan was the only daughter and rela-

tion of a dead vicar. Dying of consumption, Victoria's
mother had left her child and the petition along with a
brass button token from Victoria's father, who had just
died at sea in service to His Majesty. The records she
had found at the Royal Naval offices had snuffed out
her last hope of ever finding relations. Captain Charles
Givan had lived and died without a single relation listed
in his records.

"What is going on in that head of yours?" His voice
was low, his expression eerily calm, but he refused to
wait for an answer. "Victoria, gather your affairs. We
leave this afternoon. If the weather holds, we can be in
London tomorrow—can secure a Special License by—"

"You are perfectly right. And after we marry, could
we hold a ball in the Beaufort London town house? I'm
certain all your friends in the House of Lords would
enjoy the honor of bowing and scraping before me. And
the gossips will be positively panting to hear all the details of how THE CATCH OF THE CENTURY was
netted by a bloody NOBODY you found on the side of
a country road!" The last she shouted at him.

"You are perfectly right," he returned, unmoved. "It
will be a beastly business."

He withstood her blast of outrage with the same calculating tactics he'd used when she had first met him.
The only difference was that she now knew how to re-
taliate.

"The boys have informed me that the cottage at Wallace Abbey is fully repaired," she said stiffly. "We will
leave your protection this afternoon. I was going to wait
until tomorrow, but I find it might be better—"

"Coward," he whispered.

"I beg your pardon?"

"You heard me."

"Look, I release you from whatever bonds of gentlemanly code you've forced upon yourself. I assure you I find none of your ideas acceptable." She sniffed.

"Victoria, listen to me. You are making a grave mistake. You could very well find yourself with child. Surely, you've considered the consequences. I hadn't thought I'd have to remind you."

"I've spent decades looking into the forlorn eyes of what some people—of your rank—call the physical evidence of sin. I assure you, I know precisely what might happen. If I do find myself in a condition, I shall find an obscure corner of England, and you shall pay for our care, which shall be but a pittance. There are plenty of war widows, and I shall play the part. The child and I shall be perfectly happy. Either way, you shall rejoin your *family*—your world, and I shall rejoin mine—eventually—at the foundling home or, if fate insists, somewhere far from anyone who would know the truth. What I will not do is accede to your wishes, which would only serve to subject us to the slow, daily torture of remembering the foolishness of a moment."

She had wounded him as effectively as she had dared. She could see it in his eyes. But really, what had he expected?

"Victoria . . . if you think for a moment that I would allow you to cower off to some godforsaken corner if you found yourself with *my* child, you do not know me. And while I had wished to keep this from you, I can see I must tell you the full truth of it. Do you know that you talk in your sleep?"

A chill of worry wound down her spine.

"Well, I'm sorry to inform that you do, and there was idle talk among the servants before I put an end to it. Your reputation will be in tatters if we do not marry." He paused and gentled his voice. "Now look, I'm sorry the idea of this marriage is so repugnant to you, but it will occur. God, woman! I should never have let you stew so long. Now, I shan't force you to leave today, but I do expect you to reconcile yourself to the grim facts of our upcoming nuptials by the time we leave at first light. Tomorrow. I will not delay this again." He turned on his heel and strode through the door without a backward glance.

Victoria bounded to the door after it shut, only to hear him bark for the servants to resume their posts. Only now they felt more like guards to keep *her* inside versus guards to keep *him* outside. She could have sworn he said something about "bread and broth, only," but then it could very well have been "break her bones, slowly."

Well, that had gone superbly well.

He had gone about it all wrong, he decided several hours later as he stood brooding and unseeing the beauty of the vista from his library window. He had the wealth of two nations, and yet he had not succeeded in the one thing that mattered. The one thing he wanted. Needed.

And yet, she was also correct. In marrying her, he might very well ruin her innate happiness. He could not easily envision her rubbing along with the members of the aristocracy. With their sharpened claws and in-grained instinct to winnow out anyone who smelled of the shop or worse, she would be ripped to ribbons in one evening. And they would do it with graciousness dripping from ear to ear. She didn't stand a chance, even if half the gentlemen in the House of Lords owed him favors or money or both.

Nothing in his life was in balance. The idea he held dear, to rejuvenate the area with a mill, was fading. His meetings, or rather his attempts to meet with his stubborn neighbor, the Earl of Wymith, had utterly failed. On his second attempt to enter the sanctified chambers of his neighbor's manor, the Wymith butler had informed His Grace that his lordship was giving him fair warning. He was lacing gun-traps on the edges of his property to ward off trespassers just as his former nemesis had done.

In the distance, a large carriage that rivaled his own inched along under the arch of tulip trees bordering the avenue leading toward the high tower of Beaulieu. Within a quarter hour, he watched two gentlemen descend from the carriage, who in turn helped two ladies find their footing. The first was a diminutive gray-haired lady, wearing an outrageously colorful gown. She carried a long-snouted, short-legged canine. Why, if he was not mistaken, it was the Dowager Duchess of Helston, followed by the fire-breathing Duke of Helston, the beautiful, blond Countess of Sheffield, and an oversized brute of a man, dressed as a gentleman. What in hell?

The library door was ajar, and he could hear the familiar demanding baritone of Helston acidly informing a footman that—*Yes, he would very much like to see His Grace, if His Grace would have time for His Grace.*

John stilled the corner of his mouth from rising as the footman gave up any pretence of maintaining the correct forms of precedence. Through the sound of footsteps mounting the marble stair, John heard the echo of the party's conversation.

"Well, at least we know the way, at this point," Helston said, dryly. "Second bloody time in less than five months. Perhaps I should scour the area for a suitable residence if this is the way it shall go from now on."

"Friendship has its costs," the other man said with a chuckle.

"The problem as I see it is that so far it's been bloody one-sided in your case, *Friend*."

"Luc! Shhh. Is this not the most magnificent . . . Oh—"

And then after a knock, which further opened the

door, Helston, the dowager with her tiny brown dog tucked under her arm, and the stranger were ushered into the library. A red-faced footman hurriedly preceded them. The countess was missing from the party.

"Pardon me, Your Grace," the footman said. "His Grace, the Duke of Helston, and Her Grace, the—"

Helston cut through the trivialities with seasoned hauteur. "He knows who we are. How the bloody are you, Beaufort? *Good of you to see us*." Amusement laced the words of the black-haired and famously black-humored Duke of Helston as he strode forward to grip John's shoulder on one side and to shake his hand with the other. "Like the new name. May I say it fits you better than the others? Although I must admit to a certain fondness for your epithet in the *Post*."

The dog barked. "Hush," Ata admonished her pet. "Antlers are our friends here, Attila. Oh, Beaufort, please pardon us," she shot a dark look toward her grandson. "May we offer our very deepest sympathies on the death of your uncle? He was a generous man—a gentleman who did not shirk from helping us in our great hour of need last winter. I fear we come on an equally important mission today."

"How may I be of service to you, madam?" John bowed deeply before her. He'd always liked the little, dark-eyed, plain-speaking dowager.

John tilted his head to glance at the towering, rugged stranger behind the two Helstons. They had forgotten to introduce the man in their obvious haste.

The dowager produced a letter from her reticule and offered it to him. "I received this letter three days ago. It was dispatched from the inn in Quesbury. I'm sorry to say it is from a woman who is very dear to us all. She had the great misfortune to become stranded with several others when the mail coach departed without them.

Oh, I told her to accept the use of our carriage before she left town, but she is so very stubborn."

"A clear case of the pot calling the kettle black," Helston drawled.

"Luc! Do be serious. I am terri—"

"I keep telling you that I have not the slightest doubt that the intrepid, flame-haired woman *I know* is perfectly fine. This is a fool's errand. Now then, Beaufort, have you seen or heard news of a Miss Victoria Givan? She was traveling with—"

"Three boys," John finished, looking up from the letter. Her handwriting was as bold and arrogant as a queen's.

The dowager placed her hand over her heart. "Oh, thank heavens. You've news of them?"

The hulking gentleman behind them moved with the speed and lethal silence of a jungle cat. "Where is she?"

"And who are you, sir?" John perused the form of the giant with all the hauteur his station permitted.

"Where is she?" he demanded again.

"You must be Miss Givan's *very* good friend. No thanks to you, she is comfortably ensconced in one of the chambers above. The boys are here, too."

The man exhaled roughly, his hand rubbing his brow. "I don't know what you're suggesting, Beaufort. But I am that grateful to you, I don't really care." The man eased back a step when John stepped forward. "I must say though, I can't like your tone, but, yes, I am her *very* good friend. That's why I'm here. Her welfare is my responsibility."

John couldn't keep the edge of anger from his bark. "You are her *benefactor*, you blackguard."

The Duke of Helston and the diminutive dowager were looking at him as if he'd lost his wits.

"Uh, no, actually. *Vic's* benefactor is the Countess of Sheffield, soon to be—"

At the sound of the nickname Victoria refused to allow him to use, he erupted. "You're the one who knows her as *Vic*? By God, I shall wash the floor with—"

"Much as I would enjoy watching some other fool take on my *friend* here," Helston interrupted abruptly, "I feel dukes should stand by one another. It's the natural order of things. I'm sorry Wallace, but I must—"

"Wallace?" John interrupted, incredulous. "*You're* Wallace?"

The dowager piped up. "Yes, so sorry. Thought you'd been introduced. He's the long-lost earl you've probably recently heard tell about—that is if you follow the gossip columns, which you should since they particularly like to report about you often enough." The dowager smiled, a pert little V of a smile. "Monstrously tall, isn't he? Don't know how the countess manages to bully him as well as she does."

Wallace smiled. "Ata, you know Grace has never bullied a fly in her entire life. She shames us all into doing the proper thing with her impeccable manners, her unsurpassed charm, her—"

"Wallace," Helston cut in with obvious boredom. "It's not at all the thing to be so obviously in love with your fiancée."

The dowager turned on her grandson. "A clear case of the pot calling the kettle—"

"Ata . . ." Helston growled. "Oh, do let's get on with it. It's almost full dark, and we should see Miss Givan, then get out of Beaufort's little hovel here. I'm famished."

John nodded almost imperceptibly to the footman hovering in the doorway, and the man undertook his bidding to arrange for the needs of their new guests without a word. And then suddenly, the ethereal beauty of the Countess of Sheffield glimmered from the hall. She walked quickly inside, forwent the courtesy of a curtsy, and went to Wallace's side. The man's attention was exclusively drawn to her, and he urged, "What is it, sweetheart?"

Her blue eyes darted to John, a worried question lurking there. "She's left."

John started. "Left?"

She searched his face, a hint of distrust in evidence. "One of your maids directed me to the ladies withdrawing, and when I asked, she explained that Victoria was indeed here. I took the liberty of going to her chamber, and I found . . ."

"What did you find, sweetheart?" Wallace asked softly.

"Knotted sheets from the window."

John could not make his feet move. "Knotted sheets? Why, the little . . ."

Wallace's eyes narrowed. "Little what, Beaufort? What have you done to her? I shall strangle you with those sheets until you cough up an offer if you've compromised her. This is the most gothic story I've ever heard. Straight from the pages of—"

"The *Canterbury Tales*," John finished. "Yes, I do believe I'm going to burn that book, if I find her. But never fear, Wallace, I'm marrying her. Even if I have to cuff and drag her every inch of the way to Gretna Green."

Wallace noticeably relaxed and continued gruffly. "You may use my smithy's *twitch* if you like. It's far superior to cuffs or rope ties."

The Countess of Sheffield's eyes softened. "Now dearest, do not give him any ideas."

"I suppose you're right, my love. But he has just voluntarily committed himself to a lifetime with Victoria. And while I adore her with every inch of my heart, she is, well, even you must admit, Grace—Victoria can be a *challenge*, at times. A wonderful, infuriating—"

"I would suggest you stop while you're ahead, Wallace," John said stiffly. "You are speaking of the soon-to-be Duchess of Beaufort. And while I may refer to my future wife as I see fit, you, on the other hand—"

Helston's brows had almost reached his hairline. He recovered and quickly stepped between them. "Enough. *Enough*. Is there no brandy to be had in this hut of yours, Beaufort?"

"Oh, this is the perfect reason to write again to dear Mr. Brown in Scotland." The dowager Duchess of Helston laughed. "Luc, do you think this might roust him from his ill will toward me?"

"For God sakes, Ata, allow Brownie the peace he has earned."

"But he loves weddings. Adores them. He'll never be able to withstand the temptation of attending now both Wallace's *and* Beaufort's weddings to two ladies from my secret circle."

"Funny," the duke replied dryly. "Brownie's never mentioned a particular fondness for such folly in the past. And since when did Miss Givan become part of your ridiculous club? She's not even a widow."

Ata blinked. "I've grown accustomed to your infernal Devil's rules. If I say Victoria doesn't need to be bereaved to be in my widows club, then so be it." The tiny dowager tilted up her nose and sniffed. "Well, I'm off to write to Mr. Brown, and you can't stop me."

The Countess of Sheffield bit her lip to keep from laughing.

"Christ. My appetite is ruined," the Duke of Helston said darkly. "There is far too much talk of weddings and happiness swirling about to my liking. When, I ask you, is tragedy to come back in style?"

Chapter Five

John had decided he would, indeed, borrow Wallace's twitch, if he ever found her.

They had searched every last mile of land separating them from the cottage near the abbey. Every dale, every hollow, every lane. She was not to be found, nor were the boys. She wasn't a fool. She'd somehow charmed one of the younger grooms into providing his services as a driver, along with two of John's best carriage horses and a simple four-wheeled dog cart. Yet none of them had returned.

He swore violently as he paced the ridge above his massive stable—the best vantage point, and sufficiently removed from the great house to allow him to mouth every obscenity he could think of. He and the other two gentlemen had ridden all afternoon, all night, looking for her and the trio of boys. Helston and the earl didn't take her disappearance nearly as seriously as he did.

And if he had had to endure their jibes another minute longer, he had thought he very well might give in to his desire to smash the dark humor from both of them. He had galloped away from them as dawn first streaked its tawny pink fingers across the horizon, their laughter floating behind him.

The sound of crickets whirred all 'round him, the sound deafening with the heat of day increasing.

Where was she?

A horse and rider appeared at the crest of the hill in front of him, and his heart pumped with renewed hope. But it was not she. The rider wore a top hat and breeches.

The man drew up and dismounted, his mare's shoulders showing a hint of lather.

Could his day grow any worse? *Apparently.*

The earl swept an exaggerated bow. "Your Grace."

"Wymith," John gritted out. "To what do I owe the pleasure?" The imposing gentleman in his prime before him resembled his forebearer about as much as John did his own—that is, not one whit.

The earl retrieved something from a saddlebag flung across his horse's flanks and dropped two feathered shapes before him.

"What on earth?"

"I think she pilfered them from one of your great rooms. Miss Givan is a very, ahem, enterprising young lady, if I do say so."

John reached to clench his hands around the stuffed forms of a preserved wood duck and pheasant. "Careful, Wymith, she is my fiancée."

"Really," he drawled. "She didn't mention that."

"And what, pray tell, did she say to you?"

The other man studied him for a moment. "That we are both hardheaded beasts who refuse to see reason."

"Hmmm."

"She insisted I see past my objections to your very obvious desire to fatten your purses by way of this proposed easement. Said we should both think to the betterment of the many people of this county who depend on us."

"Did she now?" he muttered.

"Yes."

"And?"

"And she said we should compromise and build the road and the mill half on my property and half on yours, and arrange for the majority of the profits to go to the men who work there and to the ill and infirm of Derbyshire." The earl examined his fingernails. "She also said that you had finally seen the error of your ways and those of your uncle before you—after she had fully explained in detail all of your faults—some of which, I am sorry to say, had little to do with hunting and trespassing but much to do with locks and keys."

He itched to strangle the managing little philanthropist with pockets to let.

The earl continued. "These two motheaten bits of fluff were the peace offering she insisted I accept from you. More importantly, she said I was invited to hunt in Beaulieu Park anytime I wished."

"Really?"

"She also insisted I was to condescend to wait upon you, here, as you wished to invite me to dine so we could discuss the building of the mill."

"I see."

He shrewdly stroked his jaw. "A most interesting choice, Beaufort. She has more pluck than most men."

"I know."

"Surprising how well you've done for yourself," he said. "Not much of a conversationalist, are you?"

"No."

"Well, that's fine by me. Hate chatter. Now, are you going to invite me to breakfast or not?"

"Of course." John continued without a hint of irony. "I'm *delighted* you've come."

"Well," the earl said discomfited, "I don't know about you, but I'm not inclined to have to face her again without a signed agreement. Oh, and by the by, she said to tell you that she has removed to the cottage near the abbey, and . . ."

"Yes?"

Wymith licked his lips. "She said to give you this by way of a token of her appreciation and a formal good-bye." He tendered her battered volume of the *Canterbury Tales*.

John gripped the book, his eyes challenging the earl to say another blasted word. After a decade of silence, John bowed, his eyes so tired it felt as if an ocean's worth of salt and sand resided under his lids, "I'm honored by your visit, Wymith. Do you know the Duke and Dowager Duchess of Helston? Or the Countess of Sheffield and her fiancé, the Earl of Wallace? No? *Gentle folk* . . . You shall enjoy their company. This way, now. Fancy kippers?"

Would she always know how to work on him? A part of him melted at what she had so brazenly accomplished. All that bad luck, all those horrid words . . . erased with such heaven-sent goodness and devil-made assurance.

He had tried to go without them, but that blasted herd of Victoria's acquaintances would not be put off. The tension in the first of two carriages was as tight as the noose on a dead man. And they would not leave off of the subject of the snakebite once the physician had let it slip when he had come to call.

The Earl of Wallace's baritone rumbled within the close confines of the barouche. "British vipers are very rarely fatal, especially if you administer snakeroot or clivers. You didn't try to suck the poison out, did you? Only a fool would employ that barbaric practice."

John nearly lunged at the earl. The only thing that kept him in his seat was the fact that the cottage was around the next bend in the road.

"Your lips were on her ankle, Your Grace?" Ata's eyebrows lifted. "How very . . . intimate of you."

"I've already told you, Victoria and I are to be married."

Her Grace harrumphed. "Yes, well, it's obvious she refused you." She smiled knowingly. "Perhaps you didn't ask her in the correct fashion. Did you tell her she was the most beautiful creature alive? Did you tell her you couldn't live without her? Did you tell her you lo—"

"Ata," Helston said with a sigh. "Leave the poor sod be. I agreed to prop up his spirits and bear witness to his future responsib—ahem, happiness," he continued dryly, "but I did not agree to listen to more romantic folderol."

"Well, so few men know how to go about proposals properly. 'Tis the reason there are so many spinsters. Everyone knows unmarried ladies have a superior life over married females. Gentlemen have to use every last ounce of false charm to lull a lady's senses into acceptance."

"Ata," Luc growled louder.

"Not that we ever thought that in your case, dearest. I've always suspected you blackmailed or tricked Rosamunde into having you. You probably locked her in a room with naught but bread and broth until she promised to have you. Beaufort, on the other hand, would *never* . . ." She batted her eyelashes.

John groaned at the same moment the carriage lurched to a full stop.

* * *

Victoria rubbed at a spot on the large table in the refurbished kitchen of the cottage, grateful she finally had a moment to herself. She really only had to find two last servants for this house of men and boys. A man and his wife had arrived without notice this morning, both in search of employment. Their letters of recommendation were exemplary, and Victoria had engaged them as manservant and housekeeper. There was only the cook to find, and a maid-of-all-work. The boys were now off with the architect's men, to the abbey.

Lost in her never-ending stream of thoughts regarding a certain not-to-be-borne duke, she looked up only to find the man who occupied her every thought standing before her.

She cleared her throat awkwardly. "You've come."

"Did you doubt I would?"

She tried to adopt an air of indifference to hide her ill ease. "What took you so long?"

"Your friends. And benefactor."

She frowned. "Did they come in person? Oh, I'm sorry I caused them such trouble."

"Well, at least you are capable of feeling regret for something, Victoria."

She glanced away. "I have no regrets, Your Grace."

"I told you not to call me that."

"Yes, but you've ordered me to do so many things that I cannot be blamed for not always remembering all your wishes."

He advanced toward her. "No? Well then I shall have to remind you of my wishes."

She bit her lip.

"But, first, I must thank you."

"For what?"

"For coercing the Earl of Wymith into an agreement."

"Phifft. That was child's play. I assure you it's far harder to get two hungry boys to share a slice of bread. You two were stuffed full of—"

"Victoria." He closed his eyes and shook his head. "I've known you long enough to see through your methods. I will not be put off. Now, you are not to say another word until you accept my compliments and more. If not, beware. The Earl of Wallace possesses an interesting device, which he has invited me to use if you will not hear me through."

She felt nearly ill at the thought that the duke could so easily see through her.

"Do you love him so very much?" he asked gruffly. "So much you cannot see your way to one day caring for someone else?"

Her gaze wavered the merest bit before she replied. "Yes."

He broke into a grin. "I adore that about you."

"Adore what?" she replied, irritated beyond measure.

"The fact that you lie about as well as a poacher plump with partridge in his pockets."

"Yes, well, it worked well enough on you at key moments."

His deep blue eyes scrutinized her, fraying her nerves. "Why did you run away? It's not like you."

A scratching sound came from the direction of the pantry. Victoria ignored it. "I did not run away. If I'd meant to run away I wouldn't be here now, would I?"

He took a step toward her. "Victoria, we must marry. You've never been afraid of anything in your life."

"This only proves you do not know me at all. I've been afraid my entire life."

In a moment, he had trapped her in his embrace, forcing her to accept the protection and comfort of his arms. "You were probably only afraid of being denied important things—food, shelter. Do not try and tell me you're afraid of facing down a ballroom full of puffed-up aristocrats bent on mischievous gossip. Having endured a lifetime of it, I assure you it's all meaningless chatter. Just think how you'll relish forcing them to feel guilty about their excesses and how you shall also coerce them into helping the less fortunate, just as you did the Earl of Wymith."

"And you."

He chuckled. "Yes, and me. And you shall have the pleasure of reminding me daily that I was too thick-headed to think of the solution first."

"I won't marry you no matter how hard you try to charm me," she said abruptly, and pushed against his broad, warm chest.

He shook his head. "You know, I finally find the most beautiful lady on earth—the one woman I cannot live without—the lady I was destined to—"

"Ata has been working on you, hasn't she?"

"Blast it, Victoria." He rocked his forehead in his hands. "Do not say another word, or Lord help me, I will—"

"What?" she interrupted.

"I will *love* you. Love you for the rest of my life without pause. Love you until you forget to be afraid." He paused and continued quietly, "I shall love you enough for the both of us."

She felt the burn of tears behind her eyes, the ache of holding back in her throat.

"Now do you think you could possibly accept my offer? Accept me?"

Her heart soared. "Yes. Actually it's quite convenient because—"

He rushed to gather her back into his arms. "Oh, darling . . . promise you will never, ever cause me as much worry as you did yesterday when you disappeared."

"Your know, John, you're going to have to stop asking for so many favors and promises. I already warned you how those sorts of things spoil a person. And as I recall, you said I would never have to do anything else you ever asked again . . . when the snake bit me."

"Yes, well, that was when I was sure it was a viper, and I thought you'd be dead within a day."

"That is the poorest excuse I've ever heard." Another scratching sound came from the pantry, and Victoria looked about her for the broom with a jot of fear. "What *is* that?"

He appeared completely unconcerned by the odd noise. "Darling, there are two things we must do before your dear friends descend upon us. They're waiting outside."

"Yes?" He was nuzzling her neck, making it very hard to concentrate.

"I must kiss you, and you must answer one last question."

His lips nibbled the edge of her jaw, leaving her unable to form a coherent sentence. "Hmmm. . ."

He whispered, "Who gave you those delectable little boots of yours? The Countess of Sheffield?"

"No," she murmured.

His lips were closing fast. "Don't you dare tell me it was that heathen Wallace."

"It wasn't."

"Well?" He brushed his firm lips across the top of her nose and paused. Waiting . . .

"It was the Dowager Duchess of Helston. Said they would drive men to distraction . . . And she was absolutely spot o—"

He growled and swooped in to claim his kiss . . . To claim her, as she had always hoped. It was the way of all the best *Canterbury Tales* after all, was it not?

When she felt her knees weaken, she forced her lips

from his and rested her forehead against the snowy folds of his neckcloth. He towered a good six inches above her, making a very comfortable, rock-solid support. "You know, this was much easier than I thought," she murmured.

"What was much easier?"

"Snaring the Catch of the Century."

He chuckled. "Really?"

"Yes. Everyone knows the way to engage a man's interest is to insist you'll have none of him."

"Is that so?"

"Yes."

"Well, that's not the way of it a'tall. I fell in love with you when I somehow found myself taking you sixty miles instead of sixty yards."

"No. That's the reason I fell in love with you, John."

It was as if she had struck him, he went so still. Christ, he hadn't dared to hope until now. He then crushed her to him, his arms like two iron bands about her. Until . . .

The faintest flapping or scratching noise pierced their dream.

"John . . . Have I mentioned how little I like the countryside? And all the dangers one finds in nature?" Victoria revealed, haltingly.

"Come closer. I'll protect you." He kissed her worried brow gently. "It's probably just a little, harmless mouse."

She reluctantly pushed away from his arms. "You should know better given my history. The carpenter warned there were *bats* here when they came to rebuild."

"Well, Victoria, I sucked the snakebite. Escort the bat outside, if you please." He grasped the broom and extended it to her. "If you face down your fear, my love, I shall reward you with a very long honeymoon in Beaufort House in Mayfair."

She strode over to a window and threw open the sash.

"Inviting more in are you?" He smiled that impossibly irresistible smile at her.

"Do you have a better idea?"

He went to the table, efficiently lit a candle, and gathered an empty jar from the washboard.

"I didn't know that bats dislike candlelight."

"Everyone knows bats are night creatures."

"Is this sort of like how you knew vipers prefer wooded, shady areas?"

"No, this is sort of like how I knew you might come to love me as I love you."

She looked at him, and his eyes softened. He put down the articles he had collected and pulled her back into his arms. "Actually, I have a much better idea. The Duke of Helston and the Earl of Wallace are just the sort who relish offering a *friendly* hand."

A commotion of voices drifted from the front of the cottage, and John winked, grasped her hand, and pulled her outside, through the kitchen door. Rounding the side of the house, he urged her on. "Come, darling, it's only a little farther."

"Said the devil to the innocent."

He led them to the now-empty carriage and helped her inside. "Now kiss me again," he insisted. "You know we'll not have another chance of being alone as soon as they run us to the ground. And there is plenty of room in the second carriage . . . if they don't breathe. "

"Ah, finally—your finesse—your infamous skills of diplomacy and negotiation—makes an appearance." She grasped his neckcloth and urged him closer.

John tapped three times on the ceiling of the carriage,

and the barouche moved forward. "Precisely. You have your methods, and I have mine. We shall do very well together, darling." He encircled her with his arms and lowered his lips to hers, until she finally, blessedly, allowed herself to grasp the happiness she had always deserved. Victoria kissed the man she loved with all her heart and soul and allowed the anxiety of a lifetime to flow from her breast into his, only to learn the extraordinary joy of shared dreams realized.

She whispered such words of love in his ear combined with that throaty low laughter of hers designed to melt butter and all lesser men. Holding her, kissing her, John suddenly envisioned it all. The gaggle of Helstons and Wallaces, and all the other mysterious members of the dowager duchess's secret club, regularly invading their residences for the rest of his life. Above all, he envisioned Victoria . . . and children. So very many children—some his, many not. They were crowding the empty halls of his childhood, of his past. In front of him, crowds of happiness beckoned, and he answered their call by opening his heart to the woman before him and caressing her beautiful face until she fell back into his warm embrace.

Epilogue

My dear Mr. Brown,

This is an amendment of sorts to my last letter to you—of which I have not received the pleasure of a reply. Everyone here says holding a grudge for so long is not attractive in a gentleman, but if this idea irritates you further, let it be known that I did not necessarily agree with them.

It now appears there are to be two weddings in the near future. In addition to the marriage of the Countess of Sheffield and the Earl of Wallace, Miss Victoria Givan is to be the new Duke of Beaufort's bride shortly. Very shortly, if the duke has his way. And as we well know, dukes always have their way. It is amazing how hard, and how fast these great men are falling as of late. Very unlike, ahem, resentful Scots.

I am happy to report that the new Duke of Beaufort does not possess the vile, bloodthirsty nature of his predecessors. Nor does my dear new friend, the Earl of Wymith, a man I plan to introduce to the last two widows in my club. My grandson is lukewarm on the idea. Indeed, he says he would rather settle my Elizabeth and Sarah with a small fortune instead of enduring the travails of friendship and love again.

Oh, John . . . please hurry back to town. The center aisle of St. George's is a very long one, and I shall twice require your arm to lean against. You know how frail I am these days. I do hope you are not laughing. I should not have to warn you that Attila the Dog does not take kindly to gentlemen who are unkind to me.

Do come. I shall be forced to desperate measures if you do not, and I promise you will like it even less than all that has come before—if that is possible.

Your devoted,
Ata

Want to read more about the characters in this novella and the entire secret widows club? RITA® Award-winning author **SOPHIA NASH**'s latest series for Avon Books is on shelves now! Meet Rosamunde Baird, the lady capable of taking on the austere Duke of Helston in *A Dangerous Beauty*, named Best Regency-set Historical of the Year by *Romantic Times BOOKreviews* magazine. The *Chicago Tribune* called Georgiana Wilde's and the Marquis of Ellesmere's love story in *The Kiss* "a dazzling combination of subtly complex characters, simmering sensuality, and writing that gleams with sharp wit." Or fall in love with the Countess of Sheffield and a rugged stranger in Sophia's latest story, *Love with the Perfect Scoundrel*. To learn more about the author and her books, visit *www.SophiaNash.com*.

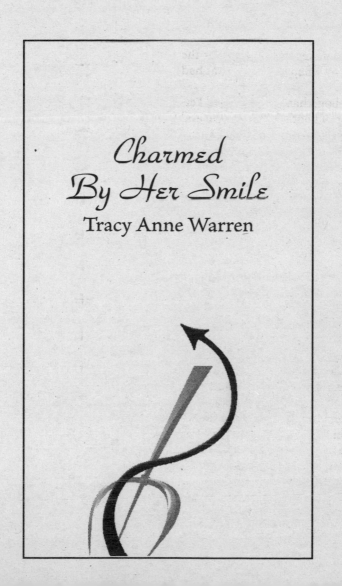

Charmed
By Her Smile

Tracy Anne Warren

Chapter One

London, England
Early August 1809

*I*ndia Byron raised a glass of champagne punch to her lips, then choked when she caught sight of a tawny-haired young man standing in the drawing-room doorway, scanning the crowd.

How did he get in here? she thought in alarm.

It was bad enough her older brother, Spence, had brought the simpleton home for the summer along with a gaggle of first-years from Oxford. But now to find him in London at a family wedding—to which he quite clearly had *not* been invited—well, it was really beyond the pale.

She knew without conceit that he was here because of her. Ever since their introduction at her father's country estate last month, he'd been mooning over her—making calves' eyes and penning dozens of truly dreadful poems written in her honor. *One more ode to my "dewy emerald eyes*," she thought, *and I'll surely be sick!*

Taking a few steps back, she maneuvered herself so she was half-hidden behind a pair of her cousins, Jack and Drake—both men too deep in conversation to notice her skulking.

The next time I see Spence, she vowed, *he's a dead man!*

Swallowing a hasty draught of punch to help bolster her nerves, she set the champagne flute down on the nearest table and glanced around for a convenient avenue of escape. Across the room, another cousin, Cade Byron, and his new wife, Meg, were holding court—the bride and groom both glowing with happiness, as they accepted the well-wishes of family and friends alike. But India didn't have time to celebrate. At that moment, she needed to save herself.

Spying an open set of French doors that led to the terrace and garden beyond, she hurried toward them. As she did, she glanced back and gasped when she saw a pair of familiar mooning hazel eyes turn her way. Breaking into a run, she wondered how she was going to elude him.

Mercy help me, I'm bored, Quentin Marlowe, 8th Duke of Weybridge, thought, as he drained the last of his champagne. Twirling the now-empty glass between his fingers, he leaned a shoulder against a foliage-covered garden arbor and gazed across the lawn toward Clybourne House.

Actually, he would rather be drinking brandy, but he supposed eleven thirty in the morning was too early for hard liquor—even for him. Brandy or not, he knew the spirits would do nothing to relieve his present ennui.

Not that his friend Cade's wedding wasn't a splendid affair—since it was—but at its heart, a reception was still just a reception. And over the course of his two-and-thirty years, he'd attended far too many weddings and wedding receptions to see this one as anything new.

Lately it seemed as if *nothing* was new.

London was invariably the same. Each spring, the Season came and went with its usual round of parties, amusements, and the annual crop of perky debutantes, all desperately searching for a husband.

Then late summer would arrive, and it was off to the country for hunting, riding, and social gatherings that would last through the autumn.

The holidays descended next, along with family and friends come to revel over cups of wassail and bicker over their differences.

Then winter set in—cold, oppressive and dreary.

Finally, spring returned and the whole cycle would begin again. Just thinking about it made him sigh.

That's the problem, he mused. *Nothing surprises me anymore. It's all just a tedious bore.*

Suddenly, a flash of white caught his eye as a young woman with fair skin and lustrous sable hair hurried from the house. Her slippered feet flew as she ran, her gaze darting right, then left, then back.

Pretty little thing, he mused. *Gorgeous, actually.* Quite likely a Byron, he guessed, especially given the multitude of them in attendance today. And young—probably not much more than eighteen, if he didn't miss the mark. Obviously, she was fleeing from something—or more likely *someone*—since it seemed probable she was being pursued by one of the other guests. A lover's game perhaps?

Shrugging, he glanced away.

He was contemplating whether or not to indulge in

one of the cheroots in his lapel pocket, when, out of the corner of his eye, he caught sight of her racing down the terrace steps and across the yard. Her pale skirts swirled around her legs, displaying her trim ankles in a most enticing way, as she moved deeper into the garden. Suddenly she lifted her head and met his gaze, espying him where he stood in the partial concealment of the leafy arbor.

Slowing, she glanced again toward the house, hesitating as though she were weighing her options. Apparently, having made up her mind, she continued on in his direction, coming to a halt barely an inch away from him.

"Quick!" she declared in a breathless voice. "Kiss me!"

One eyebrow winged skyward. "I beg your pardon?"

"No time for pardons," she admonished. "He's nearly upon us. Just do it. *Kiss me!*"

"He isn't a jealous husband, is he?" he asked with lazy amusement. "Or a lover brandishing a pistol?"

Now that really would liven up the festivities, he thought.

"No," she said. "He's just a besotted idiot who doesn't know when to go away. Hurry while there's still time. Kiss me. *Please!*"

Quentin looked down at her lovely heart-shaped face and into the depths of her beseeching green eyes. His gaze roamed lower, tracing across the adorable sweep of her nose, the refined curves of her cheekbones, then over her full, rosy lips which were parted in rapt anticipation.

Despite his better judgment, he was intrigued. Even more, he had a sudden craving to find out if her mouth tasted as ripe and delicious as it looked.

"Well," he drawled, warming to the possibilities. "Who am I to deny a lady?"

Taking her in his arms, he pressed his lips to hers.

The spark was instantaneous; a jolt of pleasure so intense it blazed through him like a rippling summer heat, saturating his blood and sinking deep into his vitals. As for her mouth, she tasted like honey and wine, with a lightness that made him think of pure springwater. Wanting a deeper draught to quench his sudden thirst, he traced his tongue along her lower lip and urged her mouth to open.

She gave an answering sigh of delight and began to respond. But just as quickly, she pressed her palms to his chest and broke away. She didn't draw back very far, however—their faces remaining close. "Is he still there?" she whispered.

He who?

For a moment, Quentin didn't understand the question. Then memory returned. Glancing up, he surveyed the garden. "Brown hair? Lanky build? Wounded expression like a puppy that just got kicked?"

She gave a faint nod.

"Then yes, he's still there. Shall we continue, since he doesn't look sure yet whether to stay or go?"

She paused, her eyes wide and slightly bemused. He wondered if she was about to refuse, when she nodded and slid her arms around his shoulders. "Yes. Kiss me again."

With a smile, he bent to do as she commanded.

Sensing her distraction over the other man, he kept their kiss brief this time. Light, playful, and undemanding. She relaxed, growing increasingly more confident and pliant inside his embrace.

Leaving his lips against hers so they were barely brushing, he flicked another glance upward. "Now he looks like a furious, wounded puppy," he murmured. "Mad enough to chew off his own tail. Sure you aren't trying to make him jealous?"

Her sweet breath puffed against his mouth. "No! I just want him gone since he's been plaguing me this past month entire. Truly, I have tried to be nice, but he just will not take the hint."

He gave her another plucking, lingering kiss. "Don't look now, but I think your wish has been granted. He's turned around and is walking back to the house—or should I say stomping back. Ah, there, he's gone inside."

"Thank heavens," India declared, tension flowing from her in voluble waves that reached all the way to her toes.

For a moment she considered looking over her shoulder to verify that Peter, "the Pest," was truly gone, but she didn't want to take the chance of ruining her good fortune. Instead she gazed up into the face of the stranger, who still held her within his arms.

Arresting was the best way to describe him, she decided, since he wasn't handsome in the conventional sense. His nose was too long and hawkish for one, his chin too square. His bone structure looked chiseled, as though it had been hewn from a rough block of granite. Contrarily, his lips were elegant, capable of being seductive or stern, she was sure, depending upon his whim. As for his eyes, they were dark—the color of freshly brewed coffee—with a pair of formidable brows that arched like raven's wings above his penetrating gaze.

His most remarkable feature, by far though, was his hair. Thick and soft with a stubborn hint of wave, his close-cropped locks were so dark a brown as to appear black. But the true surprise lay at his temples, where twin streaks of silver gleamed as though painted there by a master's hand.

Her fingers tingled with the need to touch, to glide through those pale strands and see if they were as luxurious as they promised to be. Instead, she left her hands where they rested on the wide expanse of his large male shoulders—her body nestled against his long, powerful frame.

"Lately, I've come to realize how the poor fox must feel during hunting season," she remarked, trying to steer her thoughts back to her recent escape from her unwanted admirer's attentions, rather than dwelling on the overwhelming sensuality of the man in whose arms she stood.

"That bad, hmm?" he asked.

"Worse." She paused. "I suppose you think I'm cruel?"

His dark gaze turned gentle. "Not at all. Sometimes stronger deterrents than words are required."

"Exactly. And I have you to thank. I am greatly in your debt."

"No need. Believe me, the past few minutes have been my express pleasure."

Her pulse gave a dangerous thump. "Yes, well, now that he is gone, I suppose I ought to be returning inside."

"I wouldn't go just yet," he warned. "Not until he's had time to call for his carriage."

Tiny lines formed over the bridge of her nose. "Oh, mayhap you're right. Still, you should probably release me, now that Peter is gone."

He stroked a hand over her back in a way that made her want to purr like a cat. "All the more reason to keep you right where you are. I kissed you for his sake. Now, I want a kiss of my own. After all, you did make mention of being in my debt."

"Yes, but you said there was no need for gratitude—"

His teeth flashed in a wicked grin, his arms tightening as he turned her more fully into the concealing shade of the arbor. "I changed my mind."

Then, before she could draw another breath, his lips claimed hers again.

Delight burst like fireworks through her veins, the sensation of his touch every bit as shocking and thrilling as the first time she'd felt it.

When she'd asked him to kiss her, she'd assumed their embrace would be quick and to the point. He'd give her a simple, ordinary kiss that would last just long enough to discourage her unwanted suitor. Then she would thank him and be on her way back to the reception. No harm. No fuss.

But nothing of the sort had occurred.

Like a sky crackling with electricity just before a storm, a sizzle had gone through her body the instant his mouth touched hers. Her nerve endings had come alive, senses inundated with one glorious rush of pleasure after another.

Somehow she'd found the strength to break that initial embrace—and the second one as well—keeping enough of her wits about her to remember the reason she was in his arms at all. But this time she knew she was in trouble.

He was a complete stranger, and yet she was comfortable with him in ways that made no sense. His faintest touch left her vulnerable and unsure, but still she knew instinctively that she'd found a safe harbor in his arms.

Nevertheless, being alone with him was insane and foolhardy. She was only eighteen, not even officially out, yet here she was breaking every one of Society's most sacred rules. Letting him help her get rid of Peter was one thing. Letting him kiss her senseless was quite another!

Push him away, she told herself. *Say no while you still can.*

But already it was too late, a heated shudder rippling over her skin like a fever, as he intensified their kiss. Slanting his mouth over hers, he claimed her, using a subtle pressure that made her gasp.

The moment her lips parted, his tongue came inside to glide in hot, wet, satiny circles that reduced her mind to mush. She whimpered as he feasted on her, the flavor of his kiss as intoxicating as the most potent liquor, and as effervescent as the finest French champagne.

Tightening her arms around his shoulders, she held on as he ravished her mouth, yielding to his smallest command, reveling in his possession. Responding to his tutelage, she followed his lead as he slowly, patiently taught her the finer points of kissing. He was the first man to ever really kiss her—since she supposed a couple of childish pecks under the mistletoe didn't count. And given his obvious skills, she realized just how much more she had to learn.

A long minute later, he slid his hands low and cupped her bottom to press her more fully against him. She startled, growing momentarily tense in his embrace. He did as well, his muscles tightening, even as his hold on her relaxed.

With a groan, he wrenched himself away. His eyes were dark and lambent as they met her own, his eyelids heavy with clear passion. "My thanks for the kiss, dear girl," he rasped on a husky tone. "I can safely say that you and I are more than even now."

Abruptly, sanity came rushing back, along with a cascade of heat that crept into her face. Smiling, he stroked the edge of a finger over one hot cheek, his skin cool against her burning flesh.

"You're as sweet as you are pretty. Run on now before I give your cousins real cause to come after me with a shotgun."

She swayed on her feet, not sure whether to go or fling herself back into his arms.

Whirling, she sprinted away, forcing herself not to look around to catch one last glimpse of him.

* * *

Quentin rested a fist against one of the wooden slats that formed the arbor and watched her flee.

The instant he let her go, he wanted her back, his body protesting the decision to release her. But despite his less-than-savory reputation when it came to women, he wasn't in the habit of ravishing innocent young ladies, however tempting they might be.

Damn and blast, I wanted her though, he thought, knowing he'd be trapped in the arbor until the most pressing evidence of his arousal cooled. Even then, it would be wise to take his leave. If he returned to the reception and saw her there, who knows what impulses might arise to tempt him—and her—again.

She might be young and inexperienced, but she was passionate—wildly so—the sensation of her fresh, un-tutored kisses still burning on his lips. Whatever man earned the right to take her to his bed would be a lucky fellow indeed. But such pleasure would only be granted at the expense of a wedding ring—and that was a price he was most unwilling to pay.

No, despite her natural charm and vivacity, he was better off forgetting her. He'd worked the trick numerous times before with other women—the delicious Miss Byron would be no different.

Even so, as he reached into his coat pocket to extract the cheroot he'd earlier planned to smoke, he couldn't help but be struck by one salient fact.

I'm not the least bit bored anymore.

Chapter Two

*I*ʼve laid out yer favorite white muslin gown with the little green scribbly-things all over it," her maid informed India two weeks later, as she walked out of the bathing chamber into the well-appointed guest room where she would be staying.

India laughed. "Those are Grecian keys, not *scribbly-things*," she teased. Crossing to the bed, she removed her dressing gown, then reached for the fresh linen shift lying across the cheery yellow counterpane.

"Well, they looks like scribbly-things to me," her maid replied. "I've set out yer green slippers as well. The rest I've yet to unpack and press. A great lot of bother all this traveling to and fro is if ye asks me, just fer a few days' visit. But I expect ye'll have a fine time all the same."

"As will you. Dorset is always delightful in August. I

hear there are bathing machines in Lyme Regis, which is only a few miles distant."

The servant gave a snort. "Bathing machines. Drowning traps is more like. And indecent to boot with the ladies stripped down to their unmentionables." She bustled across to the open wardrobe to hang a gown. "But I do like a sea breeze, I confess. Here now, enough of such talk. Let me get you dressed and ready so you can join the others. Surely they're all near arrived by now."

India herself had arrived only a couple hours ago, having made the journey from London with her aunt Ava—the Dowager Duchess of Clybourne—and cousin Mallory. From the start, she'd been excited about the invitation to attend the Pettigrews' country party. But now that she was here, she was even more grateful and determined to enjoy herself—hoping the respite would be just what she needed to clear the memories of a certain dark-haired gentleman from her mind.

Each night she dreamed of him—her stranger from the garden—his gravelly voice murmuring in her ear, his kisses sweeping her away into realms of forbidden pleasure where only the two of them dwelled.

But such phantasms were just that—fantasies that were best forgotten, as was the man himself. He'd helped her get rid of Peter, whom she hadn't seen since the day of the reception. And now she needed to set her stranger aside as well.

Forcing him from her thoughts, she turned and let her maid assist her into her gown.

Twenty minutes later, she went downstairs. She found herself alone, however, the hour apparently too early yet for the others to have left the sanctuary of their own bedchambers.

Deciding to explore a bit, she wandered along the spacious corridors and elegantly furnished rooms, stopping every once in a while to admire a particularly attractive piece of artwork or an interesting architectural element. Eventually she found the library. Strolling inside, she began perusing the books on the shelves.

She'd just taken down a volume of poetry by Wordsworth, when she heard muffled footfalls on the carpet behind her. Eager for the company, she turned with an expectant smile, but her good humor plummeted at sight of the rangy young man who had entered the room. The book she held fell to the floor with a thump.

"Here, allow me to get that for you," declared an overly earnest voice she'd hoped never to hear again. Her lips tightened as she watched Peter—the Pest— Harte hurry forward to retrieve the book.

Before he could do so, however, she dipped down and snatched up the volume. "No need," she announced. "I have it."

He stopped and rocked back on his heels, an injured expression on his long, almost cherubic countenance. "You ought to have let me do that for you, Miss Byron. That's what gentlemen are for. To aid a lady in her hour of need."

Willpower and good manners were all that kept her from rolling her eyes. *Hour of need, really!*

"Well, lucky me," she said. "Disaster has been averted."

He gave her a happy smile, the faintly mocking quality of her retort having apparently escaped him.

Good heavens, I have to get away and get away now! she thought.

"I'm sorry, but my cousin is waiting for me above stairs," she said on a quick improvisation. "I was just going to take this . . . this book to her. I must go immediately."

"May I say you're looking splendid," he declared, as though she hadn't spoken at all. "Do you know it's been two weeks since last we met?"

Yes, I know. Two wonderful, glorious weeks.

"How I've missed you, Miss Byron. I have been bereft without sight of your exquisite beauty. Truly, you are a rare pearl among a vast sea of female oysters."

Female oysters?

"Inspired by such thoughts, I have written a poem to express my feelings."

"No, no poems!" she stated, holding up a hand. "This book, you see." She waved the volume in the air. "I really have no time to spare in its urgent delivery."

His round chin jutted forward, clearly annoyed that his quest was being met with resistance. "But surely you can remain a bit longer."

"I am sorry, I cannot." She moved to depart.

He stepped forward and blocked her path. "But I must be permitted to speak. I shall read only the opening few stanzas. You will see—" He began reaching into his pocket.

"No! Don't!" she stated. "Do not read that poem."

For a long moment, he stood silent, then slowly lowered his hand to his side. "Very well, if that is what you wish. Though I must tell you that it's one of my best," he said in a clearly petulant voice. "Even so, I insist you hear me out in plain language, since you deny me the right to express my emotions in verse."

He paced a few steps, then stopped. "Although I am loath to say, I've been deuced upset—pardon my language—ever since that day at the reception." He crossed his arms over his slender chest, his high forehead wrinkling with irritation. "I was most shocked . . . wounded, and yes, appalled by your brazen behavior. Yet in spite of your . . . indiscretion, I have decided to forgive you."

Her mouth fell open. "*What!*"

"Which is why I am here."

She frowned as a sudden thought occurred. "Now that you mention it, how is it that you *are* here? I didn't think you were even acquainted with the Pettigrews."

A sheepish look came over this face. "I'm not, but my aunt is, and I wrangled an invitation through her. Auntie Ethel is a bosom friend of Lady Pettigrew's, don't you know."

No, I didn't, she bemoaned silently. *If I had, I would never have come.*

"When I told my aunt of my intention to marry you," he continued, "she was most obliging on my behalf."

Air whooshed out of her lungs. "*You told her what?*"

"Now, don't ruffle up so, my love. All will be well, you will see."

Her fingers squeezed so hard against the book she held that her knuckles turned white. "I am not your love, and you had no right to discuss such matters with your aunt, especially since we are *not* engaged."

Ruddy color crept into his fair cheeks. "I didn't say we were. Only that I hoped we would be soon."

She trembled, outraged frustration churning through her like a bad case of dyspepsia. "Mr. Harte—"

"Peter," he interjected on an optimistic note.

"*Mr. Harte.* I have tried to be understanding and patient over these last weeks. Believe me, I am sensible of the honor of your proposal and have no wish to injure your feelings. However, I must tell you that your suit is not welcome."

For a moment, he hung his head, shoulders slumping in dejection. "You are only being modest—"

"I assure you, I am not. My recent *indiscretion,* as you called it, certainly ought to have proven that much to you. Now, I bid you good day and hope this is the end of the matter." Clutching the volume of poetry to her chest, she started toward the door.

"No," he said.

She halted, turning back. "Pardon?"

His thin shoulders drew straight, his voice gaining volume and strength. "I said no. You are too important to me to simply give up. I refuse to cede the field of romantic conquest without a fight. Providence has placed us here together in this house for the next week—time that will allow me to woo you and prove that I am worthy of your love."

Horrified shock rippled over her skin, a sick lump dropping to the bottom of her stomach like a wad of old biscuit dough.

"Yes," he continued, renewed confidence ringing in his tone. "I will demonstrate my affection and win you to my side. By week's end, you will have forgotten all about that fellow you were kissing in the garden and want only *my* kisses."

"Believe me, I shall not."

"What was his name anyway? That *man,*" he asked, practically spitting out the last word.

This cannot be happening, she thought in near panic. "His name is not important. And you are wrong about the other," she declared. "The man you saw, he . . . he . . ." *Yes? Think quick!* "He is practically my betrothed," she stated.

"What!"

"Yes," she went on, scrambling wildly to come up with her next excuse. "He is a friend of the family, and I've known him for years. We met again earlier this summer on a visit . . . b-before you arrived at the house

. . . and he has been mad for me ever since. I expect him to make an offer at any moment."

His tawny brows drew close, the bridge of his aquiline nose wrinkling in consternation. "Spence didn't say anything about your being courted by someone else."

"Of course, he didn't. I am not· yet out, so nothing official can be said at present. And Spencer was away from the house at the time, so even he doesn't know. But this man . . . he is very serious about me and *very* jealous. So you see why you must end this futile pursuit. I belong to someone else."

There! she thought. *Surely that will send him on his way.*

His lower lip quivered, large hands clenched at his sides. "Well, you don't belong to him yet, and I have this week to prove the superiority of my affection. Anyway, if he's so in love with you, where is he? This *almost betrothed* of yours?"

She gripped the book more tightly, wishing she could use it to whack Peter over the head. Instead, she forced herself to think fast again. "He . . . um . . . he is delayed by business. But he'll be here. I'm just not sure when."

Never was when, but in the meantime, maybe she could use the threat of her stranger's arrival to hold the Pest at bay. She only hoped her stalling tactics would work. Otherwise, she didn't like to contemplate the days ahead.

"I need to take this book upstairs, if you'll recall," she said.

He gave a sharp, almost pugnacious nod, then thrust his hands into his pockets.

Turning, she hurried to the door. Walking at a clip, she moved down the hall and into the corridor beyond. She turned one corner, then another, head down as she searched for the main staircase. She had nearly reached it, or so she hoped, when she rounded another corner and barreled straight into something. *Or rather someone.*

"Oh, good heavens!" she said, as the man with whom she'd collided reached out to steady her. Tipping back her head to issue an apology, she met a pair of warm, coffee brown eyes.

Eyes she'd seen only last night in her dreams.

She drew in a sharp breath, the compelling magnetism of his dark, distinctive features and vital personality even more powerful than she recalled—and even more appealing.

His lips curved into a slow smile. "Well, hello again," he drawled. "I must say, you and I seem to meet in the most unconventional of ways."

Her heart pounded in her chest. "You're here," she marveled.

His smile widened. "I am indeed. Were you expecting me?"

"No," she said, recovering a measure of her equilibrium. "But I am incredibly glad to see you. We need to talk."

Chapter Three

Surprised again, Quentin thought, as he let the incomparable Miss Byron lead him into a nearby drawing room.

And to think I very nearly decided not to come.

He'd accepted the Pettigrews' invitation to their country party ages ago, but after receiving a rather cryptic note from his friend Jack Byron last week—informing him that he would not be able to attend as planned—Quentin had considered sending his regrets.

But now he was pleased he hadn't—sensing the boredom that had been creeping back upon him lately melt away like a clump of snow dropped onto a blazing hearth. He could almost feel the sizzle.

What is she up to this time? he wondered. In spite of the loud peal of several internal warning bells, he knew he had to find out.

He watched as she crossed to a window that overlooked

the sprawling green lawn beyond. Stopping, she laid the book she was holding on a nearby chair before turning around. "It would seem I am in need of your assistance again," she stated, glancing up to meet his gaze.

He strode forward, halting less than a foot away from her. "More kisses, is it?" he said, unable to resist the urge to tease her a bit. He forced back a grin, as a telltale wash of pink stained her cheeks.

"No." She gave him a look of reproach, followed by another that seemed curiously chagrined. "This time I need you to pretend to be wildly enamored of me and on the verge of proposing marriage."

His jaw grew slack. Recovering quickly, he gave her a long stare. "Might you care to repeat that?"

"Only if you are hard of hearing, which I can tell you are not. Truly, I apologize in advance for springing this on you so abruptly, but I haven't much time."

"You never do," he remarked with a sardonic twist.

She ignored his comment, and continued, "You see, he's back!"

"Who is back?"

"Peter Harte. The simpleton who was trailing me at the reception."

"The wounded puppy, you mean?"

She nodded. "Precisely. He procured an invitation from Lady Pettigrew to attend this party for the sole purpose of seeking me out again. Only minutes ago, he cornered me in the library to say he has forgiven me for kissing you that day in the garden and that he plans to win me away from you."

"And he believes I am pursuing you because of our kiss?"

Her skin glowed with fresh color. "Well, in part. And also because I may have told him we are very nearly engaged."

He raised a brow. "Good Lord!"

"Also, you've known my immediate family for years," she said, as she continued reciting her litany of deceits. "And when the two of us met again earlier this summer at my father's house, the sparks flew."

She isn't far wrong about that, he mused. *Every time we meet, sparks do fly.* Although right now, he was trying to decide which emotion had the upper hand— irritation or amusement. "Anything else we did together that I should know about?"

Her lovely full lips drew tight in concentration. "Not that I can think of."

"How reassuring."

Their gazes met, her green eyes beseeching once more. "Oh, do please forgive me. I never meant to involve you, but he simply would not take no for an answer. What else was I to do?"

He could think of several options but decided to keep his mouth shut for the time being. Honestly, he'd never met a more impetuous minx, nor one so brazen. *Why then, do I find her so delightful?*

"I realize it's asking a great deal," she said, laying a hand on his sleeve. "But couldn't you court me for a little while? Just until Peter goes away again. I expect once he sees us together, he'll storm off like he did before, and that will be the end of the matter."

And if it isn't? Quentin considered. Was he willing to spend the next week dancing attendance on her? Devoting his time and risking comment over his supposed pursuit of a girl who was barely out of the schoolroom? Then again, he'd never cared much for other people's opinions, so why should he start now?

Of course, he could do the easy, straightforward thing and have a chat with the encroaching puppy. He had no doubt a few well-chosen words would convince Peter

Harte to leave Miss Byron alone. And if that still wasn't sufficient, he knew that Lord Pettigrew would be only too happy to kick him out at Quentin's request.

But where will that leave me for the week?

He'd barely arrived, and already he was feeling vastly entertained by her antics. When he considered the situation, he realized he rather fancied the notion of spending the next week in mock pursuit of the irrepressible Miss Byron. Her suggestion promised to provide a game that was both lively and delicious—as well as the opportunity to flirt with her as much as he wished.

So why not indulge?

There was his earlier vow to keep his distance from her, he admitted, but he could handle himself. Their encounter this week would amount to no more than an innocent, casual dalliance. Once over, the two of them would part with smiles and fond recollections—neither the worse for the experience.

"So," she asked with a sweetly expectant murmur. "Will you help me?"

"Given all you've told me, my dear girl, how can I possibly refuse?"

Her eyes brightened, sparkling with delight as she let out a happy little laugh. The sound went straight through him, leaving in its wake a sudden craving to hear it once again.

He was just about to make the attempt, when another young woman walked into the room. A young woman he knew quite well.

"Quentin!" Lady Mallory Byron exclaimed, her lovely features lighting with undisguised pleasure. "You've arrived. Oh, it's so good to see you. Come here this instant and give me a hug."

* * *

So his name is Quentin, India thought. *At least I know that much now.*

She watched him go to her cousin, her chest tightening in a strangely uncomfortable way, as he enveloped Mallory in a warm, heartfelt embrace. Moments later she relaxed, however, when it became apparent that his and Mallory's affection went no deeper than that of platonic friends.

Clearly, the two of them were comfortable with each other, but in a manner that reminded her of the way Mallory behaved around her brothers. Fleetingly, she considered the Banbury tale she'd told about his having been a longtime friend of her own branch of the family. If that were actually true, might the two of them now share the same kind of casual relationship he enjoyed with her cousin?

As soon as the thought crossed her mind though, she dismissed it, knowing she was far too aware of him as a man ever to be able to see him in such a light—not even if she had known him since infancy.

"So you've both met, I see," Mallory said, separating from Quentin before motioning India forward to join them. "Was it just now?"

India was trying to decide how to answer, when he stepped into the breach.

"Actually, Miss Byron and I have not been formally introduced," he said. "Perhaps you would care to do the honors."

"Oh, of course. It would be my pleasure," Mallory said, her eyes brightening. "Your Grace, allow me to present Miss India Byron. India is my first cousin from Uncle Charles' side of the family, if you didn't know. India, this inestimable gentleman is Quentin Marlowe, His Grace, the Duke of Weybridge."

"Weybridge!" India said without thinking. "You're Weybridge?"

He raised one dark brow. "Indeed. Have you some prior knowledge of me?" *Other than our secret pact and the torrid kisses we shared in the garden of your cousins' London town house,* his gaze seemed to say.

She swallowed. "No, none really. Only what is said in the Society pages."

Which, as it happened, was a very great deal indeed. Even as sheltered as she was, she'd read enough about him to fill a book—and a very naughty one at that. His exploits with sword and pistols were legendary, as were his impressive skills at driving horses and playing cards. He was even better known for his liaisons with women—worldly, experienced beauties, who were reported on occasion to swoon at his mere entrance into a room. No wonder she'd melted at his first touch—and his second and third.

Warmth spread through her body, making her wish she'd brought her fan. *To think I've been consorting with "Devil Weybridge" himself.*

His eyes narrowed, his countenance taking on a sardonic cast. "So, you read the Society pages, do you?"

She shifted her feet. "Well, there isn't a great deal else to do in the country, Your Grace."

His features didn't soften. "And your mother approves of you filling your head full of scandal broth and tawdry gossip?"

Her gaze darted to Mallory, who was looking on with amazed curiosity. She would find no help there, she realized. Straightening her shoulders, she continued. "Actually, Mama and I read the papers together every morning over breakfast. The Society pages are her very favorite."

His lips tightened.

"Oh, but I am sure what is printed about *you* is nothing but half-truths and lies," she rushed to assure.

"What those publications claim to be news *is* mainly a collection of half-truths and lies." His warm brown eyes met hers, something shifting deep in his gaze. "But in my case, you'd be wise to believe every word."

Then he winked.

Surprise leapt through her, together with the sudden realization that he'd only been teasing her.

While she visibly recovered, he began to laugh. "This gathering may prove memorable yet. Come, Miss Byron, let me procure a libation for you." He offered his arm. "You will excuse us, will you not, Lady Mallory?"

Mallory blinked, looking from one to the other of them for a long moment. "Of course. In fact, I see Mama and Major Hargreaves have arrived and are talking across the way. I believe I shall join them."

Only after Mallory left did India notice how many other guests were now assembled in the room. She'd been so engrossed in her conversation with Quentin that she hadn't even been aware of their entrance. Among their number stood Peter Harte, who was glaring across at her and Quentin with a disapproving frown.

What would Peter think when he learned his competition was none other than Devil Weybridge himself? Considering Quentin's reputation, she hoped Peter would decide he was beaten before he'd even begun.

Cheered by the thought, she took Quentin's arm.

"India, hmm?" he said, as they crossed the room together. "It's a lovely name, but if you don't mind my saying, a rather unusual one as well."

"Oh, I don't mind. And it would be unusual, except for the fact that I've always believed it demonstrates a marked lack of originality on my parents' part."

"How so?"

"Because my father was stationed with the military in India at the time of my birth, and it's where I was born. I've always been grateful he wasn't assigned to a post in Egypt or Gibraltar, or just think of the name I'd have now."

He laughed, his deep brown eyes twinkling with undisguised humor. "The prospect does give one pause. Although I must say you would have made a very pretty Gibraltara, or Egyptia perhaps?"

"Please, don't even jest," she said with a mock shudder. "The thought is too dreadful to contemplate. Believe me, I like India just fine."

Their gazes met. "I like India, too," he said in a serious tone. "In fact, the more I know of her, the more I am finding to admire."

Her heart pounded, the smile sliding from her mouth as she lost herself in his beautiful eyes.

"I've brought you a lemonade, Miss Byron," interrupted a defiant, young male voice. "I thought you looked a bit warm and in need of refreshment."

Turning her head, she saw Peter Harte hovering close by. "Mr. Harte," she said.

"Here"—he thrust the glass toward her—"this is for you."

Seeing no other option, she accepted the beverage.

The moment she did, Quentin reached out and gently removed it from her hand, setting it onto a nearby tray. "Miss Byron doesn't care for lemonade. She told me she is more in the mood for tea."

Peter bristled, thrusting out his chin. "And who are you to decide what Miss Byron does and does not like?"

"The gentleman she has chosen to procure refreshments for her this evening." Using a look only a duke could carry off, Quentin stared down his nose with bored hauteur. "And you are, sir?"

Peter shifted, clearly discomfited. "Peter Harte, Esquire."

"Ah," Quentin replied. "Come, my dear India. Let us get that tea for you."

Recovering herself, she moved to obey.

"And who are you, sir?" Peter demanded, obviously not about to be put off.

Quentin stopped and turned back. "I am Weybridge. Anything else you should like to know?"

Wheels turned almost visibly inside Peter's brain as he pondered the import of Quentin's reply. His eyes widened as comprehension dawned. Mouth agape, he stared.

"I thought not," Quentin said.

Turning again, he led her away.

"That was amazing," she whispered. "I've never seen him rendered speechless."

"It was one way of handling him. We'll see how long it lasts."

"Surely, that will do the trick, and he will cease this futile pursuit."

"Perhaps. For now though, my dear, you have some tea to drink."

Chapter Four

Peter Harte stared at them through dinner and cards that evening, then again through breakfast the following morning—his relentless hazel gaze so intrusive it nearly put India off her eggs and buttered toast.

For his part, Quentin took it all in stride, seeming to find humor in the other man's fulminating glances when he wasn't otherwise occupied lavishing attention on her.

And lavish attention he did, turning the full force of his magnetic personality her way like the warmth of a brilliant sun. When she'd asked him to pretend to court her, she hadn't realized exactly what that might entail. Yet she could marshal no complaint, quite unable to resist his sophisticated charm and scintillating conversation, regardless of how out of her depth it occasionally left her feeling.

She had to admit to a sensation of relief, however, when Lady Pettigrew announced shortly after breakfast that the gentlemen would be taking to the fields to hunt wildfowl. She was sorry Quentin would be away, but under the circumstances it was worth the loss, since she would be spared Peter's petulant stares and glares for an entire afternoon. And so with smiles and waves, she and the other ladies saw the men off, remaining behind to indulge in archery and watercolor painting.

Nearly three hours later, India was adding a flourish of vermilion to her watercolor paper when she heard the unmistakable sounds of barking dogs and male voices.

"Home already, are they?" declared Lady Pettigrew. "I wonder if they had any luck? Usually they're out far longer than this."

Over the rise they came. As the group drew nearer, hunting rifles bent open over their elbows, it became apparent that a mishap had befallen the party.

Or rather *one* of the party.

Resembling a drenched cat and looking every inch as miserable, Peter Harte was soaked through. His hair was plastered to his head like a monk's cap, while his once-fashionable country attire clung to his lanky frame in a most uncomfortable manner. To make matters worse, he was stained brown as a nut, doused in a slick gleam of mud that coated him from head to toe.

Laying down her brush, India stood, along with a few of the other ladies.

The Ossley sisters—a pair of young women, who looked so much alike she was never quite sure which one she was addressing—hurried toward the men. The two of them made noises of sympathy, clucking and cooing over Peter, even as they made certain not to get too close for fear of staining their gowns with a stray fleck of mud.

"Stars above. What in the world happened to you, Mr. Harte?" Aunt Ava asked from her seat next to Lady Pettigrew.

A few of the men chuckled under their breaths at the question, obviously amused by whatever it was that had happened.

"He landed himself in the bog, that's what," Lord Pettigrew answered, when Peter did not speak up. "He and Weybridge were competing for the most birds taken, and were tied at six each, when Harte had to try bagging one more. Didn't listen when I told him not to wander off to the east, but he went regardless. Not three minutes later, he was plunged up to his neck in weeds and muck."

"Dear me," Lady Pettigrew said.

Dear me indeed, India thought, lifting a hand to cover a smile.

"If not for Weybridge and the rather ingenious use of some fallen tree branches, Harte would probably still be stuck in the quagmire. We were talking about sending for a pair of oxen and a pulley when the duke saved the day."

The men laughed—all of them except Quentin, who remained straight-faced and silent. As for Peter, his cheeks turned pink as a boiled lobster under his coating of grime.

India almost felt sorry for him since she knew exactly why he'd been so determined to take that last bird. He'd wanted to return the valiant warrior and show off for her. Instead, he'd only made a spectacle of himself—and a filthy one at that.

"At least we came away with an excellent brace of birds," Lord Pettigrew continued, turning to address his wife. "Tell Cook to add duck and partridge to tomorrow night's repast. There should be plenty for all. Now come along, Harte, before that muck dries so hard you need a bootjack to scrape it off."

With a muffled curse, Peter turned and stalked away. The Misses Ossley followed, skipping along next to him, while they peppered him with a barrage of sympathetic remarks. Unfortunately, Peter didn't seem to appreciate their comments in the least.

Lord Pettigrew and the other men soon followed. As they did, Quentin strolled up to India, leaning close so their words could not be overheard. "Harte is nothing if not entertaining."

"And determined," she replied. "It must have been quite a sight watching him fall into that bog."

"And even more of one getting him out." Quentin grinned, showing his teeth in an irresistible smile that had India smiling back.

Sweeping him with a glance, she noticed streaks of mud on his coat, sleeves, and boots. "Perhaps I ought not mention the fact, Your Grace, but it appears you have carried back a trace of the bog on you as well."

He shrugged. "Nothing a hot bath and a change of attire won't rectify."

An image of him stripped to the skin and stepping into a bath caused her blood to flow faster. She could only imagine how breathtaking he would look without so much as a stitch of clothing on his body.

Quentin arched a brow, his eyes glinting. "Sixpence for your thoughts."

She glanced away, grateful her cheeks were already flushed pink from the hot August sun. "My thoughts are nothing special. I was only wondering how much longer before nuncheon is served."

"Liar," he said, a low laugh rumbling from his chest.

"Save me a seat at the table, hmm? Until then, pray enjoy your watercolor painting. That's quite a nice start you've made."

Pleasure slid through her. "Thank you, Your Grace."

With another light chuckle, he made her a bow, then sauntered away.

She watched until he disappeared, certain that painting would be the farthest thing from her mind.

"Allow me to turn the pages for you, Miss Byron," Peter Harte declared as India took a seat in front of the pianoforte after dinner that evening.

She held back a sigh as she arranged the skirts of her ivory silk gown. "How kind of you to offer, but this tune is a familiar one. I shall do quite well on my own."

"Nonetheless, I wouldn't feel right leaving you to manage by yourself. I am certain you will find my services of great use."

I am sure I shall not, she thought.

But he had already taken up a position behind her left shoulder, and short of leaping up and pushing him away, she saw little recourse but to accept his offer with silent grace.

After opening the musical score on the stand, she took a moment to glance across the guest-filled drawing room. Her gaze went unerringly to Quentin, finding him seated on the other side of the room next to Mallory and Major Hargreaves. Her cousin's dark head was bent close to the major's guinea gold one, the two of them deep in conversation.

Quentin, however, was looking straight at her. Deciding to take advantage of the opportunity, she shot him a clear "rescue me" look.

To her consternation, he merely shrugged and smiled.

Responding before she thought, she stuck her tongue

out at him praying afterward that no one else had seen.

His grin stretched wide, chest moving in a silent laugh, as he relaxed back in his chair. From all appearances he looked ready to enjoy the coming entertainment, having apparently decided to abandon her for the time being.

Forcing her gaze away, she stared for a moment at her skirt.

"He'll never come up to scratch, you know."

"What?" Her gaze shot to Peter's.

"Weybridge," he said in a low voice. "He isn't the marrying kind, despite what he may have convinced you to believe. You would be far better off accepting my marriage proposal."

"We've had this discussion before, Mr. Harte. Many times before. Now, everyone is waiting for me to begin."

And they were, gazes turning her way in anticipation of her performance. Suddenly, she was grateful she'd chosen a song she had often played before; otherwise, she would surely have made a fool of herself.

As it was, she bobbled the first flourish of notes before she settled into the rhythm.

"Aren't you glad now that I'm here to help?" Peter murmured, clearly unaware of his implied insult to her playing.

She didn't answer, concentrating on getting through the piece—and then getting rid of Peter. She shot another glance at Quentin. Their gazes met again, his dark eyes warm with obvious enjoyment.

Is Peter right that Quentin isn't the marrying kind?

Very likely, she decided, given everything she knew about him. But what did it matter since he wasn't actually courting her. They were only passing a brief span of time together, then they would part, possibly forever.

Staring hard at the music, she realized she was nearly at the end of the last stanza on that sheet. "The page, Mr. Harte," she chastened in an uncharacteristically impatient tone. "Are you following the notes?"

"Oh, yes, of course." But it was obvious he had not been, fumbling with the paper as he leaned over to turn the score a few beats too late.

Luckily, her playing was almost automatic by then, giving her confidence that she would be able to finish the song and not disgrace herself too badly in the attempt.

Finally, she played the final chord, smiling with relief that the performance was through.

Her fellow house guests broke into appreciative applauses.

"Bravo!" Peter called in a loud voice, beating his hands together with an excess of enthusiasm. "Excellent! Outstanding!"

She climbed to her feet. "Thank you," she said in a quiet voice. "But my playing was nothing more than adequate. Pray do not give it more credit than it deserves."

"But I'm not. It was wonderful! Perfection itself. As are you, lovely, unassuming Miss Byron."

She stared at him, suddenly alarmed by the notion that he and others might think she was being deliberately self-effacing in order to elicit his praise. She cringed at the very idea.

"Your beauty, your talent, your grace knows no rival," he continued, his voice carrying across the room. "You are like a goddess brought down to earth."

"Mr. Harte, enough. Please," she whispered, wanting to flee from him but knowing it would only draw more attention their way.

He waved his arms in a fulsome arc. "But why should I cease when I speak only the truth? You are too modest, that is all. Too modest to know the full extent of your own brilliance. Do you know, I think I feel a verse coming upon me."

No, anything but that!

She was about to hurry away, when Quentin appeared at her side.

"Miss Byron," he said in a low tone, as he reached out to take her arm. "I believe you promised to join me for a cup of tea and a sweetmeat. I have a spot on the settee all picked out."

Peter puffed out his chest. "I say. The lady and I were having a conversation, you know."

"Yes, you *were* having a conversation, but it is now at an end. In case you weren't aware, Miss Ossley is waiting to entertain us all, and you are keeping her from doing so."

"Oh, I . . . well, no, I didn't realize," Peter sputtered.

"Miss Ossley." Quentin motioned to the girl.

She walked forward, together with her sister, the pair of them moving into place at the pianoforte. One sat while the other whispered something in her ear. The pair of them giggled.

"Mr. Harte," one of the girls called. "Would you turn the pages for us like you did Miss Byron? We would be ever so grateful." They whispered something to each other again, then released another round of giggles.

Peter frowned, his irritation clear. But manners dictated he could do nothing but accept. Mumbling something inaudible under his breath, he went to do as he was bade.

"And so, you escape once again," Quentin murmured in India's ear, as he drew her away.

"Yes, though you certainly took your time about it," she said, releasing a pent-up sigh of relief. "Actually, I oughtn't even speak to you after your desertion."

He flashed her an inquiring look. "And what would you have had me do? Battle him for the right to stand next to you while you performed? I don't believe either of us would have benefited from that kind of scene. I do apologize, though, for not reaching you a minute sooner. Had I been quicker, I could have spared you and the rest of us his public soliloquy. Forgive me. Please."

The starch came out of her shoulders. "You are forgiven. But don't leave me again. I expect you to stick close by my side for the remainder of the party."

He bent nearer, his warm breath whispering against her ear. "I can think of nowhere else I would rather be than close to you."

Her heart knocked hard beneath her breast.

"Here we are," he declared, arriving in front of a small couch upholstered in burgundy damask. "I thought this settee would give us a chance to talk without being overheard."

She stared at the settee, noticing that the narrow piece of furniture was made to seat two—only two and rather snugly at that. Her mouth grew dry, breath suddenly thin inside her lungs.

Unable to form the necessary words, she nodded and let him seat her, then himself. His large frame filled the space, one powerful thigh lolling a hairbreadth from her own.

Glancing around, she looked to see if anyone else was watching them, but no one was. Despite being in a drawing room with more than two dozen people, the corner felt amazingly private. Amazingly intimate. Vaguely, she became aware of one of the Ossley sisters launching into a painfully slow rendition of a Mozart adagio.

"I asked one of the footmen to bring us tea and something sweet. You like marchpane, do you not?"

"Y-yes."

And truthfully, she did like marchpane, though at present she suspected she might have been willing to agree to nearly anything he asked.

Glancing up, she lost herself for a moment in the rich brown depths of his eyes. *He is magnificent,* she thought, wishing as she had once before that she could reach up and thread her fingers through his luxurious black hair and the silvery wings that feathered out from his temples.

"You do play well," he said.

"What?" Her brows drew together, needing a moment to adjust to the sudden change in conversation.

"I greatly enjoyed your performance on the pianoforte. Although, as you said yourself, it was not without fault."

"A gentleman would not point out such things."

"A gentleman like Harte, you mean? We haven't been acquainted long, but I know you well enough to tell that you don't care for false flattery."

She toyed with a piece of ribbon on her dress. "You are right, I do not."

"Then you will believe me, when I say you play well, and that I would never turn down an opportunity to hear you perform."

She met his gaze again and smiled. "And I would never refuse to do so, were you my audience, Your Grace."

"Quentin," he said in a throaty tone. "In private you must always call me Quentin."

I do already, she thought, *in my mind and my heart.*

A footman approached just then, making her realize she'd forgotten there were other people in the room.

"Oh, here is our tea," she said with forced cheer. "And the comfits, as you promised. They look delicious."

Quentin leaned nearer. "But not as delicious as you."

She shivered, her arm pressing against his side.

"Nevertheless," he said, pulling slightly away again. "I shall have to content myself with these. Let us indulge, India. I fear we shall need the sustenance with yet another Miss Ossley waiting to entertain us."

She blinked, then laughed. Taking a piece of marchpane from the plate, she bit in and let the sugary almond confection melt against her tongue.

Chapter Five

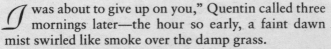

I was about to give up on you," Quentin called three mornings later—the hour so early, a faint dawn mist swirled like smoke over the damp grass.

Turning from where he'd been waiting near a small copse of trees, he watched her hurry down the stone steps at the front of the house. As she moved, the skirts of her simple blue day dress billowed around her in a most becoming way, revealing brief, tempting glimpses of her calves and the sturdy brown, kidskin half boots covering her feet.

At least she's dressed appropriately for an outing, he thought, shifting the pair of fishing rods and the tackle basket in his hand.

"Sorry I'm late," she said, drawing to a halt at his side. "I'm not used to waking up while it's still night outside." She raised a hand to cover the yawn that caught her, moisture brimming in her eyes.

"The fish bite best when it's early. If you'd rather go back to bed, there's still time to hurry inside again without anyone being the wiser."

She shook her head. "Oh no, not after overhearing Peter tell Lady Pettigrew last night that he plans to remain at home with the ladies today. If he's staying with the women, then I'm going with the men! Besides, after I told Mallory that I was sneaking out with you, she decided to come along as well."

"She's already gone down to the stream. I saw her with Hargreaves and a couple of the others not ten minutes past. We're the last of the group, I believe."

"Then let us go too before it gets light enough for Peter to look out his window and see us."

Quentin nodded, knowing he wouldn't be surprised if Harte did exactly that.

Despite his original agreement to help free India from Harte's unwanted attentions, he hadn't initially realized just how persistent, nor how annoying "Peter the Pest" could be.

But over the course of the past few days, Quentin had received a firsthand education on the subject. Rather than cause Harte to withdraw in defeat, Quentin's attentions toward India only seemed to inflame him, goading Harte to compete against him with the determination of a knight questing after a grail. Not only was Harte interested in wresting India from his supposed grasp, he wanted to beat Quentin at any activity in which the two of them were engaged.

Quentin had in no way actively sought the rivalry, but neither had he backed down from it. To date, the two of them had faced off over everything from whist to cricket, charades and crambo to horseback riding and golf. Then, of course, there was the infamous hunting expedition. Even now, Harte received an occasional jibe from one of the other men over his memorable, murky swim in the bog.

At first, Quentin had been amused by the young man's efforts to compete against him, especially considering that Harte never managed to win any of their encounters. He'd tried to be tolerant as well, attributing Harte's obsessiveness to youthful excess and a lack of experience. But lately he simply found him tedious and a bit pathetic.

No wonder poor India was at her wits' end. Harte wouldn't take no for an answer, not even when the truth was plain for all to see. Everyone in attendance knew that India Byron wasn't romantically interested in Peter Harte. The man needed to accept reality and move on.

Yet despite all the bother, Quentin couldn't complain about the time he was spending with India. Each day with her was a new adventure. Every hour an exciting delight. Witty, intelligent, and filled with a zest for life, she made him feel young and alive in ways he'd forgotten he could be. She made him realize there were myriad pleasures to be had, if one only took the time to look.

And look he did, not only at the world as she showed it to him, but at her as well. Despite his resolve to take matters between them no farther than a bit of harmless flirting, he found himself wanting more. Wanting her. Desiring her with a need that seemed to deepen by the day. So far, he'd held his longing in check, refusing to give in to the desire that burned inside him like a barely banked fire.

If she weren't such an innocent, he would have taken her already. He knew she was far from immune to him and that he would have no difficulty acquiring an invitation to her bed. But she *was* innocent. Which meant he would have to leave her sexual awakening to the man who would one day become her husband, whoever he might be.

Scowling at the thought, he forced himself back to the topic at hand. "You're right," he said. "No time to dawdle. We have fish to catch. You have been fishing before, have you not?"

"Of course. With my brothers. But I fear I must warn you that I can't bear baiting the hook. You'll have to do it for me."

He smiled. "Too squeamish?"

"No. I feel sorry for the worms. Imagine being skewered, then fed to a fish. Poor things." She shuddered.

Laughing, he held out a hand.

After a moment, she took it, and together they set out after the others.

"I think I've got one!" India declared nearly two hours later as she stood with her boots braced in the soft, grass-covered bank that overlooked the gently eddying stream.

She and Quentin were alone, the pair of them having walked some distance upstream from the others in order to find a calm spot where the fish were likely to be hungry and plentiful. Apparently, their strategy was working, since he'd already caught a lovely trout not more than fifteen minutes ago, and now she had a bite as well.

Tightening her grip on her fishing rod, she pulled back on the line and worked to reel in her catch. The lancewood pole bobbed sharply, confirming her suspicion that she had a lively one. The pliable wood quivered, the line growing taut as the fish struggled to escape.

"Keep at it," Quentin encouraged from where he stood several feet to her left. "Don't let him snag you up on a rock and break away."

Out of the corner of her eye, she saw Quentin secure

his own fishing rod. Then she had no more time to watch him, since she was far too busy reeling in her line to pay attention to anything else—not even another enjoyable perusal of Quentin Marlowe's striking physique.

Having dressed with sport in mind, he wore a fawn waistcoat and breeches with a pair of knee-high black Hessians on his feet. And although he'd arrived wearing a coat, he'd stripped that off an hour earlier after seeking her permission to do so. As he'd told her, the sleeves were far too confining for fishing and the material far too warm for the rising August temperatures.

"Must be a big one," he remarked, as he drew up beside her.

Moments later, the fish popped out of the water, wriggling wildly on the hook. She fought to maintain the upper hand.

Quentin moved past her and steadied his feet on a rock along the edge of the stream, before leaning forward to grab the line and secure her catch. "What a beauty!" he called, holding the dripping fish aloft. "Two pounds if I don't miss my guess. We certainly won't be going back emptyhanded."

She smiled, pleased by her success. "I wish my brothers were here to see. They'd be green as chive cheese."

"Competitive, are they?"

"Horribly. Especially when it comes to sport. I've long ago washed my hands of their wagers and wrangling. Still a fish like this deserves some recognition, do you not think?"

"Indeed, it does. If you'd like I could frank a letter to each of them, providing a detailed description and an ink rendering of your catch. Or maybe an advertisement in the *Times* would be more fitting. I have a caption in mind already. *Lady wishes her brothers to know that she is the better angler!*"

She laughed at his good-natured teasing, watching as he went to the creel he'd brought and laid the fish inside next to his own catch.

"Following on your earlier remark about cheese," he ventured. "What would you say to a small repast?"

"You brought food?"

"I most certainly did. No respectable angler ever comes out without something to eat."

Her stomach rumbled in approval of the idea. "Then I'd say you're brilliant, that's what. I've been famished for ages, but assumed we'd have to wait to return to the house."

"Nothing of the sort. Let's dip our hands clean in the stream, then we shall dine in style. Or at least on that big rock over there. I believe it looks wide enough to share."

Glancing across, she studied the large chunk of granite and agreed, noting that it was about the size of Lady Pettigrew's settee without the upholstery.

Minutes later found them seated next to each other, her feet dangling a couple inches above the ground. He handed her a handkerchief with a wedge of cheddar and a hunk of crisp, yeasty bread nestled inside. The rich, salty aromas made her mouth water.

Unable to wait an instant longer, she dived into the simple meal, finding it heavenly. "Umm, delicious," she pronounced after a first swallow.

He ate a bite of the serving he'd prepared for himself, then nodded in agreement. "Just right on a fine summer morning."

They fell silent for a brief time, while they both enjoyed the meal, comfortable and relaxed with each other. She felt as though they'd shared moments like this a hundred times before. And yet in truth they were still strangers, their acquaintance numbered by mere days.

But still it feels like more, she thought. *It feels like eternity. I'm being silly,* she told herself, shaking off the sensation.

In two days more, the country party would end, and she and Quentin would return to their usual lives and activities. She realized she didn't know what those were for him. Suddenly, she wanted to hear everything about him before it was too late to ask.

"Tell me about your estate," she said, breaking off a small bite of bread without eating it.

He glanced over at her. "What do you want to know?"

"Anything. Everything. I only know that it is located in Herefordshire near the Welsh border and that you have over five hundred tenants and a hundred servants to see to the Keep."

His mouth curved into a wide smile. "You already seem well acquainted with the subject. Gossip pages again?"

"They're very informative, as I've told you. Nevertheless, they only present facts without any real substance or detail. What's it like there in the winter, for instance?"

"Cold, as I believe winter generally is."

She shot him a look. "Don't be flippant, Your Grace."

"Quentin," he corrected in a warm drawl.

"Don't be flippant, *Quentin.* You know what I mean. Do you take sleigh rides or skate on a pond? How do you pass the holidays? Do you have lots of family?"

His expression sobered. "Two brothers, but they are often away. When my parents were alive, we all used to celebrate Christmas at Weybridge Keep, but those days are long since past. Now, I generally stay in London. What of you?"

"Oh, we always go to Braebourne to Cousin Edward's estate. The family wouldn't think to do otherwise."

"I am sure it's delightful."

"It is. You should—"

He raised a brow. "I should what?"

She had been ready to say, "you should come," but then realized the implications of such an invitation. What would he think of her wanting to see him again? Especially since she'd just been asking questions about his estate? Would he wonder if she suddenly had designs upon him? Had hopes of marrying him?

But of course I don't, she admonished. Quentin was dashing and seductive and entirely capable of winning the hand of any woman he chose. But the idea of a serious attachment between them was absurd. His courting of her was only make-believe, after all.

Yet what if it wasn't? What if he really was pursuing me and truly wanted me for his wife?

A potent longing tightened like a vise around her heart, leaving her with an unexpected awareness that such a wish was exactly what she wanted. Quite intensely, in fact. Lowering her gaze, she stared hard at her toes and struggled to collect her tattered emotions.

"What is it I should do?" he inquired again, his words returning her to their conversation.

She searched for an answer, forcing a smile. "Do? Why see if there's anything left in that basket. I'm still hungry."

He chuckled. "I believe there's an orange."

"Perfect." *I only hope I can choke it down, along with my foolish dreams.*

Sitting quietly, she let him peel and section the fruit, then pass her a serving. Thanking him, she forced herself to eat a slice.

Juice squirted in a crazy arch as she bit in, a few droplets sliding down her cheek. She raised a hand to wipe them away, but he stopped her.

"Here," he said. "Allow me."

Her eyelids fluttered slightly, her pulse thudding in her throat as she held still. Using the edge of his handkerchief, he leaned close and pressed the fine linen against her damp skin.

"All done?" she asked with an odd quaver in her voice.

"Not quite," he said. "I think I may have missed a spot."

She glanced up and into his eyes. A tingle sizzled down her spine at the acute need she saw in his gaze. Need for her.

Then his mouth was on her skin, his tongue gliding over the spot where the orange juice had been. "Sweet," he murmured. "So very sweet."

Her toes curled, and her eyelids fell closed, her breath catching on a harsh inhale.

Nuzzling her cheek, he pressed a series of lingering kisses against her flesh in a seemingly random pattern that led slowly to her mouth. Her senses spun in crazy circles, his touch everything she remembered and more. She still had dreams of him, but those paled in comparison to the reality of his touch, her memories no more than weak facsimiles of real passion and ardent need. A sigh escaped her, a ragged snippet of sound that verged on a moan. Enthralled, she waited for his kiss, yearned for his possession.

Finally, his mouth met hers, plundering with a leisurely thoroughness that made her ache. Dark, sultry, and delectable, she couldn't get enough, her desire heightened by the power of not just her need, but her emotions. He was everything she wanted. Everything she craved. Everything she . . . loved?

Yes—she sighed in her mind—*I do love him.*

Leaning closer, she kissed him back, pleasure tossing her like a feather adrift in a tempest. He reached up and cupped the back of her head, angling his mouth over hers to deepen their embrace. But a few moments later, he paused, his mouth growing still against her own.

Suddenly, he pulled away.

Before she had time to recover, he was on his feet. "Forgive me, India," he said in a gruff tone. "I acted before I thought and had no right to take advantage."

"But you were—"

"I was wrong. We're here alone, and I gave in to temptation. Believe me though, it won't happen again."

Won't it? she thought in abject disappointment, her spirits deflating like the bubbles in a glass of old champagne.

"I should check my line," he said. "I left the hook in the water and might have a bite by now."

Is he talking about fishing? Now? It would seem he was, she realized, watching as he strode down the bank to the stream, then leaned over to take up his fishing rod.

All the bright light faded from the day, despite the fact that the actual sun continued to blaze as strongly as ever overhead. And though it was August, with heat rippling in the air, a chill crept upon her like a bitter winter wind.

Cold and bereft, she stood, but didn't move forward, realizing she no longer felt certain of anything.

Chapter Six

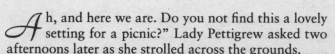

*A*h, and here we are. Do you not find this a lovely setting for a picnic?" Lady Pettigrew asked two afternoons later as she strolled across the grounds.

Walking next to Lady Pettigrew, with her aunt on the other side, India cast an idle glance around. The vista was stunning, but she took little notice of it, scarcely looking at either the majestic ocean waves crashing in the distance or at the ruins of the fifteenth-century monastery that rose over the landscape in jagged columns of weatherbeaten gray stone. Normally she would have been brimming with interest and excitement over the outing, but today she was having a hard time working up the necessary enthusiasm. Nevertheless, she forced herself to smile.

"Yes, it's quite lovely," she agreed. Tipping her parasol slightly to one side, she glanced around in a furtive search for Quentin.

Although she'd ridden here with him in his curricle, he'd lost no time excusing himself soon after their arrival. Having escorted her to her aunt, he stayed just long enough to exchange a few pleasantries, then bowed and left to assist some of the men, who were busy setting up for a game of cricket.

On the surface, everything between them was fine, his attentions to her as marked as before. But underneath nothing was the same. The easy, flirtatious friendship they'd shared at the start had vanished in the aftermath of their kiss by the stream. She wanted to draw him closer but couldn't find a way. While he seemed determined to maintain a kind of invisible barrier between them—a circumstance that let her know exactly how relieved he would be to leave her behind when the party ended tomorrow.

Sighting him several yards away, she couldn't help but stare.

How splendid he looks, she thought. His bold, darkly arresting features and natural strength cast every other man around him into the shade. But there was more to Quentin than just a pleasing face and physique—there was the dynamic inner man as well. As she now knew, he was intelligent and charming, worldly, with a self-effacing sense of humor and a surprising appreciation of the absurd. To some he might appear cynical, even jaded, but underneath he possessed a gentle compassion and a generous heart. She only wished he wanted to share that heart with her.

Her fingers clenched around the wooden parasol handle she held, longing rising inside her in a now-familiar ache. With a sigh, she turned away.

"Is everything all right, dear?" Aunt Ava murmured in a soothing voice. "You seem a bit blue-deviled today. I'm not used to seeing you without your usual, jolly smile."

She gazed at the older woman, a part of her wanting badly to confide. Instead, she forced a happier expression onto her face. "Only a bit wistful over thoughts of home. I have not seen my little sisters in more than a month's time, and as much as I am enjoying myself here, I shall be glad to be back among everything and everyone familiar."

"Well, of course you shall. Although, might I venture to wonder if mayhap there is another reason as well?" Her aunt's shrewd gaze drifted away, settling for a brief, but pointed, moment on Quentin. She raised an inquiring brow.

India glanced away. "No, it's nothing like that . . . nothing serious that is. Nor do I wish it to be."

Liar.

Aunt Ava gave her a kindly smile. "It's just as well, I suppose. He is a good man and an excellent friend to my sons, but he's complicated. Despite his title, I suspect only the very deepest love will ever induce him to marry. And that love will need to be returned in even greater measure by his bride. So it is good that what's between you is nothing serious. You are young yet, India. You have time."

But I have no time, she thought with a sudden bleakness. *Since he has already stolen my heart.*

To her relief, everyone's attention was soon called by Lady Pettigrew informing her guests that their picnic luncheon was served.

The rest of the afternoon passed at a leisurely pace— the food delicious, the games entertaining, the ruins providing an intriguing tableau on which to climb and comment. India spent little time with Quentin, passing much of her day with Mallory and the Misses Ossley, as they sat on lawn blankets chatting and cheering their chosen men on to victory in the cricket match.

Hours later, she stood, brushing off her skirts, as everyone readied themselves to depart. She sensed a man approach and glanced up. Her shoulders drooped when she saw it wasn't Quentin. "Oh, hallo, Mr. Harte."

"Miss Byron." He sent her a toothy smile. "May I say you're looking as lovely as a newly opened rose today."

She said nothing.

Apparently taking her silence as encouragement, he tugged at his coat sleeves and straightened to his full height. "I was wondering . . . that is I hoped I might persuade you to drive back with me. This is our last outing together for a while, after all."

Drive back with him? Absolutely not.

But then her gaze drifted toward Quentin, watching him laugh at some remark made by Philipa Stockton—a very attractive, very widowed, female guest.

Does he want her?

She frowned, not at all liking the direction of her thoughts. Emotions churning, she found herself suddenly anxious to depart. "Yes, all right. You may see me home."

"I assumed you wouldn't—" he began. "What did you say?"

She looked at his astonished face. "I said yes. I am ready to depart whenever you are."

"Then let us away immediately!" Grinning from ear to ear, he offered her his arm.

What in the blazes does she think she's about? Quentin wondered, as he watched India walk across the field with Peter Harte of all people.

Has the puppy coerced her into it?

But she didn't appear upset, nor was she turning back

to send him a "help me" look. In fact, she wasn't sending him any looks at all.

He shouldn't be surprised by her reproof, he supposed, not given his lack of attention toward her today. But ever since that kiss by the stream, he'd known he needed to put some distance between them.

He hadn't even meant to kiss her, it had just happened. And once he'd tasted her lips again, he'd been lost. Tearing himself away from her had been a wrenching experience, one he'd found nearly impossible to manage. But manage he had.

Yes, he wanted her—so badly he ached. But where would it lead? She might fascinate him now, but what of later? Surely his interest would fade. No, he decided, it was best to make a clean break while it could still be done. Which is why he forced himself not to stride across the grounds after her, especially when he saw Harte hand her up into his curricle.

Let them go, he told himself. *Let her go. It's best for us both.*

Twenty minutes later, India gazed around at the passing countryside, aware she didn't recognize anything about her surroundings. "Mr. Harte, are you certain this is the way to the Pettigrews'? I don't recall following this path earlier today."

He tossed her a quick glance, then looked ahead again. "Well now, that's because it isn't. I decided to take a detour. But not to worry, I'll have you back soon enough."

"A detour, but—"

"There's a stretch of land just ahead with a superlative view of the ocean. Glorious cliffs. I thought you might enjoy seeing them."

"I would have appreciated it more had you thought to advise me of your plan before we set out." Her mouth tightened, deeply regretting her impulsive decision to let him drive her home. "As beautiful as the view may be," she continued, "I don't think we have time to tarry. My aunt is expecting me and will wonder where I am."

"We'll only be a little late. Nothing to cause concern."

"Still—"

"Here we are." With a quiet command to his horse, he brought the curricle to a stop. After securing the reins around the brake, he leaned back and took a dramatic breath of the salt-scented air. "Ah, isn't this spectacular?"

She couldn't help but agree. The rugged cliffs formed a majestic curve that hugged the grassy green landscape, while below lay a narrow strip of toast-colored sand beach. Beyond stretched the ocean, shimmering blue as far as the eye could see. Yet, lovely as the view might be, the landscape was empty, the only sign of human habitation a small cottage perched on a similar jut of land some miles in the distance.

"It is breathtaking, however—"

Before she could finish her comment, he vaulted from the carriage and hurried around to her side. "Come," he entreated, stretching up a hand. "Let us walk a few yards."

"Mr. Harte—"

"Five minutes. Surely you can spare five minutes?"

Five minutes, hmm? If it would appease him enough to get him moving again, she supposed it was worth the delay. Besides, if she didn't agree, she feared he would keep her here arguing for double that amount of time. Placing her hand in his, she allowed him to help her to the ground.

She strolled next to him, the sea breeze ruffling her pale yellow muslin skirts.

"Have I told you how beautiful you are?" he said.

"On innumerable occasions."

"Then let this be another. You are as radiant—"

"*Please*, Mr. Harte—"

"Peter," he implored, turning his earnest gaze on her. "I so wish you would call me Peter."

"Mr. Harte, while I thank you for your kind words, I have no need of flattery."

"Perhaps not, but you are worthy regardless, in spite of your unwise preference for Weybridge." He slowed to kick at a feathery tuft of grass. "Although I could not help but notice a slight cooling between the two of you lately. Have you quarreled?"

She glanced toward her slippers. "Not at all."

"Is it because he's leaving tomorrow without making you an offer?"

"His intentions remain as fixed as ever." *And they do,* she thought, *since he's never intended to marry me.*

"He ought to have secured your hand, if he means to do so. He's too arrogant by half, you know."

"He's a duke. All dukes are arrogant. It's in their nature."

"Still, he doesn't deserve you."

She continued their walk, hoping the five minutes was nearly over.

He kicked more grass. After another few feet, he stopped and turned to face her, catching hold of her hand before she could prevent it. "Miss Byron," he said. "I know you have not favored my suit in the past, but my feelings for you remain as strong as ever."

Oh, heavens, surely not again!

"I love you with a passion for the ages," he continued.

"From the very depths of my bones and the heart of my marrow . . ."

Heart of his marrow? Where does he come up with such folderol?

". . . As Romeo loved Juliet. As Tristan loved Isolde. As Paris loved Helen . . ."

She held her tongue, struck by the irony that all the love affairs he mentioned had tragic ends.

"You must give me some right to hope," he went on. "Some sign that you may yet return my love with affection of your own. If you want me to change, I'll change. If it's riches you desire, I will obtain them for you. Whatever you want, you have only to say, and it will be yours."

Gazing into his pleading eyes, she felt her chest tighten. Even now, she believed he was in the grip of an intense, but fleeting, infatuation that would end the moment she was out of his sight for more than a few days. But what if she was wrong? What if she was un-derestimating the strength of his emotions? *If he feels even a glimmer of what I feel for Quentin, then he has my profound sympathy and understanding.*

"Mr. Harte—"

"Peter."

She exhaled a slow breath. "Peter. I wish I could tell you what you want to hear. I wish I could return your affection. How much easier everything would be if I could. But I am afraid I do not love you, and no amount of time or persuasion will change my mind. I am sorry. Truly I am."

His face hardened, anger flashing in his gaze. "I don't want your pity. I want your love. And if you won't give it to me, I'll take it. I'll make you love me one way or another."

Without warning, he hauled her into his arms and

kissed her, grinding his lips against hers with a force that made her stomach roil. Twisting in his grip, she fought for freedom.

"Stop!" she panted, turning her head to evade him.

But he followed, smearing his wet mouth over hers in several clumsy forays. Increasing the pressure of his kiss, he tried to force his tongue into her mouth. Without thinking, she raised a hand and slapped him, cutting him hard across the face and ear.

He reared back, an ugly red mark staining his skin.

"I said stop!" she yelled, breaking free with a fierce shove. "How dare you touch me. Don't you *ever* do something like that again."

"But India—"

"Don't! Do not speak my name. In fact, don't ever speak to me again. I have tried to be considerate, putting up with you these past weeks, but I've had all I can take. Leave me alone, do you hear? Leave me alone, or I shall tell my father what you've done. And I shall tell Spence as well. He won't like it. He might even demand satisfaction, and I know he's twice the swordsman you are."

His cheeks burned, a sullen expression turning his eyes dark and mean. "Leave you alone? Fine, then, I shall. I wash my hands of you, Miss Byron. You are on your own." Spinning on his heels, he stalked to the carriage and leapt inside.

She followed, wondering how she was going to endure the ride home. But she needn't have worried, since seconds later he gave the reins a sharp flick and set his horse in motion.

"Wait!" she called, incredulous that he was abandoning her. She took several running steps after the departing vehicle, but it was already too late. The curricle sped faster, racing away into the distance.

Why that vile little worm, she thought, fury bubbling through her like acid. She stood for a long moment, trembling despite the warmth of the day. Gazing at her surroundings, she wondered where she was.

Miles and miles from the Pettigrews', that's where.

What's more, she had no means of transportation and no way of obtaining any, since her pin money was inside her reticule. The reticule she'd left in his carriage.

What am I to do now?

Surveying the empty fields ahead, she realized there was only one choice. Walk. And hope someone came along to aid her. Or that Peter changed his mind and returned for her. But somehow, she knew he wouldn't.

With a sigh of resignation, she set out. She hadn't gone far when she noticed a bank of fat gray clouds rolling in overhead, the wind whipping harder at her skirts.

Oh, wonderful. Rain. Can this day possibly get any better?

Chapter Seven

A little over an hour later, Quentin cornered Peter Harte in an unoccupied corridor not far from the Pettigrews' drawing room. "Where is she, Harte?" he demanded on a low growl.

"*She* who?" Harte said in apparent confusion—an act Quentin didn't believe for an instant.

"You know exactly who. Miss Byron."

The younger man shrugged, his gazing darting sideways. "How should I know? Haven't seen her lately."

He leaned closer, using his greater height in a way he knew to be intimidating. "Lately or since the picnic? I watched you hand her into your carriage, but no one has seen her since."

After the outing, Quentin had driven straight back to the Pettigrews'. While the other guests continued to arrive, he'd gone upstairs to his bedchamber to change his clothes. On his return downstairs, he'd seen Harte, but not India. At the time, he assumed she'd already retired to her room to nap and relax before dinner like many of the other ladies, and thought nothing of her absence.

But as the minutes continued to tick past, he began to wonder.

And worry.

Perhaps it was some sixth sense, but his gut told him something wasn't right. Having learned long ago always to trust his instincts, he went back upstairs and knocked on her door. Her maid answered, informing him that Miss India hadn't yet returned. Even more deeply concerned, he'd set out in search of Harte.

"So," he now insisted. "Where is India? You did bring her home, did you not?"

A muscle twitched in Harte's cheek. "Of course I brought her home. I'm sure she's around here somewhere. Probably off gabbing with one of the other girls. You know how females are. Now, if you don't mind, I'm on my way to the drawing room for a libation."

When Harte started to move around him, he grabbed his arm and pushed him back against the wall. "You're lying. I can see it on your ferrety little face. Out with it, or so help me I'll make sure you're drinking your meals through a straw for the next several weeks."

Harte's eyes rounded, the heightened color in his face draining to white. "I . . . I . . ."

A sick sensation twisted inside Quentin's vitals, his grip on Harte's arm tightening so much the other man let out a yelp of pain. "You what? What have you done with her? If you've hurt her I'll—"

"No, no, of course I didn't hurt her. What do you take me for? I would never injure Miss Byron."

Relief swept through him. "Well, then, let's have it. And I want the truth this time."

"I . . . I . . . left her."

He scowled. "What do you mean, *left her*?"

"We had a quarrel . . . and well . . . in the heat of the moment, I drove off. B-but I'm sure she'll find her way back," Harte rushed to assure. "She's pr-probably found a ride with a farmer or tradesman and is walking through the door even as we speak."

Quentin stared, wondering if Harte was daft or just stupid? *Has he any idea of the potential danger he's placed her in?*

The younger man let out a fresh yelp, as Quentin's grip tightened another inch. "You mean you abandoned her? That she's out there alone somewhere right now, while you were about to have drinks and dinner with the rest of the guests? Why you insufferable toad. You're beneath contempt. While I can still stand to look at you, tell me everything that happened today between you and India, and don't leave out so much as a single detail."

Harte gulped and began his recitation. By the time he was done, the sick sensation had blossomed once again inside Quentin's gut. His hands fisted, terrified to know that India was alone and lost in unfamiliar country, miles away from the nearest town. The thought of what could happen to her, especially if she were to be set upon by highwaymen or other unsavory types . . . well, he didn't want to contemplate the possibilities.

With a hard shove, he pushed Harte away.

The other man curled against the wall, gingerly rubbing his bruised arm.

"You're not to say a word of this to anyone, do you hear?" he told him in a menacing tone. "Well, do you?"

Harte nodded.

"You're to pack your bags and clear out now. I don't care what excuse you use so long as neither my name nor Miss Byron's is included. Then I want you gone."

Harte straightened in clear surprise. "W-what do you mean, gone?"

"Out! Right now. You won't even have time for that libation you were craving. Or at least, you won't if you have any sense, since I expect to find you gone long before my return. If I see so much as your shadow when I get back, well, I won't be responsible for my actions."

Beads of nervous sweat gleamed on Harte's brow, as he nodded for a second time. "All right, I'll go."

"Good." He took a couple steps away, then swung around again. "Oh, and Harte."

The man glanced up. "What?"

"This." Using his fisted knuckles, he punched him square in the face.

"*Ow!*" Harte cried, reeling away as he raised a hand to cover his cheek. "What'd you do that for?"

"That was for India. I thought she deserved a measure of retribution after everything you've put her through. Now, get out of my sight before I decide to take my own pound of flesh."

Harte's hazel eyes goggled—or at least one of them did, since the other was busy swelling shut and turning the color of a squashed blackberry. With a whimper, he wheeled around and fled down the hall.

Quentin didn't remain long enough to watch him further, turning instead on his boot heel to go find India.

India stopped and took off her slipper, then turned it over to shake out a pebble. As she did, a fierce gust of wind rose up, slamming her so hard it nearly ripped the silken shoe out of her hand. Managing somehow to hold on, she quickly slid her foot into the slipper once more and retied the ribbons, her skirts whirling in a frenzied dance around her ankles.

Straightening, she took a moment to survey the fields

of windblown grass and the empty road ahead. With a sigh, she started forward again. But with every step, her chest grew tighter, burgeoning alarm threatening to squeeze the breath from her lungs.

She'd been walking for nearly an hour and hadn't caught so much as a glimpse of another person. Besides the occasional bird and rabbit, the only animals she'd encountered were a few sheep on a distant hill, but no farmstead or farmer. Worse yet, she was irretrievably lost.

Initially, she'd followed the marks left by Peter's carriage, but far too soon those faded away, leaving her unsure which direction to go. After another quarter mile, she was well and truly lost, having no idea whether she was walking toward the Pettigrews' or away.

Perhaps she should have stopped at that point and waited for someone to find her. But what if no one did? Because as much as she told herself not to worry, she couldn't help but fear nightfall, wondering what she would do if she was still out here alone when the sun sank from the sky for the day.

And so she'd continued on.

Luckily, it was summer, so there was still plenty of light. Or rather, there would have been plenty of light were it not for the increasingly angry band of storm clouds gathering overhead. She kept expecting the rain to start, but so far it had held off. Judging by the rapidly blackening sky, though, she knew her reprieve couldn't last too much longer.

Blast Peter Harte! When she got back, she was going to make him wish he'd never laid eyes on her. Until then, she had no choice but to continue on and pray someone would come to her rescue.

Five minutes later she was still walking, her bonnet-covered head lowered against the wind, when she heard a rumbling sound coming up behind her—a noise that sounded distinctly like carriage wheels.

Turning around, her heart quickened with relief when she saw a curricle. She raised an arm to signal the driver, but to her dawning joy she realized she had no need. The vehicle slowed, its large male occupant reassuringly familiar.

Quentin! He's come for me!

Drawing his horses to a stop, he secured the reins; the leather carriage hood he'd pulled up against the weather shaking in the wind. "India. Thank God," he said, jumping out of the vehicle and coming to her side. "I've been searching everywhere for you."

He opened his arms, and she went into them without a moment's hesitation, reveling in his warmth and strength as her fears dissolved like so much pixie dust. "How did you know?"

"Where to find you, you mean? It was Harte. When I noticed you were missing, he and I had a talk."

So Quentin realized I was gone and came looking. Pleasure spread through her at the knowledge. "He told you what he did?"

"Not without a bit of persuasion, but I wrung the truth from him soon enough. Although I have to say you're a fair distance from where he said he left you. A good thing I decided to drive east a couple extra miles, or else I might have been searching for you half the night."

She trembled, a grateful lump forming in her throat to know he wouldn't have given up looking for her no matter how long it took.

"Come, though," he said. "We can talk later. Right now, we need to be on our way back before this storm decides to let loose."

As though prompted by his words, a cluster of fat

raindrops splattered to the ground, another one landing in a wet plop against her cheek. As the water slid over her skin, a second cluster of drops fell in an abrupt staccato.

Three seconds later, the sky split wide and turned everything as wet as a sea.

Together they raced for the carriage, Quentin tossing her up onto the seat as quickly as he could before climbing in after her. With rain pelting them in a fury, he set the horses in motion. The curricle's hood provided some measure of protection, but not enough to keep them dry. Especially not with the wind blowing the rain toward them rather than away.

Thunder crashed in an earsplitting boom, making the horses shy in fright. Quentin kept them steady, but not without a great deal of effort and skilled control. "We need to find shelter," he shouted over the storm, as he continued to urge the team forward.

Only there was no shelter—or at least not the sort that came by way of a barn or house.

India hung on, gripping the edge of the seat as he steered the curricle off the road toward a large stand of old-growth trees. Towering fifty feet tall or more, the oaks' thick limbs formed a massive canopy of heavy branches and interwoven green leaves.

Driving beneath, he turned the team and the carriage so that both were protected from the brunt of the wind. Now buffered, the rain lessened to a steady patter, a hush descending around them despite the continuing storm. Thunder boomed again but from a greater distance this time.

"We'll wait until the worst is over," he said, taking off his hat and giving it a shake. "These summer squalls flare up fast and pass through just as quickly. Twenty minutes or so, and it'll likely be nothing more than an annoying drizzle." Quentin paused for a few seconds. "You're freezing," he observed with husky concern. "Here, let's get you warm before you take your death." Shifting on the seat, he took off his long surtout of light-weight wool. "Come here," he said, urging her to him.

She nodded and wrapped her arms around herself as a shiver made gooseflesh rise on her damp skin. Her dress was damp as well, the thin muslin that had been so comfortable earlier in the day, now cold and clinging.

"But I'll get you wet."

"Don't be foolish." Reaching out, he tugged her closer, fitting her against his chest as he swept his coat over them both.

Blissful warmth flowed through her, his male scent and the sensation of his firm-muscled body as intoxicating as a tumbler of hot mulled wine. Closing her eyes, she burrowed nearer, her shivers easing instantly.

"That pretty bonnet of yours needs to come off," he said. "It's poking me in the cheek."

"Oh, I'm sorry. Let me—"

"No, let me," he hushed, his fingers going to the ribbon under her chin to pull it loose. Her bonnet soon joined his hat on the empty space beside her, then she forgot all about such matters, as he settled her comfortably against him again.

"Better?" she asked.

"Perfect."

Quiet descended, the muffled roar of the storm and the rustling leaves providing the only sound.

"Quentin?" she ventured after a time.

"Hmm?"

"I . . . well . . . thank you. Thank you for coming after me," she said. "I don't know what I would have done if you hadn't found me. I was so lost and alone, and I would have been caught in this dreadful storm. With night coming on I—"

"You would have managed somehow," he interrupted in a gentle voice. "You're a very resilient young woman. But I'm sorry for everything you've gone through today. I should never have let you leave with Harte this afternoon. When I saw you climb into his carriage, I ought to have stopped it immediately and insisted I be the one to drive you back."

"I didn't realize you'd noticed since you were busy talking to that widow," she said, a glimmer of her earlier jealousy returning.

"What widow?"

"The one with the fluttery blue eyes and the big . . ." She paused, searching for an acceptable term. "Bodice."

His mouth turned up in amusement. "Bodice, hmm? I have to admit I didn't pay much attention to either her eyes or her . . . bodice. I was too busy watching you at the time."

"Were you?"

He nodded, shifting slightly so she could meet his gaze, his irises a rich, luminous brown that gleamed even in the storm-darkened light. "I probably shouldn't admit this, but I spend a great deal of time watching you. So much so lately that I find myself in a fair way to becoming bewitched. There's just something about you, India, that has a way of casting a spell over a man."

Casting a spell? she thought. *What does he mean? Might he have feelings for me, after all?* Her heart careened into a mad zigzagging rhythm, slowing only when she realized he might simply mean that he desired her.

And if that was all, then what?

"I told your aunt I was coming to look for you," he

said, stroking her arm with a gentle, gliding touch that was no doubt meant to be soothing.

It wasn't.

A rash of tingles broke out all over her skin, waves of hot and cold assailing her like alternating tides.

"She was greatly alarmed to know what had occurred," he continued, "but agreed it would be best to let me recover you rather than alert the entire household to the situation. She's putting out the story that you took a bit too much sun at the picnic and decided to spend the evening in your room. So you needn't worry for your reputation. It's safe."

"But what of you? Won't you be missed at dinner?"

"I told Lord Pettigrew I had urgent business. Which, as it happens, I did. I just didn't mention that you were my business this evening."

"Then no one but Aunt Ava knows we're here together?" Her pulse hurried faster.

He shook his head. "No one else except Harte, and he left tonight as well."

"He did? But why?" she asked, surprise further diverting her attention.

"Because I persuaded him that remaining wouldn't be conducive to his continued good health. Of course, the black eye I gave him didn't hurt in reinforcing his decision to leave."

Her mouth fell open. "You gave him a black eye?"

"For abandoning you today? I most certainly did. Considering the shameful way he treated you, he should count himself lucky not to have come away with far worse."

Warmth of another kind spread through her. Not only had Quentin worried and searched for her, he'd also exacted a measure of retribution on her behalf. Perhaps it was unworthy of her to applaud such violence, but she was glad he'd stood up for her honor. Her very own knight—without any need for the shining armor.

She stroked an idle hand across his chest, pausing to toy with one of the gold buttons on his jacket. "I realize we haven't known each other long—scarcely three weeks, and not even that if you don't count our first meeting—"

"How could I not count our first meeting?" he drawled in a throaty tone. "It was one of the most memorable of my life."

And mine, she thought, powerful memories sweeping through her. Memories of their first glance. Their first touch. Their first kiss.

"I know it's too soon," she went on, tracing the pattern on his silk waistcoat. "But I have a deep regard for you. Actually, it's more than regard—much, much more. Quentin, I think . . . no, I'm quite certain that I lo—"

"Don't," he murmured, laying his fingers over her mouth. "Don't say it."

"But why?" she said, freeing her lips from beneath his touch. "Why, when it's true?"

"Because it isn't true. This week has been a place out of time, and whatever you think you're feeling isn't real. Once you return home to your usual life, you'll see I'm right. You'll realize everything we've done, everything we've felt, is little more than a fantasy."

"But it's not."

"India—"

"No. You're wrong. How can you say this isn't real?" Lifting her hand, she trailed her fingers across his cheek. "Can you not feel this?"

She brushed her thumb over his lower lip.

"Or this?" She kissed his chin before feathering more kisses along the faintly bristled edge of his jaw. "How is this not real?"

"Don't," he whispered, his eyelids dropping low. "Stop this before we both do something we'll regret."

"But I won't regret a thing," she told him, threading her fingers into the silvery strands of hair that grew in among the black. "I can't." Sliding her fingers deeper, she cupped his head and tugged him closer. "Not when I love you."

He groaned, and she felt a shudder go through him. Then, with the force of the storm still raging around them, he captured her lips beneath his own.

Pleasure assailed her—hot, heady, and instantaneous. Surrendering without so much as a hint of caution, she wound her arms around his neck and pressed her mouth more fully against his.

With her lips parted, she invited him in, eager to claim and be claimed, in any way he desired. Closing her eyes, she followed his command, letting him draw her deeper into a world of sultry heat and indescribable bliss. A moan hummed low in her throat, then another when he reached up and covered one of her breasts with his palm.

Her body throbbed, shivery tremors racing in riotous arcs across her skin. Her nipples drew into taut peaks beneath the damp material of her gown, every new touch of his fingers leaving her in a welter of anticipation for the next. She whimpered, unprepared for the yawning need that poured through her. Using slow, measured strokes and leisurely circles, he caressed her flesh in ways that left her flushed and half-mad with desire.

Their kiss turned frenzied, an ardent joining that drove the very air from her lungs. Growing bolder, she intensified their embrace, turning their kisses into an unspoken challenge to see who could bring the other the greater pleasure.

Point to Quentin, she thought on a gasp as he caught

her lower lip between his teeth to worry the tender flesh in a gentle but incredibly erotic way. Releasing her lip, he soothed the abused spot with a warm, wet stroke of his tongue before taking her mouth again in a kiss that was both dark and enthralling.

She shuddered, her head lolling back as he scattered kisses across her cheeks and chin and throat. Apparently unsatisfied at having her still seated next to him, he drew her up and across his lap. Cradling her close, he plundered her mouth again.

Distantly, she sensed him unfastening the buttons on the back of her gown, then tugging open the laces of her stays. Without warning, cool air wafted over her exposed breasts, her bare nipples tightening in a way that was almost painful. But then she had no more time to think, helpless to do anything but feel, as he bent and pressed his open mouth to her breasts—first one, then the other, savoring her as though he'd been invited to a feast.

Heat engulfed her like a fiery explosion, each draw of his lips, every devilish swirl of his tongue making her writhe with the most profound delight. And yet she ached, the place between her legs growing damp in the most amazing and disturbing manner. She shifted her legs, restless and craving more.

An enervating quiver chased over her body as he tongued one sensitive tip and suckled even more fervently at her flesh. Her senses spun, her nerve endings burning to the point where she feared she might actually turn to flame. Then his hand slipped under her skirts to introduce her to an entirely new level of torment.

Gliding slowly upward, he trailed his fingers along her calf and knee, pausing for brief moments along the way to draw tantalizing circles on her with the flat of his hand. She trembled when he reached her thigh.

Catching her lip between her teeth, she waited in rapt suspense as he stroked her flesh.

A gasp burst from her throat, when she felt him slide his palm behind her to caress the bare curve of her bottom. He played there for several long moments, fondling her with a kind of possessive intimacy that was as shocking as it was intense.

Pleasure surged like a rising tide, a raw quiver crashing through her body, as his hand moved again and settled against her nether curls. Continuing to suckle deeply at her breast, he parted her most tender flesh and slid his fingers along her slick core.

She bucked at the sensation, undone by both his touch and her own sizzling need. A keening moan sang from her mouth, her surrender complete, as he opened her wider and sank a single finger deep inside.

Slowly, he raised his head. "Open your eyes."

Her lids stayed shut, breath soughing audibly from her parted lips. "I—I c-can't."

"Open your eyes, India."

Somehow she found the strength to look at him this time. "W-why?"

"Because," he intoned in a near growl. "I want to see you. I want to watch you reach your peak."

Her peak? What does he mean?

Then he began stroking her, gliding deep inside to massage her willing flesh. He used the rest of his fingers on her as well, painting her with her own moisture until she thought she might go insane.

She gazed at him, staring half-delirious into his beautiful dark eyes.

"That's it," he coaxed, as he increased his stroke, rubbing her in a way that drew wild little pants from her lips.

Just when she thought she could take no more, he

thrust a second finger into her and sent her hurtling over some invisible edge.

She wailed, her entire body convulsing, as the most-astonishing pleasure poured through her, rapture that bathed her in what felt like a dazzling golden light. She hung on, giddy and weak and utterly in love. She could do this with Quentin forever. Anywhere, anytime, he wished.

Suddenly he was kissing her, taking her mouth in ravenous draughts that left her no time to recover. Not that she wanted to, quite the opposite.

Removing his hand from between her legs, he shifted her, sliding her up and over him so she straddled his hips. His hand went between them, working to open the buttons on his falls.

But even as he did, he suddenly stopped, his entire frame growing rigid. Breaking off their kiss, he turned his head away and sucked in a harsh breath. "Bloody hell," he cursed.

She frowned. "Quentin?"

Cursing again, he closed his eyes for a long moment, then ever so gently lifted her so that she was sitting beside him again. "I can't," he said between clenched teeth.

"Can't what?"

"Take you, that's what." He paused and gulped down a deep breath. "The rain appears to have lessened. Let's get you dressed, so we can be on our way again."

By Christ, what's wrong with me? he berated himself, as he took up the reins with shaking hands. *How could I have forgotten for a single instant that she's a virgin? Worse still, how could he have been so lost to passion that he'd been on the verge of taking her—in a curricle no less!*

He knew he should offer for her. After the liberties he'd just enjoyed, she had every reason to expect a marriage proposal. But despite her protestations of love, she was young—too young to really know her own mind.

She hadn't even had a London Season. Hadn't yet been able to test her wings and take her pick of men. Did he have the right to step in and claim her before she knew who she was and what she wanted?

The barbarian inside him said *yes*. The civilized man disagreed. *No*, he told himself, *for her own good, and mine as well, I should set her free*. A few weeks from now, she'll thank me. By next spring, she'll be glad she hadn't let a whirlwind romance with a virtual stranger determine the rest of her life.

And what of me?

What of him? *I'm infatuated, that's all*. Once she returned home, and he wasn't in her company for long hours each day, her allure would fade. Lovely, effervescent, and delightful as India Byron might be, she would quickly become no more important to him than any other woman. And when they next met, they would do so as ordinary acquaintances—albeit ones who had shared an intense, though brief, passion.

Watching the now-lazily-falling rain, he forced down a sigh. Shifting his glance, he saw that she was once again properly attired. Even her bonnet was back on her head, with the ribbon tied in a pretty bow beneath her chin. Reaching for his surtout, he draped the woolen garment over her.

"But haven't you need of your coat?" she protested in a soft voice. Her luminous green eyes met his, the impact of her gaze seeming to reach into his soul.

Lust. Nothing more than lust, he told himself.

"I won't have you taking a chill," he said, his words sounding gruff, even to his own ears.

Giving the reins a sharp snap, he maneuvered the carriage back onto the road and set out for the Pettigrews'.

With darkness having fallen, India followed Quentin inside through a servants' entrance at the rear of the house. Careful to be quiet, the two of them made their way up another back staircase, then down the corridor toward their rooms. Luckily, they didn't encounter anyone along the way. All the guests were downstairs eating dinner, while the servants were busy seeing to their needs.

Reaching the door to her bedchamber, she stopped, then gazed up at Quentin.

"I'll send word to your aunt that we have returned," he said. "I'm sure she'll be along to look in on you as soon as she can. In the meantime, have your maid bring you something to eat. You must be famished by now."

Actually, food was the farthest thing from her mind, her body still aglow from their passionate encounter in his carriage. He'd been so silent on the journey back, though. Was it because of his frustration at having to put such an abrupt halt to their lovemaking?

Were it not for his restraint, she would have surrendered her virginity to him, and gladly. Maybe she should have told him that then. Mayhap she ought to tell him that now. As brazen as it might sound aloud, she wanted him to be her first.

Her only.

She was trying to find the words when he reached out and caught her hand inside his own.

"I want you to know that what happened between us this evening was my doing and mine alone," he said. "You are to assume none of the responsibility, do you understand? You're lovely, India. Sweet and delightful and innocent in every way."

"But I'm not," she said, recalling how she'd coaxed him to kiss her and the wanton manner in which she'd responded to his every touch. "N-not innocent, that is."

He smiled. "But you are, my dear girl. And that's how I want you to stay."

"But—"

"Go to your room, eat your dinner, and get some sleep. Everything will seem clearer in the morning."

She thrust out her lower lip. "You make me sound like a child."

A rueful laugh rolled from his throat before his gaze darkened with a sensuality she was quickly coming to recognize. "Never fear. I'm well aware you're a woman. A wonderful, mesmerizing woman, who will continue to grow more beautiful and enchanting with each passing day."

Lifting her hand, he closed his eyes and pressed his lips against her palm for a long moment. "Sleep well, India. Dream of sweet thoughts and cherished wishes."

She trembled, wanting to throw her arms around him and hold him close. Instead, she forced herself to remain still, as he released her hand and took a few steps back. "Good night," she said.

"Good night." With a last look, he turned and strode away.

Setting a hand on the door handle to her bedchamber, she stood for a long moment before finally going inside.

She awakened early the next morning and rose from bed, anxious to dress quickly and go downstairs. She wanted to find Quentin so they could talk before everyone else joined them for breakfast. Otherwise, she knew she would be compelled to wait for an opportunity to speak with him alone—and risk missing the chance entirely.

Practically running, she flew down the staircase and into the main hall. One of the Pettigrews' liveried footmen watched her come to a gliding halt, her slippers skating lightly over the polished marble floor.

"Excuse me, but could you tell me if any of the guests have come downstairs yet?"

"One or two," the young man said with an encouraging smile. "Who are ye looking for, Miss?"

"The Duke of Weybridge. He's tall and dark with very brown eyes."

"I know 'im. But I'm afraid you've missed him."

"What do you mean? Missed him?" she asked, an odd clenching sensation flexing beneath her breasts.

"He left not long after first light. Helped him out m'self with his luggage and such."

"Are you quite sure it was His Grace?"

"Can't miss the silver in that hair o'his. Aye, I'm sure it was him."

A buzzing rang in her ears, and she swayed.

"Here now, Miss, are ye awright?" He reached a hand toward her, as if concerned she might fall.

She drew away, collecting herself enough to meet his concerned gaze. "Yes. I am quite well."

Only she wasn't. Quentin was gone.

Chapter Eight

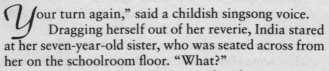

"$\mathcal{Y}$our turn again," said a childish singsong voice.

Dragging herself out of her reverie, India stared at her seven-year-old sister, who was seated across from her on the schoolroom floor. "What?"

"It's your turn," Poppy Byron said with a measure of exasperation. "We're playing spillikins, remember?"

"Oh, yes, of course. I wasn't attending as I should. My apologies."

The younger girl's dark brows drew together. "You haven't been attending a lot of things lately," she muttered under her breath.

"What is that supposed to mean? And yes, I heard you."

Poppy glanced up. "Sorry. It's just that you haven't seemed yourself the last few weeks. Ever since you came back from that visit with Aunt Ava, you've been . . ."

"Yes? What have I been?"

"Sad. You never laugh anymore. Not like you used to. Why don't you laugh anymore, India?"

Lowering her gaze, she stared at the jumbled mass of wooden jackstraws scattered over the broad oak flooring. "I laugh when someone says something funny," she defended. Reaching toward a spillikin with a painted blue tip, she lifted one away. "And I'm not sad."

But she was sad, and they both knew it, no matter how hard she tried to conceal her feelings.

In the nearly three months since she'd returned home from the Pettigrews', she'd been melancholy.

At first, she'd tried to pretend nothing was wrong, going out of her way to be sunny and cheerful, as she threw herself into the usual round of family activities with an almost frightening zeal. Yet inwardly she was miserable, only allowing her real feelings to escape at night, when she was certain she was alone.

The first week after Quentin left, her emotions ran the gambit from anger to despair. One moment she would be furious, berating him for his callousness and the shabby manner in which he had used her, then departed—recalling that he hadn't even given her the courtesy of a note.

But in the next breath, she would be sunk in misery, telling herself the fault was her own for being careless enough to fall in love with him. Suppose he *had* written her a note, or had even stayed to tell her good-bye. What might he have said that wouldn't have crushed her just as much as his leaving? How could words have possibly softened the agonizing blow of knowing he did not love her in return?

He'd said what they shared was nothing more than a fantasy. But for her, every moment, every emotion, was as real as the moon and as radiant as the stars.

Finally, her tears had dried, and in their wake, she'd

taken a vow to forget him—as he no doubt had already forgotten her. But as the days moved past, and her life resumed its natural course, her devotion for him did not fade. If anything, her love strengthened. Try as she might, she could not free herself from her memories of their days together—thoughts of him embedded deep into her bones, her love for him inextricably entwined around her soul.

Forcing a smile, she looked across at her sister. "I just have a great deal on my mind these days, that's all."

"Like going to London in the spring?"

"Yes. Exactly."

"I wish *I* could go to London for the Season," Poppy said with a wistful sigh.

"That day shall come soon enough. Pray do not be so impatient." *I certainly wish I didn't have to go, since I shall be expected to seek out a husband—a man who will not be Quentin Marlowe.*

And what if she saw him there? How would she bear such an encounter?

She was just about to reach for a new spillikin stick when two pairs of slippered feet came stamping through the doorway. Her sisters—Anna and Janey—raced in, sliding to an abrupt, skirt-swinging halt.

"India, India, you shall never guess!" twelve-year-old Janey declared, breathless from her apparently mad dash up the stairs.

India met her gaze. "Never guess what?"

"That we have a visitor and you are to come downstairs immediately."

Her lips tightened on a repressed sigh. "What sort of visitor? Has the squire called again?"

"No," stated Anna, in the exaggeratedly calm voice she had taken to using since turning fifteen last month.

"The visitor is a gentleman, and Mama says you are to put on your best frock and join them as soon as may be."

"A gentleman? What's his name?"

"Well, we do not know, nor what he looks like, since he arrived before we had a chance to see," Anna continued. "But he is closeted with Papa in his study at this very minute."

India scowled at that bit of news.

"You don't suppose he's here to propose to you?" Janey said on a giggle. "Oh, heavens, what if it's one of those fellows Spence brought home last summer? Maybe the one with the chuckleheaded expression who followed you around spouting poetry wherever he went."

Peter Harte!

India felt her eyes widen with alarm. Good Lord, surely he didn't have the temerity to come seeking her father's permission to ask for her hand? Not after he'd been so thoroughly dismissed the last time they'd met? Then again, Peter Harte never had been one to take no for an answer.

Well, she thought rising to her feet, *he's going to learn his lesson once and for all.* She would go downstairs all right and see to it he was sent packing!

Storming from the room, she headed for the stairs.

Her sisters followed. Down one flight they went, to the second floor, like ducks in a row.

"What about your gown?" Anna called when India didn't turn in the direction of her bedchamber.

Her dress was an old, comfortable moss green kerseymere she'd worn dozens of times, eminently suitable for afternoons at home. "My attire is perfectly fine."

Perfectly fine for the likes of Peter Harte, that is.

She continued on down the next flight of stairs, her sisters at her heels. When they reached the main floor, she stopped and turned. "You had all best stay here. Mama won't approve if we all go in."

"Of course not," Anna said, cloaking herself in a mantle of dignity. "I shall take the girls into the music room."

"Where you can try listening through the wall," India observed with a knowing look.

"Exactly!" Janey piped.

India couldn't help but grin. "Do not let Mama catch you."

But as she walked toward her father's study, her smile fell away, her affront returning full force.

She met her mother in front of the closed study doors.

"There you are," her mother said in a quiet voice, her gaze sweeping down. "What is that you have on? Did the girls not tell you to change your gown?"

"I can go back up if you like—"

"No, no there's no time. He's been in with your father for fifteen minutes now as it is. I can't imagine they have much more to discuss."

Fifteen minutes? What could Peter the Pest have had to talk to her father about for fifteen minutes?

"Go on. Go in," her mother encouraged with a wide smile, her blue eyes twinkling with anticipation.

Does Mama approve his suit? She'd never thought her mother much cared for Peter, nor that her father had a good opinion of him either, come to think. But maybe a formal declaration made all the difference.

Well, I shall put a stop to his overtures. Now and for good!

Giving a brief knock, she opened the door and stepped inside.

The room was large, with her father's desk positioned so that he faced anyone who entered. A pair of upholstered armchairs was set in front of it, their high backs angled in a way that concealed the occupants.

Without making any real attempt to identify the visitor—of whom all she could make out was a pair of booted feet—she marched up to her father. "Papa, I understand you wish to see me?"

Gazing her way, he smiled and stood. "Ah, India. Good, you are here. We have a guest who has come all this way for a visit. He informs me he is acquainted with you."

"Well, yes, of course, he is. But there has been some mistake and whatever he has told you, I trust you will disregard it."

Her father's thick salt-and-pepper brows rose on his forehead. "What's that now?"

"This gentleman is here under an erroneous assumption. And I would have you ask him to—"

"Ask me to what?" remarked a well-remembered voice.

From out of the chair he rose, large and dark and so exceptionally magnificent that for a moment she forgot how to draw her next breath. Her lips parted. "*Quentin.*"

She stared, her senses alive as she drank in the sight of his beloved face. Then abruptly she remembered herself and the fact that they were not alone. "I m-mean, Your Grace. How do you do?" Lowering her gaze to the carpet, she sank into a deep curtsy.

Quentin returned the gesture with a bow. "Miss Byron. A pleasure as always."

A silence fell, her father looking between them, as he crossed his arms over his stocky chest. "So, what is this you were saying, India?"

Her gaze darted his way, as she inwardly kicked herself for her impetuous assumptions. "N-nothing. Nothing of any import, that is. Pray forget I spoke."

A slight smile turned up the corners of Quentin's mouth. Apparently choosing to withhold comment, however, he laid a hand on the back of his chair instead.

"Yes, well, if that's the case, then let's move along," her father stated. "His Grace and I were just discussing agriculture."

Agriculture!

"It would seem your father takes a lively interest in the latest cultivation methods for turnips," Quentin observed in an even tone.

"A good cash crop, turnips. Beneficial for both man and beast," her father asserted in a speech she had heard him make many times before. "But I daresay that's not what brought Weybridge to our doorstep." He cleared his throat. "It seems the duke would like a word with you, India, and I have agreed that he may have it."

Her heart hammered in her chest.

Casting speculative glances between her and Quentin again, her father came around from behind his desk. "Your mother said something about rounding up a tray of tea and sandwiches. I think I'll just go see how she's coming with those."

Sending her a reassuring smile, her father left, closing the double doors at his back.

The ticking of the clock that stood in the far corner of the room seemed to increase its volume, together with that of a bird warbling a tune from its perch on a branch outside one of the windows.

Folding her hands in front of her, she waited, more awkward in Quentin's presence than she could ever remember being. But then perhaps that was because she couldn't decide whether she ought to run out of the room or run instead into his arms.

Of course if she did that, she might also find herself begging, and she still possessed enough pride to forgo such a pitiable display. Possible, too, was the chance that her parents were wrong and that Quentin wished to speak to her for a completely different reason than they assumed. Although what that reason might be, she couldn't imagine. Unless he was here to apologize for leaving without a word that day.

Something inside her shriveled at the notion.

"How have you been, India?" he asked in a rich, mellow tone that made her quiver deep inside.

Been? she thought. *Desolate. That's how I've been.*

Instead, she sent him what she hoped was a carefree smile. "Quite well. Excellent, in fact."

His gaze sought hers, a deep glint in his coffee-hued eyes that she couldn't quite interpret. "You look wonderful. Even more beautiful than I remember."

She buried a hand against her skirt. "And what of you, Your Grace? How have you been these past months?"

"Less than good, actually."

"What do you mean?" she asked, lines creasing her forehead in sudden concern. "You haven't been ill, have you?"

"No, not physically ill. Not unless you consider unhappiness a disease. Because if that's the case, then you might say I'm in a very bad way indeed."

She stared, her pulse thudding harder in her veins.

"I thought I was doing the right thing when I left you in August," he continued. "I told myself it was for both of our good, and that a clean break was exactly what we needed. Once parted, we'd count ourselves lucky over our easy escape. After all, who bases their lives on little more than a week's acquaintance? What kind of foundation would it provide for a relationship?"

He pulled in a ragged breath. "Since then, I've come to realize that I made the biggest mistake of my life. No matter how I've tried, I can't get you out of my mind or my heart. You haunt me, India, and without you, I'm scarcely fit for anything."

Reaching into his pocket, he withdrew a ring. The

brilliant square-cut emerald winked like a cat's eye in the milky afternoon light.

Her heart did a flip, not quite able to believe all the things he was saying.

"I suppose I'm a selfish bastard to claim you before you've even had a chance to step out in the world and spread your wings," he went on. "But I cannot do without you. I love you, and I've come to understand that it's not the length of time that matters but the depth of the devotion. Seven days or seventy years, it won't change how I feel. Tell me it's not too late, sweetheart. Tell me you still hold the same regard for me that you did all those months ago. Marry me, India Byron, and make me a happy man."

A full-body shiver went through her, emotions pouring over her with such force that she feared she might burst apart. Suddenly, her earlier question repeated in her head, and all at once she knew exactly where to run.

Taking three huge steps, she sprinted forward, then launched herself into his arms. He caught her safely, clutching her against his strong chest, as she wrapped her arms around him.

Her lips went to his. Or maybe his went to hers, the two of them kissing with a wild, ravenous joy. Closing her eyes, she let the rapture soar within her, knowing she would never find anything more perfect than the beauty of his touch. Kissing him harder, she felt all the past weeks' misery fall away.

At length, he broke their kiss, a bit winded as he met her gaze. "So, do I take it that's a yes?"

"Of course it's a yes!" she retorted. "Yes, yes, yes, yes, yes, yes, yes! Did I say it enough? One time for each day we were together at the Pettigrews'?"

"I believe you managed. And you still love me, in spite of the way I left?"

"I shouldn't," she told him with a mildly reproving look. "You were cruel, you know."

He grew solemn. "I know, and I'm sorry. From now on, I'll do everything in my power to make it up to you."

"Well, I won't stop you, if you insist. But right now, I'm just too happy to stay angry. I've been so miserable. You'll never know just how much."

"If you've been anything like me, I do," he said with complete sincerity.

"Swear you'll never leave me again."

"I swear and gladly."

He kissed her once more, neither of them coming up for air for quite some while.

"Are you sure?" he murmured against her lips.

"About what?" she asked on a dreamy sigh, almost delirious with pleasure.

"The engagement. We can postpone it if you want. The delay will probably kill me, but we can wait to make the announcement until after you've had your Season. So long as I know it'll be my ring on your finger, I shall willingly suffer any deprivation on your behalf."

"I most certainly am not postponing the engagement or the wedding!" she stated with a firm shake of her head. "We shall spend the Season together where I can enjoy the delights of London as your bride. Besides, I'll make a much bigger splash that way. Society will find the new Duchess of Weybridge far more impressive than plain Miss Byron." She flashed him a saucy grin.

He grinned back. "Believe me, darling, there's nothing plain about you. There never was, and there never shall be."

"Oh, I just remembered," she said. "Where is my ring?"

For a moment, he looked nonplussed. "I believe in all excitement, I dropped it. Here, let me look."

Releasing her, he stepped back, while she did the

same. The emerald sparkled where it lay on the carpet.

Bending, Quentin picked it up. "Shall we try this again?"

Trembling with happiness, she held out her hand.

He smiled, his dark eyes aglow with love. "Will you marry me, India?"

"Yes, Quentin. I will." She watched, beaming as he slid the gold-and-gemstone circlet onto her finger.

"I'll never take it off," she said with a husky catch of emotion in her voice.

"And I shall never let you."

Drawing her back into his arms, he captured her mouth for a long, lingering kiss. Her senses swam, giddy with bliss. When he cupped her breast in his palm, she arched into his touch, then reached up to thread her fingers into his hair. Slanting her mouth against his, she let him take her flying, tingling from head to toe and drunk with delight.

At length, he drew away. "Hmm, we'd better stop while I still have the strength," he groaned, his words heavy with repressed desire. "Speaking of which, is there any other way out of here besides the door?"

"Just the windows. Why?"

"Because I'm sure your father is about to name his seconds, we've been in here so long. If I didn't already want to marry you, I'd have to do so now just for propriety's sake."

She gave a little snort. "You'd find some other way. You're a very persuasive sort of man, Your Grace. I have no doubt Mama and the girls will be wrapped firmly around your finger by the end of the evening."

"Perhaps. But there's only one woman I care to have wrapped around my finger, and that's you."

"You're in luck then, since I'm wrapped tight, and shall stay that way. Now and forever, my love."

TRACY ANNE WARREN grew up in a small central Ohio town. After working for a number of years in finance, she quit her day job to pursue her first love—writing romance novels. Warren lives in Maryland with three exuberant young Siamese cats and windows full of gorgeous orchids and African violets. When she's not writing, she enjoys reading, watching movies, and dreaming up the characters for her next book. Visit her website at *www.tracyannewarren.com*.

*Next month, don't miss these exciting new
love stories only from
Avon Books*

Obsession Untamed by Pamela Palmer
Delaney Randall is snatched from her apartment one night by
Tighe, a dangerous Feral Warrior—one of an elite band of
immortals who can change shape at will. He needs Delaney's
help to track a dark fiend, but soon becomes wild with an obsession for her that is as untamed as his heart.

Since the Surrender by Julie Anne Long
Captain Chase Eversea receives a mysterious message summoning him to a London rendezvous . . . where he encounters the
memory of his most wicked indiscretion in the flesh: Rosalind
March—the only woman he could never forget.

The Infamous Rogue by Alexandra Benedict
The daughter of a wealthy bandit, Sophia Dawson once lost
herself in the arms of Black Hawk, the most infamous pirate ever
to command the high seas. Now she is determined to put her
sinful past behind her and marry a well-born nobleman, but her
ex-lover has returned for revenge . . .

Beauty and the Duke by Melody Thomas
Ten years ago they were young lovers, sharing sinful touches and
desperate ecstasy. But he was bound by his promise to wed
another. Now they say he's cursed, that any woman who shares
his bed will meet an untimely end. Should Christine be afraid of
the devil duke and his ravenous desire?

Avon Romances
the best in
exceptional authors and unforgettable novels!

At Avon Books, we know your passion for romance—once you finish one of our novels, you find yourself wanting more.

May we tempt you with . . .

- **Excerpts** from our upcoming releases.

- Entertaining **extras**, including authors' personal photo albums and book lists.

- Behind-the-scenes **scoop** on your favorite characters and series.

- **Sweepstakes** for the chance to win free books, romantic getaways, and other fun prizes.

- Writing **tips** from our authors and editors.

- **Blog** with our authors and find out why they love to write romance.

- **Exclusive content** that's not contained within the pages of our novels.

Join us at
www.avonbooks.com

AVON

An Imprint of HarperCollins*Publishers*
www.avonromance.com

Available wherever books are sold or please call 1-800-331-3761 to order.

FTH 0708